"A writer of considerabl
long series of novels and sto
magazines for the next twe
builder of semi-realistic rom

Neither was his hero, Jimmie Dale, The Gray Seal."

- Robert Sampson

"Few characters as obscure as Canadian novelist Frank L. Packard's gentleman cracksman, Jimmie Dale the Gray Seal, have had the impact and long term import of this one. Almost unknown today, Packard and his creation not only exerted a tremendous influence on the pulps he came from, but established many of the tropes of the modern superhero in comic books.

From his secret lair, the Sanctuary, his multiple identities, and his calling card, a gray diamond paper seal, Jimmie Dale set the pattern for the mystery men and super heroes who will follow.

Norvell Page, who took over the Spider from R.T.M Scott (creator of Aurelius Smith aka Secret Service Smith), was a particular fan of the Gray Seal and used many of Packard's ideas in the Spider's saga."

- David L. Vineyard

"Other writers ripped off so much Frank Packard it ain't funny. I want to give Packard due, he was the first in this genre."

- Steve Hoffman

"While Packard may have borrowed from Raffles, Arsène Lupin, and other similar characters of the late Edwardian period in creating his own version of the gentleman thief who fights crime there can be no doubt that in Jimmie Dale we see the origin of the hero pulp characters culminating in The Shadow, The Spider, and even Batman."

- J. F. Norris

"If there had been great controversy over the creation of The Lone Ranger, there can be none about the (Green) Hornet. It was George W. Trendle's idea, aided and abetted somewhat by a book he came across called *The Adventures of Jimmie Dale*."

- Dick Osgood

"Walt (Disney) loved the fictional character, Jimmie Dale, Alias the Gray Seal, and as a boy would re-enact those adventures with his boyhood friend, Walt Pfieffer.

"One of the projects that Walt proposed to NBC was a series to be called *Jimmie Dale, Alias the Gray Seal* but the network felt the concept was not what the public expected from Disney and rejected the proposal."

- Wade Sampson

"Packard's writing had a raw vitality and a sense of mood which is still appealing even in today's age of entertainment overkill... If Packard had not existed, would the Spider have his seal? The Shadow his slouch hat? Lamont Cranston his Cobalt Club? The Phantom his disguises? Or any of them their secret identities?"

-Don Hutchison

"Lee Falk's primary influence when creating The Phantom was actually Jimmie Dale, the Gray Seal (Frank Packard's character who also inspired the Green Hornet). Falk's original title for his strip was "The Gray Ghost" (before the strip was retitled by KFS *) who left a seal (with The Phantom's death-head) as his calling card, repeating Jimmie Dale's M.O. Also, The Phantom's alter ego was originally to be Jimmy Wells, before Lee came up with the Ghost Who Walks jungle background four months into the daily strip. Though Jimmie Dale is largely forgotten today, the character was a huge influence on The Shadow, The Phantom, the Spider and the aforementioned Green Hornet."

-Anthony Tollin

* King Features Syndicate

"Packard's books are deemed a critical bridge between late 1800s Victorian era style writings and the newer grittier Rogue school of the 1930s and 1940s. His city of New York is immoral and dirty with evil-smelling tenements, the back alleys the haunts of dope fiends, thieves and murderers. Jimmie Dale's life's work and passion was to clean it up, usually with a happy ending."

- Jim Skaggs

THE COMPLETE ADVENTURES OF JIMMIE DALE

VOLUME ONE

An Annotated Compilation of the Novels featuring the Gray Seal and the Tocsin

BY FRANK L. PACKARD

Edited by Michael Howard
Cover painting by Doug Klauba
Book design by Melissa Tilley

TABLE OF CONTENTS:

A BRIEF BIOGRAPHY OF FRANK L. PACKARD

THE ADVENTURES OF JIMMIE DALE

PART ONE: THE MAN IN THE CASE

PART TWO: THE WOMAN IN THE CASE

A Brief Biography of Frank L. Packard

Frank Lucius Packard was born in Montreal, Quebec, on February 2, 1877. His father, Lucius Henry Packard, was an American who founded a shoe polish company in Boston after the Civil War. Around 1870 Lucius made a trip to Montreal and decided to permanently relocate there. Montreal was a thriving center of shoe manufacturing at that time - and the residence of Mary Francis Joslin who Lucius married in 1875.

Frank attended a number of Montreal area schools as a child, including a French Protestant establishment where he gained a fluency with that language. After completing high school he passed into McGill University in 1893. Four years later he graduated with a Bachelor of Science degree in Engineering. For the 1897-1898 academic year he took a post-graduate course in Electrical Engineering at the University of Liege in Belgium.

As a young man Frank Packard held a number of different jobs. On summer breaks from McGill he worked for the Canadian Pacific Railway. This gave him a familiarity with trains and railroad men that would play a large part in his future career as an author. After college he went to Savannah, Georgia where the city's electrical grid was being converted from an overhead system to one underground. More engineering work followed, this time in Stoughton, Massachusetts where he had many paternal relatives. By 1902 he was managing the family shoe polish company in Boston.

His dissatisfaction with the business world is shown by his habit of rising at 4:00 am and getting in a few hours of writing before starting his management duties. Engineering majors are not traditionally known for their literary ability but Packard won a prize for best University essay while at McGill so clearly his affinity for the written word began early in life.

In 1906 *Munsey's* published his short story "Corporal Bob," which would be the first of over 150 appearances for Packard in various American magazines. His earliest short fiction pieces were railroad adventures, fifteen of which were gathered in his first book, *On the Iron at Big Cloud* (1911). Although he continued to draw inspiration from the railways after that, notably in the later novels *The Wire Devils* (1918) and *The Night Operator* (1919), he also wrote thrillers about South Sea islands and the badlands of Manhattan. His inspiration for the former was a trip on a freighter across the Pacific in 1912 and 1913. For the latter Packard's son indicates that his father was at one time "almost living in a police precinct station" in New York City.

Packard was not an overnight success. His financial records show he earned just $2,600.00 in 1912-1913 (that's the equivalent of $67,760 in 2018). By 1927-1928 however, that figure had jumped to $25,500 ($644,960). *The Miracle Man* (1914) is considered his first commercial success. In that novel a gang of small-time New York crooks plan to exploit a blind faith-healer in rural Maine but instead find themselves healed both spiritually and physically. The theme of redemption occurs in several more of Packard's works, including *Greater Love Hath No Man* (1913), *The Sin That Was His* (1917), and arguably, the entire Gray Seal series. He produced 32 books in all, which appeared in at least eight languages besides English. During his lifetime more than four million copies of his books were sold. Between 1915 and 1932 twelve movies were made based on Packard's short stories and novels. *The Miracle Man* was actually filmed twice and the earlier 1919 version is said to have launched the career of actor Lon Chaney. It also became a successful Broadway play under the supervision of George Cohan.

But his most popular creation was Jimmie Dale, a well-to-do clubman who fought crime in the guise of the Gray Seal. Five books about the character were published, beginning with *The Adventures of Jimmie Dale* in 1917. That same year saw the release of a sixteen-chapter silent movie serial titled *Jimmie Dale Alias the Gray Seal.*

Presumably Packard was familiar with Edwardian Age characters like A. J. Raffles, Jimmy Valentine, Arsène Lupin, and the Scarlet Pimpernel. Certain traces of each of those figures can be seen in the formation of the Gray Seal. But Packard broke new ground by combining them into the first masked hero to battle crime in a modern big city. That concept not only directly influenced 1930s figures like the Shadow and the Green Hornet, it also played a significant role in the comic book superhero explosion that followed. In subsequent decades there were literally hundreds of writers in a wide variety of media that - knowingly or not - employed some part of Packard's Gray Seal template to their own series characters.

However, one component of his work was simply too radical for a majority of his emulators. Jimmie Dale had many heroic traits to his credit: courage, resourcefulness, compassion, mechanical aptitude, and athletic prowess among them. Even so, it is only through the superior intellectual abilities of the woman he at first knows only as the Tocsin that the Gray Seal can triumph over that seemingly endless horde of grasping, ruthless villains that threaten society in early Twentieth Century New York. Packard was at work on a sixth Jimmie Dale novel when he died on February 17, 1942.

Packard's first wife, Gertrude Edwards, died in a drowning accident in 1901. They had only been married for three months. In 1910 he married

Marguerite Pearl Macintyre, who would herself become a writer later in life. They had three sons and a daughter together. Their first child, Lucius Henry Packard, was quoted earlier in this piece. Lucius was born in May 1914, the month and year that also saw the debut of the Gray Seal in a magazine short story. Jimmie Dale went on to cast a very long shadow over popular culture for the next century, but when Lucius died in 2006 his obituary in the *Montreal Gazette* made no mention of either the Gray Seal or his creator.

Michael Howard
Troy, Michigan
September 2018

THE

ADVENTURES OF

JIMMIE DALE

BY FRANK L. PACKARD

Author of "The Miracle Man," "Greater Love Hath No Man,"
etc.

PART ONE: THE MAN IN THE CASE

(The material comprising Part One of this book first appeared in *People's Ideal Fiction Magazine* between May 1914 and March 1915 under the series label "The Professional Adventures of Jimmie Dale." {"It was another Jimmie Dale now—the professional Jimmie Dale. Quick as a cat, active, lithe, he was over a six-foot fence in the rear of a building in a flash... "} With the July 1914 issue the magazine title was shortened to just *People's*.)

PART ONE: THE MAN IN THE CASE

CHAPTER I

THE GRAY SEAL [1]

(By my reckoning the events of this chapter occur on Thursday, July 22, 1915 and Friday, July 23, 1915. These dates, and the ones that will appear at the start of each subsequent chapter, are derived not just from information found in the five published Jimmie Dale novels, but from various unpublished works by Packard as well. It was the latter material which convinced me the dating of this novel had to be set after it first appeared in print. Since Dale never meets a historical personage in the series and because the only time a specific date is mentioned is way off in Book Five, readers can feel free to ignore my 'retconning' chronology. If a timeline based solely on printed writings is preferred then just subtract two years from the dates I supply. A future volume of this compilation will offer a more detailed explanation of how I devised the timeline.)

AMONG New York's fashionable and ultra-exclusive clubs, the St. James stood an acknowledged leader—more men, perhaps, cast an envious eye at its portals, of modest and unassuming taste, as they passed by on Fifth Avenue, than they did at any other club upon the long list that the city boasts. True, there were more expensive clubs upon whose membership roll scintillated more stars of New York's social set, but the St. James was distinctive. It guaranteed a man, so to speak—that is, it guaranteed a man to be innately a gentleman. It required money, it is true, to keep up one's membership, but there were many members who were not wealthy, as wealth is measured nowadays—there were many, even, who were pressed sometimes to meet their dues and their house accounts, but the accounts were invariably promptly paid. No man, once in, could ever afford, or ever had the desire, to resign from the St. James Club. Its

---

1 According to a sales ledger that survives among Packard's private papers the first installment of this book ("The Gray Seal") was submitted for magazine publication on July 12, 1913. It was immediately accepted and he was paid $160. That's the equivalent of $4,000 in 2018.

membership was cosmopolitan; men of very walk in life passed in and out of its doors, professional men and business men, physicians, artists, merchants, authors, engineers, each stamped with the "hall mark" of the St. James, an innate gentleman. To receive a two weeks' out-of-town visitor's card to the St. James was something to speak about, and men from Chicago, St. Louis, or San Francisco spoke of it with a sort of holier-than-thou air to fellow members of their own exclusive clubs, at home again. [2]

Is there any doubt that Jimmie Dale was a gentleman—an *innate* gentleman? Jimmie Dale's father had been a member of the St. James Club, and one of the largest safe manufacturers of the United States, a prosperous, wealthy man, and at Jimmie Dale's birth he had proposed his son's name for membership. It took some time to get into the St. James; there was a long waiting list that neither money, influence, nor pull could alter by so much as one iota. Men proposed their sons' names for membership when they were born as religiously as they entered them upon the city's birth register. At twenty-one Jimmie Dale was elected to membership; and, incidentally, that same year, graduated from Harvard. [3] It was Mr. Dale's desire that his son should enter the business and learn it from the ground up, and Jimmie Dale, for four years thereafter, had followed his father's wishes. Then his father died. Jimmie Dale had leanings toward more artistic pursuits than business. [4] He was credited

---

[2] No connection is ever made to the St. James Club of London which was founded in 1857. Other prestigious gentlemen's clubs located on Manhattan's Fifth Avenue included the Knickerbocker Club, the Metropolitan Club, and the University Club.

[3] I calculate that Dale was at Harvard from 1907 to 1911. His contemporaries there would have included poets T. S. Eliot and Alan Seeger, journalists John Reed and Walter Lippmann, humorist Robert Benchley, and Ernst Hanfstaengl who would later become a confidant of Adolf Hitler.

[4] Nobody would make the claim that the Gray Seal novels are autobiographical but Frank Packard does share some similarities with Jimmie Dale. Both are the sons of prosperous business owners although Lucius Packard produced shoe polish rather than safes. Jimmie and Frank each declined to continue with the family business and both rejected their father's beliefs in other ways as well. Lucius was a devout Baptist while Frank was an agnostic as an adult. As for Jimmie Dale, when a safe manufacture's son decided to become an infamous cracksman, clearly there is some deep-seated resentment there. The implication is that young Jimmie felt forced into a business career he did not want but it seems doubtful he was consciously aware of the true impulses that gave birth to his extralegal activities.

with sketching a little, writing a little; [5] and he was credited with having received a very snug amount from the combine to which he sold out his safe-manufacturing interests. He lived a bachelor life—his mother had been dead many years [6]—in the house that his father [7] had left him on Riverside Drive, [8] kept a car or two and enough servants to run his ménage smoothly, and serve a dinner exquisitely when he felt hospitably inclined.

Could there be any doubt that Jimmie Dale was innately a gentleman?

It was evening, and Jimmie Dale sat at a small table in the corner of the St. James Club dining room. Opposite him sat Herman Carruthers, a

---

[5] References to Dale's artistic inclinations will occur through this series but there are no further mentions of him as an author. However, every scene in every Gray Seal book is told only through his point of view, albeit with a third person narrative voice. So perhaps an argument could be made that Jimmie himself wrote up these adventures and that Frank Packard was the "literary agent."

[6] Packard's mother died when he was eleven days old.

[7] No names are given for either parent and no other relatives are ever mentioned. The published Gray Seal saga encompasses more than a half-million words and there is only a single instance where he is called "James" so perhaps that was his father's name.

Author Philip José Farmer in his short story "The Grant-Robeson Papers" hints that Jimmie Dale is a cousin to Lamont Cranston, AKA The Shadow. Farmer's Wold Newton literary concept theorizes that many popular Nineteenth and Twentieth Century heroes and villains are actually related to each other. However, while he offers highly detailed genealogies for Tarzan and Doc Savage the Dale-Cranston connection is not elaborated on. Perhaps the suggested family tie was motivated simply by the many parallels between the Gray Seal book series and the magazine version of The Shadow written (usually) by Walter B. Gibson. As pulp scholar Will Murray notes, "Frank L. Packard, creator of Jimmie Dale, alias the Grey (sic) Seal, was a strong influence on Walter's Shadow stories." One example would be that the St. James Club was the obvious inspiration for Gibson's Cobalt Club.

[8] Elsewhere in this novel the house is placed just north of where Riverside Drive and West 98th Street meet but the neighborhood description given by Packard differs significantly from the New York you and I can visit – or research historically. A residence on Riverside Drive rather than say Gramercy Park or lower Fifth Avenue implies the Dales are "new money" but later in this novel we are told the Dale name had "for generations in New York been the family pride."

young man of his own age, about twenty-six, [9] a leading figure in the newspaper world, whose rise from reporter to managing editor of the morning *News-Argus* [10] within the short space of a few years had been almost meteoric.

They were at coffee and cigars, and Jimmie Dale was leaning back in his chair, his dark eyes [11] fixed interestedly on his guest.

Carruthers, intently engaged in trimming his cigar ash on the edge of the Limoges china saucer of his coffee set, looked up with an abrupt laugh.

"No; I wouldn't care to go on record as being an advocate of crime," he said whimsically; "that would never do. But I don't mind admitting quite privately that it's been a positive regret to me that he has gone."

"Made too good 'copy' to lose, I suppose?" suggested Jimmie Dale quizzically. "Too bad, too, after working up a theatrical name like that for him – the Gray Seal – rather unique! Who stuck that on him – you?"

Carruthers laughed – then, grown serious, leaned toward Jimmie Dale.

"You don't mean to say, Jimmie, that you don't know about that, do you?" he asked incredulously. "Why, up to a year ago the papers were full of him."

"I never read your beastly agony columns," said Jimmie Dale, with a cheery grin.

"Well," said Carruthers, "you must have skipped everything but the stock reports then."

"Granted," said Jimmie Dale. "So go on, Carruthers, and tell me about him – I dare say I may have heard of him, since you are so distressed about it, but my memory isn't good enough to contradict anything you may have to say about the estimable gentleman, so you're safe."

Carruthers reverted to the Limoges saucer and the tip of his cigar.

"He was the most puzzling, bewildering, delightful crook in the annals of crime," said Carruthers reminiscently, after a moment's silence. "Jimmie, he was the king-pin of them all. Clever isn't the word for him, or dare-devil isn't either. I used to think sometimes his motive was more than

---

9 Dale and Carruthers both probably have 1889 birthdates.

10 Possibly affiliated in some way with the Nineteenth Century newspaper the *Brooklyn Daily News-Argus.*

11 Brown, it is presumed but we're never told for certain.

half for the pure deviltry of it, to laugh at the police and pull the noses of the rest of us that were after him. I used to dream nights about those confounded gray seals of his—that's where he got his name; he left every job he ever did with a little gray paper affair, fashioned diamond-shaped, stuck somewhere where it would be the first thing your eyes would light upon when you reached the scene, and—"

"Don't go so fast," smiled Jimmie Dale. "I don't quite get the connection. What did you have to do with this—er—Gray Seal fellow? Where do you come in?"

"I? I had a good deal to do with him," said Carruthers grimly. "I was a reporter when he first broke loose, and the ambition of my life, after I began really to appreciate what he was, was to get him—and I nearly did, half a dozen times, only—"

"Only you never quite did, eh?" cut in Jimmie Dale slyly. "How near did you get, old man? Come on, now, no bluffing; did the Gray Seal ever even recognise you as a factor in the hare-and-hound game?"

"You're flicking on the raw, Jimmie," Carruthers answered, with a wry grimace. "He knew me, all right, confound him! He favoured me with several sarcastic notes—I'll show 'em to you some day—explaining how I'd fallen down and how I could have got him if I'd done something else." Carruthers' fist came suddenly down on the table. "And I would have got him, too, if he had lived."

"Lived!" ejaculated Jimmie Dale. "He's dead, then?"

"Yes," averted Carruthers; "he's dead."

"H'm!" said Jimmie Dale facetiously. "I hope the size of the wreath you sent was an adequate tribute of your appreciation."

"I never sent any wreath," returned Carruthers, "for the very simple reason that I didn't know where to send it, or when he died. I said he was dead because for over a year now he hasn't lifted a finger."

"Rotten poor evidence, even for a newspaper," commented Jimmie Dale. "Why not give him credit for having, say—reformed?"

Carruthers shook his head. "You don't get it at all, Jimmie," he said earnestly. "The Gray Seal wasn't an ordinary crook—he was a classic. He was an artist, and the art of the thing was in his blood. A man like that could no more stop than he could stop breathing—and live. He's dead; there's nothing to it but that—he's dead. I'd bet a year's salary on it."

"Another good man gone wrong, then," said Jimmie Dale capriciously. "I suppose, though, that at least you discovered the 'woman in the case'?"

Carruthers looked up quickly, a little startled; then laughed shortly.

"What's the matter?" inquired Jimmie Dale.

"Nothing," said Carruthers. "You kind of got me for a moment, that's all. That's the way those infernal notes from the Gray Seal used to end up: 'Find the lady, old chap; and you'll get me.' He had a damned patronising familiarity that would make you squirm."

"Poor old Carruthers!" grinned Jimmie Dale. "You did take it to heart, didn't you?"

"I'd have sold my soul to get him—and so would you, if you had been in my boots," said Carruthers, biting nervously at the end of his cigar.

"And been sorry for it afterward," supplied Jimmie Dale.

"Yes, by Jove, you're right!" admitted Carruthers, "I suppose I should. I actually got to love the fellow—it was the *game*, really, that I wanted to beat."

"Well, and how about this woman? Keep on the straight and narrow path, old man," prodded Jimmie Dale.

"The woman?" Carruthers smiled. "Nothing doing! I don't believe there was one—he wouldn't have been likely to egg the police and reporters on to finding her if there had been, would he? It was a blind, of course. He worked alone, absolutely alone. That's the secret of his success, according to my way of thinking. There was never so much as an indication that he had had an accomplice in anything he ever did."

Jimmie Dale's eyes travelled around the club's homelike, perfectly appointed room. He nodded to a fellow member here and there, then his eyes rested musingly on his guest again.

Carruthers was staring thoughtfully at his coffee cup.

"He was the prince of crooks and the father of originality," announced Carruthers abruptly, following the pause that had ensued. "Half the time there wasn't any more getting at the motive for the curious things he did, than there was getting at the Gray Seal himself."

"Carruthers," said Jimmie Dale, with a quick little nod of approval, "you're positively interesting to-night. But, so far, you've been kind of scouting around the outside edges without getting into the thick of it. Let's have some of your experiences with the Gray Seal in detail; they ought to make ripping fine yarns."

"Not to-night, Jimmie," said Carruthers; "it would take too long." He pulled out his watch mechanically as he spoke, glanced at it—and pushed back his chair. "Great Scott!" he exclaimed. "It's nearly half-past nine. I'd no idea we had lingered so long over dinner. I'll have to hurry; we're a morning paper, you know, Jimmie."

"What! Really! Is it as late as that." Jimmie Dale rose from his chair as Carruthers stood up. "Well, if you must –"

"I must," said Carruthers, with a laugh.

"All right, O slave." Jimmie Dale laughed back – and slipped his hand, a trick of their old college days together, through Carruthers' arm as they left the room.

He accompanied Carruthers downstairs to the door of the club, and saw his guest into a taxi; then he returned inside, sauntered through the billiard room, and from there into one of the cardrooms, where, pressed into a game, he played several rubbers of bridge before going home.

It was, therefore, well on toward midnight when Jimmie Dale arrived at his house on Riverside Drive, and was admitted by an elderly manservant. [12]

"Hello, Jason," said Jimmie Dale pleasantly. "You still up!"

"Yes, sir," replied Jason, who had been valet to Jimmie Dale's father before him. "I was going to bed, sir, at about ten o'clock, when a messenger came with a letter. Begging your pardon, sir, a young lady, and –"

"Jason" – Jimmie Dale flung out the interruption, sudden, quick, imperative – "what did she look like?"

"Why – why, I don't exactly know as I could describe her, sir," stammered Jason, taken aback. "Very ladylike, sir, in her dress and appearance, and what I would call, sir, a beautiful face."

"Hair and eyes – what color?" demanded Jimmie Dale crisply. "Nose, lips, chin – what shape?"

"Why, sir," gasped Jason, staring at his master, "I – I don't rightly know. I wouldn't call her fair or dark, something between. I didn't take particular notice, and it wasn't overlight outside the door."

"It's too bad you weren't a younger man, Jason," commented Jimmie Dale, with a curious tinge of bitterness in his voice. "I'd have given a year's income for your opportunity to-night, Jason."

"Yes, sir," said Jason helplessly.

"Well, go on," prompted Jimmie Dale. "You told her I wasn't home, and she said she knew it, didn't she? And she left the letter that I was on no account to miss receiving when I got back, though there was no need

---

12 In a radio adaption of this chapter that Packard wrote in the 1930s he puts Jason's age at about seventy. It's assumed that Jason is his surname but that's never specifically stated.

of telephoning me to the club—when I returned would do, but it was imperative that I should have it then—eh?"

"Good Lord, sir!" ejaculated Jason, his jaw dropped, "that's exactly what she did say."

"Jason," said Jimmie Dale grimly, "listen to me. If ever she comes here again, inveigle her in. If you can't inveigle her, use force; capture her, pull her in, do anything—do anything, do you hear? Only don't let her get away from you until I've come."

Jason gazed at his master as though the other had lost his reason.

"Use force, sir?" he repeated weakly—and shook his head. "You—you can't mean that, sir."

"Can't I?" inquired Jimmie Dale, with a mirthless smile. "I mean every word of it, Jason—and if I thought there was the slightest chance of her giving you the opportunity, I'd be more imperative still. As it is—where's the letter?"

"On the table in your studio, sir," said Jason, mechanically.

Jimmie Dale started toward the stairs—then turned and came back to where Jason, still shaking his head heavily, had been gazing anxiously after his master. Jimmie Dale laid his hand on the old man's shoulder.

"Jason," he said kindly, with a swift change of mood, "you've been a long time in the family—first with father, and now with me. You'd do a good deal for me, wouldn't you?"

"I'd do anything in the world for you, Master Jim," said the old man earnestly.

"Well, then, remember this," said Jimmie Dale slowly, looking into the other's eyes, "remember this—keep your mouth shut and your eyes open. It's my fault. I should have warned you long ago, but I never dreamed that she would ever come here herself. There have been times when it was practically a matter of life and death to me to know who that woman is that you saw to-night. That's all, Jason. Now go to bed."

"Master Jim," said the old man simply, "thank you, sir, thank you for trusting me. I've dandled you on my knee when you were a baby, Master Jim. I don't know what it's about, and it isn't for me to ask. I thought, sir, that maybe you were having a little fun with me. But I know now, and you can trust me, Master Jim, if she ever comes again."

"Thank you, Jason," said Jimmie Dale, his hand closing with an appreciative pressure on the other's shoulder "Good-night, Jason."

Upstairs on the first landing, Jimmie Dale opened a door, closed and locked it behind him—and the electric switch clicked under his fingers. A glow fell softly from a cluster of shaded ceiling lights. It was a large room, a very large room, running the entire depth of the house, and the effect of apparent disorder in the arrangement of its appointments seemed to breathe a sense of charm. There were great cozy, deep, leather-covered lounging chairs, a huge, leather-covered davenport, and an easel or two with half-finished sketches upon them; the walls were panelled, the panels of exquisite grain and matching; in the centre of the room stood a flat-topped rosewood desk; upon the floor was a dark, heavy velvet rug; and, perhaps most inviting of all, there was a great, old-fashioned fireplace at one side of the room.

For an instant Jimmie Dale remained quietly by the door, as though listening. Six feet he stood, muscular in every line of his body, like a well-trained athlete with no single ounce of superfluous fat about him – the grace and ease of power in his poise. His strong, clean-shaven face, as the light fell upon it now, was serious – a mood that became him well – the firm lips closed, the dark, reliant eyes a little narrowed, a frown on the broad forehead, the square jaw clamped.

Then abruptly he walked across the room to the desk, picked up an envelope that lay upon it, and, turning again, dropped into the nearest lounging chair.

There had been no doubt in his mind, none to dispel. It was precisely what he had expected from almost the first word Jason had spoken. It was the same handwriting, the same texture of paper, and there was the same old haunting, rare, indefinable fragrance about it. Jimmie Dale's hands turned the envelope now this way, now that, as he looked at it. Wonderful hands were Jimmie Dale's, with long, slim, tapering fingers whose sensitive tips seemed now as though they were striving to decipher the message within.

He laughed suddenly, a little harshly, and tore open the envelope. Five closely written sheets fell into his hand. He read them slowly, critically, read them over again; and then, his eyes on the rug at his feet, he began to tear the paper into minute pieces between his fingers, depositing the pieces, as he tore them, upon the arm of his chair. The five sheets demolished, his fingers dipped into the heap of shreds on the arm of the chair and tore them over and over again, tore them until they were scarcely larger than bits of confetti, tore at them absently and mechanically, his eyes never shifting from the rug at his feet.

Then with a shrug of his shoulders, as though rousing himself to present reality, a curious smile flickering on his lips, he brushed the pieces of paper into one hand, carried them to the empty fireplace, laid them down in a little pile, and set them afire. Lighting a cigarette, he watched them burn until the last glow had gone from the last charred scrap; then he crunched and scattered them with the brass-handled fender brush, and, retracing his steps across the room, flung back a portière from where it hung before a little alcove, and dropped on his knees in front of a round, squat, barrel-shaped safe — one of his own design and planning in the years when he had been with his father.

His slim, sensitive fingers played for an instant among the knobs and dials that studded the door, guided, it seemed by the sense of touch alone — and the door swung open. Within was another door, with locks and bolts as intricate and massive as the outer one. This, too, he opened; and then from the interior took out a short, thick, rolled-up leather bundle tied together with thongs. He rose from his knees, closed the safe, and drew the portière across the alcove again. With the bundle under his arm, he glanced sharply around the room, listened intently, then, unlocking the door that gave on the hall, he switched off the lights and went to his dressing room, that was on the same floor. Here, divesting himself quickly of his dinner clothes, he selected a dark tweed suit with loose-fitting, sack coat from his wardrobe, and began to put it on.

Dressed, all but his coat and vest, he turned to the leather bundle that he had placed on a table, untied the thongs, and carefully opened it out to its full length — and again that curious, cryptic smile tinged his lips. Rolled the opposite away from that in which it had been tied up, the leather strip made a wide belt that went on somewhat after the fashion of a life preserver, the thongs being used for shoulder straps — a belt that, once on, the vest would hide completely, and, fitting close, left no telltale bulge in the outer garments. It was not an ordinary belt; it was full of stout-sewn, up-right little pockets all the way around, and in the pockets grimly lay an array of fine, blued-steel, highly tempered instruments — a compact, powerful burglar's kit. [13]

The slim, sensitive fingers passed with almost a caressing touch over the vicious little implements, and from one of the pockets extracted a thin, flat metal case. This Jimmie Dale opened, and glanced inside — between sheets of oil paper lay little rows of *gray, adhesive, diamond-shaped seals.*

---

[13] The Gray Seal's standard equipment includes up to twelve lockpicks of various sizes, a hand drill and a saw (both with detachable handles), glass cutter, wire cutters, skeleton keys, a steel wedge, handcuffs, a crowbar, and a length of stout cord. And, remarkably enough given that he is a frequent target of guns wielded by the law and the lawless alike, nitroglycerin ("soup"). According to the magazine version of this novel the belt has "dozens" of pockets.

Jimmie Dale snapped the case shut, returned it to its recess, and from another took out a black silk mask. He held it up to the light for examination.

"Pretty good shape after a year," muttered Jimmie Dale, replacing it.

He put on the belt, then his vest and coat. From the drawer of his dresser he took an automatic revolver [14] and an electric flashlight, slipped them into his pocket, and went softly downstairs. From the hat stand he chose a black slouch hat, pulled it well over his eyes — and left the house.

Jimmie Dale walked down a block, then hailed a bus and mounted to the top. [15] It was late, and he found himself the only passenger. He inserted his dime in the conductor's little resonant-belled cash receiver, and then settled back on the uncomfortable, bumping, cushionless seat.

On rattled the bus; it turned across town, passed the Circle, and headed for Fifth Avenue — but Jimmie Dale, to all appearances, was quite oblivious of its movements.

It was a year since she had written him. *She!* Jimmie Dale did not smile, his lips were pressed hard together. Not a very intimate or personal appellation, that — but he knew her by no other. It *was* a woman, surely — the hand-writing was feminine, the diction eminently so — and had *she* not come herself that night to Jason! He remembered the last letter, apart from the one to-night, that he had received from her. It was a year ago now — and the letter had been hardly more than a note. The police had worked themselves into a frenzy over the Gray Seal, the papers had grown absolutely maudlin — and she had written, in her characteristic way:

Things are a little too warm, aren't they, Jimmie? Let's let them cool for a year.

Since then until to-night he had heard nothing from her. It was a strange compact that he had entered into — so strange that it could never

---

14 Packard, like Walter Gibson after him, uses automatic and revolver interchangeably in his stories. Either Packard didn't understand that they are two different types of handguns or Jimmie Dale's weapon of choice actually is that rare hybrid firearm, the automatic-revolver. The Landstad 1900 from Norway is a possible candidate. Regards of what he was armed with, New York State's Sullivan Act of 1911 made it illegal for a citizen to possess a concealed weapon without licensing by the police.

15 Millionaire he may be but Dale frequently uses public transportation.

have known, could never know a parallel—unique, dangerous, bizarre, it was all that and more. It had begun really through his connection with his father's business—the business of manufacturing safes that should defy the cleverest criminals—when his brains, turned into that channel, had been pitted against the underworld, against the methods of a thousand different crooks from Maine to California, the report of whose every operation had reached him in the natural course of business, and every one of which he had studied in minutest detail. It had begun through that—but at the bottom of it was his own restless, adventurous spirit.

He had meant to set the police by the ears, using his gray-seal device both as an added barb and that no innocent bystander of the underworld, innocent for once, might be involved—he had meant to laugh at them and puzzle them to the verge of madness, for in the last analysis they would find only an abortive attempt at crime—and he had succeeded. And then he had gone too far—and he had been caught—by *her*. That string of pearls, which, to study whose effect facetiously, he had so idiotically wrapped around his wrist, and which, so ironically, he had been unable to loosen in time and had been forced to carry with him in his sudden, desperate dash to escape from Marx's the big jeweler's, in Maiden Lane, whose strong room he had toyed with one night, had been the lever which, *at first*, she had held over him.

The bus was on Fifth Avenue now, and speeding rapidly down the deserted thoroughfare. Jimmie Dale looked up at the lighted windows of the St. James Club as they went by, smiled whimsically, and shifted in his seat, seeking a more comfortable position.

She had caught him—how he did not know—he had never seen her—did not know who she was, though time and again he had devoted all his energies for months at a stretch to a solution of the mystery. The morning following the Maiden Lane affair, indeed, before he had breakfasted, Jason had brought him the first letter from her. It had started by detailing his every move of the night before—and it had ended with an ultimatum: "The cleverness, the originality of the Gray Seal as a crook lacked but one thing," she had naively written, "and that one thing was that his crookedness required a leading string to guide it into channels that were worthy of his genius." [16] In a word, *she* would plan the coups, and he would act at her dictation and execute them—or else how did twenty years in Sing Sing for that little Maiden Lane affair appeal to him? He was

---

[16] Jimmie Dale's strong moral code is on display throughout the series but apparently it never occurred to him to use the Gray Seal persona to help people in trouble until blackmailed into doing so.

to answer by the next morning, a simple "yes" or "no" in the personal column of the morning *News-Argus*.

A threat to a man like Jimmie Dale was like flaunting a red rag at a bull, and a rage ungovernable had surged upon him. Then cold reason had come. He was caught – there was no question about that – she had taken pains to show him that he need make no mistake there. Innocent enough in his own conscience, as far as actual theft went, for the pearls would in due course be restored in some way to the possession of their owner, he would have been unable to make even his own father, who was alive then, believe in his innocence, let alone a jury of his peers. Dishonour, shame, ignominy, a long prison sentence, stared him in the face, and there was but one alternative – to link hands with this unseen, mysterious accomplice. Well, he could at least temporise, he could always "queer" a game in some specious manner, if he were pushed too far. And so, in the next morning's *News-Argus*, Jimmie Dale had answered "yes." And then had followed those years in which there had been *no* temporising, in which every plan was carried out to the last detail, those years of curious, unaccountable, bewildering affairs that Carruthers had spoken of, one on top of another, that had shaken the old headquarters on Mulberry Street [17] to its foundations, until the Gray Seal had become a name to conjure with. And, yes, it was quite true, he had entered into it all, gone the limit, with an eagerness that was insatiable.

The bus had reached the lower end of Fifth Avenue, passed through Washington Square, and stopped at the end of its run. Jimmie Dale clambered down from the top, threw a pleasant "good-night" to the conductor, and headed briskly down the street before him. A little later he crossed into West Broadway, and his pace slowed to a leisurely stroll.

Here, at the upper end of the street, was a conglomerate business section of rather inferior class, catering doubtless to the poor, foreign element that congregated west of Broadway proper, and to the south of Washington Square. The street was, at first glance, deserted; it was dark and dreary, with stores and lofts on either side. An elevated train roared by overhead, with a thunderous, deafening clamour. Jimmie Dale, on the right-hand side of the street, glanced interestedly at the dark store windows as he went by. And then, a block ahead, on the other side, his eyes rested on an approaching form. As the other reached the corner and paused, and the light from the street lamp glinted on brass buttons,

---

[17] New York City Police Headquarters shifted from 300 Mulberry Street to 240 Centre on November 29, 1909.

Jimmie Dale's eyes narrowed a little under his slouch hat. The policeman, although nonchalantly swinging a nightstick, appeared to be watching him.

Jimmie Dale went on half a block farther, stooped to the sidewalk to tie his shoe, glanced back over his shoulder – the policeman was not in sight – and slipped like a shadow into the alleyway beside which he had stopped.

It was another Jimmie Dale now – the professional Jimmie Dale. Quick as a cat, active, lithe, he was over a six-foot fence in the rear of a building in a flash, and crouched a black shape, against the back door of an unpretentious, unkempt, dirty, secondhand shop that fronted on West Broadway – the last place certainly in all New York that the managing editor of the *News-Argus*, or any one else, for that matter, would have picked out as the setting for the second debut of the Gray Seal.

From the belt around his waist, Jimmie Dale took the black silk mask, and slipped it on; and from the belt, too, came a little instrument that his deft fingers manipulated in the lock. A curious snipping sound followed. Jimmie Dale put his weight gradually against the door. The door held fast.

"Bolted," said Jimmie Dale to himself.

The sensitive fingers travelled slowly up and down the side of the door, seeming to press and feel for the position of the bolt through an inch of plank – then from the belt came a tiny saw, thin and pointed at the end, that fitted into the little handle drawn from another receptacle in the leather girdle beneath the unbuttoned vest.

Hardly a sound it made as it bit into the door. Half a minute passed – there was the faint fall of a small piece of wood – into the aperture crept the delicate, tapering fingers – came a slight rasping of metal – then the door swung back, the dark shadow that had been Jimmie Dale vanished and the door closed again.

A round, white beam of light glowed for an instant – and disappeared. A miscellaneous, lumbering collection of junk and odds and ends blocked the entry, leaving no more space than was sufficient for bare passageway. Jimmie Dale moved cautiously – and once more the flashlight in his hand showed the way for an instant – then darkness again.

The cluttered accumulation of secondhand stuff in the rear gave place to a little more orderly arrangement as he advanced toward the front of the store. Like a huge firefly, the flashlight twinkled, went out, twinkled again, and went out. He passed a sort of crude, partitioned-off apartment that did duty for the establishment's office, a sort of little boxed-in place it was, about in the middle of the floor. Jimmie Dale's light played on it for a moment, but he kept on toward the front door without any pause.

Every movement was quick, sure, accurate, with not a wasted second. It had been barely a minute since he had vaulted the back fence. It was hardly a quarter of a minute more before the cumbersome lock of the front door was unfastened, and the door itself pulled imperceptibly ajar.

He went swiftly back to the office now – and found it even more of a shaky, cheap affair than it had at first appeared; more like a box stall with windows around the top than anything else, the windows doubtless to permit the occupant to overlook the store from the vantage point of the high stool that stood before a long, battered, wobbly desk. There was a door to the place, too, but the door was open and the key was in the lock. The ray of Jimmie Dale's flashlight swept once around the interior – and rested on an antique, ponderous safe.

Under the mask Jimmie Dale's lips [18] parted in a smile that seemed almost apologetic, as he viewed the helpless iron monstrosity that was little more than an insult to a trained cracksman. Then from the belt came the thin metal case and a pair of tweezers. He opened the case, and with the tweezers lifted out one of the gray-coloured, diamond-shaped seals. Holding the seal with the tweezers, he moistened the gummed side with his lips, then laid it on a handkerchief which he took from his pocket, and clapped the handkerchief against the front of the safe, sticking the seal conspicuously into place. Jimmie Dale's insignia bore no finger prints. The microscopes and magnifying glasses at headquarters had many a time regretfully assured the police of that fact. [19]

And now his hands and fingers seemed to work like lightning. Into the soft iron bit a drill – bit in and through – bit in and through again. It was dark, pitch black – and silent. Not a sound, save the quick, dull rasp of the ratchet – like the distant gnawing of a mouse! Jimmie Dale worked fast – another hole went through the face of the old-fashioned safe – and then suddenly he straightened up to listen, every faculty tense, alert, and strained, his body thrown a little forward. *What was that!*

---

[18] Contemporary illustrations of the Gray Seal - including the 1917 movie serial - show him wearing a domino mask that is little more than a ring of fabric around each eye but Packard consistently describes the mask as covering most of the face.

[19] Dale is always careful about leaving fingerprints on his gray paper seals but is described handling door knobs and every other object he encounters as the Gray Seal without apparent concern. Since he never seems to wear gloves we just have to presume his other precautions are implied rather than shown.

From the alleyway leading from the street without, through which he himself had come, sounded the stealthy crunch of feet. Motionless in the utter darkness, Jimmie Dale listened — there was a scraping noise in the rear — someone was climbing the fence that he had climbed!

In an instant the tools in Jimmie Dale's hands disappeared into their respective pockets beneath his vest — and the sensitive fingers shot to the dial on the safe.

"Too bad," muttered Jimmie Dale plaintively to himself. "I could have made such an artistic job of it — I swear I could have cut Carruthers' profile in the hole in less than no time — to open it like this is really taking the poor old thing at a disadvantage."

He was on his knees now, one ear close to the dial, listening as the tumblers fell, while the delicate fingers spun the knob unerringly — the other ear strained toward the rear of the premises.

Came a footstep — a ray of light — a stumble — nearer — the newcomer was inside the place now, and must have found out that the back door had been tampered with. Nearer came the steps — still nearer — and then the safe door swung open under Jimmie Dale's hand, and Jimmie Dale, that he might not be caught like a rat in a trap, darted from the office — but he had delayed a little too long.

From around the cluttered piles of junk and miscellany swept the light — full on Jimmie Dale. Hesitation for the smallest fraction of a second would have been fatal, but hesitation was something that in all his life Jimmie Dale had never known. Quick as a panther in its spring, he leaped full at the light and the man behind it. The rough voice, in surprised exclamation at the sudden discovery of the quarry, died in a gasp.

There was a crash as the two men met — and the other reeled back before the impact. Onto him Jimmie Dale sprang, and his hands flew for the other's throat. It was an officer in uniform! Jimmie Dale had felt the brass buttons as they locked. In the darkness there was a queer smile on Jimmie Dale's tight lips. It was no doubt *the* officer whom he had passed on the other side of the street.

The other was a smaller man than Jimmie Dale, but powerful for his build — and he fought now with all his strength. This way and that the two men reeled, staggered, swayed, panting and gasping; and then — they had lurched back close to the office door — with a sudden swing, every muscle brought into play for a supreme effort, Jimmie Dale hurled the other from him, sending the man sprawling back to the floor of the office, and in the winking of an eye had slammed shut the door and turned the key.

There was a bull-like roar, the shrill *cheep-cheep-cheep* of the patrolman's whistle, and a shattering crash as the officer flung his body against the partition — then the bark of a revolver shot, the tinkle of breaking glass, as the man fired through the office window—and past Jimmie Dale, speeding now for the front door, a bullet hummed viciously.

Out on the street dashed Jimmie Dale, whipping the mask from his face—and glanced like a hawk around him. For all the racket, the neighbourhood had not yet been aroused—no one was in sight. From just overhead came the rattle of a downtown elevated train. In a hundred-yard sprint, Jimmie Dale raced it a half block to the station, tore up the steps—and a moment later dropped nonchalantly into a seat and pulled an evening newspaper from his pocket.

Jimmie Dale got off at the second station down, crossed the street, mounted the steps of the elevated again, and took the next train uptown. His movements appeared to be somewhat erratic—he alighted at the station next above the one by which he had made his escape. Looking down the street it was too dark to see much of anything, but a confused noise as of a gathering crowd reached him from what was about the location of the secondhand store. He listened appreciatively for a moment.

"Isn't it a perfectly lovely night?" said Jimmie Dale amiably to himself. "And to think of that cop running away with the idea that I didn't see him when he hid in a doorway after I passed the corner! Well, well, strange—isn't it?"

With another glance down the street, a whimsical lift of his shoulders, he headed west into the dilapidated tenement quarter that huddled for a handful of blocks near by, just south of Washington Square. It was a little after one o'clock in the morning now and the pedestrians were casual. Jimmie Dale read the street signs on the corners as he went along, turned abruptly into an intersecting street, counted the tenements from the corner as he passed, and—for the eye of any one who might be watching—opened the street door of one of them quite as though he were accustomed and had a perfect right to do so, and went inside.

It was murky and dark within; hot, unhealthy, with lingering smells of garlic and stale cooking. He groped for the stairs and started up. He climbed one flight, then another—and one more to the top. Here, treading softly, he made an examination of the landing with a view, evidently, to obtaining an idea of the location and the number of doors that opened off from it.

His selection fell on the third door from the head of the stairs—there were four all told, two apartments of two rooms each. He paused for an instant to adjust the black silk mask, tried the door quietly, found it unlocked, opened it with a sudden, quick, brisk movement—and, stepping in side, leaned with his back against it.

"Good-morning," said Jimmie Dale pleasantly.

It was a squalid place, a miserable hole, in which a single flickering, yellow gas jet gave light. It was almost bare of furniture; there was nothing but a couple of cheap chairs, a rickety table—unpawnable. A boy, he was hardly more than that, perhaps twenty-two, from a posture in which he was huddled across the table with head buried in out-flung arms, sprang with a startled cry to his feet.

"Good-morning," said Jimmie Dale again. "Your name's Hagan, Bert Hagan—isn't it? And you work for Isaac Brolsky in the secondhand shop over on West Broadway—don't you?"

The boy's lips quivered, and the gaunt, hollow, half-starved face, white, ashen-white now, was pitiful.

"I—I guess you got me," he faltered "I—I suppose you're a plain-clothes man, though I never knew dicks wore masks."

"They don't generally," said Jimmie Dale coolly. "It's a fad of mine—Bert Hagan."

The lad, hanging to the table, turned his head away for a moment—and there was silence.

Presently Hagan spoke again. "I'll go," he said numbly. "I won't make any trouble. Would—would you mind not speaking loud? I—I wouldn't like her to know."

"Her?" said Jimmie Dale softly.

The boy tiptoed across the room, opened a connecting door a little, peered inside, opened it a little wider—and looked over his shoulder at Jimmie Dale.

Jimmie Dale crossed to the boy, looked inside the other room—and his lip twitched queerly, as the sight sent a quick, hurt throb through his heart. A young woman, younger than the boy, lay on a tumble-down bed, a rag of clothing over her—her face with a deathlike pallor upon it, as she lay in what appeared to be a stupor. She was ill, critically ill; it needed no trained eye to discern a fact all too apparent to the most casual observer. The squalor, the glaring poverty here, was even more pitifully in evidence than in the other room—only here upon a chair beside the bed was a cluster of medicine bottles and a little heap of fruit.

Jimmie Dale drew back silently as the boy closed the door.

Hagan walked to the table and picked up his hat.

"I'm—I'm ready," he said brokenly. "Let's go."

"Just a minute," said Jimmie Dale. "Tell us about it."

"Twon't take long," said Hagan, trying to smile. "She's my wife. The sickness took all we had. I—I kinder got behind in the rent and things. They were going to fire us out of here—to-morrow. And there wasn't any money for the medicine, and – and the things she had to have. Maybe you wouldn't have done it – but I did. I couldn't see her dying there for the want of something a little money'd buy – and – and I couldn't" – he caught his voice in a little sob – "I couldn't see her thrown out on the street like that."

"And so," said Jimmie Dale, "instead of putting old Isaac's cash in the safe this evening when you locked up, you put it in your pocket instead – eh? Didn't you know you'd get caught?"

"What did it matter?" said the boy. He was twirling his misshapen hat between his fingers. "I knew they'd know it was me in the morning when old Isaac found it gone, because there wasn't anybody else to do it. But I paid the rent for four months ahead to-night, and I fixed it so's she'd have medicine and things to eat. I was going to beat it before daylight myself – I" – he brushed his hand hurriedly across his cheek – "I didn't want to go – to leave her till I had to."

"Well, say" – there was wonderment in Jimmie Dale's tones, and his English lapsed into ungrammatical, reassuring vernacular – "ain't that queer! Say, I'm no detective. Gee, kid, did you think I was? Say, listen to this! I cracked old Isaac's safe half an hour ago – and I guess there won't be any idea going around that you got the money and I pulled a lemon. Say, I ain't superstitious, but it looks like luck meant you to have another chance, don't it?"

The hat dropped from Hagan's hands to the floor, and he swayed a little.

"You – you ain't a dick!" he stammered. "Then how'd you know about me and my name when you found the safe empty? Who told you?"

A wry grimace spread suddenly over Jimmie Dale's face beneath the mask, and he swallowed hard. Jimmie Dale would have given a good deal to have been able to answer that question himself.

"Oh, that!" said Jimmie Dale. "That's easy – I knew you worked there. Say, it's the limit, ain't it? Talk about your luck being in, why all you've got to do is to sit tight and keep your mouth shut, and you're safe as a church. Only say, what are you going to do about the money, now you've got a four months' start and are kind of landed on your feet?

"Do?" said the boy. "I'll pay it back, little by little. I meant to. I ain't no –" He stopped abruptly.

"Crook," supplied Jimmie Dale pleasantly. "Spit it right out, kid; you won't hurt my feelings none. Well, I'll tell you – you're talking the way I like to hear you – you pay that back, slide it in without his knowing it, a bit at a time, whenever you can, and you'll never hear a yip out of me; but if you don't, why it kind of looks as though I have a right to come down your street and get my share or know the reason why—eh?"

"Then you never get any share," said Hagan, with a catch in his voice. "I pay it back as fast as I can."

"Sure," said Jimmie Dale. "That's right—that's what I said. Well, so long—Hagan." And Jimmie Dale had opened the door and slipped outside.

An hour later, in his dressing room in his house on Riverside Drive, Jimmie Dale was removing his coat as the telephone, a hand instrument on the table, rang. Jimmie Dale glanced at it—and leisurely proceeded to remove his vest. Again the telephone rang. Jimmie Dale took off his curious, pocketed leather belt—as the telephone repeated its summons. He picked out the little drill he had used a short while before, and inspected it critically—feeling its point with his thumb, as one might feel a razor's blade. Again the telephone rang insistently. He reached languidly for the receiver, took it off its hook, and held it to his ear.

"Hello!" said Jimmie Dale, with a sleepy yawn. "Hello! Hello! Why the deuce don't you yank a man out of bed at two o'clock in the morning and have done with it, and—eh? Oh, that you, Carruthers?"

"Yes," came Carruthers' voice excitedly. "Jimmie, listen—listen! The Gray Seal's come to life! He's just pulled a break on West Broadway!"

"Good Lord!" gasped Jimmie Dale. "You don't say!"

CHAPTER II

BY PROXY

(Thursday 7/29/1915 to Friday 7/30/1915)

THE most puzzling bewildering, delightful crook in the annals of crime," Herman Carruthers, the editor of the *Morning News-Argus*, had called the Gray Seal; and Jimmie Dale smiled a little grimly now as he recalled the occasion of a week ago at the St. James Club over their after-dinner coffee. That was before his second debut, with Isaac Brolsky's poverty-stricken premises over on West Broadway as a setting for the break.

She had written: "Things are a little too warm, aren't they, Jimmie? Let's let them cool for a year." Well, they had cooled for a year, and Carruthers as a result had been complacently satisfied in his own mind that the Gray Seal was dead — until that break at Isaac Brolsky's over on West Broadway!

Jimmie Dale's smile was tinged with whimsicality now. The only effect of the year's inaction had been to usher in his renewed activity with a furor compared to which all that had gone before was insignificant. Where the newspapers had been maudlin, they now raved — raved in editorials and raved in headlines. It was an impossible, untenable, unbelievable condition of affairs that this Gray Seal, for all his incomparable cleverness, should flaunt his crimes in the faces of the citizens of New York. One could actually see the editors writhing in their swivel chairs as their fiery denunciations dripped from their pens! What was the matter with the police? Were the police children; or, worse still, imbeciles — or, still worse again, was there some one "higher up" who was profiting by this rogue's work? New York would not stand for it — New York would most decidedly not — and the sooner the police realised that fact the better! If the police were helpless, or tools, the citizens of New York were not, and it was time the citizens were thoroughly aroused.

There was a way, too, to arouse the citizens, that was both good business from the newspaper standpoint, and efficacious as a method. Carruthers, of the *Morning News-Argus*, had initiated it. The *Morning News-Argus* offered twenty-five thousand dollars' reward for the capture of the Gray Seal! Other papers immediately followed suit in varying amounts. The authorities, State and municipal, goaded to desperation, did likewise, and the five million men, women, and children of New York were automatically metamorphosed into embryonic sleuths. New York was aroused.

Jimmie Dale, alias the Gray Seal, member of the ultra-exclusive St. James Club, the latter fact sufficient in itself to guarantee his social standing, graduate of Harvard, inheritor of his deceased father's immense wealth amassed in the manufacture of burglar-proof safes, some of the most ingenious patents on which were due to Jimmie Dale himself, figured with a pencil on the margin of the newspaper he had been reading, using the arm of the big, luxurious, leather-upholstered lounging chair as a support for the paper. The result of his calculations was eighty-five thousand dollars. [20]

He brushed the paper onto the Turkish rug, dove into the pocket of his dinner jacket for his cigarettes, and began to smoke as his eyes strayed around the room, his own particular den in his fashionable Riverside Drive residence.

Eighty-five thousand dollars' reward! Jimmie Dale blew meditative rings of cigarette smoke at the fireplace. What would she say to that? Would she decide it was "too hot" again, and call it off? It added quite a little hazard to the game—*quite* a little! If he only knew who "she" was! It was a strange partnership—the strangest partnership that had ever existed between two human beings.

He turned a little in his chair as a step sounded in the hallway without—that is, Jimmie Dale caught the sound, muffled though it was by the heavy carpet. Came then a knock upon the door.

"Come in," invited Jimmie Dale.

It was old Jason, the butler. The old man was visibly excited, as he extended a silver tray on which lay a letter.

Jimmie Dale's hand reached quickly out, the long, slim tapering fingers closed upon the envelope—but his eyes were on Jason significantly, questioningly.

"Yes, Master Jim," said the old man, "I recognised it on the instant, sir. After what you said, sir, last week, honouring me, I might say, to a certain extent with your confidence, though I'm sure I don't know what it all means, I—"

"Who brought it this time, Jason?" inquired Jimmie Dale quietly.

---

[20] That's over two million dollars in 2018 currency.

"Not the young person, begging your pardon, not the young lady, sir. A shuffer [21] in a big automobile. 'Your master at once,' he says, and shoves the letter into my hand, and was off."

"Very good, Jason," said Jimmie Dale. "You may go."

The door closed. Yes, it was from *her* – it was the same texture of paper, there was the same rare, haunting fragrance clinging to it.

He tore the envelope open, and extracted a folded sheet of paper. What was it this time? To call the partnership off again until the present furor should have subsided once more – or the skilfully sketched outline of a new adventure? Which? He glanced at the few lines written on the sheet, and lunged forward from his chair to his feet. It was neither one nor the other. It was –

Jimmie Dale's face was set, and an angry red surge swept his cheeks. His lips moved, muttering audibly fragments of the letter, as he stared at it.

" – incredible that you – a heinous thing – act instantly – this is ruin – "

For an instant – a rare occurrence in Jimmie Dale's life – he stood like a man stricken, still staring at the sheet in his hand. Then mechanically his fingers tore the paper into little pieces, and the little pieces into tiny shreds. Anger fled, and a sickening sense of impotent dismay took its place; the red left his cheeks, and in its stead a grayness came.

"Act instantly!" The words seemed to leap at him, drum at his ears with constant repetition. Act instantly! But how? How? Then his brain – that keen, clear, master brain – sprang from stunned inaction into virility again. Of course – Carruthers! It was in Carruthers' line.

He stepped to the desk – and paused with his hand extended to pick up the telephone. How explain to Carruthers that he, Jimmie Dale, already knew what Carruthers might not yet have heard of, even though Carruthers would naturally be among the first to be in touch with such affairs! No; that would never do. Better get there himself at once and trust to –

The telephone rang.

Jimmie Dale waited until it rang again, then he lifted the receiver from the hook.

"Hello?" he said.

---

21 "Shuffer" here is a slang term for chauffeur.

"Hello! Hello! Jimmie!" came a voice. "This is Carruthers. That you, Jimmie?"

"Yes," said Jimmie Dale and sat down limply in the desk chair.

"It's the Gray Seal again. I promised you I'd let you in on the ground floor next time anything happened, so come on down here quick if you want to see some of his work at firsthand."

Jimmie Dale flirted a bead of sweat from his forehead.

"Carruthers," said Jimmie languidly, "you newspaper chaps make me tired with your Gray Seal. I'm just going to bed."

"Bed nothing!" spluttered Carruthers, from the other end of the wire. "Come down, I tell you. It's worth your while—half the population of New York would give the toes off their feet for the chance. Come down, you blasé idiot! The Gray Seal has gone the limit this time—it's *murder*."

Jimmie Dale's face was haggard.

"Oh!" he said peevishly. "Sounds interesting. Where are you? I guess maybe I'll jog along."

"I should think you would!" snapped Carruthers. "You know the Palace on the Bowery? 22 Yes? Well, meet me on the corner there as soon as you can. Hustle! Good—"

"Oh, I say, Carruthers!" interposed Jimmie Dale.

"Yes?" demanded Carruthers.

"Thanks awfully for letting me know, old man."

"Don't mention it!" returned Carruthers sarcastically. "You always were a grateful beast, Jimmie. Hurry up!"

Jimmie Dale hung up the receiver of the city 'phone, and took down the receiver of another, a private-house installation, and rang twice for the garage.

"The light car at once, Benson," he ordered curtly. "At once!"

Jimmie Dale worked quickly then. In his dressing room, he changed from dinner clothes to tweeds; spent a second or so over the contents of a locked drawer in the dresser, from which he selected a very small but serviceable automatic, and a very small but highly powerful magnifying

---

22 The Bowery and the Lower East Side are the primary settings for this series. Packard lived in New York from 1907 or 1908 to the end of 1910 and it can probably be said that the Gray Seal's New York best resembles the city in those years. Even by then the Tenderloin had surpassed the Bowery as the vice center of Manhattan but Packard never references that neighborhood.

glass whose combination of little round lenses worked on a pivot, and, closed over one another, were of about the compass of a quarter of a dollar.

In three minutes he was outside the house and stepping into the car, just as it drew up at the curb.

"Benson," he said tersely to his chauffeur, "drop me one block this side of the Palace on the Bowery – and forget there was ever a speed law enacted. Understand?"

"Very good, sir," said Benson, touching his cap. "I'll do my best, sir."

Jimmie Dale, in the tonneau, stretched out his legs under the front seat, and dug his hands into his pockets – and inside the pockets his hands were clenched and knotted fists.

Murder! At times it had occurred to him that there was a possibility that some crook of the underworld would attempt to cover his tracks and take refuge from pursuit by foisting himself on the authorities as the Gray Seal. That was a possibility, a risk always to be run. But that *murder* should be laid to the Gray Seal's door! Anger, merciless and unrestrained, surged over Jimmie Dale.

There was peril here, live and imminent. Suppose that some day he should be caught in some little affair, recognised and identified as the Gray Seal, there would be the charge of murder hanging over him – and the electric chair to face!

But the peril was not the only thing. Even worse to Jimmie Dale's artistic and sensitive temperament was the vilification, the holding up to loathing, contumely, and abhorrence of the name, the stainless name, of the Gray Seal. It *was* stainless! He had guarded it jealously – as a man guards the woman's name he loves.

Affairs that had mystified and driven the police distracted with impotence there had been, many of them; and on the face of them – crimes. But no act ever committed had been in reality a crime – none without the highest of motives, the righting of some outrageous wrong, the protection of some poor stumbling fellow human.

That had been his partnership with her. How, by what amazing means, by what power that smacked almost of the miraculous she came in touch with all these things and supplied him with the data on which to work he did not know – only that, thanks to her, there were happier hearts and happier homes since the Gray Seal had begun to work. "Dear Philanthropic Crook," she often called him in her letters. And now – it was *murder!*

Take Carruthers, for instance. For years, as a reporter before he had risen to the editorial desk, he had been one of the keenest on the scent of the Gray Seal, but always for the sake of the game – always filled with admiration, as he said himself, for the daring, the originality of the most puzzling, bewildering, delightful crook in the annals of crime. Carruthers was but an example. Carruthers now would hunt the Gray Seal like a mad dog. The Gray Seal, to Carruthers and every one else, would be the vilest name in the land – a synonym for murder.

On the car flew – and upon Jimmie Dale's face, as though chiselled in marble, was a look that was not good to see. And a mirthless smile set, frozen, on his lips.

"I'll get the man that did this," gritted Jimmie Dale between his teeth. "I'll *get* him! And, when I get him, I'll wring a confession from him if I have to swing for it!"

The car swept from Broadway into Astor Place, on down the Bowery, and presently stopped.

Jimmie Dale stepped out. "I shall not want you any more, Benson," he said. "You may return home."

Jimmie Dale started down the block – a nonchalant Jimmie Dale now, if anything, bored a little. Near the corner, a figure, back turned, was lounging at the edge of the sidewalk. Jimmie Dale touched the man on the arm.

"Hello, Carruthers!" he drawled.

"Ah, Jimmie!" Carruthers turned with an excited smile. "That's the boy! You've made mighty quick time."

"Well, you told me to hurry," grumbled Jimmie Dale. "I'm doing my best to please you to-night. Came down in my car, and got summoned for three fines to-morrow."

Carruthers laughed. "Come on," he said; and, linking his arm in Jimmie Dale's, turned the corner, and headed west along the cross street. "This is going to make a noise," he continued, a grim note creeping into his voice. "The biggest noise the city has ever heard. I take back all I said about the Gray Seal. I'd always pictured his cleverness as being inseparable with at least a decent sort of man, even if he was a rogue and a criminal, but I'm through with that. He's a rotter and a hound of the rankest sort! I didn't think there was anything more vulgar or brutal than murder, but he's shown me that there is. A guttersnipe's got more decency! To murder a man and then boastfully label the corpse is –"

"Say, Carruthers," said Jimmie Dale plaintively, suddenly hanging back, "I say, you know, it's – it's all right for you to mess up in this sort of thing, it's your beastly business, and I'm awfully damned thankful to you for giving me a look-in, but isn't it—er—rather *infra dig* [23] for me? A bit morbid, you know, and all that sort of thing. I'd never hear the end of it at the club—you know what the St. James is. Couldn't I be Merideth Stanley Annstruther, or something like that, one of your new reporters, or something like that, you know?"

Carruthers chuckled. "Sure, Jimmie," he said. "You're the latest addition to the staff of the *News-Argus.* Don't worry; the incomparable Jimmie Dale won't figure publicly in this."

"It's awfully good of you," said Jimmie gratefully. "I have to have a notebook or something, don't I?"

Carruthers, from his pocket, handed him one. "Thanks," said Jimmie Dale.

A little way ahead, a crowd had collected on the sidewalk before a doorway, and Carruthers pointed with a jerk of his hand.

"It's in Moriarty's place—a gambling hell," he explained. "I haven't got the story myself yet, though I've been inside, and had a look around. Inspector Clayton discovered the crime, and reported it at headquarters. I was at my desk in the office when the news came, and, as you know the interest I've taken in the Gray Seal, I decided to 'cover' it myself. When I got here, Clayton hadn't returned from headquarters, so, as you seemed so keenly interested last week, I telephoned you. If Clayton's back now we'll get the details. Clayton's a good fellow with the 'press,' and he won't hold anything out on us. Now, here we are. Keep close to me, and I'll pass you in."

They shouldered through the crowd and up to an officer at the door. The officer nodded, stepped aside, and Carruthers, with Jimmie Dale following, entered the house.

They climbed one flight, and then another. The card-rooms, the faro, stud, and roulette layouts were deserted, save for policemen here and there on guard. Carruthers led the way to a room at the back of the hall, whose door was open and from which issued a hubbub of voices—one voice rose above the others, heavy and gratingly complacent.

"Clayton's back," observed Carruthers.

They stepped over the threshold, and the heavy voice greeted them.

"Ah, here's Carruthers now! H'are you, Carruthers? They told me you'd been here, and were coming back, so I've been keeping the boys

---

[23] Shortened from "infra dignitatem" which is Latin for "beneath one's dignity."

waiting before handing out the dope. You've had a look at that—eh?" He flung out a fat hand toward the bed.

The voices rose again, all directed at Carruthers now.

"Bubble's burst, eh, Carruthers? What about the 'Prince of Crooks'? Artistry in crime, wasn't it, you said?" They were quoting from his editorials of bygone days, a half dozen reporters of rival papers, grinning and joshing him good-naturedly, seemingly quite unaffected by what lay within arm's reach of them upon the bed.

Carruthers smiled a little wryly, shrugged his shoulders—and presented Jimmie Dale to Inspector Clayton.

"Mr. Matthewson, [24] a new man of ours—inspector."

"Glad to know you, Mr. Matthewson," said the inspector.

Jimmie Dale found his hand grasped by another that was flabby and unpleasantly moist; and found himself looking into a face that was red, with heavy rolls of unhealthy fat terminating in a double chin and a thick, apoplectic neck—a huge, round face, with rat's eyes.

Clayton dropped Jimmie Dale's hand, and waved his own in the air. Jimmie Dale remained modestly on the outside of the circle as the reporters gathered around the police inspector.

"Now, then," said Clayton coarsely, "the guy that's croaked there is Metzer, Jake Metzer. Get that?"

Jimmie Dale, scribbling hurriedly in his notebook like all the rest, turned a little toward the bed, and his lower jaw crept out the fraction of an inch. Both gas jets in the room were turned on full, giving ample light. A man fully dressed, a man of perhaps forty, lay upon his back on the bed, one arm outflung across the bedspread, the other dangling, with fingers just touching the floor, the head at an angle and off the pillow. It was as though he had been carried to the bed and flung upon it after the deed had been committed. Jimmie Dale's eyes shifted and swept the room. Yes, everything was in disorder, as though there had been a struggle—a chair upturned, a table canted against the wall, broken pieces of crockery from the washstand on the carpet, and—

"Metzer was a stool pigeon, see?" went on Clayton, "and he lived here. Moriarty wasn't on to him. Metzer stood in thick with a wider circle of crooks than any other snitch in New York."

Jimmie Dale, still scribbling as Clayton talked, stepped to the bed and leaned over the murdered man. The murder had been done with a

---

[24] Curious that no one on the scene associated this alias with Christy Mathewson, future Hall of Fame baseball player who was active from 1900 to 1916. Packard himself, having lived the majority of his life in Canada, favored golf and curling.

blackjack evidently—a couple of blows. The left side of the temple was crushed in. Right in the middle of the forehead, pasted there, a gray-colored, diamond shaped paper seal flaunted itself—the device of the Gray Seal. In Jimmie Dale' hand, hidden as he turned his back, the tiny combination of powerful lenses was focused on the seal.

Clayton guffawed. "That's right!" he called out. "Take a good look. That's a bright young man you've got, Carruthers."

Jimmie Dale looked up a little sheepishly—and got a grin from the assembled reporters, and a scowl from Carruthers.

"Now, then," continued Clayton, "here's the facts—as much of 'em as I can let you boys print at present. You know I'm stretching a point to let you in here—don't forget that when you come to write up the case— honour where's honour's due, you know. Well, me and Metzer there was getting ready to close down on a big piece of game, and I was over here in this room talking to him about it early this afternoon. We had it framed to get our man to-night—see? I left Metzer, say, about three o'clock, and he was to show up over at headquarters with another little bit of evidence we wanted at eight o'clock to-night."

Jimmie Dale was listening—to every word. But he stooped now again over the murdered man's head deliberately, though he felt the inspector's rat's eyes upon him—stooped, and, with his finger nail, lifted back the right-hand point of the diamond-shaped seal where it bordered a faint thread of blood on the man's forehead.

There was a bull-like roar from the inspector, and he burst through the ring of reporters, and grabbed Jimmie Dale by the shoulder.

"Here you, what in hell are you doing!" he spluttered angrily.

Embarrassed and confused, Jimmie Dale drew back, glanced around, and smiled again a little sheepishly as his eyes rested on the red-flushed jowl of the inspector.

"I—I wanted to see how it was stuck on," he explained inanely.

"Stuck on!" bellowed Clayton. "I'll show you how it's *stuck* on, if you monkey around here! Don't you know any better than that! Where were you dragged up anyway? The coroner hasn't been here yet. You're a hot cub of a reporter, you are!" He turned to Carruthers. "Y'ought to get out printed instructions for 'em before you turn 'em loose!" he snapped.

Carruthers' face was red with mortification. There was a grin, expanded, on the faces of the others.

"Stand away from that bed!" roared Clayton at Jimmie Dale. "And if you go near it again, I'll throw you out of here bodily!"

Jimmie Dale edged away, and, eyes lowered, fumbled nervously with the leaves of his notebook.

Clayton grunted, glared at Jimmie Dale for an instant viciously — and resumed his story.

"I was saying," he said, "that Metzer was to come to headquarters at eight o'clock this evening. Well, he didn't show up. That looked queer. It was mighty important business. We was after one of the biggest hauls we'd ever pulled off. I waited till nine o'clock, an hour ago, and I was getting nervous. Then I started over here to find out what was the matter. When I got here I asked Moriarty if he'd seen Metzer. Moriarty said he hadn't since I was here before. He was a little suspicious that I had something on Metzer — see? Well, by pumping Moriarty, he admitted that Metzer had had a visitor about an hour after I left."

"Who was it? Know what his name is, inspector?" asked one of the reporters quickly.

Inspector Clayton winked heavily. "Don't be greedy, boys," he grinned.

"You mean you've got him?" burst out another one of the men excitedly.

"Sure! Sure, I've got him." Inspector Clayton waved his fat hand airily. "Or I will have before morning — but I ain't saying anything more till it's over." He smiled significantly. "Well, that's about all. You've got the details right around you. I left Moriarty downstairs and came up here, and found just what you see — Metzer laying on the bed there, and the gray seal stuck on his forehead — and" — he ended abruptly — "I'll have the Gray Seal himself behind the bars by morning."

A chorus of ejaculations rose from the reporters, while their pencils worked furiously.

Then Jimmie Dale appeared to have an inspiration. Jimmie Dale turned a leaf in his notebook and began to sketch rapidly, cocking his head now on one side now on the other. With a few deft strokes he had outlined the figure of Inspector Clayton. The reporter beside Jimmie Dale leaned over to inspect the work, and another did likewise. Jimmie Dale drew in Clayton's face most excellently, if somewhat flatteringly; and then, with a little flourish of pride, wrote under the drawing: "The Man Who Captured the Gray Seal."

"That's a cracking good sketch!" pronounced the reporter at his side. "Let the inspector see it."

"What is it?" demanded Clayton, scowling.

Jimmie Dale handed him the notebook modestly.

Inspector Clayton took it, looked at it, looked at Jimmie Dale; then his scowl relaxed into a self-sufficient and pleased smile, and he grunted approvingly.

"That's the stuff to put over," he said. "Mabbe you're not much of a reporter, but you can draw. Y're all right, sport — y're all right. Forget what I said to you a while ago."

Jimmie Dale smiled too — deprecatingly. And put the notebook in his pocket.

An officer entered the room hurriedly, and, drawing Clayton aside, spoke in an undertone. A triumphant and malicious grin settled on Clayton's features, and he started with a rush for the door.

"Come around to headquarters in two hours, boys," he called as he went out, "and I'll have something more for you."

The room cleared, the reporters tumbling downstairs to make for the nearest telephones to get their "copy" into their respective offices.

On the street, a few doors up from the house where they were free from the crowd, Carruthers halted Jimmie Dale.

"Jimmie," he said reproachfully, "you certainly made a mark of us both. There wasn't any need to play the 'cub' so egregiously. However, I'll forgive you for the sake of the sketch — hand it over, Jimmie; I'm going to reproduce it in the first edition."

"It wasn't drawn for reproduction, Carruthers — at least not yet," said Jimmie Dale quietly.

Carruthers stared at him. "Eh?" he asked blankly.

"I've taken a dislike to Clayton," said Jimmie Dale whimsically. "He's too patently after free advertising, and I'm not going to help along his boost. You can't have it, old man, so let's think about something else. What'll they do with that bit of paper that's on the poor devil's forehead up there, for instance."

"Say," said Carruthers, "does it strike you that you're acting queer? You haven't been drinking, have you, Jimmie?"

"What'll they do with it?" persisted Jimmie Dale.

"Well," said Carruthers, smiling a little tolerantly, "they'll photograph it and enlarge the photograph, and label it 'Exhibit A' or 'Exhibit B' or something like that — and file it away in the archives with the fifty or more just like it that are already in their collection."

"That's what I thought," observed Jimmie Dale. He took Carruthers by the lapel of the coat. "I'd like a photograph of that. I'd like it so much that I've got to have it. Know the chap that does that work for the police?"

"Yes," admitted Carruthers.

"Very good!" said Jimmie Dale crisply, "Get an extra print of the enlargement from him then — for a consideration — whatever he asks — I'll pay for it."

"But what for?" demanded Carruthers. "I don't understand."

"Because," said Jimmie Dale very seriously, "put it down to imagination or whatever you like, I think I smell something fishy here."

"You *what!*" exclaimed Carruthers in amazement. "You're not joking, are you, Jimmie?"

Jimmie Dale laughed shortly. "It's so far from a joke," he said, in a low tone, "that I want your word you'll get that photograph into my hands by to-morrow afternoon, no matter what transpires in the meantime. And look here, Carruthers, don't think I'm playing the silly thickhead, and trying to mystify you. I'm no detective or anything like that. I've just got an idea that apparently hasn't occurred to any one else — and, of course, I may be all wrong. If I am, I'm not going to say a word even to you, because it wouldn't be playing fair with some one else; if I'm right the *Morning News-Argus* gets the biggest scoop of the century. Will you go in on that basis?"

Carruthers put out his hand impulsively. "If you're in earnest, Jimmie — you bet!"

"Good!" returned Jimmie Dale. "The photograph by to-morrow afternoon then. And now — "

"And now," said Caruthers, "I've got to hurry over to the office and get a write-up man at work. Will you come along, or meet me at headquarters later? Clayton said in two hours he'd — "

"Neither," said Jimmie Dale. "I'm not interested in headquarters. I'm going home."

"Well, all right then," Carruthers returned. "You can bank on me for to-morrow. Good-night, Jimmie."

"Good-night, old man," said Jimmie Dale, and, turning, walked briskly toward the Bowery.

But Jimmie Dale did not go home. He walked down the Bowery for three blocks, crossed to the east side, and turned down a cross street. Two blocks more he walked in this direction, and halfway down the next. Here he paused an instant — the street was dimly lighted, almost dark, deserted. Jimmie Dale edged close to the houses until his shadow blended with the shadows of the walls — and slipped suddenly into a pitch-black areaway.

He opened a door, stepped into an unlighted hallway where the air was close and evil smelling, mounted a stairway, and halted before another door on the first landing. There was the low clicking of a lock, three times repeated, and he entered a room, closing and fastening the door behind him.

Jimmie Dale called it his "Sanctuary." [25] In one of the worst neighbourhoods of New York, where no questions were asked as long as the rent was paid, it had the further advantage of three separate exits – one by the areaway where he had entered; one from the street itself; and another through a back yard with an entry into a saloon that fronted on the next street. It was not often that Jimmie Dale used his Sanctuary, but there had been times when it was no more nor less than exactly what he called it – a sanctuary!

He stepped to the window, assured himself that the shade was down – and lighted the gas, blinking a little as the yellow flame illuminated the room.

It was a rough place, dirty, uninviting; a bedroom, furnished in the most scanty fashion. Neither, apparently, was there anything suspicious about it to reward one curious enough to break in during the owner's absence – some rather disreputable clothes hanging on the wall, and flung untidily across the bed – that was all.

Alone now, Jimmie Dale's face was strained and anxious and, occasionally, as he undressed himself, his hands clenched until his knuckles grew white. The gray seal on the murdered man's forehead was a *genuine gray seal* – one of Jimmie Dale's own. There was no doubt of that – he had satisfied himself on that point.

Where had it come from? How had it been obtained? Jimmie Dale carefully placed the clothes he had taken off under the mattress, pulled a disreputable collarless flannel shirt over his head, and pulled on a disreputable pair of boots. There were only two sources of supply. His own – and the collection that the police had made, which Carruthers had referred to.

Jimmie Dale lifted a corner of the oilcloth in a corner of the room, lifted a piece of the flooring, lifted out a little box which he placed upon the rickety table, and sat down before a cracked mirror. Who was it that would have access to the gray seals in the possession of the police, since, obviously, it was one of those that was on the dead man's forehead? The

---

[25] Based on descriptions presented in this novel I place the tenement building at either 66 or 68 East Fourth Street but again, Packard's geography does not always correspond to "real life" New York. Dale's Sanctuary is generally considered the inspiration for The Shadow's Sanctum.

answer came quick enough—came with the sudden out-thrust of Jimmie Dale's lower jaw. *One of the police themselves*—no one else. Clayton's heavy, cunning face, Clayton's shifty eyes, Clayton's sudden rush when he had touched the dead man's forehead, pictured themselves in a red flash of fury before Jimmie Dale. There was no mask now, no facetiousness, no acted part—only a merciless rage, and the muscles of Jimmie Dale's face quivered and twitched. *Murder,* foisted, shifted upon another, upon the Gray Seal—making of that name a calumny—ruining forever the work that she and he might do!

And then Jimmie Dale smiled mirthlessly, with thinning lips. The box before him was open. His fingers worked quickly—a little wax behind the ears, in the nostrils, under the upper lip, deftly placed-hands, wrists, neck, throat, and face received their quota of stain, applied with an artist's touch—and then the spruce, muscular Jimmie Dale, transformed into a slouching, vicious-featured denizen of the underworld, [26] replaced the box under the flooring, pulled a slouch hat over his eyes, extinguished the gas, and went out.

Jimmie Dale's range of acquaintanceship was wide—from the upper strata of the St. James Club to the elite of New York's gangland. And, adored by the one, he was trusted implicitly by the other—not understood, perhaps, by the latter, for he had never allied himself with any of their nefarious schemes, but trusted implicitly through long years of personal contact. It had stood Jimmie Dale in good stead before, this association, where, in a sort of strange, carefully guarded exchange, the news of the underworld was common property to those without the law. To New York in its millions, the murder of Metzer, the stool pigeon, would be unknown until the city rose in the morning to read the sensational details over the breakfast table; here, it would already be the topic of whispered conversations, here it had probably been known long before the police had discovered the crime. Especially would it be expected to be known to Pete Lazanis, commonly called the Runt, who was a power below the dead line [27] and, more pertinent still, one in whose confidence Jimmie Dale had rejoiced for years.

---

[26] We're never told where Dale learned these makeup techniques. Perhaps he participated in amateur dramatics with the Hasty Pudding Theatrical Society at Harvard.

[27] The Dead Line was created by Police Official Thomas Byrnes in the 1880s to mark the upper end of Manhattan's financial district. Since criminals were supposed to stay north of that district it's doubtful that the Runt had influence south of that boundary. Packard will continue to confuse the geography of that artificial barrier throughout this novel.

Jimmie Dale, as Larry the Bat – a euphonious "monaker" bestowed possibly because this particular world knew him only by night – began a search for the Runt. From one resort to another he hurried, talking in the accepted style through one corner of his mouth [28] to hard-visaged individuals behind dirty, reeking bars that were reared on equally dirty and foul-smelling sawdust-strewn floors; visiting dance halls, secretive back rooms, and certain Chinese pipe joints.

But the Runt was decidedly elusive. There had been no news of him, no one had seen him – and this after fully an hour had passed since Jimmie Dale had left Carruthers in front of Moriarty's. The possibilities however were still legion – numbered only by the numberless dives and dens sheltered by that quarter of the city.

Jimmie Dale turned into Chatham Square, heading for the Pagoda Dance Hall. A man loitering at the curb shot a swift, searching glance at him as he slouched by. Jimmie Dale paused in the doorway of the Pagoda and looked up and down the street. The man he had passed had drawn a little closer; another man in an apparently aimless fashion lounged a few yards away.

"Something up," muttered Jimmie Dale to himself. "Lansing, of headquarters, and the other looks like Milrae."

Jimmie Dale pushed in through the door of the Pagoda. A bedlam of noise surged out at him – a tin-pan piano and a mandolin were going furiously from a little raised platform at the rear; in the centre of the room a dozen couples were in the throes of the tango and the bunny-hug; around the sides, at little tables, men and women laughed and applauded and thumped time on the tabletops with their beer mugs; while waiters, with beer-stained aprons and unshaven faces, juggled marvelous handfuls of glasses and mugs from the bar beside the platform to the patrons at the tables.

Jimmie Dale's eyes swept the room in a swift, comprehensive glance, fixed on a little fellow, loudly dressed, who shared a table halfway down the room with a woman in a picture hat, and a smile of relief touched his lips. The Runt at last!

He walked down the room, caught the Runt's eyes significantly as he passed the table, kept on to a door between the platform and the bar,

---

[28] Learning to speak from the side of your mouth helped convicts appear to comply with the "rule of silence" in place in most prisons of this era.

opened it, and went out into a lighted hallway, at one end of which a door opened onto the street, and at the other a stairway led above.

The Runt joined him. "Wot's de row, Larry?" inquired the Runt.

"Nuthin' much," said Jimmie Dale. "Only I t'ought I'd let youse know. I was passin' Moriarty's an' got de tip. Say, some guy's croaked Jake Metzer dere."

"Aw, ferget it!" observed the Runt airily. "Dat's stale. I was wise to dat hours ago."

Jimmie Dale's face fell. "But I just come from dere," he insisted; "an' de harness bulls [29] only just found it out."

"Mabbe," grunted the Runt. "But Metzer got his early in de afternoon—see?"

Jimmie Dale looked quickly around him—and then leaned toward the Runt.

"Wot's de lay, Runt?" he whispered.

The Runt pulled down one eyelid, and, with his knowing grin, the cigarette, clinging to his upper lip, sagged down in the opposite corner of his mouth.

Jimmie Dale grinned, too—in a flash inspiration had come to Jimmie Dale.

"Say, Runt"—he jerked his head toward the street door—"wot's de fly cops [30] doin' out dere?"

The grin vanished from the Runt's lips. He stared for a second wildly at Jimmie Dale, and then clutched at Jimmie Dale's arm.

"De *wot?*" he said hoarsely.

"De fly cops," Jimmie Dale repeated in well-simulated surprise. "Dey was dere when I come in—Lansing an' Milrae, an—"

The Runt shot a hurried glance at the stairway, and licked his lips as though they had gone suddenly dry.

"My Gawd, I—" He gasped, and shrank hastily back against the wall beside Jimmie Dale.

The door from the street had opened noiselessly, instantly. Black forms bulked there—then a rush of feet—and at the head of half a dozen men, the face of Inspector Clayton loomed up before Jimmie Dale. There was a

---

29 In this context a uniformed police officer.

30 Plainclothes detectives.

second's pause in the rush; and, in the pause, Clayton's voice, in a vicious undertone:

"You two ginks open your traps, and I'll run you both in!"

And then the rush passed, and swept on up the stairs.

Jimmie Dale looked at the Runt. The cigarette dangled limply; the Runt's eyes were like a hunted beast's.

"Dey got him!" he mumbled. "It's Stace – Stace Morse. He come to me after croakin' Metzer, an' he's been hidin' up dere all afternoon."

Stace Morse – known in gangland as a man with every crime in the calendar to his credit, and prominent because of it! Something seemed to go suddenly queer inside of Jimmie Dale. Stace Morse! Was he wrong, after all? Jimmie Dale drew closer to the Runt.

"Yer givin' me a steer, ain't youse?" He spoke again from the corner of his mouth, almost inaudibly. "Are youse sure it was Stace croaked Metzer? Wot fer? How'd yer know?"

The Runt was listening, his eyes strained toward the stairs. The hall door to the street was closed, but both were quite well aware that there was an officer on guard outside.

"He told me," whispered the Runt. "Metzer was fixin' ter snitch on him ter-night. Dey've got de goods on Stace, too. He made a bum job of it."

"Why didn't he get out of de country den when he had de chanst, instead of hangin' around here all afternoon?" demanded Jimmie Dale.

"He was broke," the Runt answered. "We was gettin' de coin fer him ter fade away wid ter-night, an' – "

A revolver shot from above cut short his words. Came then the sound of a struggle, oaths, the shuffling tread of feet – but in the dance hall the piano still rattled on, the mandolin twanged, voices sang and applauded, and beer mugs thumped time.

They were on the stairs now, the officers, half carrying, half dragging some one between them – and the man they dragged cursed them with utter abandon. As they reached the bottom of the stairs, Jimmie Dale caught sight of the prisoner's face – not a prepossessing one – villainous, – low-browed, contorted with a mixture of fear and rage.

"It's a lie! A lie! A lie!" the man shrieked. "I never seen him in me life – blast you! – curse you! – d'ye hear!"

Inspector Clayton caught Jimmie Dale and the Runt by the collars.

"There's nothing to interest you around here!" he snapped maliciously. "Go on, now – beat it!" And he pushed them toward the door.

They had heard the disturbance in the dance hall now and the occupants were swarming to the sidewalk. A patrol wagon came around the corner. In the crowd Jimmie Dale slipped away from the Runt.

Was he wrong, after all? A fierce passion seized him. It was Stace Morse who had murdered Metzer, the Runt had said. In Jimmie Dale's brain the words began to reiterate themselves in a singsong fashion: "It was Stace Morse. It was Stace Morse." Then his lips drew tight together. *Was* it Stace Morse? He would have given a good deal for a chance to talk to the man—even for a minute. But there was no possibility of that now. Later, to-morrow perhaps, if he was wrong, after all!

Jimmie Dale returned to the Sanctuary, removed from his person all evidences of Larry the Bat—and from the Sanctuary went home to Riverside Drive.

In his den there, in the morning after breakfast, Jason, the butler, brought him the papers. Three-inch headlines in red ink screamed, exulted, and shrieked out the news that the Gray Seal, in the person of Stace Morse, fence, yeggman and murderer, had been captured. The public, if it had held any private admiration for the one-time mysterious crook could now once and forever disillusion itself. The Gray Seal was Stace Morse—and Stace Morse was of the dregs of the city's scum, a pariah, an outcast, with no single redeeming trait to lift him from the ruck of mire and slime that had strewn his life from infancy. The face of Inspector Clayton, blandly self-complacent, leaped out from the paper to meet Jimmie Dale's eyes—and with it a column and a half of perfervid eulogy.

Something at first like dismay, the dismay of impotency, filled Jimmie Dale—and then, cold, leaving him unnaturally calm, the old merciless rage took its place. There was nothing to do now but wait—wait until Carruthers should send that photograph. Then if, after all, he were wrong—then he must find some other way. But was he wrong! The notebook that Carruthers had given him, open at the sketch he had made of Clayton, lay upon the desk. Jimmie Dale picked it up—he had already spent quite a little time over it before breakfast—and examined it again minutely, even resorting to his magnifying glass. He put it down as a knock sounded at the door, and Jason entered with a silver card tray. From Carruthers already! Jimmie Dale stepped quickly forward—and then Jimmie Dale met the old man's eyes. It wasn't from Carruthers—it was from *her!*

"The same shuffer brought it, Master Jim," said Jason.

Jimmie Dale snatched the envelope from the tray, and waved the other from the room. As the door closed, he tore open the letter. There was just a single line:

Jimmie – Jimmie, you haven't failed, have you?

Jimmie Dale stared at it. Failed! Failed – *her!* The haggard look was in his face again. It was the bond between them that was at stake – the Gray Seal – the bond that had come, he knew for all time in that instant, to mean his life.

"God knows!" he muttered hoarsely, and flung himself into a lounging chair, still staring at the note.

The hours dragged by. Luncheon time arrived and passed – and then by special messenger the little package from Carruthers came.

Jimmie Dale started to undo the string, then laid the package down, and held out his hands before him for inspection. They were trembling visibly. It was a strange condition for Jimmie Dale either to witness or experience, unlike him, foreign to him.

"This won't do, Jimmie," he said grimly, shaking his head.

He picked up the package again, opened it, and from between two pieces of cardboard took out a large photographic print. A moment, two, Jimmie Dale examined it, used the magnifying glass again; and then a strange gleam came into the dark eyes, and his lips moved.

"I've won," said Jimmie Dale, with ominous softness. "I've *won!*"

He was standing beside the rosewood desk, and he reached for the phone. Carruthers would be at home now – he called Carruthers there. After a moment or two he got the connection.

"This is Jimmie, Carruthers," he said. "Yes, I got it. Thanks. . . . Yes. . . . Listen. I want you to get Inspector Clayton, and bring him up here at once. . . . What? No, no – no! . . . How? . . . Why – er – tell him you're going to run a full page of him in the Sunday edition, and you want him to sit for a sketch. He'd go anywhere for that. . . . Yes. . . . Half an hour. . . . *Yes.* . . . Good-bye."

Jimmie Dale hung up the receiver; and, hastily now, began to write upon a pad that lay before him on the desk. The minutes passed. As he wrote, he scored out words and lines here and there, substituting others. At the end he had covered three large pages with, to any one but himself, an indecipherable scrawl. These he shoved aside now, and, very carefully, very legibly, made a copy on fresh sheets. As he finished, he heard a car draw up in front of the house. Jimmie Dale folded the copied sheets neatly, tucked them in his pocket, lighted a cigarette, and was lolling lazily in his chair as Jason announced: "Mr. Carruthers, sir, and another gentleman to see you."

"Show them up, Jason," instructed Jimmie Dale.

Jimmie Dale rose from his chair as they came in. Jason, well-trained servant, closed the door behind them.

"Hello, Carruthers; hello, inspector," said Jimmie Dale pleasantly, and waved them to seats. "Take this chair, Carruthers." He motioned to one at his elbow. "Glad to see you, inspector — try that one in front of the desk, you'll find it comfortable."

Carruthers, trying to catch Jimmie Dale's eye for some sort of a cue, and, failing, sat down. Inspector Clayton stared at Jimmie Dale.

"Oh, it's *you*, eh?" His eyes roved around the room, fastened for an instant on some of Jimmie Dale's work on an easel, came back finally to Jimmie Dale — and he plumped himself down in the chair indicated. "Thought you was more'n a cub reporter," he remarked, with a grin. "You were too slick with your pencil. Pretty fine studio you got here. Carruthers says you're going to draw me."

Jimmie Dale smiled — not pleasantly — and leaned suddenly over the desk.

"Yes," he said slowly, a grim intonation in his voice, "going to draw you — *true to life*."

With an exclamation, Clayton slued around in his chair, half rose, and his shifty eyes, small and cunning, bored into Jimmie Dale's face.

"What d'ye mean by that?" he snapped out.

"Just exactly what I say," replied Jimmie Dale curtly. "No more, no less. But first, not to be too abrupt, I want to join with the newspapers in congratulating you on the remarkable — shall I call it celerity, or acumen? — with which you solved the mystery of Metzer's death, and placed the murderer behind the bars. It is really remarkable, inspector, so remarkable, in fact, that it's almost — *suspicious*. Don't you think so? No? Well, that's what Mr. Carruthers was good enough to bring you up here to talk over — in an intimate and confidential way, you know."

Inspector Clayton surged up from his chair to his feet, his fists clenched, the red sweeping over his face — and then he shook one fist at Carruthers.

"So that's your game, is it!" he stormed. "Trying to crawl out of that twenty-five thousand reward, eh? And as for you" — he turned on Jimmie Dale — "you've rigged up a nice little plant between you, eh? Well, it won't work — and I'll make you squirm for this, both of you, damn you, before I'm through!" He glared from one to the other for a moment — then swung on his heel. "Good-afternoon, gentlemen," he sneered, as he started for the door.

He was halfway across the room before Jimmie Dale spoke.

"Clayton!"

Clayton turned. Jimmie Dale was still leaning over the desk, but now one elbow was propped upon it, and in the most casual way a revolver covered Inspector Clayton.

"If you attempt to leave this room," said Jimmie Dale, without raising his voice, "I assure you that I shall fire with as little compunction as though I were aiming at a mad dog – and I apologise to all mad dogs for coupling your name with them." His voice rang suddenly cold. "Come back here, and sit down in that chair!"

The colour ebbed slowly from Clayton's face. He hesitated – then sullenly retraced his steps; hesitated again as he reached the chair, and finally sat down.

"What – what d'ye mean by this?" he stammered, trying to bluster.

"Just this," said Jimmie Dale. "That I accuse you of the murder of Jake Metzer – *it was you who murdered Metzer.*"

"Good God!" burst suddenly from Carruthers.

"You lie!" yelled Clayton – and again he surged up from his chair.

"That is what Stace Morse said," said Jimmie Dale coolly. "Sit down!"

Then Clayton tried to laugh. "You're – you're having a joke, ain't you? It was Stace – I can prove it. Come down to headquarters, and I can prove it. I got the goods on him all the way. I tell you" – his voice rose shrilly – "it was Stace Morse."

"You are a despicable hound," [31] said Jimmie Dale, through set lips. "Here" – he handed the revolver over to Carruthers – "keep him covered, Carruthers. You're going to the *chair* for this, Clayton," he said, in a fierce monotone. "The chair! You can't send another there in your place – this time. Shall I draw you now – true to life? You've been grafting for years on every disreputable den in your district. Metzer was going to show you up; and so, Metzer being in the road, you removed him. And you seized on the fact of Stace Morse having paid a visit to him this afternoon to fix the crime on – Stace Morse. Proofs? Oh, yes, I know you've manufactured proofs enough to convict him – if there weren't stronger proofs to convict *you.*"

"Convict *me!*" Clayton's lower jaw hung loosely; but still he made an effort at bluster. "You haven't a thing on me – not a thing – not a thing."

Jimmie Dale smiled again – unpleasantly.

---

[31] Dale frequently refers to people he doesn't like as hounds or curs so it's doubtful he was a dog lover.

"You are quite wrong, Clayton. See—here." He took a sheet of paper from the drawer of his desk.

Clayton reached for it quickly. "What is it?" he demanded.

Jimmie Dale drew it back out of reach.

"Just a minute," he said softly. "You remember, don't you, that in the presence of Carruthers here, of myself, and of half a dozen reporters, you stated that you had been alone with Metzer in his room at three o'clock yesterday, and that it was you—alone—who found the body later on at nine o'clock? Yes? I mention this simply to show that from your own lips the evidence is complete that you had an *opportunity* to commit the crime. Now you may look at this, Clayton." He handed over the sheet of paper.

Clayton took it, stared at it, turning it over from first one side to the other. Then a sort of relief seemed to come to him and he gulped.

"Nothing but a damned piece of blank paper!" he mumbled.

Jimmie Dale reached over and took back the sheet.

"You're wrong again, Clayton," he said calmly. "It *was* quite blank before I handed it to you—but not now. I noticed yesterday that your hands were generally moist. I am sure they are more so now—excitement, you know. Carruthers, see that he doesn't interrupt."

From a drawer, Jimmie Dale took out a little black bottle, the notebook he had used the day before, and the photograph Carruthers had sent him. On the sheet of paper Clayton had just handled, Jimmie Dale sprinkled a little powder from the bottle.

"Lampblack," explained Jimmie Dale. He shook the paper carefully, allowing the loose powder to fall on the desk blotter—and held out the sheet toward Clayton. "Rather neat, isn't it? A very good impression, too. Your thumb print, Clayton. Now don't move. You may look—not touch." He laid the paper down on the desk in front of Clayton. Beside it he placed the notebook, open at the sketch—a black thumb print now upon it. "You recall handling this yesterday, I'm sure, Clayton. I tried the same experiment with the lampblack on it this morning, you see. And this" — beside the notebook he placed the police photograph; that, too, in its enlargement, showed, sharply defined, a thumb print on a diamond-shaped background. "You will no doubt recognise it as an official photograph, enlarged, taken of the gray seal on Metzer's forehead—*and the thumb print of Metzer's murderer.* You have only to glance at the little scar at the edge of the centre loop to satisfy yourself that the three are identical. Of course, there are a dozen other points of similarity equally indisputable, but—"

Jimmie Dale stopped. Clayton was on his feet—rocking on his feet. His face was deathlike in its pallor. Moisture was oozing from his forehead.

"I didn't do it! I didn't do it!" he cried out wildly. "My God, I tell you, I *didn't* do it—and—and—that would send me to the chair."

"Yes," said Jimmie Dale coldly, "and that's precisely where you're going—to the chair."

The man was beside himself now—racked to the soul by a paroxysm of fear.

"I'm innocent—innocent!" he screamed out. "Oh, for God's sake, don't send an innocent man to his death. [32] It *was* Stace Morse. Listen! Listen! I'll tell the truth." He was clawing with his hands, piteously, over the desk at Jimmie Dale. "When the big rewards came out last week I stole one of the gray seals from the bunch at headquarters to—to use it the first time any crime was committed when I was sure I could lay my hands on the man who did it. Don't you see? Of course he'd deny he was the Gray Seal, just as he'd deny that he was guilty—but I'd have the proof both ways and—and I'd collect the rewards, and—and—" The man collapsed into the chair.

Carruthers was up from his seat, his hands gripping tight on the edge of the desk as he leaned over it.

"Jimmie—Jimmie—what does this mean?" he gasped out.

Jimmie Dale smiled—pleasantly now.

"That he has told the truth," said Jimmie Dale quietly. "It is quite true that Stace Morse committed the murder. Shows up the value of circumstantial evidence though, doesn't it? This would certainly have got him off, and convicted Clayton here before any jury in the land. But the point is, Carruthers, that Stace Morse *isn't* the Gray Seal—and that the Gray Seal is *not* a murderer."

Clayton looked up. "You—you believe me?" he stammered eagerly.

Jimmie Dale whirled on him in a sudden sweep of passion.

"*No,* you cur!" he flashed. "It's not you I believe. I simply wanted your confession before witnesses." He whipped the three written sheets from his pocket. "Here, substantially, is that confession written out." He passed it to Carruthers. "Read it to him, Carruthers."

Carruthers read it aloud.

"Now," said Jimmie Dale grimly, "this spells ruin for you, Clayton. You don't deserve a chance to escape prison bars, but I'm going to give

---

[32] No doubt Clayton is thinking here of New York police lieutenant Charles Becker who at the time I set this chapter is in Sing Sing Prison awaiting execution for a murder many believe he did not commit.

you one, for you're going to get it pretty stiff, anyhow. If you refuse to sign this, I'll hand you over to the district attorney in half an hour, and Carruthers and I will swear to your confession; on the other hand, if you sign it, Carruthers will not be able to print it until to-morrow morning, and that gives you something like fourteen hours to put distance between yourself and New York. Here is a pen – if you are quick enough to take us by surprise once you have signed, you might succeed in making a dash for that door and effecting your escape – without forcing us to compound a felony – understand?"

Clayton's hand trembled violently as he seized the pen. He scrawled his name – looked from one to the other – wet his lips – and then, taking Jimmie Dale at his word, rushed for the door – and the door slammed behind him.

Carruthers' face was hard. "What did you let him go for, Jimmie?" he said uncompromisingly.

"Selfishness. Pure selfishness," said Jimmie Dale softly. "They'd guy me unmercifully if they ever heard of it at the St. James Club. The honour is all yours, Carruthers. I don't appear on the stage. That's understood? Yes? Well, then" – he handed over the signed confession – "is the 'scoop' big enough?"

Carruthers fingered the sheets, but his eyes in a bewildered way searched Jimmie Dale's face.

"Big enough!" he echoed, as though invoking the universe. "It's the biggest thing the newspaper game has ever known. But how did you come to do it? What started you? Where did you get your lead?"

"Why, from you, I guess, Carruthers," Jimmie Dale answered thoughtfully, with artfully puckered brow. "I remembered that you had said last week that the Gray Seal never left finger marks on his work – and I saw one on the seal on Metzer's forehead. Then, you know, I lifted one corner where the seal overlapped a thread of blood, and, underneath, the thread of blood wasn't in the slightest disturbed; so, of course, I knew the seal had been put on quite a long time after the man was dead – not until the blood had dried thoroughly, to a crust, you know, so that even the damp surface of the sticky side of the seal hadn't affected it. And then, I took a dislike to Clayton somehow – and put two and two together, and took a flyer in getting him to handle the notebook. I guess that's all – no other reason on earth. Jolly lucky, don't you think?"

Carruthers didn't say anything for a moment. When he spoke, it was irrelevantly.

"You saved me twenty-five thousand dollars on that reward, Jimmie."

"That's the only thing I regret," said Jimmie Dale brightly. "It wasn't nice of you, Carruthers, to turn on the Gray Seal that way. And it strikes me you owe the chap, whoever he is, a pretty emphatic exoneration after what you said in this morning's edition."

"Jimmie," said Carruthers earnestly. "You know what I thought of him before. It's like a new lease of life to get back one's faith in him. You leave it to me. I'll put the Gray Seal on a pedestal to-morrow that will be worthy of the immortals — you leave it to me."

And Carruthers kept his word. Also, before the paper had been an hour off the press, Carruthers received a letter. It thanked Carruthers quite genuinely, even if couched in somewhat facetious terms, for his "sweeping vindication," twitted him gently for his "backsliding," begged to remain "his gratefully," and in lieu of signature there was a gray-coloured piece of paper shaped like this:

Only there were no fingerprints on it.

CHAPTER III

THE MOTHER LODE

(Friday 7/30/1915 to Saturday 7/31/1915)

IT was the following evening, and they had dined together again at the St. James Club—Jimmie Dale, and Carruthers of the *Morning News-Argus*. From Clayton and a discussion of the Metzer murder, the conversation had turned, not illogically, upon the physiognomy of criminals in general. Jimmie Dale, lazily ensconced now in a lounging chair in one of the club's private library rooms, flicked a minute speck of cigar ash from the sleeve of his dinner jacket, and smiled whimsically across the table at his friend.

"Oh, I dare say there's a lot in physiognomy, Carruthers," he drawled. "Never studied the thing, you know—that is, from the standpoint of crime. Personally, I've only got one prejudice: I distrust, on principle, the man who wears a perennial and pompous smirk—which isn't, of course, strictly speaking, physiognomy at all. You see, a man can't help his eyes being beady or his nose pronounced, but pomposity and a smirk, now—" Jimmie Dale shrugged his shoulders.

Carruthers laughed—and then glanced ludicrously at Jimmie Dale, as the door, ajar, was pushed open, and a man entered.

"Speaking of angels," murmured Jimmie Dale—and sat up in his chair. "Hello, Markel!" he observed casually, "You've met Carruthers, of the *News-Argus*, haven't you?"

Markel was fat and important; he had beady black eyes, fastidiously trimmed whiskers—and a pronounced smirk. [33]

Markel blew his nose vigorously, coughed asthmatically, and held out his hand.

---

[33] Black eyes are a common trait Packard gives to his villains, along with stereotypically Jewish attributes. Of all the obstacles that Frank Packard will on occasion present to less forgiving Twenty-first Century readers - verbose narrative style, histrionic storytelling techniques, clunky dialogue - his worst trait of all is perpetuating Anti-Semitic literary conventions.

In the original magazine version of this chapter it's obtrusive side whiskers that Dale objects to.

"Of course, certainly," said he effusively. "I've met Carruthers several times – used his sheet more than once to advertise a new bond flotation."

The dominant note in Markel's voice was an ingratiating and unpleasant whine, and Carruthers nodded, not very cordially – and shook hands.

Markel went back to the door, closed it carefully, and returned to the table.

"Fact is," he smiled confidentially, "I saw you two come in here a few minutes ago, and I've got something that I thought Carruthers might be glad to have for his society column – say, in the Sunday edition."

He dove into the inside pocket of his coat, produced a large morocco leather jeweller's case, and, holding it out over the table between Carruthers and Jimmie Dale, suddenly snapped the cover open – and then, with a complacent little chuckle that terminated in another fit of coughing, spilled the contents on the table under the electric reading lamp.

Like a thing of living, pulsing fire it rolled before their eyes – a magnificent diamond necklace, of wondrous beauty, gleaming and scintillating as the light rays shot back from a thousand facets.

For a moment, both men gazed at it without a word.

"Little surprise for my wife," volunteered Markel, with a debonair wave of his pudgy hand, and trying to make his voice sound careless.

The case lay open – patently displaying the name of the most famous jewelry house in America. Jimmie Dale's eyes fixed on Markel's whiskers where they were brushed outward in an ornate and fastidious gray-black sweep.

"By Jove!" he commented. "You don't do things by halves, do you, Markel?"

"Two hundred and ten thousand dollars I paid for that little bunch of gewgaws," said Markel, waving his hand again. Then he clapped Carruthers heartily on the shoulder. "What do you think of it, Carruthers – eh? Say, a photograph of it, and one of Mrs. Markel – eh? Please her, you know – she's crazy on this society stunt – all flubdub to me of course. How's it strike you, Carruthers?"

Carruthers, very evidently, liked neither the man nor his manners, but Carruthers, above everything else, was a gentleman.

"To be perfectly frank with you, Mr. Markel," he said a little frigidly, "I don't believe in this sort of thing. It's all right from a newspaper standpoint, and we do it; but it's just in this way that owners of valuable jewelry lay themselves open to theft. It simply amounts to advising every crook in the country that you have a quarter of a million at his disposal, which he can carry away in his vest pocket, once he can get his hands on it – and you invite him to try."

Jimmie Dale laughed. "What Carruthers means, Markel, is that you'll have the Gray Seal down your street. Carruthers talks of crooks generally, but he thinks in terms of only one. He can't help it. He's been trying so long to catch the chap that it's become an obsession. Eh, Carruthers?"

Carruthers smiled seriously. "Perhaps," he admitted. "I hope, though, for Mr. Markel's sake, that the Gray Seal won't take a fancy to it – if he does, Mr. Markel can say good-bye to his necklace."

"Pouf!" coughed Markel arrogantly. "Overrated! His cleverness is all in the newspaper columns. If he knows what's good for him, he'll know enough to leave this alone."

Jimmie Dale was leaning over the table poking gingerly with the tip of his forefinger at the centre stone in the setting, revolving it gently to and fro in the light – a very large stone, whose weight would hardly be less than fifteen carats. Jimmie Dale lowered his head for a closer examination – and to hide a curious, mocking little gleam that crept into his dark eyes.

"Yes, I should say you're right, Markel," he agreed judicially. "He ought to know better than to touch this. It – it would be too hard to dispose of."

"I'm not worrying," declared Markel importantly.

"No," said Jimmie Dale. "Two hundred and ten thousand, you said. Any special – er – significance to the occasion, if the question's not impertinent? Birthday, wedding anniversary – or something like that?"

"No, nothing like that!" Markel grinned, winked secretively, and rubbed his hands together. "I'm feeling good, that's all – I'm going to make the killing of my life to-morrow."

"Oh!" said Jimmie Dale.

Markel turned to Carruthers. "I'll let you in on that, too, Carruthers, in a day or two, if you'll send a reporter around – financial man, you know. It'll be worth your while. And now, how about this? What do you say to a little article and the photos next Sunday?"

There was a slight hint of rising colour in Carruthers' face.

"If you'll send them to the society editor, I've no doubt he'll be able to use them," he said brusquely.

"Right!" said Markel, and coughed, and patted Carruthers' shoulder patronisingly again. "I'll just do that little thing." He picked up the necklace, dangled it till it flashed and flashed again under the light, then restored it very ostentatiously to its case, and the case to his pocket.

"Thanks awfully, Carruthers," he said, as he rose from his chair. "See you again, Dale. Good-night!"

Carruthers glared at the door as it closed behind the man.

"Say it!" prodded Jimmie Dale sweetly. "Don't feel restrained because you are a guest—I absolve you in advance."

"Rotter!" said Carruthers.

"Well," said Jimmie Dale softly. "You see—Carruthers?"

Carruthers' match crackled savagely as he lighted a cigar.

"Yes, I see," he growled. "But I don't see—you'll pardon my saying so—how vulgarity like that ever acquired membership in the St. James Club."

"Carruthers," said Jimmie Dale plaintively, "you ought to know better than that. You know, to begin with, since it seems he has advertised with you, that he runs some sort of brokerage business in Boston. He's taken a summer home up here on Long Island, and some misguided chap put him on the club's visitor's list. His card will *not* be renewed. Sleek customer, isn't he? Trifle familiar—I was only introduced to him last night."

Carruthers grunted, broke his burned match into pieces, and began to toss the pieces into an ash tray.

Jimmie Dale became absorbed in an inspection of his hands—those wonderful hands with long, slim, tapering fingers, whose clean, pink flesh masked a strength and power that was like to a steel vise. [34]

Jimmie Dale looked up. "Going to print a nice little story for him about the 'costliest and most beautiful necklace in America'?" he inquired innocently.

Carruthers scowled. "No," he said bluntly. "I am not. He'll read the *News-Argus* a long time before he reads anything about that, Jimmie."

But therein Carruthers was wrong—the *News-Argus* carried the "story" of Markel's diamond necklace in three-inch "caps" in red ink on the front page in the next morning's edition—and Carruthers gloated over it because the morning *News-Argus* was the *only* paper in New York that did. Carruthers was to hear more of Markel and Markel's necklace than he thought, though for the time being the subject dropped between the two men.

It was still early, barely ten o'clock, when Carruthers left the club, and, preferring to walk to the newspaper offices, refused Jimmie Dale's offer of

---

[34] Walter Gibson describes The Shadow's hands in a similar manner.

his limousine. It was but five minutes later when Jimmie Dale, after chatting for a moment or two with those about in the lobby, in turn sought the coat room, where Markel was being assisted into his coat.

"Getting home early, aren't you, Markel?" remarked Jimmie Dale pleasantly.

"Yes," said Markel, and ran his fingers fussily, comb fashion, through his whiskers. "Quite a little run out to my place, you know – and with, you know what, I don't care to be out too late."

"No, of course," concurred Jimmie Dale, getting into his own coat.

They walked out of the club together, and Markel climbed importantly into the tonneau of a big gray touring car. "Ah – home, Peters," he sniffed at his chauffeur; and then, with a grandiloquent wave of his hand to Jimmie Dale: "'Night, Dale."

Jimmie Dale smiled with his eyes – which were hidden by the brim of his hat.

"Good-night, Markel," he replied, and the smile crept curiously to the corners of his mouth as he watched the gray car disappear down the street.

A limousine drew up, and Benson, Jimmie Dale's chauffeur, opened the door.

"Home, Mr. Dale?" he asked cheerily, touching his cap.

"Yes, Benson – home," said Jimmie Dale absently, and stepped into the car.

It was a luxurious car, as everything that belonged to Jimmie Dale was luxurious – and he leaned back luxuriously on the cushions, extended his legs luxuriously to their full length, plunged his hands into his overcoat pockets – and then a change stole strangely, slowly over Jimmie Dale.

The sensitive fingers of his right hand in the pocket had touched, and now played delicately over a sealed envelope that they had found there, played over it as though indeed by the sense of touch alone they could read the contents – and he drew his body gradually erect.

It was another of those mysterious missives from – her. The texture of the paper was invariably the same – like this one. How had it come there? Collusion with the coat boy at the club? That was hardly probable. Perhaps it had been there before he had entered the club for dinner – he remembered, now, that there had been several people passing, and that he had been jostled slightly in crossing the sidewalk. What, however, did it matter? It was there mysteriously, as scores of others had come to him mysteriously, with never a clew to her identity, to the identity of his – he smiled a little grimly – accomplice in crime.

He took the envelope from his pocket and stared at it. His fingers had not been at fault – it was one of hers. The faint, elusive, exquisite fragrance of some rare perfume came to him as he held it.

"I'd give," said Jimmie Dale wistfully to himself – "I'd give everything I own to know who you are – and some day, please God, I will know."

Jimmie Dale tore the envelope very gently, as though the tearing almost were an act of desecration – and extracted the letter from within. He began to read aloud hurriedly and in snatches:

"DEAR PHILANTHROPIC CROOK: Charleton Park Manor – Markel's house is the second one from the gates on the right-hand side – library leads off reception hall on left, door opposite staircase – telephone in reception hall near vestibule entrance, left-hand side – safe is one of your father's make, No. 14,321 – clothes closet behind the desk – probably will be kept in cash box – five servants; two men, three maids – quarters on top story – Markel and wife occupy room over library – French windows to dining room on opposite side of the house – opening on the lawn – get it *to-night,* Jimmie – *to-morrow would be too late* – dispose of it – see fit – Henry Wilbur, Marshall Building, Broadway – fifth story – "

Through the glass-panelled front of the car, Jimmie Dale could see his chauffeur's back, and the hand that held the letter dropped now to his side, and Jimmie Dale stared – at his chauffeur's back. Then, presently, he read the letter again, as though committing it to memory now; and then, tearing the paper into tiny shreds, as he did with every one of her communications, he reached out of the window and allowed the little pieces to filter gradually from his hand.

The Gray Seal! He smiled in his whimsical way. If it were ever known! He, Jimmie Dale, with his social standing, his wealth, his position – the Gray Seal! Not a police official, not a secret-service bureau probably in the civilised world, but knew the name – not a man, woman, or child certainly in this great city around him but to whom it was as familiar as their own! Danger? Yes. A battle of wits? Yes. His against everybody's – even against Carruthers', his old college chum! For, even as a reporter, before he had risen to the editorial desk, and even now that he had, Carruthers had been one of the keenest on the scent of the Gray Seal.

Danger? Yes. But it was worth it! Worth it a thousand times for the very lure of the danger itself; but worth it most of all for his association with her who, by some amazing means, verging indeed on the miraculous, came into touch with all these things, and supplied him with the data on which to work – that always some wrong might be righted, or gladness come where there had been gloom before, or hope where there had been despair—that into some fellow human's heart should come a gleam of sunshine. Yes, in spite of the howls of the police, the virulent diatribes of the press, an angry public screaming for his arrest, conviction, and punishment, there were those perhaps who even on their bended knees at night asked God's blessing on—the Gray Seal!

Was it strange, then, after all, that the police, seeking a clew through motive, should have been driven to frenzy on every occasion in finding themselves forever confronted with what, from every angle they were able to view it, was quite a purposeless crime! On one point only they were right, the old dogma, the old, old cry, old as the institution of police, older than that, old since time immemorial—*cherchez la femme!* Quite right—but also quite purposeless! Jimmie Dale's eyes grew wistful. He had been "hunting for the woman in the case" himself, now, for months and years indefatigably, using every resource at his command—quite purposelessly.

Jimmie Dale shrugged his shoulders. Why go over all this to-night— there were other things to do. She had come to him again—and this time with a matter that entailed more than ordinary difficulty, more than usual danger, that would tax his wits and his skill to the utmost, not only to succeed, but to get out of it himself with a whole skin. Markel—eh? Jimmie Dale leaned back in his seat, clasped his hands behind his head—and his eyes, half closed now, were studying Benson's back again through the plate-glass front.

He was still sitting in that position as the car approached his residence on Riverside Drive—but, as it came to a stop, and Benson opened the door, it was a very alert Jimmie Dale that stepped to the sidewalk.

"Benson," he said crisply, "I am going downtown again later on, but I shall drive myself. Bring the touring car around and leave it in front of the house. I'll run it into the garage when I get back—you need not wait up."

"Very good, sir," said Benson.

In the hallway, Jason, the butler, who had been butler to Jimmie Dale's father before him, took Jimmie Dale's hat and coat.

"It's a fine evening, Master Jim," said the privileged old man affectionately.

Jimmie Dale took out his silver cigarette case, selected a cigarette, tapped it daintily on the cover of the case—and accepted the match the old man hastily produced.

"Yes, Jason." said Jimmie Dale, pleasantly facetious, "it *is* a fine night, a glorious night, moon and stars and a balmy breeze—quite too fine, indeed, to remain indoors. In fact, you might lay out my gray ulster; I think I will go for a spin presently, when I have changed."

"Yes, sir," said Jason. "Anything else, Master Jim?"

"No; that's all, Jason. Don't sit up for me — you may go to bed now."

"Thank you, sir," said the old man.

Jimmie Dale went upstairs, opened the door of his own particular den on the right of the landing, stepped inside, closed the door, switched on the light — and Jimmie Dale's debonair nonchalance dropped from him as a mask instantly — and it was another Jimmie Dale — the professional Jimmie Dale.

Quick now in every action, he swung aside the portière that curtained off the squat, barrel-shaped safe in the little alcove, opened the safe, took out that curious leather girdle with its kit of burglar's tools, added to it a flashlight and an automatic revolver, closed the safe — and passed into his dressing room. Here, he proceeded to divest himself rapidly of his evening clothes, selecting in their stead a suit of dark tweed. He heard Jason come up the stairs, pass along the hall, and mount the second flight to his own quarters; and presently came the sound of an automobile without. The dressing room fronted on the Drive — Jimmie Dale looked out. Benson was just getting out of the touring car. Slipping the leather girdle, then, around his waist, Jimmie Dale put on his vest, then his coat — and walked briskly downstairs.

Jason had laid out a gray ulster on the hall stand. Jimmie Dale put it on, selected a leather cap with motor-goggle attachment that pulled down almost to the tip of his nose, tucked a slouch hat into the pocket of the ulster, and, leaving the house, climbed into his car.

He glanced at his watch as he started — it was a quarter of eleven. Jimmie Dale's lips pursed a little.

"I guess it'll make a night of it, and a tight squeeze, at that, to get back under cover before daylight," he muttered. "I'll have to do some tall speeding."

But at first, across the city and through Brooklyn, for all his impatience, it was necessarily slow — after that, Jimmie Dale took chances, and, once on the country roads of Long Island, the big, powerful car tore through the night like a greyhound whose leash is slipped.

A half hour passed — Jimmie Dale's eyes shifting occasionally from the gray thread of road ahead of him under the glare of the dancing lamps, to the road map spread out at his feet, upon which, from time to time, he focused his pocket flashlight. And then, finally, he slowed the car to a snail's pace — he should be very near his destination — that very ultra-exclusive subdivision of Charleton Park Manor.

On either side of the road now was quite a thickly set stretch of wooded land, rising slightly on the right — and this Jimmie Dale scrutinised sharply. In fact, he stopped for an instant as he came opposite to a wagon track — it seemed to be little more than that — that led in through the trees.

"If it's not too far from the seat of war," commented Jimmie Dale to himself, as he went on again, "it will do admirably."

And then, a hundred yards farther on, Jimmie Dale nodded his head in satisfaction — he was passing the rather ornate stone pillars that marked the entrance to Charleton Park Manor, and on which the initial promoters of the subdivision, the real-estate people, had evidently deemed it good advertising policy to expend a small fortune.

Another hundred yards farther on, Jimmie Dale turned his car around and returned past the gates to the wagon track again. The road was deserted — not a car nor a vehicle of any description was in sight. Jimmie Dale made sure of that — and in another instant Jimmie Dale's own car, every light extinguished, had vanished — he had backed it up the wagon track, just far enough in for the trees to screen it thoroughly from the main road.

Nor did Jimmie Dale himself appear again on the main road — until just as he emerged close to the gates of Charleton Park Manor from a short cut through the woods. Also, he was without his ulster now, and the slouch hat had replaced the motor cap.

Jimmie Dale, in the moonlight, took stock of his surroundings, as he passed in at a businesslike walk through the gates. It was a large park, if that name could properly be applied to it at all, and the houses — he caught sight of one set back from the driveway on the right — were quite far apart, each in its own rather spacious grounds among the trees.

"The second house on the right," her letter had said. Jimmie Dale had already passed the first one — the next would be Markel's then — and it loomed ahead of him now, black and shadowy and unlighted.

Jimmie Dale shot a glance around him — there was stillness, quiet everywhere — no sign of life — no sound.

Jimmie Dale's face became tense, his lips tight — and he stepped suddenly from the sidewalk in among the trees. They were not thick here, of course, the trees, and the turf beneath his feet was well kept — and, therefore, soundless. He moved quickly now, but cautiously, from tree to tree, for the moonlight, flooding the lawn and house, threw all objects into bold relief.

A minute, two, three went by — and a shadow flitted here and there across the light-green sward, like the moving of the trees swaying in the breeze — and then Jimmie Dale was standing close up against one side of the house, hidden by the protecting black shadows of the walls.

But here, for a moment, Jimmie Dale seemed little occupied with the house itself – he was staring down past its length to where the woods made a heavy, dark background at the rear. Then he turned his head, to face directly to the main road, then back again slowly, as though measuring an angle. Jimmie Dale had no intention of making his escape by the roundabout way in which he had been forced to come in order to make certain of locating the right house, the second one from the gates – and he was getting the bearings of his car and the wagon track now.

"I guess that'll be about right," Jimmie Dale muttered finally.

"And now for – "

He slipped along the side of the house and halted where, almost on a level with the ground, the French windows of the dining room opened on the lawn. Jimmie Dale tried them gently. They were locked.

An indulgent smile crept to Jimmie Dale's lips – and his hand crept in under his vest. It came out again – not empty – and Jimmie Dale leaned close against the window. There was a faint, almost inaudible, scratching sound, then a slight, brittle crack – and Jimmie Dale laid a neat little four-inch square of glass on the ground at his feet. Through the aperture he reached in his hand, turned the key that was in the lock, turned the bolt-rod handle, pushed the doors silently open – wide open – left them open – and stepped into the room.

He could see quite well within, thanks to the moonlight. Jimmie Dale produced a black silk mask from one of the little leather pockets, adjusted it carefully over his face, and crossed the room to the hall door. He opened this – wide open – left it open – and entered the hall.

Here it was dark – a pitch blackness. He stood for a moment, listening – utter silence. And then – alert, strained, tense in an instant, Jimmie Dale crouched against the wall – and then he smiled a little grimly. It was only some one coughing upstairs – Markel – in his sleep, perhaps, or, perhaps – in wakefulness.

"I'm a fool!" confided Jimmie Dale to himself, as he recognised the cough that he had heard at the club. "And yet – I don't know. One's nerves get sort of taut. Pretty stiff business. If I'm ever caught, the penitentiary sentence I get will be the smallest part of what's to pay."

A round button of light played along the wall from the flashlight in his hand – just for an instant – and all was blackness again. But in that instant Jimmie Dale was across the hall, and his fingers were tracing the telephone connection from the instrument to where the wires disappeared in the baseboard of the floor. Another instant, and he had severed the wires with a pair of nippers.

Again the quick, firefly gleam of light to locate the stair case and the library door opposite to it—and, moving without the slightest noise, Jimmie Dale's hand was on the door itself. Again he paused to listen. All was silence now.

The door swung under his hand, and, left open behind him, he was in the room. The flashlight winked once—suspiciously. Then he snapped its little switch, keeping the current on, and the ray dodged impudently here and there all over the apartment.

The safe was set in a sort of clothes closet behind the desk, she had said. Yes, there it was—the door, at least. Jimmie Dale moved toward it—and paused as his light swept the top of the intervening desk. A mass of papers, books, and correspondence littered it untidily. The yellow sheet of a telegram caught Jimmie Dale's eye.

He picked it up and glanced at it. It read:

"Vein uncovered to-day. Undoubtedly mother lode. Enormously rich. Put the screws on at once.   THURL."

Under the mask, Jimmie Dale's lips twitched.

"I think, Markel, you miserable hound," said he softly, "that God will forgive me for depriving you of a share of the profits. Two hundred and ten thousand, I think it was, you said the sparklers cost." A curious little sound came from Jimmie Dale's lips—like a chuckle.

Jimmie Dale tossed the telegram back on the desk, moved on behind the desk, opened the door of the closet that had been metamorphosed into a vault—and the white light travelled slowly, searchingly, critically over the shining black-enamelled steel, the nickelled knobs, and dials of a safe that confronted him.

Jimmie Dale nodded at it—familiarly, grimly.

"It's number one-four-three-two-one, all right," he murmured. "And one of the best we ever made. Pretty tough. But I've done it before. Say, half an hour of gentle persuasion. It would be too bad to crack it with 'soup'—besides, that's crude—Carruthers would never forgive the Gray Seal for that!"

The light went out—blackness fell. Jimmie Dale's slim, sensitive fingers closed on the dial's knob, his head touched the steel front of the safe as he pressed his ear against it for the tumblers' fall.

And then silence. It seemed to grow heavier, that silence, with each second—to palpitate through the quiet house—to grow pregnant, premonitory of dread, of fear—it seemed to throb in long undulations, and the stillness grew *loud*. A moonbeam filtered in between the edge of the drawn shade and the edge of the window. It struggled across the floor in a wavering path, strayed over the desk, and died away, shadowy and formless, against the blackness of the opened recess door, against the blackness of the great steel safe, the blackness of a huddled form crouched against it. Only now and then, in a strange, projected, wraithlike effect, the moon ray glinted timidly on the tip of a nickel dial, and, ghostlike, disclosed a human hand.

Upstairs, Markel coughed again. Then from the safe a whisper, heavy-breathed as from great exertion:

"Missed it!"

The dial whirled with faint, musical, little metallic clicks; then began to move slowly again, very, very slowly. The moonbeam, as though petulant at its own abortive attempt to satisfy its curiosity, retreated back across the floor, and faded away.

Blackness!

Time passed. Then from the safe again, but now in a low gasp, a pant of relief:

"Ah!"

The ear might barely catch the sound – it was as of metal sliding in well-oiled grooves, of metal meeting metal in a padded thud. The massive door swung outward. Jimmie Dale stood up, easing his cramped muscles, and flirted the sweat beads from his forehead.

After a moment, he knelt again. There was still the inner door – but that was a minor matter to Jimmie Dale compared with what had gone before.

Stillness once more – a long period of it. And then again that cough from above – a prolonged paroxysm of it this time that went racketing through the house.

Jimmie Dale, in the act of swinging back the inner door of the safe, paused to listen, and little furrows under his mask gathered on his forehead. The coughing stopped. Jimmie Dale waited a moment, still listening – then his flashlight bored into the interior of the safe.

"The cash box, probably," quoted Jimmie Dale, beneath his breath – and picked it up from where it lay in the bottom compartment of the safe.

The lock snipped under the insistent probe of a delicate little blued-steel instrument, and Jimmie Dale lifted the cover. There was a package of papers and documents on top, held together with elastic bands. Jimmie Dale spent a moment or two examining these, then his fingers dived down underneath, and the next minute, under the flashlight, the morocco leather case open, the diamond necklace was sparkling and flashing on its white satin bed.

"A tempting little thing, isn't it?" said Jimmie Dale gently. "It was really thoughtful of you, Markel, to buy that this afternoon!"

Jimmie Dale replaced the necklace in the cash box, set the cash box on the floor, closed the inner door of the safe, and swung the outer door a little inward – but left it flauntingly ajar. Then from a pocket of the leather girdle beneath his vest he produced his small, thin, flat, metal case. From this, from between sheets of oil paper, with the aid of a pair of tweezers, he lifted out a gray, diamond-shaped seal. Jimmie Dale was apparently fastidious. He held the seal with the tweezers as he moistened the adhesive side with his tongue, laid the seal on his handkerchief, and pressed the handkerchief firmly against the safe – as usual, Jimmie Dale's insignia bore no finger prints as it lay neatly capping the knob of the dial.

He reached down, picked up the cash box – and then, for the second time that night, held suddenly tense, alert, listening, his every muscle taut. A door opened upstairs. There came a murmur of voices. Then a momentary lull.

Jimmie Dale listened. Like a statue he stood there in the black, absolutely motionless – his head a little forward and to one side. Nothing – not a sound. Then a very low, curious, swishing noise, and a faint creak. *Somebody was coming down the stairs!*

Jimmie Dale moved stealthily from the recess, and noiselessly to the desk. Very faintly, but distinctly now, came a pad of either slippered or bare feet on the stairway carpet. Like a cat, soundless in his movements, Jimmie Dale crept toward the door of the room. Down the stairs came that pad of feet; occasionally came that swishing sound. Nearer the door crept Jimmie Dale, and his lips were thinned now, his jaws clamped. How near were they together, he and this night prowler? At times he could not hear the other at all, and, besides, the heavy carpet made the judgment of distance an impossibility. If he could gain the hall, and, in the darkness, elude the other, the way of escape through the dining room was open. And then, within a few feet of the door, Jimmie Dale halted abruptly, as a woman's voice rose querulously from the hallway above:

"You are making a perfect fool of yourself, Theodore Markel! Come back here to bed!"

Jimmie Dale's face hardened like stone – the answer came almost from the very threshold in front of him:

"I can't sleep, I tell you" – it was Markel's voice, in a disgruntled snarl. "I was a fool to bring the confounded thing home. I'm going to take the library couch for the rest of the night."

It happened quick, then — quick as the winking of an eye. Two sharp, almost simultaneous, clicks of the electric-light buttons pressed by Markel, and the hall and library were a flood of light — and Jimmie Dale leaped forward to where, in dressing gown and pajamas, blankets and bedding over one arm, a revolver dangling in the other hand, Markel stood full before the door in the hallway without.

There was a wild yell of terror and surprise from Markel, then a deafening roar and a spit of flame from his revolver — a bitter, smothered exclamation from Jimmie Dale as the cash box crashed to the floor from his left hand, and he was upon the other like a tiger.

With the impact, both men went to the floor, grappled, and rolled over and over. Half mad with fear, shock, and surprise, Markel fought like a maniac, and his voice, in gasping shouts, rang through the house.

A minute, two passed — and the men rolled about the hall floor. Markel, over middle age and unheathily fat, against Jimmie Dale's six feet of muscle — only Jimmie Dale's left hand, dripping a red stream now, was almost useless.

From above came wild confusion — women's voices in little shrieks; men's voices shouting in excitement; doors opening, running feet. And then Jimmie Dale had snatched the revolver from the floor where Markel had dropped it in the scuffle, and was pressing it against Markel's forehead — and Markel, terror-stricken, had collapsed in a flabby, pliant heap.

Jimmie Dale, still covering Markel with the weapon, stood up. The frightened faces of women protruded over the banisters above. The two men-servants, at best none too enthusiastically on the way down, stopped as though stunned as Jimmie Dale swung the revolver upon them.

Then Jimmie Dale spoke — to Markel — pointing the weapon at Markel again.

"I don't like you, Markel," he said, with cold impudence. "The only decent thing you'll ever do will be to die — and if those men of yours on the stairs move another step it will be your death warrant. Do you understand? I would suggest that you request them to stay where they are."

Cold sweat was on Markel's face as he stared into the muzzle of the revolver, and his teeth chattered.

"Go back!" he screamed hysterically at the servants. "Go back! Sit down! Don't move! Do what he tells you!"

"Thank you!" said Jimmie Dale grimly. "Now, get up yourself!"

Markel got up.

Jimmie Dale backed to the library door, picked up the cash box, tucked it under his left armpit, and faced those on the stairs.

"Mr. Markel and I are going out for a little walk," he announced coolly. "If one of you make a move or raise an alarm before your master comes back, I shall be obliged, in self-defence, to shoot—Mr. Markel. Mr. Markel quite understands that—I am sure. Do you not, Mr. Markel?"

"Helen," screamed Markel to his wife, "don't let 'em move! For God's sake, do as he says!"

Jimmie Dale's lips, just showing beneath the edge of his mask, broadened in a pleasant little smile.

"Will you lead the way, Mr. Markel?" he requested, with ironic deference. "Through the dining room, please. Yes, that's right!"

Markel walked weakly into the dining room, and Jimmie Dale followed. A prod in the back from the revolver muzzle, and Markel stepped through the French windows and out on the lawn. Jimmie Dale faced the other toward the woods at the rear of the house.

"Go on!" Jimmie Dale's voice was curt now, uncompromising. "And step lively!"

They passed on along the side of the house and in among the trees. Fifty yards or so more, and Jimmie Dale halted. He backed Markel up against a large tree—not over gently.

"I—I say"—Markel's teeth were going like castanets. "I—"

"You'll oblige me by keeping your mouth shut," observed Jimmie Dale politely—and he whipped the cord of Markel's dressing gown loose and began to tie the man to the tree. "You have many unpleasant characteristics, Markel—your voice is one of them. Shall I repeat that I do not like you?" He stepped to the back of the tree. "Pardon me if I draw this uncomfortably tight. I don't think you can reach around to the knot. No? The trunk is too large? Quite so!" He stepped around to face Markel again—the man was thoroughly frightened, his face was livid, his jaw sagged weakly, and his eyes followed every movement of the revolver in Jimmie Dale's hand in a sort of miserable fascination. Jimmie Dale smiled unhappily. "I am going to do something, Markel, that I should advise no other man to do—I am going to put you on your honour! For the next fifteen minutes you are not to utter a sound. Do you understand?"

"Y-yes," said Markel hoarsely.

"No," said Jimmie Dale sadly, "I don' think you do. Let me be painfully explicit. If you break your vow of silence by so much as a second, then to-morrow, or the next day, or the day after, at my convenience, Markel, you and I will meet again—for the *last* time. There can be no possible misapprehension on your part now—Markel?"

"N-no," – Markel could scarcely chatter out the word.

"Quite so," said Jimmie Dale, in velvet tones. He stood for an instant looking at the other with cool insolence; then: "Good-night, Markel" – and five minutes later a great touring car was tearing New Yorkward over the Long Island roads at express speed.

It was one o'clock in the morning as Jimmie Dale swung the car into a cross street off lower Broadway, and drew up at the curb beside a large office building. He got out, snuggled the cash box under his ulster, went around to the Broadway entrance, glanced up to note that a light burned in a fifth-story window, and entered the building.

The hallway was practically in darkness, one or two incandescents only threw a dim light about. Jimmie Dale stopped for a moment at the foot of the stairs, beside the elevator well, to listen – if the watchman was making rounds, it was in another part of the building Jimmie Dale began to climb.

He reached the fifth floor, turned down the corridor, and halted in front of a door, through the ground-glass panel of which a light glowed faintly – as though coming from an inner office beyond. Jimmie Dale drew the black silk mask from his pocket, adjusted it, tried the door, found it unlocked, opened it noiselessly, and stepped inside. Across the room, through another door, half open, the light streamed into the outer office, where Jimmie Dale stood.

Jimmie Dale stole across the room, crouched by the door to look into the inner office – and his face went suddenly rigid.

"Good God!" he whispered. "As bad as that!" – but it was a nonchalant Jimmie Dale to all outward appearances that, on the instant, stepped unconcernedly over the threshold.

An elderly man, white-haired, kindly-faced, kindly-eyed, save now that the face was drawn and haggard, the eyes full of weariness, was standing behind a flat-topped desk, his fingers twitching nervously on a revolver in his hand. He whirled, with a startled cry, at Jimmie Dale's entrance, and the revolver clattered from his fingers to the floor.

"I am afraid," said Jimmie Dale, smiling pleasantly, "that you were going to shoot yourself. Your name is Wilbur, Henry Wilbur, isn't it?"

Unmanned, trembling, the other stood – and nodded mechanically.

"It's really not a nice thing to do," said Jimmie Dale confidentially. "Makes a mess, you see, too" – he was pulling off his motor gauntlet, his ulster, his jacket, and, having set the cash box on the desk, was rolling back his sleeve as he spoke. "Had a little experience myself this evening." He held out his hand that, with the forearm, was covered with blood. "A little above the wrist—fortunately only a flesh wound—a little memento from a chap named Markel, and—"

"*Markel!*" The word burst, quivering, from the other's lips.

"Yes," said Jimmie Dale imperturbably. "Do you mind if I wash a bit—and could you oblige me with a towel, or something that would do for a bandage?"

The man seemed dazed. In a subconscious way, he walked from the desk to a little cupboard, and took out two towels.

Jimmie Dale stooped, while the other's back was turned, picked up the revolver from the floor, and slipped it into his trousers pocket.

"Markel?" said Wilbur again, the same trembling anxiety in his voice, as he handed Jimmie Dale the towels and motioned toward a washstand in the corner of the room. "Did you say Markel—Theodore Markel?"

"Yes," said Jimmie Dale, examining his wound critically.

"You had trouble—a fight with him? Is he—he—dead?"

"No," said Jimmie Dale, smiling a little grimly. "He's pretty badly hurt, though, I imagine—but not in a physical way."

"Strange!" whispered Wilbur, in a numbed tone to himself; and he went back and sank down in his desk chair. "Strange that you should speak of Markel—strange that you should have come here to-night!"

Jimmie Dale did not answer. He glanced now and then at the other, as he deftly dressed his wrist—the man seemed on the verge of collapse, on the verge of a nervous breakdown. Jimmie Dale swore softly to himself. Wilbur was too old a man to be called upon to stand against the trouble and anxiety that was mirrored in the misery in his face, that had brought him to the point of taking his own life.

Jimmie Dale put on his coat again, walked over to the desk, and picked up the 'phone.

"If I may?" he inquired courteously—and confided a number to the mouthpiece of the instrument.

There was a moment's wait, during which Wilbur, in a desperate sort of way, seemed to be trying to rally himself, to piece together a puzzle, as it were; and for the first time he appeared to take a personal interest in the masked figure that leaned against his desk. He kept passing his hands across his eyes, staring at Jimmie Dale.

Then Jimmie Dale spoke—into the 'phone.

"*Morning News-Argus* office? Mr. Carruthers, please. Thank you."

Another wait—then Jimmie Dale's voice changed its pitch and register to a pleasant and natural, though quite unrecognisable bass.

76

"Mr. Carruthers? Yes. I thought it might interest you to know that Mr. Theodore Markel purchased a very valuable diamond necklace this afternoon. . . . Oh, you knew that, did you? Well, so much the better; you'll be all the more keenly interested to know that it is no longer in his possession. . . . I beg pardon? Oh, yes, I quite forgot – this is the Gray Seal speaking. . . . Yes. . . . The Gray Seal. . . . I have just come from Mr. Markel's country house, and if you hurry a man out there you ought to be able to give the public an exclusive bit of news, a scoop, I believe you call it – you see, Mr. Carruthers, I am not ungrateful for, I might say, the eulogistic manner in which the *Morning News-Argus* treated me in that last affair, and I trust I shall be able to do you many more favours – I am deeply in your debt. And, oh, yes, tell your reporter not to overlook the detail of Mr. Markel in his pajamas and dressing gown tied to a tree in his park – Mr. Markel might be inclined to be reticent on that point, and it would be a pity to deprive the public of any – er – 'atmosphere' in the story, you know. . . . What? . . . No; I am afraid Mr. Markel's 'phone is – er – out of order. . . . Yes. . . . And, by the way, speaking of 'phones, Mr. Carruthers, between gentlemen, I know you will make no effort under the circumstances to discover the number I am calling from. Good-night, Mr. Carruthers." Jimmie Dale hung the receiver abruptly on the hook.

"You see," said Jimmie Dale, turning to Wilbur – and then he stopped. The man was on his feet, swaying there, his face positively gray.

"My God!" Wilbur burst out. "What have you done? A thousand times better if I had shot myself, as I would have done in another moment if you had not come in. I was only ruined then – I am disgraced now. You have robbed Markel's safe – I am the one man in the world who would have a reason above all others for doing that – and Markel knows it. He will accuse me of it. He can prove I had a motive. I have not been home to-night. Nobody knows I am here. I cannot prove an alibi. What have you done!"

"Really," said Jimmie Dale, almost plaintively, swinging himself up on the corner of the desk and taking the cash box on his knee, "really, you are alarming yourself unnecessarily. I – "

But Wilbur stopped him. "You don't know what you are talking about!" Wilbur cried out, in a choked way; then, his voice steadying, he rushed on: "Listen! I am a ruined man, absolutely ruined. And Markel has ruined me – I did not see through his trick until too late. Listen! For years, as a mining engineer, I made a good salary – and I saved it. Two years ago I had nearly seventy thousand dollars – it represented my life work. I bought an abandoned mine in Alaska for next to nothing – I was certain it was rich. A man by the name of Thurl, Jason T. Thurl, another mining engineer, a steamer acquaintance, was out there at the time – he was a partner of Markel's, though I didn't know it then. I started to work the mine. It didn't pan out. I dropped nearly every cent. Then I struck a small vein that temporarily recouped me, and supplied the necessary funds with which to go ahead for a while. Thurl, who had tried to buy the mine out from under my option in the first place, repeatedly then tried to buy it from me at a ridiculous figure. I refused. He persisted. I refused – I was confident, I *knew* I had one of the richest properties in Alaska."

Wilbur paused. A little row of glistening drops had gathered on his forehead. Jimmie Dale, balancing Markel's cash box on one knee, drummed softly with his finger tips on the cover.

"The vein petered out," Wilbur went on. "But I was still confident. I sank all the proceeds of the first strike – and sank them fast, for unaccountable accidents that crippled me both financially and in the progress of the work began to happen." Wilbur flung out his hands impotently. "Oh, it's a long story – too long to tell. Thurl was at the bottom of those accidents. He knew as well as I did that the mine was rich – better than I did, for that matter, for we discovered before we ran him out of Alaska that he had made secret borings on the property. But what I did not know until a few hours ago was that he had actually uncovered what we uncovered only yesterday – the mother lode. He was driving me as fast as he could into the last ditch – for Markel. I didn't know until yesterday that Markel had anything to do with it. I struggled on out there, hoping every day to open a new vein. I raised money on everything I had, except my insurance and the mine – and sank it in the mine. No one out there would advance me anything on a property that looked like a failure, that had once already been abandoned. I have always kept an office here, and I came back East with the idea of raising something on my insurance. Markel, quite by haphazard as I then thought, was introduced to me just before we left San Francisco on our way to New York. On the run across the continent we became very friendly. Naturally, I told him my story. He played sympathetic good fellow, and offered to lend me fifty thousand dollars on a demand note. I did not want to be involved for a cent more than was necessary, and, as I said, I hoped from day to day to make another strike. I refused to take more than ten thousand. I remember now that he seemed strangely disappointed."

Again Wilbur stopped. He swept the moisture from his forehead – and his fist, clenched, came down upon the desk.

"You see the game!" – there was bitter anger in his voice now. "You see the game! He wanted to get me in deep enough so that I couldn't wriggle out, deeper than ten thousand that I could get at any time on my insurance, he wanted me where I couldn't get away – and he got me. The first ten thousand wasn't enough. I went to him for a second, a third, a fourth, a fifth – hoping always that each would be the last. Each time a new note, a demand note for the total amount, was made, cancelling the former one. I didn't know his game, didn't suspect it—I blessed God for giving me such a friend—until this, or, rather, yesterday afternoon, when I received a telegram from my manager at the mine saying that he had struck what looked like a very rich vein—the mother lode. And"—Wilbur's fist curled until the knuckles were like ivory in their whiteness—"he added in the telegram that Thurl had wired the news of the strike to a man in New York by the name of Markel. Do you see? I hadn't had the telegram five minutes, when a messenger brought me a letter from Markel curtly informing me that I would have to meet my note to-morrow morning. I can't meet it. He knew I couldn't. With wealth in sight—I'm wiped out. A *demand* note, a call loan, do you understand—and with a few months in which to develop the new vein I could pay it readily. As it is—I default the note—Markel attaches all I have left, which is the mine. The mine is sold to satisfy my indebtedness. Markel buys it in legally, upheld by the law—and acquires, *robs* me of it, and—"

"And so," said Jimmie Dale musingly, "you were going to shoot yourself?"

Wilbur straightened up, and there was something akin to pathetic grandeur in the set of the old shoulders as they squared back.

"Yes!" he said, in a low voice. "And shall I tell you why? Even if, which is not likely, there was something reverting to me over the purchase price, it would be a paltry thing compared with the mine. I have a wife and children. If I have worked for them all my life, could I stand back now at the last and see them robbed of their inheritance by a black-hearted scoundrel when I could still lift a hand to prevent it! I had one way left. What is my life? I am too old a man to cling to it where they are concerned. I have referred to my insurance several times. I have always carried heavy insurance"—he smiled a little curious, mirthless smile—"*that has no suicide clause.*" He swept his hand over the desk, indicating the papers scattered there. "I have worked late to-night getting my affairs in order. My total insurance is fifty-two thousand dollars, though I couldn't *borrow* anywhere near the full amount on it—but at my death, paid in full, it would satisfy the note. My executors, by instruction would pay the note—and no dollar from the mine, no single grain of gold, not an ounce of quartz, would Markel ever get his hands on, and my wife and children would be saved. That is—"

His words ended abruptly—with a little gasp. Jimmie Dale had opened the cash box and was dangling the necklace under the light—a stream of fiery, flashing, sparkling gems.

Then Wilbur spoke again, a hard, bitter note in his voice, pointing his hand at the necklace.

"But now, on top of everything, you have brought me disgrace — because you broke into his safe to-night for *that!* He would and will accuse me. I have heard of you — the Gray Seal — you have done a pitiful night's work in your greed for that thing there."

"For this?" Jimmie Dale smiled ironically, holding the necklace up. Then he shook his head. "I didn't break into Markel's safe for this — it wouldn't have been worth while. It's only paste."

"Paste!" exclaimed Wilbur, in a slow way.

"Paste," said Jimmie Dale placidly, dropping the necklace back into its case. "Quite in keeping with Markel, isn't it — to make a sensation on the cheap?"

"But that doesn't change matters!" Wilbur cried out sharply, after a numbed instant's pause. "You still broke into the safe, even if you didn't know then that the necklace was paste."

"Ah, but, you see — I did know then," said Jimmie Dale softly. "I am really — you must take my word for it — a very good judge of stones, and I had — er — seen these before."

Wilbur stared — bewildered, confused.

"Then why — what was it that —"

"A paper," said Jimmie Dale, with a little chuckle — and produced it from the cash box. "It reads like this: 'On demand, I promise to pay —' "

"My note!" It came in a great, surging cry from Wilbur; and he strained forward to read it.

"Of course," said Jimmie Dale. "Of course — your note. Did you think that I had just happened to drop in on you? Now, then, see here, you just buck up, and — er — smile. There isn't even a possibility of you being accused of the theft. In the first place, Markel saw quite enough of me to know that it wasn't you. Secondly, neither Markel nor any one else would ever dream that the break was made for anything else but the necklace, with which you have no connection — the papers were in the cash box and were just taken along with it. Don't you see? And, besides, the police, with my very good friend, Carruthers at their elbows, will see very thoroughly to it that the Gray Seal gets full and ample credit for the crime. But" —

Jimmie Dale pulled out his watch, and yawned under his mask — "it's getting to be an unconscionable hour — and you've still a letter to write."

"A letter?" Wilbur's voice was broken, his lips quivering.

"To Markel," said Jimmie Dale pleasantly. "Write him in reply to his letter of the afternoon, and post it before you leave here — just as though you had written it at once, promptly, on receipt of his. He will still get it on the morning delivery. State that you will take up the note immediately on presentation at whatever bank he chooses to name. That's all. Seeing that he hasn't got it, he can't very well present it—can he? Eventually, having—er—no use for fake diamonds, I shall return the necklace, together with the papers in his cash box here—including your note."

"Eventually?" Uncomprehendingly, stumblingly, Wilbur repeated the word.

"In a month or two or three, as the case may be," explained Jimmie Dale brightly. "Whenever you insert a personal in the *News-Argus* to the effect that the mother lode has given you the cash to meet it." He replaced the note in the cash box, slipped down to his feet from the desk—and then he choked a little. Wilbur, the tears streaming down his face, unable to speak, was holding out his hands to Jimmie Dale. "I—er—good-night!" said Jimmie Dale hurriedly—and stepped quickly from the room.

Halfway down the first flight of stairs he paused. Steps, running after him, sounded along the corridor above; and then Wilbur's voice.

"Don't go—not yet," cried the old man. "I don't understand. How did you know—who told you about the note?"

Jimmie Dale did not answer—he went on noiselessly down the stairs. His mask was off now, and his lips curved into a strange little smile.

"I wish I knew," said Jimmie Dale wistfully to himself.

CHAPTER IV

THE COUNTERFEIT FIVE

(Monday 8/30/1915 to Tuesday 8/31/1915)

IT was still early in the evening, but a little after nine o'clock. The Fifth Avenue bus wended its way, jouncing its patrons, particularly those on the top seats, across town, and turned into Riverside Drive. A short distance behind the bus, a limousine rolled down the cross street leisurely, silently.

As the lights of passing craft on the Hudson and a myriad scintillating, luminous points dotting the west shore came into view, Jimmie Dale rose impulsively from his seat on the top of the bus, descended the little circular iron ladder at the rear, and dropped off into the street. It was only a few blocks farther to his residence on the Drive, and the night was well worth the walk; besides, restless, disturbed, and perplexed in mind, the walk appealed to him.

He stepped across to the sidewalk and proceeded slowly along. A month had gone by and he had not heard a word from—*her*. The break on West Broadway, the murder of Metzer in Moriarty's gambling hell, the theft of Markel's diamond necklace had followed each other in quick succession—and then this month of utter silence, with no sign of her, as though indeed she had never existed.

But it was not this temporary silence on her part that troubled Jimmie Dale now. In the years that he had worked with this unknown, mysterious accomplice of his whom he had never seen, there had been longer intervals than a bare month in which he had heard nothing from her—it was not that. It was the failure, total, absolute, and complete, that was the only result for the month of ceaseless, unremitting, doggedly-expended effort, even as it had been the result many times before, in an attempt to solve the enigma that was so intimate and vital a factor in his own life.

If he might lay any claims to cleverness, his resourcefulness, at least, he was forced to admit, was no match for hers. She came, she went without being seen—and behind her remained, instead of clews to her identity, only an amazing, intangible mystery, that left him at times appalled and dismayed. How did she know about those conditions in West Broadway, how did she know about Metzer's murder, how did she know about

Markel and Wilbur—how did she know about a hundred other affairs of the same sort that had happened since that night, years ago now, when out of pure adventure he had tampered with Marx's, the jeweller's strong room in Maiden Lane, and she had, mysteriously then, too, solved *his* identity, discovered him to be the Gray Seal?

Jimmie Dale, wrapped up in his own thoughts, entirely oblivious to his surroundings, traversed another block. There had never been since the world began, and there would never be again, so singular and bizarre a partnership as this—of hers and his. He, Jimmie Dale, with his strange double life, one of New York's young bachelor millionaires, one whose social status was unquestioned; and she, who—who *what?* That was just it! Who what? What was she? What was her name? What one personal, intimate thing did he know about her? And what was to be the end? Not that he would have severed his association with her—not for worlds!— though every time, that, by some new and curious method, one of her letters found its way into his hands, outlining some fresh coup for him to execute, his peril and danger of discovery was increased in staggering ratio. To-day, the police hunted the Gray Seal as they hunted a mad dog; the papers stormed and raved against him: in every detective bureau of two continents he was catalogued as the most notorious criminal of the age—and yet, strange paradox, no single crime had ever been committed!

Jimmie Dale's strong, fine-featured face lighted up. Crime! Thanks to her, there were those who blessed the name of the Gray Seal, those into whose lives had come joy, relief from misery, escape from death even— and their blessings were worth a thousandfold the risk and peril of disaster that threatened him at every minute of the day.

"Thank God for her!" murmured Jimmie Dale softly. "But—but if I could only find her, see her, know who she is, talk to her, and hear her voice!" Then he smiled a little wanly. "It's been a pretty tough month— and nothing to show for it!"

It had! It had been one of the hardest months through which Jimmie Dale had ever lived. The St. James, that most exclusive club, his favourite haunt, had seen nothing of him; the easel in his den, that was his hobby, had been untouched; there had been days even when he had not crossed the threshold of his home. Every resource at his command he had called into play in an effort to solve the mystery. For nearly the entire month, following first this lead and then that, he had lived in the one disguise that he felt confident she knew nothing of—that was, or, rather, had become, almost a dual personality with him. From the Sanctuary, that miserable and disreputable room in a tenement on the East Side, a tenement that had three separate means of entrance and exit, he had emerged day after day as Larry the Bat, a character as well known and as well liked in the exclusive circles of the underworld as was Jimmie Dale in the most exclusive strata of New York's society and fashion. And it had been useless—all useless. Through his own endeavours, through the help of his friends of the underworld, the lives of half a dozen men, Bert Hagan's on West Broadway, for instance, Markel's, and others', had been laid bare to the last shred, but nowhere could be found the one vital point that linked their lives with hers, that would account for her intimate knowledge of them, and so furnish him with the clew that would then with certainty lead him to a solution of her identity.

It was baffling, puzzling, unbelievable, bordering, indeed, on the miraculous—herself, everything about her, her acts, her methods, her cleverness, intangible in one sense, were terrifically real in another. Jimmie Dale shook his head. The miraculous and this practical, everyday life were wide and far apart. There was nothing miraculous about it—it was only that the key to it was, so far, beyond his reach.

And then suddenly Jimmie Dale shrugged his shoulders in consonance with a whimsical change in both mood and thought.

"Larry the Bat is a hard taskmaster!" he muttered facetiously. "I'm afraid I'm not very presentable this evening—no bath this morning, and no shave, and, after nearly a month of make-up, that beastly grease paint gets into the skin creases in a most intimate way." He chuckled as the thought of old Jason, his butler, came to him. "I saw Jason, torn between two conflicting emotions, shaking his head over the black circles under my eyes last night—he didn't know whether to worry over the first signs of a galloping decline, or break his heart at witnessing the young master he had dandled on his knees going to the damnation bowwows and turning into a confirmed roué! I guess I'll have to mind myself, though. Even Carruthers detached his mind far enough from his editorial desk and the hope of exclusively publishing the news of the Gray Seal's capture in the *Morning News-Argus*, to tell me I was looking seedy. It's wonderful the way a little paint will metamorphose a man! Well, anyway, here's for a good hot tub to-night, and a fresh start!"

He quickened his pace. There were still three blocks to go, and here was no hurrying, jostling crowd to impede his progress; indeed, as far as he could see up the Drive, there was not a pedestrian in sight. And then, as he walked, involuntarily, insistently, his mind harked back into the old groove again.

"I've tried to picture her," said Jimmie Dale softly to himself. "I've tried to picture her a hundred, yes, a thousand times, and —"

A bus, rumbling cityward, went by him, squeaking, creaking, and rattling in its uneasy joints—and out of the noise, almost at his elbow it seemed, a voice spoke his name—and in that instant intuitively he *knew*, and it thrilled him, stopped the beat of his heart, as, dulcet, soft, clear as the note of a silver bell it fell—and only one word:

"Jimmie!"

He whirled around. A limousine, wheels just grazing the curb, was gliding slowly and silently past him, and from the window a woman's arm, white-gloved and dainty, was extended, and from the fingers to the pavement fluttered an envelope—and the car leaped forward.

For the fraction of a second, Jimmie Dale stood dazed, immovable, a gamut of emotions, surprise, fierce exultation, amazement, a strange joy, a mighty uplift, swirling upon him—and then, snatching up the envelope from the ground, he sprang out into the road after the car. It was the one chance he had ever had, the one chance she had ever given him, and he had seen—a white gloved arm! He could not reach the car, it was speeding away from him like an arrow now, but there was something else that would do just as well, something that with all her cleverness she had overlooked—the car's number dangling on the rear axle, the rays of the little lamp playing on the enamelled surface of the plate! Gasping, panting, he held his own for a yard or more, and there floated back to him a little silvery laugh from the body of the limousine, and then Jimmie Dale laughed, too, and stopped—it was No. 15,836!

He stood and watched the car disappear up the Drive. What delicious irony! A month of gruelling, ceaseless toil that had been vain, futile, useless—and the key, when he was not looking for it, unexpectedly, through no effort of his, was thrust into his hand—No. 15,836!

Jimmie Dale, the gently ironic smile still on his lips, those slim, supersensitive fingers of his subconsciously noting that the texture of the envelope was the same as she always used, retraced his steps to the sidewalk.

"Number fifteen thousand eight hundred and thirty-six," said Jimmie Dale aloud—and halted at the curb as though rooted to the spot. It sounded strangely familiar, that number! He repeated it over again slowly: "One-five-eight-three-six." And the smile left his lips, and upon his face came the look of a chastened child. She had used a duplicate plate! Fifteen thousand eight hundred and thirty-six was the number of one of his own cars—his own particular runabout!

For a moment longer he stood there, undecided whether to laugh or swear, and then his eyes fastened mechanically on the envelope he was twirling in his fingers. Here, at least, was something that was not elusive; that, on the contrary, as a hundred others in the past had done, outlined probably a grim night's work ahead for the Gray Seal! And, if it were as those others had been, every minute from the moment of its receipt was precious time. He stepped under the nearest street light, and tore the envelope open.

"Dear Philanthropic Crook," it began—and then followed two closely written pages. Jimmie Dale read them, his lips growing gradually tighter, a smouldering light creeping into his dark eyes, and once he emitted a short, low whistle of consternation—that was at the end, as he read the post-script that was heavily underscored: "Work quickly. They will raid to-night. Be careful. Look out for Kline, he is the sharpest man in the United States secret service."

For a brief instant longer, Jimmie Dale stood under the street lamp, his mind in a lightning-quick way cataloguing every point in her letter, viewing every point from a myriad angles, constructing, devising, mapping out a plan to dove-tail into them—and then Jimmie Dale swung on a downtown bus. There was neither time nor occasion to go home now—that marvellous little kit of burglar's tools that peeped from their tiny pockets in that curious leather undervest, and that reposed now in the safe in his den, would be useless to him to-night; besides, in the breast pocket of his coat, neatly folded, was a black silk mask, and, relics of his role of Larry the Bat, an automatic revolver, an electric flashlight, a steel jimmy, and a bunch of skeleton keys, were distributed among the other pockets of his smart tweed suit.

Jimmie Dale changed from the bus to the subway, leaving behind him, strewn over many blocks, the tiny and minute fragments into which he had torn her letter; at Astor Place he left the subway, walked to Broadway, turned uptown for a block to Eighth Street, then along Eighth Street almost to Sixth Avenue—and stopped.

A rather shabby shop, a pitiful sort of a place, displaying in its window a heterogeneous conglomeration of cheap odds and ends, ink bottles, candy, pencils, cigarettes, pens, toys, writing pads, marbles, and a multitude of other small wares, confronted him. Within, a little, old, sweet-faced, gray-haired woman stood behind the counter, pottering over the rearrangement of some articles on the shelves.

"My word!" said Jimmie Dale softly to himself. "You wouldn't believe it, would you! And I've always wondered how these little stores managed to make both ends meet. Think of that old soul making fifteen or twenty thousand dollars from a layout like this—even if it has taken her a lifetime!"

Jimmie Dale had halted nonchalantly and unconcernedly by the curb, not too near the window, busied apparently in an effort to light a refractory cigarette; and then, about to enter the store, he gazed aimlessly across the street for a moment instead. A man came briskly around the corner from Sixth Avenue, opened the store door, and went in.

Jimmie Dale drew back a little, and turned his head again as the door closed — and a sudden, quick, alert, and startled look spread over his face.

The man who had entered bent over the counter and spoke to the old lady. She seemed to listen with a dawning terror creeping over her features, and then her hands went piteously to the thin hair behind her ears. The man motioned toward a door at the rear of the store. She hesitated, then came out from behind the counter, and swayed a little as though her limbs would not support her weight.

Jimmie Dale's lips thinned.

"I'm afraid," he muttered slowly, "I'm afraid that I'm too late even now." And then, as she came to the door and turned the key on the inside: "Pray Heaven she doesn't turn the light out — or somebody might think I was trying to break in!"

But in that respect Jimmie Dale's fears were groundless. She did not turn out either of the gas jets that lighted the little shop; instead, in a faltering, reluctant sort of manner, she led the way directly through the door in the rear, and the man followed her.

The shop was empty — and Jimmie Dale was standing against the door on the outside. His position was perfectly natural — a hundred passers-by would have noted nothing but a most commonplace occurrence — a man in the act of entering a store. And, if he appeared to fumble and have trouble with the latch, what of it! Jimmie Dale, however, was not fumbling — hidden by his back that was turned to the street, those wonderful fingers of his, in whose tips seemed embodied and concentrated every one of the human senses, were working quickly, surely, accurately, without so much as the wasted movement of a single muscle.

A faint tinkle — and the key within fell from the lock to the floor. A faint click — and the bolt of the lock slipped back. Jimmie Dale restored the skeleton keys and a little steel instrument that accompanied them to his pocket — and quietly opened the door. He stepped inside, picked up the key from the floor, inserted it in the lock, closed the door behind him, and locked it again.

"To guard against interruption," observed Jimmie Dale, a little quizzically.

He was, perhaps, thirty seconds behind the others. He crossed the shop noiselessly, cautiously, and passed through the door at the rear. It opened into a short passage that, after a few feet, gave on a sort of corridor at right angles — and down this latter, facing him, at the end, the door of a lighted room was open, and he could see the figure of the man who had entered the shop, back turned, standing on the threshold. Voices, indistinct, came to him.

The corridor itself was dark; and Jimmie Dale, satisfied that he was fairly safe from observation, stole softly forward. He passed two doors on his left—and the curious arrangement of the building that had puzzled him for a moment became clear. The store made the front of an old tenement building, with apartments above, and the rear of the store was a sort of apartment, too—the old lady's living quarters.

Step by step, testing each one against a possible creaking of the floor, Jimmie Dale moved forward, keeping close up against one wall. The man passed on into the room—and now Jimmie Dale could distinguish every word that was being spoken; and, crouched up, in the dark corridor, in the angle of the wall and the door jamb itself, could see plainly enough into the room beyond. Jimmie Dale's jaw crept out a little.

A young man, gaunt, pale, wrapped in blankets, half sat, half reclined in an invalid's chair; the old lady, on her knees, the tears streaming down her face, had her arms around the sick man's neck; while the other man, apparently upset at the scene, tugged vigorously at long, gray mustaches.

"Sammy! Sammy!" sobbed the woman piteously. "Say you didn't do it, Sammy—say you didn't do it!"

"Look here, Mrs. Matthews," said the man with the gray mustaches gently, "now don't you go to making things any harder. I've got to do my duty just the same, and take your son."

The young man, a hectic flush beginning to burn on his cheeks, gazed wildly from one to the other.

"What—what is it?" he cried out.

The man threw back his coat and displayed a badge on his vest.

"I'm Kline of the secret service," he said gravely. "I'm sorry, Sammy, but I want you for that little job in Washington at the bureau—before you left on sick leave!"

Sammy Matthews struggled away from his mother's arms, pulled himself forward in his chair—and his tongue licked dry lips.

"What—what job?" he whispered thickly.

"You know, don't you?" the other answered steadily. He took a large, flat pocketbook from his pocket, opened it, and took out a five-dollar bill. He held this before the sick man's eyes, but just out of reach, one finger silently indicating the lower left-hand corner.

Matthews stared at it for a moment, and the hectic flush faded to a grayish pallor, and a queer, impotent sound gurgled in his throat.

"I see you recognise it," said the other quietly. "It's open and shut, Sammy. That little imperfection in the plate's got you, my boy."

"Sammy! Sammy!" sobbed the woman again. "Sammy, say you didn't do it!"

"It's a lie!" said Matthews hoarsely. "It's a lie! That plate was condemned in the bureau for that imperfection — condemned and destroyed."

"Condemned *to be* destroyed," corrected the other, without raising his voice. "There's a little difference there, Sammy — about twenty years' difference — in the Federal pen. But it wasn't destroyed; this note was printed from it by one of the slickest gangs of counterfeiters in the United States — but I don't need to tell you that, I guess you know who they are. I've been after them a long time, and I've got them now, just as tight as I've got you. Instead of destroying that plate, you stole it, and disposed of it to the gang. How much did they give you?"

Matthews' face seemed to hold a dumb horror, and his fingers picked at the arms of the chair. His mother had moved from beside him now, and both her hands were patting at the man's sleeve in a pitiful way, while again and again she tried to speak, but no words would come.

"It's a lie!" said Matthews again, in a colourless, mechanical way.

The man glanced at Mrs. Matthews as he put the five-dollar note back into his pocket, seemed to choke a little, shook his head, and all trace of the official sternness that had crept into his voice disappeared.

"It's no good," he said in a low tone. "Don't do that, Mrs. Matthews, I've got to do my duty." He leaned a little toward the chair. "It's dead to rights, Sammy. You might as well make a clean breast of it. It was up to you and Al Gregor to see that the plate was destroyed. It *wasn't* destroyed; instead, it shows up in the hands of a gang of counterfeiters that I've been watching for months. Furthermore, I've got the plate itself. And finally, though I haven't placed him under arrest yet for fear you might hear of it before I wanted you to and make a get-away, I've got Al Gregor where I can put my hands on him, and I've got his confession that you and he worked the game between you to get that plate out of the bureau and dispose of it to the gang."

"Oh, my God!" — it came in a wild cry from the sick man, and in a desperate, lurching way he struggled up to his feet. "Al Gregor said that? Then — then I'm done!" He clutched at his temples. "But it's not true — it's not true! If the plate was stolen, and it must have been stolen, or that note wouldn't have been found, it was Al Gregor who stole it — I didn't, I tell you! I knew nothing of it, except that he and I were responsible for it and — and I left it to him — that's the only way I'm to blame. He's caught, and he's trying to get out of it with a light sentence by pretending to turn State's evidence, but — but I'll fight him — he can't prove it — it's only his word against mine, and—"

The other shook his head again.

"It's no good, Sammy," he said, a touch of sternness back in his tones again. "I told you it was open and shut. It's not only Al Gregor. One of the gang got weak knees when I got him where I wanted him the other night, and he swears that you are the one who *delivered* the plate to them. Between him and Gregor and what I know myself, I've got evidence enough for any jury against every one of the rest of you."

Horror, fear, helplessness seemed to mingle in the sick man's staring eyes, and he swayed unsteadily upon his feet.

"I'm innocent!" he screamed out. "But I'm caught, I'm caught in a net, and I can't get out—they lied to you—but no one will believe it any more than you do and—and it means twenty years for me—oh, God!—twenty years, and—" His hands went wriggling to his temples again, and he toppled back in a faint into the chair.

"You've killed him! You've killed my boy!" the old lady shrieked out piteously, and flung herself toward the senseless figure.

The man jumped for the table across the room, on which was a row of bottles, snatched one up, drew the cork, smelled it, and ran back with the bottle. He poured a little of the contents into his cupped hand, held it under young Matthews' nostrils, and pushed the bottle into Mrs. Matthews' hands.

"Bathe his forehead with this, Mrs. Matthews," he directed reassuringly. "He'll be all right again in a moment. There, see—he's coming around now."

There was a long, fluttering sigh, and Matthews opened his eyes; then a moment's silence; and then he spoke, with an effort, with long pauses between the words:

"Am—I—to—go—now?"

The words seemed to ring absolute terror in the old lady's ears. She turned, and dropped to her knees on the floor.

"Mr. Kline, Mr. Kline," she sobbed out, "oh, for God's love, don't take him! Let him off, let him go! He's my boy—all I've got! You've got a mother, haven't you? You know—" The tears were streaming down the sweet, old face again. "Oh, won't you, for God's dear name, won't you let him go? Won't—"

"Stop!" the man cried huskily. He was mopping at his face with his handkerchief. "I thought I was case-hardened, I ought to be—but I guess I'm not. But I've got to do my duty. You're only making it worse for Sammy there, as well as me."

Her arms were around his knees now, clinging there.

"Why can't you let him off!" she pleaded hysterically. "Why can't you! Why can't you! Nobody would know, and I'd do anything – I'd pay anything – anything – I'll give you ten – fifteen thousand dollars!"

"My poor woman," he said kindly, placing his hand on her head, "you are talking wildly. Apart altogether from the question of duty, even if I succeeded in hushing the matter up, I would probably at least be suspected and certainly discharged, and I have a family to support – and if I were caught I'd get ten years in the Federal prison for it. I'm sorry for this; I believe it's your boy's first offence, and if I could let him off I would."

"But you can – you can!" she burst out, rocking on her knees, clinging tighter still to him, as though in a paroxysm of fear that he might somehow elude her. "It will kill him – it will kill my boy. And you can save him! And even if they discharged you, what would that mean against my boy's life! You wouldn't suffer, your family wouldn't suffer, I'll – I'll take care of that – perhaps I could raise a little more than fifteen thousand – but, oh, have pity, have mercy – don't take him away!"

The man stared at her a moment, stared at the white face on the reclining chair – and passed his hand heavily across his eyes.

"You will! You will!" It came in a great surging cry of joy from the old lady. "You will – oh, thank God, thank God! – I can see it in your face!"

"I – I guess I'm soft," he said huskily, and stooped and raised Mrs. Matthews to her feet. "Don't cry any more. It'll be all right – it'll be all right. I'll – I'll fix it up somehow. I haven't made any arrests yet, and – well, I'll take my chances. I'll get the plate and turn it over to you to-morrow, only – only it's got to be destroyed in my presence."

"Yes, yes!" she cried, trying to smile through her tears – and then she flung her arms around her son's neck again. "And when you come to-morrow, I'll be ready with the money to do my share, too, and –"

But Sammy Matthews shook his head.

"You're wrong, both of you," he said weakly. "You're a white man, Kline. But destroying that plate won't save me. The minute a single note printed from it shows up, they'll know back there in Washington that the plate was stolen, and –"

"No; you're safe enough there," the other interposed heavily.

"Knowing what was up, you don't think I'd give the gang a chance to get them into circulation, do you? I got them all when I got the plate. And" – he smiled a little anxiously – "I'll bring them here to be destroyed with the plate. It would finish me now, as well as you, if one of them ever showed up. Say," he said suddenly, with a catch in his breath, "I—I don't think I know what I'm doing."

Mrs. Matthews reached out her hands to him.

"What can I say to you!" she said brokenly, "What—"

Jimmie Dale drew back along the wall. A little way from the door he quickened his pace, still moving, however, with extreme caution. They were still talking behind him as he turned from the corridor into the passageway leading to the store, and from there into the store itself. And then suddenly, in spite of caution, his foot slipped on the bare floor. It was not much—just enough to cause his other foot, poised tentatively in air, to come heavily down, and a loud and complaining creak echoed from the floor.

Jimmie Dale's jaws snapped like a steel trap. From down the corridor came a sudden, excited exclamation in the little old lady's voice, and then her steps sounded running toward the store. In the fraction of a second Jimmie Dale was at the front door.

"Clumsy, blundering fool!" he whispered fiercely to himself as he turned the key, opened the door noiselessly until it was just ajar, and turned the key in the lock again, leaving the bolt protruding out. One step backward, and he was rapping on the counter with his knuckles. "Isn't anybody here?" he called out loudly. "Isn't any—oh!"—as Mrs. Matthews appeared in the back doorway. "A package of cigarettes, please."

She stared at him, a little frightened, her eyes red and swollen with recent crying.

"How—how did you get in here?" she asked tremendously.

"I beg your pardon?" inquired Jimmie Dale, in polite surprise.

"I—I locked the door—I'm sure I did," she said, more to herself than to Jimmie Dale, and hurried across the floor to the door as she spoke.

Jimmie Dale, still politely curious, turned to watch her. For a moment bewilderment and a puzzled look were in her face—and then a sort of surprised relief.

"I must have turned the key in the lock without shutting the door tight," she explained, "for I knew I turned the key."

Jimmie Dale bent forward to examine the lock—and nodded.

"Yes," he agreed, with a smile. "I should say so." Then, gravely courteous: "I'm sorry to have intruded."

"It is nothing," she answered; and, evidently anxious to be rid of him, moved quickly around behind the counter. "What kind of cigarettes do you want?"

"Egyptians—any kind," said Jimmie Dale, laying a bill on the counter.

He pocketed the cigarettes and his change, and turned to the door.

"Good-evening," he said pleasantly – and went out.

Jimmie Dale smiled a little curiously, a little tolerantly. As he started along the street, he heard the door of the little shop close with a sort of supercareful bang, the key turned, and the latch rattle to try the door – the little old lady was bent on making no mistake a second time!

And then the smile left Jimmie Dale's lips, his face grew strained and serious, and he broke into a run down the block to Sixth Avenue. Here he paused for an instant – there was the elevated, the surface cars – which would be the quicker? He looked up the avenue. There was no train coming; the nearest surface car was blocks away. He bit his lips in vexation – and then with a jump he was across the street and hailing a passing taxicab that his eyes had just lighted on.

"Got a fare?" called Jimmie Dale.

"No, sir," answered the chauffeur, bumping his car to an abrupt halt.

"Good!" Jimmie Dale ran alongside, and yanked the door open. "Do you know where the Palace Saloon on the Bowery is?"

"Yes, sir," replied the man.

Jimmie Dale held a ten-dollar bank note up before the chauffeur's eyes.

"Earn that in four minutes, then," he snapped – and sprang into the cab.

The taxicab swerved around on little better than two wheels, started on a mad dash down the Avenue – and Jimmie Dale braced himself grimly in his seat. The cab swerved again, tore across Waverly Place, [35] circuited Washington Square, crossed Broadway, and whirled finally into the upper end of the Bowery.

Jimmie Dale spoke once – to himself – plaintively.

"It's too bad I can't let old Carruthers in on this for a scoop with his precious *Morning News-Argus* – but if I get out of it alive myself, I'll do well! Wonder if the day'll ever come when he finds out that his very dear friend and old college pal, Jimmie Dale, is the Gray Seal that he's turned himself inside out for about four years now to catch, and that he'd trade his soul with the devil any time to lay hands on! Good old Carruthers! 'The most puzzling, bewildering, delightful crook in the annals of crime' – am I?"

---

[35] This lower Manhattan street is mentioned a number of times in the novel. In the United States Census of 1910 Packard is shown living in an apartment building at 101 Waverly Place which is between 5th and 6th Avenues.

The cab drew up at the curb. Jimmie Dale sprang out, shoved the bill into the chauffeur's hand, stepped quickly across the sidewalk, and pushed his way through the swinging doors of the Palace Saloon. Inside leisurely and nonchalantly, he walked down past the length of the bar to a door at the rear. This opened into a passageway that led to the side entrance of the saloon on the cross street. Jimmie Dale emerged from the side entrance, crossed the street, retraced his steps to the Bowery, crossed over, and walked rapidly down that thoroughfare for two blocks. Here he turned east into the cross street; and here, once more, his pace became leisurely and unhurried.

"It's a strange coincidence, though possibly a very happy one," said Jimmie Dale, as he walked along, "that it should be on the same street as the Sanctuary — ah, this ought to be the place!"

An alleyway, corresponding to the one that flanked the tenement where, as Larry the Bat, he had paid room rent as a tenant for several years, in fact, the alleyway next above it, and but a short block away, intersected the street, narrow, black, and uninviting. Jimmie Dale, as he passed, peered down its length.

"No light — that's good!" commented Jimmie Dale to himself. Then: "Window opens on alleyway ten feet from ground — shoe store, Russian Jew, in basement — go in front door — straight hallway — room at end — Russian Jew probably accomplice — be careful that he does not hear you moving overhead" — Jimmie Dale's mind, with that curious faculty of his, was subconsciously repeating snatches from her letter word for word, even as he noted the dimly lighted, untidy, and disorderly interior of what, from strings of leather slippers that decorated the cellarlike entrance, was evidently a cheap and shoddy shoe store in the basement of the building.

The building itself was rickety and tumble-down, three stories high, and given over undoubtedly to gregarious foreigners of the poorer class, a rabbit burrow, as it were, having a multitude of roomers and lodgers. There was nothing ominous or even secretive about it — up the short flight of steps to the entrance, even the door hung carelessly half open.

Jimmie Dale's slouch hat was pulled a little farther down over his eyes as he mounted the steps and entered the hallway. He listened a moment. A sort of subdued, querulous hubbub seemed to hum through the place, as voices, men's, women's, and children's, echoing out from their various rooms above, mingled together, and floated down the stairways in a discordant medley. Jimmie Dale stepped lightly down the length of the hall — and listened again; this time intently, with his ear to the keyhole of the door that made the end of the passage. There was not a sound from within. He tried the door, smiled a little as he reached for his keys, worked over the lock—and straightened up suddenly as his ear caught a descending step on the stairs. It was two flights up, however—and the door was unlocked now. Jimmie Dale opened it, and, like a shadow, slipped inside; and, as he locked the door behind him, smiled once more—the door lock was but a paltry makeshift at best, but *inside* his fingers had touched a massive steel bolt that, when shot home, would yield when the door itself yielded—and not before. Without moving the bolt, he turned—and his flashlight for a moment swept the room.

"Not much like the way they describe this sort of place in storybooks!" murmured Jimmie Dale capriciously. "But I get the idea. Mr. Russian Jew downstairs makes a bluff at using it for a storeroom."

Again the flashlight made a circuit. Here, there, and everywhere, seemingly without any attempt at order, were piles of wooden shipping cases. Only the centre of the room was clear and empty; that, and a vacant space against the wall by the window.

Jimmie Dale, moving without sound, went to the window. There was a shade on it, and it was pulled down. He reached up underneath it, felt for the window fastening, and unlocked it; then cautiously tested the window itself by lifting it an inch or two—it slid easily in its grooves.

He stood then for a moment, hardfaced, a frown gathering his forehead into heavy furrows, as the flashlight's ray again and again darted hither and thither. There was nothing, absolutely nothing in the room but wooden packing cases. He lifted the cover of the one nearest to him and looked inside. It was quite empty, except for some pieces of heavy cord, and a few cardboard shoe boxes that, in turn, were empty, too.

"It's here, of course," said Jimmie Dale thoughtfully to himself. "Clever work, too! But I can't move half a hundred packing cases without that chap below hearing me; and I can't do it in ten minutes, either, which, I imagine is the outside limit of time. Fortunately, though, these cases are not without their compensation—a dozen men could hide here."

He began to move about the room. And now he stooped before one pile of boxes and then another, curiously attempting to lift up the entire pile from the bottom. Some he could not move; others, by exerting all his strength, gave a little; and then, finally, over in one corner, he found a pile that appeared to answer his purpose.

"These are certainly empty," he muttered.

There was just room to squeeze through between them and the next stack of cases alongside; but, once through, by the simple expedient of moving the cases out a little to take advantage of the angle made by the corner of the room, he obtained ample space to stand comfortably upright against the wall. But Jimmie Dale was not satisfied yet. Could he see out into the room? He experimented with his flashlight – and carefully shifted the screen of cases before him a little to one side. And yet still he was not satisfied. With a sort of ironical droop at the corners of his lips, as though suddenly there had flashed upon him the inspiration that fathered one of those whimsical ideas and fancies that were so essentially a characteristic of Jimmie Dale, he came out from behind the cases, went across the room to the case he had opened when he first entered, took out the cord and the cover of one of the cardboard shoe boxes, and with these returned to his hiding place once more.

The sounds from the upper stories of the tenement now reached him hardly at all; but from below, directly under his feet almost, he could hear some one, the proprietor of the shoe store probably, walking about.

Tense, every faculty now on the alert, his head turned in a strained, attentive attitude, Jimmie Dale threw on the flashlight's tiny switch, took that intimate and thin metal case from his pocket, extracted a diamond-shaped, gray paper seal with the little tweezers, moistened the adhesive side, and stuck it in the centre of the white cardboard-box cover, then tore the edges of the cardboard down until the whole was just small enough to slip into his pocket. Through the cardboard he looped a piece of cord, placard fashion, and with his pencil printed the four words – "with the compliments of " – above the gray seal. He surveyed the result with a grim, mirthless chuckle – and put the piece of cardboard in his pocket.

"I'm taking the longest chances I ever took in my life," said Jimmie Dale very seriously to himself, as his fingers twisted, and doubled, and tied the remaining pieces of cord together, and finally fashioned a running noose in one end. "I don't –" The cord and the flashlight went into his pocket, the room was in darkness, the black mask was whipped from his breast pocket and adjusted to his face, and his automatic was in his hand.

Came the creak of a footstep, as though on a ladder exactly below him, another, and another, receding curiously in its direction, yet at the same time growing louder in sound as if nearer the floor – then a crack of light showed in the floor in the centre of the room. This held for an instant, then expanded suddenly into a great luminous square – and through a trapdoor, opened wide now, a man's head appeared.

Jimmie Dale's eyes, fixed through the space between the piles of cases, narrowed – there was, indeed, little doubt but that the shoe-store proprietor below was an accomplice! The store served a most convenient purpose in every respect – as a secret means of entry into the room, as a sort of guarantee of innocence for the room itself. Why not! To the superficial observer, to the man who might by some chance blunder into the room – it was but an adjunct of the store itself!

The man in the trap-doorway paused with his shoulders above the floor, looked around, listened, then drew himself up, walked across the floor, and shot the heavy bolt on the door that led into the hallway of the house. He returned then to the trapdoor, bent over it, and whistled softly. Two more men, in answer to the summons, came up into the room.

"The Cap'll be along in a minute," one of them said. "Turn on the light."

A switch clicked, flooding the room with sudden brilliancy from half a dozen electric bulbs.

"Too many!" grunted the same voice again. "We ain't working to-night—turn out half of 'em."

The sudden transition from the darkness for a moment dazzled Jimmie Dale's eyes—but the next moment he was searching the faces of the three men. There were few crooks, few denizens of the crime world below the now obsolete but still famous dead line that, as Larry the Bat, he did not know at least by sight.

"Moulton, Whitie Burns, and Marty Dean," confided Jimmie Dale softly to himself. "And I don't know of any worse, except—the Cap. And gun fighters, every one of them, too—nice odds, to say nothing of—"

"Here's the Cap now!" announced one of the three. "Hello, Cap, where'd you raise the mustache?"

Jimmie Dale's eyes shifted to the trapdoor, and into them crept a contemptuous and sardonic smile—the man who was coming up now and hoisting himself to the floor was the man who, half an hour before, had threatened young Sammy Matthews with arrest.

The Cap, alias Bert Malone, alias a score of other names, closed the trapdoor after him, pulled off his mustache and gray wig, tucked them in his pocket, and faced his companions brusquely.

"Never mind about the mustache," he said curtly. "Get busy, the lot of you. Stir around and get the works out!"

"What for?" inquired Whitie Burns, a sharp, ferret-faced little man. "We got enough of the old stuff on hand now, and that bum break Gregor made when he pinched the cracked plate put the finish on that. Say, Cap—"

"Close your face, Whitie, and get the works out!" Malone cut in shortly. "We've only got the whole night ahead of us—but we'll need it all. We're going to run the queer off that cracked plate."

One of the others, Marty Dean this time, a certain brutal aggressiveness in both features and physique, edged forward.

"Say, what's the lay?" he demanded. "A joke? We printed one fiver off that plate—and then we knew enough to quit. With that crack along the corner, you couldn't pass 'em on a blind man! And Gregor saying he thought we could patch the plate up enough to get by with gives me a pain—he's got jingles in his dome factory! Run them fivers eh—say, are you cracked, too?"

"Aw, forget it!" observed Malone caustically. "Who's running this gang?" Then, with a malicious grin: "I got a customer for those fivers— fifteen thousand dollars for all we can turn out to-night. See?"

The others stared at him for a moment, incredulity and greed mingling in a curious half-hesitant, half-expectant look on their faces.

Then Whitie Burns spoke, circling his lips with the tip of his tongue:

"D'ye mean it, Cap—honest? What's the lay? How'd you work it?"

Malone, unbending with the sensation he had created, grinned again.

"Easy enough," he said offhandedly. "It was like falling off a log. Gregor said, didn't he, that the only way he had been able to get his claws on that plate was on account of young Matthews going away sick—eh? Well, the old Matthews woman, his mother, has got money—about fifteen thousand. I guess she ain't got any more than that, or I'd have raised the ante. Aw, it was easy. She threw it at me. I framed one up on them, that's all. I'm Kline, of the secret service—see? I don't suppose they'd ever seen him, though they'd know his name fast enough, but I made up something like him. I showed them where I had a case against Sammy for pinching the plate that was strong enough to put a hundred innocent men behind the bars. Of course, he knew well enough he was innocent, but he could see the twenty years I showed him with both eyes. Say, he mussed all over the place, and went and fainted like a girl. And then the old woman came across with an offer of fifteen thousand for the plate, and corrupted me." Malone's cunning, vicious face, now that the softening effects of the gray hair and mustache were gone, seemed accentuated diabolically by the grin broadening into a laugh, as he guffawed.

Marty Dean's hand swung with a bang to Malone's shoulder.

"Say, Cap—say, you're all right!" he exclaimed excitedly. "You're the boy! But what's the good of running anything off the plate before turning it over to 'em—the stuff's no good to us."

"You got a wooden nut, with sawdust for brains," said Malone sarcastically. "If he'd thought the gang of counterfeiters that was supposed to have bought the plate from him had run off only one fiver and then stopped because they say it wouldn't get by, and weren't going to run any more, and just destroy the plate like it was supposed to have been destroyed to begin with, and it all end up with no one the wiser, where d'ye think we'd have banked that fifteen thousand! I told him I had the whole run confiscated, and that the queer went with the plate, so we'll just make that little run to-night—that's why I sent word around to you this morning."

"By the jumping!" ejaculated Whitie Burns, heavy with admiration. "You got a head on you, Cap!"

"It's a good thing for some of you that I have," returned Malone complacently. "But don't stand jawing all night. Go on, now — get busy!"

There was no surprise in Jimmie Dale's face—he had chosen his position behind a pile of cases that he had been extremely careful, as a man is careful when his life hangs in the balance, to assure himself were empty. None of the four came near or touched the pile behind which he stood; but, here and there about the room, they pulled this one and that one out from various stacks. In scarcely more than a moment, the room was completely transformed. It was no longer a storeroom for surplus stock, for the storage of bulky and empty packing cases! From the cases the men had picked out, like a touch of magic, appeared a veritable printing plant, an elaborate engraver's outfit—a highly efficient foot-power press, rapidly being assembled by Whitie Burns; an electric dryer, inks, a pile of white, silk-threaded bank-note paper, a cutter, and a score of other appurtenances.

"Yes," said Jimmie Dale very gently to himself. "Yes, quite so — but the plate? Ah!" Malone was taking it out from the middle of a bundle of old newspapers, loosely tied together, that he had lifted from one of the cases.

Jimmie Dale's eyes fastened on it—and from that instant never left it. A minute passed, two, three of them—the four men were silently busy about the room—Malone was carefully cleaning the plate.

"They will raid to-night. Look out for Kline, he is the sharpest man in the United State secret service"—the warning in her letter was running through Jimmie Dale's mind. Kline—the real Kline—was going to raid the place to-night. When? At what time? It must be nearly eleven o'clock already, and—

It came sudden, quick as the crack of doom—a terrific crash against the bolted door—but the door, undoubtedly to the surprise of those without, held fast, thanks to the bolt. The four men, white-faced, seemed for an instant turned to statues. Came another crash against the door—and a sharp, imperative order to those within to open it and surrender.

"We're pinched! Beat it!" whispered Whitie Burns wildly—and dashed for the trapdoor.

Like a rat for its hole, Marty Dean followed. Malone, farther away, dropped the plate on the floor, and rushed, with Moulton beside him, after the others — but he never reached the trapdoor.

Over the crashing blows, raining now in quick succession on the door of the room, over a startled commotion as lodgers, roomers, and tenants on the floor above awoke into frightened activity with shouts and cries, came the louder crash of a pile of packing boxes hurled to the floor. And over them, vaulting those scattered in his way, Jimmie Dale sprang at Malone. The man reeled back, with a cry. Moulton dashed through the trapdoor and disappeared. The short, ugly barrel of Jimmie Dale's automatic was between Malone's eyes.

"You make a move," said Jimmie Dale, in a low sibilant way, "and I'll drop you where you stand! Put your hands behind your back — palms together!"

Malone, dazed, cowed, obeyed. A panel of the door split and rent down its length — the hinges were sagging. Jimmie Dale worked like lightning. The cord with the slip noose from his pocket went around Malone's wrists, jerked tight, and knotted; the placard, his lips grim, with no sign of humour, Jimmie Dale dangled around the man's neck.

"An introduction for you to Mr. Kline out there — that you seem so fond of!" gritted Jimmie Dale. Then, working as he talked: "I've got no time to tell you what I think of you, you pitiful hound" — he snatched up the plate from the floor and put it in his pocket — "Twenty years, I think you said, didn't you?" — his hand shot into Malone's pocket-book, and extracted the five-dollar note — "If you can open this with your toes maybe you can get away" — he wrenched the trapdoor over and slammed it shut — "good-night, Malone" — and he leaped for the window.

The door tottered inward from the top, ripping, tearing, smashing hinges, panels, and jamb. Jimmie Dale got a blurred vision of brass buttons, blue coats, and helmets, and, in the forefront, of a stocky, gray-mustached, gray-haired man in plain clothes.

Jimmie Dale threw up the window, swung out, as with a rush the officers burst through into the room and a revolver bullet hummed viciously past his ear, and dropped to the ground — into encircling arms!

"Ah, no, you don't, my bucko!" snapped a hoarse voice in his ear. "Keep quiet now, or I'll crack your bean — understand!"

But the officer, too heavy to be muscular, was no match for Jimmie Dale, who, even as he had dropped from the sill, had caught sight of the lurking form below; and now, with a quick, sudden, lithe movement he wriggled loose, his fist from a short-arm jab smashed upon the point of the other's jaw, sending the man staggering backward — and Jimmie Dale ran.

A crowd was already collecting at the mouth of the alleyway, mostly occupants of the house itself, and into these, scattering them in all directions, eluding dexterously another officer who made a grab for him, Jimmie Dale charged at top speed, burst through, and headed down the street, running like a deer.

Yells went up, a revolver spat venomously behind him, came the shrill *cheep-cheep!* of the police whistle, and heavy boots pounding the pavement in pursuit.

Down the block Jimmie Dale raced. The yells augmented in his rear. Another shot—and this time he heard the bullet buzz. And then he swerved—into the next alleyway—that flanked the Sanctuary.

He had perhaps a ten yards' lead, just a little more than the distance from the street to the side door of the Sanctuary that opened on the alleyway. And, as he ran now, his fingers tore at his clothing, loosening his tie, unbuttoning coat, vest, collar, shirt, and undershirt. He leaped at the door, swung it open, flung himself inside—and then sacrificing speed to silence, went up the stairs like a cat, cramming his mask now into his pocket.

His room was on the first landing. In an instant he had unlocked the door, entered, and locked it again behind him. From outside, an excited street urchin's voice shrilled up to him:

"He went in that door! I seen him!"

The police whistle chirped again; and then an authoritative voice:

"Get around and watch the saloon back of this, Heeney—there's a way out through there from this joint."

Jimmie Dale, divested of every stitch of clothing that he had worn, pulled a disreputable collarless flannel shirt over his head, pulled on a dirty and patched pair of trousers, and slipped into a threadbare and filthy coat. Jimmie Dale was working against seconds. They were at the lower door now. He lifted the oilcloth in the corner of the room, lifted up the loose piece of the flooring, shoved his discarded garments inside, and from a little box that was there smeared the hollow of his hand with some black substance, possessed himself of two little articles, replaced the flooring, replaced the oilcloth, and, in bare feet, stole across the room to the door. Against the door, without a sound, Jimmie Dale placed a chair, and on the chair seat he laid the two little articles he had been carrying in his hand. It was intensely black in the room, but Jimmie Dale needed no light here. From under the bed he pulled out a pair of woolen socks and a pair of congress boots, [36] both as disreputable as the rest of his attire, put them on — and very quietly, softly, cautiously, stretched himself out on the bed.

The officers were at the top of the stairs. A voice barked out:

"Stand guard on this landing, Peters. Higgins, you take the one above. We'll start from the top of the house and work down. Allow no one to pass you."

"Yes, sir! Very good, Mr. Kline," was the response.

Kline! — the sharpest man in the United States secret service, she had said. Jimmie Dale's lips set.

"I'm glad I had no shave this morning," said Jimmie Dale grimly to himself.

His fingers were working with the black substance in the hollow of his hand — and the long, slim, tapering fingers, the shapely, well-cared-for hands grew unkempt and grimy, black beneath the finger nails — and a little, too, played its part on the day's growth of beard, a little around the throat and at the nape of the neck, a little across the forehead to meet the locks of straggling and disordered hair. Jimmie Dale wiped the residue from the hollow of his hand on the knee of his trousers — and lay still.

An officer paced outside. Upstairs doors opened and closed. Gruff, harsh tones in commands echoed through the house. The search party descended to the second floor — and again the same sounds were repeated. And then, thumping down the creaking stairs, they stopped before Jimmie Dale's room. Some one tried the door, and, finding it locked, rattled it violently.

"Open the door!" It was Kline's voice.

Jimmie Dale's eyes were closed, and he was breathing regularly, though just regularly, a little slower than in natural respiration.

"Break it down!" ordered Kline tersely.

There was a rush at it — and it gave. It surged inward, knocked against the chair, upset the latter, something tinkled to the floor — and four officers, with Kline at their head, jumped into the room.

Jimmie Dale never moved. A flashlight played around the room and focused upon him — and then he was shaken roughly — only to fall inertly back on the bed again.

---

[36] Nothing to do with politics, congress boots were high shoes with elastic sides.

"I guess this is all right, Mr. Kline," said one of the officers. "It's Larry the Bat, and he's doped to the eyes. There's the stuff on the floor we knocked off the chair."

"Light the gas!" directed Kline curtly; and, being obeyed, stooped to the floor and picked up a hypodermic syringe and a small bottle. He held the bottle to the light, and read the label: *Liquor Morphinæ*. "Shake him again!" he commanded.

None too gently, a policeman caught Jimmie Dale by the shoulder and shook him vigorously – again Jimmie Dale, once the other let go his hold, fell back limply on the bed, breathing in that same, slightly slowed way.

"Larry the Bat, eh?" grunted Kline; then, to the officer who had volunteered the information: "Who's Larry the Bat? What is he? And how long have you known him?"

"I don't know who he is any more than what you can see there for yourself," replied the officer. "He's a dope fiend, and I guess a pretty tough case, though we've never had him up for anything. He's lived here ever since I've been on the beat, and that's three years or –"

"All right!" interrupted Kline crisply. "He's no good to us! You say there's an exit from this house into that saloon at the back?"

"Yes, sir but the fellow, whoever he is, couldn't get away from there. Heeney's been over on guard from the start."

"Then he's still inside there," said Kline, clipping off his words. "We'll search the saloon. Nice night's work this is! One out of the whole gang – and that one with the compliments of the Gray Seal!"

The men went out and began to descend the stairs.

"One," said Jimmie Dale to himself, still motionless, still breathing in that slow way so characteristic of the drug. "Two. Three. Four."

The minutes went by – a quarter of an hour – a half hour. Still Jimmie Dale lay there – still motionless – still breathing with slow regularity. His muscles began to cramp, to give him exquisite torture. Around him all was silence – only distant sounds from the street reached him, muffled, and at intervals. Another quarter of an hour passed – an eternity of torment. It seemed to Jimmie Dale, for all his will power, that he could not hold himself in check, that he must move, scream out even in the torture that was passing all endurance. It was silent now, utterly silent – and then out of the silence, just outside his door, a footstep creaked – and a man walked to the stairs and went down.

"Five," said Jimmie Dale to himself. "The sharpest man in the United States secret service."

And then for the first time Jimmie Dale moved – to wipe away the beads of sweat that had sprung out upon his forehead.

CHAPTER V

THE AFFAIR OF THE PUSHCART MAN

(Thursday 9/2/1915 to Friday 9/3/1915)

Larry THE BAT shambled out of the side door of the tenement into the back alleyway; shambled along the black alleyway to the street — and smiled a little grimly as a shadow across the roadway suddenly shifted its position. The game was growing acute, critical, desperate even — and it was his move.

Larry the Bat, disreputable denizen of the underworld, alias Jimmie Dale, millionaires' clubman, alias the Gray Seal, whom Carruthers of the *Morning News-Argus* called the master criminal of the age, shuffled along in the direction of the Bowery, his hands plunged deep in the pockets of his frayed and tattered trousers, where his fingers, in a curious, wistful way, fondled the keys of his own magnificent residence on Riverside Drive. It was his move — and it was an impasse, ironical, sardonic, and it was worse — it was full of peril.

True, he had outwitted Kline of the secret service two nights before, when Kline had raided the counterfeiters' den; true, he had no reason to believe that Kline suspected *him* specifically, but the man Kline wanted *had* entered the tenement that night, and since then the house had been shadowed day and night. The result was both simple and disastrous — to Jimmie Dale. Larry the Bat, a known inmate of the house, might come and go as he pleased — but to emerge from the Sanctuary in the person of Jimmie Dale would be fatal. Kline had been outwitted, but Kline had not acknowledged final defeat. The tenement had been searched from top to bottom — unostentatiously. His own room on the first landing had been searched the previous afternoon, when he was out, but they had failed to find the cunningly contrived opening in the floor under the oilcloth in the corner, an impromptu wardrobe, that would proclaim Larry the Bat and Jimmie Dale to be one and the same person — that would inevitably lead further to the establishment of his identity as the Gray Seal. In time, of course, the surveillance would cease — but he could not wait. That was the monumental irony of it — the factor that, all unknown to Kline, was forcing the issue hard now. It was his move.

Since, years ago now, as the Gray Seal, he had begun to work with *her*, that unknown, mysterious accomplice of his, and the police, stung to madness both by the virulent and constant attacks of the press and by the humiliating prod of their own failures, sought daily, high and low, with every resource at their command, for the Gray Seal, he had never been in quite so strange and perilous a plight as he found himself at that moment. To preserve inviolate the identity of Larry the Bat was absolutely vital to his safety. It was the one secret that even she, who so strangely appeared to know all else about him, he was sure, had not discovered – and it was just that, in a way, that had brought the present impossible situation to pass.

In the month previous, in a lull between those letters of hers, he had set himself doggedly and determinedly to the renewed task of what had become so dominantly now a part of his very existence – the solving of *her* identity. And for that month, as the best means to the end – means, however, that only resulted as futilely as the attempts that had gone before – he had lived mostly as Larry the Bat, returning to his home in his proper person only when occasion and necessity demanded it. He had been going home that evening, two nights before, walking along Riverside Drive, when from the window of the limousine she had dropped the letter at his feet that had plunged him into the affair of the Counterfeit Five – and he had not gone home! Eventually, to save himself, he had, in the Sanctuary, performing the transformation in desperate haste, again been forced to assume the role of Larry the Bat.

That was really the gist of it. And yesterday morning he had remembered, to his dismay, that he had had little or no money left the night before. He had intended, of course, to replenish his supply – when he got home. Only he hadn't gone home! And now he needed money – needed it badly, desperately. With thousands in the bank, with abundance even in his safe, in his own den at home, a supply kept there always for an emergency, he was facing actual want – he rattled two dimes, a nickel, and a few odd pennies thoughtfully against the keys in his pocket.

To a certain extent, old Jason, his butler, could be trusted. Jason even knew that mysterious letters of tremendous secretive importance came to the house, and the old man always meant well – but he dared not trust even Jason with the secret of his dual personality. What was he to do? He needed money imperatively – at once. Thanks to Kline, for the time being, at least, he could not rid himself of the personality of Larry the Bat by the simple expedient of slipping into the clothes of Jimmie Dale – he must live, act, and remain Larry the Bat until the secret service officer gave up the hunt. How bridge the gulf between Jimmie Dale and Larry the Bat in old Jason's eyes!

Nor was that all. There was still another matter, and one that, in order to counteract it, demanded at once a serious inroad – to the extent of a telephone call – upon his slender capital. A too prolonged and unaccounted-for absence from home, and old Jason, in his anxious, blundering solicitude, would have the fat in the fire at that end – and the city, and the social firmament thereof, would be humming with the startling news of the disappearance of a well-known millionaire. The complications that would then ensue, with himself powerless to lift a finger, Jimmie Dale did not care to think about – such a contretemps must at all hazards be prevented.

Jimmie Dale reached the corner of the street, where it intersected the Bowery, and paused languidly by the curb. No one appeared to be following. He had not expected that there would be – but it was as well to be sure. He walked then a few steps along the Bowery – and slipped suddenly into a doorway, from where he could command a view of the street corner that he had just left. At the end of ten minutes, satisfied that no one had any concern in his immediate movements, he shambled on again down the Bowery.

There was a saloon two blocks away that boasted a private telephone booth. Jimmie Dale made that his destination.

Larry the Bat was a very well-known character in that resort, and the bullet-headed dispenser of drinks behind the bar nodded unctuously to him over the heads of those clustered at the rail as he entered; Larry the Bat, as befitted one of the elite of the underworld, [37] was graciously pleased to acknowledge the proletariat salutation with a curt nod. He walked down to the end of the room, entered the telephone booth – and was carelessly careful to close the door tightly behind him.

He gave the number of his residence on Riverside Drive, and waited for the connection. After some delay, Jason's voice answered him.

"Jason," said Jimmie Dale, in matter-of-fact tones, "I shall be out of the city for another three or four days, possibly a week, and –" he stopped abruptly, as a sort of gasp came to him over the wire.

"Thank God that's you, sir!" exclaimed the old butler wildly. "I've been near mad, sir, all day!"

"Don't get excited, Jason!" said Jimmie Dale a little sharply. "The mere matter of my absence for the last two days is nothing to cause you any concern. And while I am on the subject, Jason, let me say now that I shall be glad if you will bear that fact in mind in future."

---

[37] Just how Larry earned the regard of New York's criminals is never explained. Perhaps he, like the Gray Seal, has been credited with crimes he did not actually commit. If so the police know nothing about those misdeeds since they do not treat him as a wanted man. Or a particularly dangerous one.

"Yes, sir," stammered Jason. "But, sir, it ain't that – good Lord, Master Jim, it ain't that, sir! It's – it's one of them letters."

Something like a galvanic shock seemed to jerk the disreputable, loose-jointed frame of Larry the Bat suddenly erect – and a strained whiteness crept over the dirty, unwashed face.

"Go on, Jason," said Jimmie Dale, without a quiver in his voice.

"It came this morning, sir – that shuffer with his automobile left it. I had just time to say you weren't at home, sir, and he was gone. And then, sir, there ain't been an hour gone by all through the day that a woman, sir – a lady, begging your pardon, Master Jim – hasn't rung up on the telephone, asking if you were back, and if I could get you, and where you were, and half frantic, sir, half sobbing, sometimes, sir, and saying there was a life hanging on it, Master Jim."

Larry the Bat, staring into the mouthpiece of the instrument, subconsciously passed his hand across his forehead, and subconsciously noted that his fingers, as he drew them away, were damp.

"Where is the letter now, Jason?" inquired Jimmie Dale coolly.

"Here on your desk, Master Jim. Shall I bring it to you?"

Bring it to him! How? When? Where? Bring it to him! The ghastly irony of it! Jimmie Dale tried to think – prodding, spurring desperately that keen, lightning brain of his that had never failed him yet. How bridge the gulf between Larry the Bat and Jimmie Dale in Jason's eyes – not just for the replenishing of funds now, but with a life at stake!

"No – I think not, Jason," said Jimmie Dale calmly. "Just leave it where it is. And if she telephones again, say that you have told me – that will be sufficient to satisfy any further inquiries. And Jason – "

"Yes, sir?"

"If she telephones again, try and find out where the call comes from."

"I haven't forgotten what you said once, Master Jim, sir," said the old man eagerly. "And I've been trying that sir, all day. They've all come from different pay stations, sir."

A mirthless little smile tinged Jimmie Dale's lips. Of course! He might have known! It was always that way, always the same. He was as near to the solution of her identity at that moment as he had been years ago, when she, in some mysterious way, alone of all the world, had identified him as the Gray Seal!

"Very good, Jason," he said quietly. "Don't bother about it any more. It will be all right. You can expect me when you see me. Good-night." He hung the receiver on the hook, walked out of the booth, and mechanically reached the street.

All right! It was far from "all right" – very far from it. It was no trivial thing, that letter; they never had been trivial things, those letters of hers, that involved so often a matter of life and death – as this one now, perhaps, as her actions would seem to indicate, involved life and death more urgently than any that had gone before. It was far from all right – at a moment when his own position, his own safety, was at best but a desperate chance; when his every energy, brain, wit, and cunning were taxed to the utmost to save himself! And yet, somehow, some way, at any cost, he must get that letter – and at any cost he must act upon it! To fail her was to fail utterly in everything that failure in its most miserable, its widest sense, implied – failure in that which rose paramount to every other consideration in life!

Fail her! Jimmie Dale's lips thinned into a hard, drawn line – and then parted slowly in a curiously whimsical smile. It would be a strange burglary that he had decided upon, in order that he might not fail her – stranger than any the Gray Seal had ever committed, and, in some respects, even more perilous!

He started along the Bowery, walking briskly now, toward the nearest subway station, at Astor Place, his mind for the moment electing to face the situation in a humour as whimsical as his smile. Supposing that, as Larry the Bat, he were caught and arrested during the next hour, in Jimmie Dale's residence on Riverside Drive! With his arrest as Larry the Bat, Jimmie's Dale would automatically disappear. Would follow then the suspicion that Jimmie Dale, the millionaire, had met with foul play, and as time went on, and Jimmie Dale, being then in prison as Larry the Bat, did not reappear, the assurance of it; then the certainty that suspicion would focus on Larry the Bat as being connected with the millionaire's death, since Larry the Bat had been caught in Jimmie Dale's home – and he would be accused of his own murder! It was quite humourous, of course, quite grotesquely bizarre – but it was equally an exceedingly grim possibility! There were drawbacks to a dual personality!

"In a word," confided Jimmie Dale softly to himself, and a serious light crept into the dark, steady eyes, "I'm in a bit of a nasty mess!"

At Astor Place he entered the subway; at Fourteenth Street he changed to an express, and at Ninety-sixth Street he got out. It was but a short walk west to Riverside Drive, and from there his house was only a few blocks farther on.

Jimmie Dale did not slouch now. And for all his disreputable attire, incongruous as it was in that neighbourhood, few people that he passed paid any attention to him, none gave him more than a casual glance – Jimmie Dale swung along, upright, with no attempt to make himself inconspicuous, hurrying a little, as one intent upon a definite errand. As he neared his house he slowed his pace a little until a couple, who were passing in front of it, had gone on; then he went up the steps, but noiselessly as a shadow now, to the front door, opened it softly, closed it softly behind him, and crouched for a moment in the vestibule.

Through the monogrammed lace on the plate glass of the inner doors he could see, a little indistinctly, into the reception hall beyond. The hall was empty. Jason, for that matter, would be the only one likely to be about; the other servants would have no business there in any case, and whether in their quarters above or below, they had their own stairs at the rear.

Jimmie Dale inserted the key in the spring lock, and opened the door a cautious fraction of an inch—to listen. There was no sound—yes, a subdued murmured—the servants were downstairs in the basement. He slipped inside, slipped, in a flash, across the hall, and, treading like a cat, went up the stairs. He scarcely seemed to breathe until, with a little sigh of relief, he stood inside his den on the first floor, with the door shut behind him.

"I must speak to Jason about being a little more watchful," muttered Jimmie Dale facetiously. "Here's all my property at the mercy of—Larry the Bat!"

An instant he stood by the door, looking about him—in the bright moonlight streaming in through the side windows the room's appointments stood out in soft shadows, the huge davenport, the great, luxurious easy-chairs, an easel with a half-finished canvas, as he had left it; the big, flat-topped, rosewood desk, the open fireplace—and then, his steps silent on the thick velvet rug under foot, he walked quickly to the desk.

Yes, there it was—the letter. He placed it hurriedly in his pocket—the moonlight was not strong enough to read by, and he dared not turn on the lights.

And now money—funds. In the alcove behind the portière, Jimmie Dale dropped on his knees before the squat, barrel-shaped safe, and opened it. He reached inside, took out a package of banknotes, placed the bills in his pocket—and hesitated a moment. What else would he require? What act did that letter call upon the Gray Seal to perform in the next few hours? Jimmie Dale stared thoughtfully into the interior of the safe. Whatever it was, it must be performed in the role of Larry the Bat, for though he could get into his dressing room now, and become Jimmie Dale again, there were still those watchers outside the Sanctuary—*they* must not become suspicious—and if Larry the Bat disappeared mysteriously, Larry the Bat would be the man that Kline and the secret service of the United States would never cease hunting for, and that would mean that he could never reassume a character that was as necessary for his protection as breath was to life, so long as the Gray Seal worked. True, he could change now to Jimmie Dale, but he would have to change back again and return to the Sanctuary before morning, as Larry the Bat – and remain there until Kline, beaten, called off his human bloodhounds. No, a change was not to be thought of.

What, then, would he require – that compact little kit of burglar tools, rolled in its leather jacket, that, unrolled slipped about his body like a close-fitting undervest? As well to take it anyway. He removed his coat and vest, took out the leather bundle from the safe, untied the thongs that bound it together, unrolled it, passed it around his body, life belt fashion, secured the thongs over his shoulders, and put on his coat and vest again. A revolver, a flashlight? He had both – at the Sanctuary, under the flooring – but there were duplicates here! He slipped them into his pockets. Anything else – to forestall and provide for any possible contingency? He hesitated again for a moment, thinking, then slowly closed the inner door of the safe, locked it, swung the outer door shut – and, in the act of twirling the knobs, sprang suddenly to his feet. Sharp, shrill in the stillness of the room, the telephone bell on the desk rang out clamourously.

Jimmie Dale's face set hard, as he leaped out from behind the curtain – had Jason heard it! It rang again before he could reach the desk – was ringing as he snatched the receiver from the hook.

"Yes, yes!" he called, in a low, guarded, hasty way, into the mouthpiece. "Hello! What is it?" And then one hand, resting on the desk, closed around the edge, and tightened until the skin over the knuckles grew ivory white. It was – *she!* She! It was *her* voice – he had only heard it once in all his life – that night, two nights before, in a silvery laugh from the limousine as it had sped away from him down the road – but he knew! It thrilled him now with a mad rhapsody, robbing him for the moment of every thought save that she was living, real, existent – that it was *her* voice. "It's you – *you!*" he said hoarsely.

"Oh, Jimmie – you at last!" – it came in a little gasping cry of relief. "The letter –"

"Yes, I've got it – it's all right – it's all right" – the words would not seem to come fast enough in his desperate haste. "But it's you now. Listen! Listen!" he pleaded. "Tell me who you are! My God! how I've tried to find you, and –"

That rippling, silvery laugh again, but now, too, it seemed to his eager ear, with just the faintest note of wistfulness in it.

"Some day, Jimmie. That letter now. It –"

Jimmie Dale straightened up suddenly — Jason's steps, running, sounded outside the room along the corridor — there was not an instant to lose.

"Hang up! Good-bye! Danger! Don't ring again!" he whispered hurriedly, and, with a miserable smile, replacing the receiver bitterly on the hook, he jumped for the curtain.

He reached it none too soon. The door opened, an electric-light switch clicked, and the room was flooded with light. Jason, still running, headed for the desk.

"It'll be her again!" Jimmie Dale heard the old man mutter, as from the edge of the portière he watched the other's actions.

Jason picked up the telephone.

"Hello! Hello!" he called — then began to click impatiently with the receiver hook. "Hello! . . . Who? . . . Central? . . . I don't want any number — somebody was calling here. . . . What? . . . Nobody on the wire!"

He set the telephone back on the desk with a bewildered air.

"That's queer!" he exclaimed. "I could have sworn I heard it ring twice, and —" He stopped abruptly, and, leaning across the desk, hung there, wide-eyed, staring, while a sickly pallor began to steal into his face. "The letter!" he mumbled wildly. "The letter — Master Jim's letter — the letter — it's *gone!*"

Trembling, excited, the old man began to search the desk, then down on his knees on the floor under it; and then, growing more frantic with every instant, rose and began to hunt around the room in an agitated, aimless fashion.

Jason's distress was very real — he was almost beside himself now with fear and anxiety. A whimsical, affectionate smile played over Jimmie Dale's lips at the old man's antics — and changed suddenly into one of consternation. Jason was making directly now for the curtain behind which he stood! Perhaps, though, he would pass it by, and — Jason's hand reached out and grasped the portière.

"Jason!" said Jimmie Dale sharply.

The old man staggered back as though he had been struck, tried to speak, choked, and gazed at the curtain with distended eyes.

"Is — is that you, sir — Master Jim — behind the curtain there?" he finally blurted out. "I — sir — you gave me a start — and the letter, Master Jim —"

"Don't lose your head, Jason," said Jimmie Dale coolly. "I've got the letter. Now do as I bid you."

"Yes — Master Jim," faltered the old man.

"Pull down the window shades and draw the portière together," directed Jimmie Dale.

Jason, still overwrought and excited, obeyed a little awkwardly.

"Now the lights, Jason," instructed Jimmie Dale. "Turn them off, and go and sit down in that chair at the desk."

Again Jason obeyed, stumbling in the darkness as he returned from the electric-light switch at the farther end of the room. He sat down in the chair.

Larry the Bat stepped out from behind the curtain. "I came for that letter, Jason," he explained quietly. "I am going out again now. I may be back to-morrow; I may not be back for a week. You will say nothing, not a word, of my having been here to-night. Do you understand, Jason?"

"Yes, sir," said Jason; then hesitantly: "Would you mind saying, sir, when you came in?"

"It's of no consequence, Jason – is it?"

"No, sir," said Jason.

Jimmie Dale smiled in the darkness.

"Jason!"

"Yes, sir."

"I wish you to remain where you are, without leaving that chair, for the next ten minutes." He moved across the room to the door. "Good-night, Jason," he said.

"Good-night, Master Jim – good-night, sir – oh, Lord!"

Jimmie Dale did not require that ten minutes; it was a very wide margin of safety to obviate the possibility of Jason, from a window, detecting the exit of a disreputable character from the house – in three minutes he was turning the corner of the first cross street and walking rapidly away from Riverside Drive.

In the subway station Jimmie Dale read the letter – read it twice over, as he always read those strange epistles of hers that opened the door to new peril, new danger to the Gray Seal, but too, that seemed somehow to draw tighter, in a glad, big way, the unseen bond between them; read it, as he always read those letters, almost subconsciously committing the very words to memory with that keen faculty of brain of his. But now as he began to tear the sheet and envelope into minute particles, a strained, hard look was on his face and in his eyes, and his lips, half parted, moved a little.

THE ADVENTURES OF JIMMIE DALE – PART ONE: THE MAN IN THE CASE

"It's a death warrant," muttered Jimmie Dale. "I—I guess to-night will see the end of the Gray Seal. She says I needn't do it, [38] but I guess it's worth the risk—a human life!" A downtown express roared into the station.

"What time is it?" Jimmie Dale asked the guard, as he stepped aboard.

"'Bout midnight," the man answered tersely.

The forward car was almost empty, and Jimmie Dale chose a seat by himself. How did she know? How did she know not only this, but the hundred other affairs that she had outlined in those letters of hers? By what means, superhuman, indeed, it seemed, did she—Jimmie Dale jerked himself erect suddenly. What good did it do to speculate on that now, when every minute was priceless? What was *he* to do, how was he to act, what plan could he formulate and carry out, and *win* against odds that, at the outset, were desperate enough even to forecast almost certain failure—and death!

Who would ever have suspected old Tom Ludgate, known for years throughout the squalour of the East Side as old Luddy, the pushcart man, of having a bag of unset diamonds under his pillow—or under the sack, rather, that he probably used for a pillow! What a queer thing to do! But then, old Luddy was a character—apparently always in the most poverty-stricken condition, apparently hardly more than keeping body and soul together, trusting no one, and obsessed by the dread that by depositing in a bank some one would discover that he had money, and attempt to force it from him, he had put his savings, year after year, for twenty years, twenty-five years, perhaps, into unset stones —diamonds. How had she found that out?

---

[38] Of course it's long past the time here that Dale has to be blackmailed into following the instructions of this mysterious woman, but was it ever morally right for her to risk his life even if in the cause of justice? A debatable point but consider that the Gray Seal was in operation for some time before she learned or at least exploited his true identity. Remember also that Carruthers mentioned he had almost caught the Gray Seal "half a dozen times." Those near misses can't involve her missions of mercy because obviously the authorities wouldn't, couldn't know about them in advance. So they apparently occurred before she recruited him. And what would Carruthers use to bait his traps? The public reputation of the Gray Seal, about which we are told Dale "regarded it jealously-as a man guards the woman's name he loves." Those plots presumably would have been subtler than a "I know the Gray Seal wouldn't dare to steal *this* necklace... " sort of enticement but even so it appears that his ego prompted him to make rash decisions about objects to target – on multiple occasions. So, coming under new management was probably a lucky thing for Jimmie Dale.

Jimmie Dale sank into a deeper reverie. He could steal them all right, and they would be well worth the stealing – old Luddy had done well, and lived and existed on next to nothing – the stones, she said, were worth about fifteen thousand dollars. Not so bad, even for twenty-five years of vegetable selling from a pushcart! He could steal them all right; it would tax the Gray Seal's ingenuity little to do so simple a thing as that, but that was not all, nor, indeed, hardly a factor in it – it was vital that if he were to succeed at all he must steal them *publicly,* as it were.

And after that – *what?* His own chances were pretty slim at best. Jimmie Dale, staring at the grayness of the subway wall through the window, shook his head slowly – then, with a queer little philosophical shrug of his shoulders, he smiled gravely, seriously. It was all a part of the game, all a part of the life – of the Gray Seal!

It was half-past twelve, or a little later, as nearly as he could judge, for Larry the Bat carried no such ornate thing in evidence as a watch, as he halted at the corner of a dark, squalid street in the lower East Side. It was a miserable locality – in daylight humming with a cosmopolitan hive of pitiful humans dragging out as best they could an intolerable existence, a locality peopled with every nationality on earth, their community of interest the struggle to maintain life at the lowest possible expenditure, where necessity even was pared and shaved down to a minimum; but now, at night time, or rather in the early-morning hours, the darkness, in very mercy, it seemed, covered it with a veil, as it were, and in the quiet that hung over it now hid the bald, the hideous, aye, and the piteous, too, from view.

It was a narrow street, and the row of tenement houses, each house almost identical with its neighbour, that flanked the pavement on either side, seemed, from where Jimmie Dale stood looking down its length, from the corner, to converge together at a point a little way beyond, giving it an unreal, ominous, cavernlike effect. And, too, there seemed something ominous even in its quiet. It was as though one sensed acutely the crouching of some Thing in its lair – waiting silently, viciously, with sullen patience.

A footstep sounded – another. Jimmie Dale drew quickly back around the corner into an areaway. Two men passed – in helmets – swinging their nightsticks – that beat was always policed in pairs!

They passed on, turned the corner, and went down the narrow cross street that Jimmie Dale had just been inspecting. He started to follow – and drew back again abruptly. A form flitted suddenly across the road and disappeared in the darkness in the officers' wake – ten yards behind the first another followed – at the same interval of distance still another – and yet still one more – four in all.

The darkness hid all six, the two policemen, the four men behind them – the only sounds were the *officers'* footsteps dying away in the distance.

Jimmie Dale's fingers were mechanically testing the mechanism of the automatic in his pocket.

"The Skeeter's gang!" he muttered to himself. "Red Mose, the Midget, Harve Thoms – and the Skeeter! The worst apaches in the city of New York; death contractors – the lowest bidders! Professional assassins, and a man's life any time for twenty-five dollars! I wonder – I've never done it yet – but I wonder if it would be a crime in God's sight if one shot – *to kill!*"

Jimmie Dale was at the corner again – again the street before him was black, deserted, empty. He chose the right-hand side, and, well in the shadow of the houses, as an extra precaution, stole along silently. He stopped finally before one where, in the doorway, hung a little sign. Jimmie Dale mounted the porch, and with his eyes close to the sign could just make out the larger words in the big printed type:

ROOM TO RENT

TOP FLOOR

Jimmie Dale nodded. That was right. The first house on the right-hand side, with the room-to-rent sign, her letter had said. His fingers were testing the doorknob. The door was not locked.

"Naturally, it wouldn't be locked," Jimmie Dale told himself grimly – and stepped inside.

He stood for an instant without movement, every faculty on the alert. Far up above him a step, guarded though his trained ear made it out to be, creaked faintly upon the stairs – there was no other sound. The creaking, almost inaudible at its loudest, receded farther up – and silence fell.

In the darkness, noiselessly, Jimmie Dale groped for the stairway, found it, and began to ascend. The minutes passed – it seemed a minute even from step to step, and there were three flights to the top! There must be no creaking this time – the slightest sound, he knew well enough, would be not only fatal to the work he had to do, but probably fatal to himself as well. He had been near death many times – the consciousness that he was nearer to it now, possibly, than he had ever been before, seemed to stimulate his senses into acute and abnormal energy. And, too, the physical effort, as, step by step, the flexed muscles relaxing so slowly, little by little, gradually, each time as he found foothold on the step higher up, was a terrific strain. At the top his face was bathed in perspiration, and he wiped it off with his coat sleeve.

It was still dark here, intensely dark, and his eyes, though grown accustomed to it, could make out nothing but the deeper shadow of the walls. But thanks to her, always a mistress of accurate and minute detail, he possessed a mental plan of his surroundings. The head of the stairs gave on the middle of the hallway – the hallway ran to his right and left. To his right, on the opposite side of the hall, was the door of old Luddy's squalid two-room apartment.

For a moment Jimmie Dale stood hesitant – a sudden perplexity and anxiety growing upon him. It was strange! What did it mean? He had nerved himself to a quick, desperate attempt, trusting to surprise and his own wit and agility for victory – there had seemed no other way than that, since he had seen those four men at the corner – since they were *ahead* of him. True, they were not much ahead of him, not enough to have accomplished their purpose – and, furthermore, they were not in that room. He knew that absolutely, beyond question of doubt. He had listened for just that all the nerve-racking way up the stairs. But where were they? There was no sound – not a sound – just blackness, dark, impenetrable, utter, that began to palpitate now.

It came in a whisper, wavering, sibilant – from his left. A sort of relief, fierce in the breaking of the tense expectancy, premonitory in the possibilities that it held, swept Jimmie Dale. He crept along the hall. The whisper had come from that room, presumably empty – that was for rent!

By the door he crouched – his sensitive fingers, eyes to Jimmie Dale so often – feeling over jamb and panels with a delicate, soundless touch. The door was just ajar. The fingers crept inside and touched the knob and lock – there was no key within.

The whispering still went on – but it seemed like a screaming of vultures now in Jimmie Dale's ears, as the words came to him.

"Aw, say, Skeeter, dis high-brow stunt gives me de pip! Me fer goin' in dere an' croakin' de geezer reg'lar, widout de frills. Who's to know? Say, just about two minutes, an' we're beatin' it wid de sparklers."

An inch, a half inch at a time, the knob slowly, very, very slowly turning, the door was being closed by the crouched form on the threshold.

"Close yer trap, Mose!" came a fierce response. "We ain't fixed the lay all day for nothin'. There ain't a soul on earth knows he's got any sparklers, 'cept us. If there was, it would be different – then they'd know that was what whoever did it was after, see?"

The door was closed – the knob slowly, very, very slowly being released again. From one of the leather pockets under Jimmie Dale's vest came a tiny steel instrument that he inserted in the key-hole.

The same voice spoke on:

"That's what we're croaking him for, 'cause nobody knows about them diamonds, and so's he can't *tell* anybody afterward that any were pinched. An' that's why it's got to look like he just got tired of living and did it himself. I guess that'll hold the police when they find the poor old duck hanging from the ceiling, with a bit of cord around his neck, and a chair kicked out from under his feet on the floor. Ain't you got the brains of a louse to see that?"

"Sure" — the whisper came dully, in grudging intonation through the panels – the door was locked. "Sure, but it's de hangin' 'round waitin' to get busy that's gettin' me goat, an' — "

Jimmie Dale straightened up and began to retreat along the corridor. A merciless rage was upon him now, every fiber of his being seemed to tingle and quiver with it – the damnable, hellish ingenuity of it all seemed to choke and suffocate him.

"Luck!" muttered Jimmie Dale between his clenched teeth. "Oh, the blessed luck to get that door locked! I've got time now to set the stage for my own get-away before the showdown!"

He stole on along the corridor. Excerpts from her letter were running through his brain: "It would do no good to warn him, Jimmie – the Skeeter and his gang would never let up on him until they got the stones. . . . It would do no good for you to steal them first, for they would only take that as a ruse of old Luddy's, and murder the man first and hunt afterward. . . . In some way you must let the Skeeter *see* you steal them, make them think, make them certain that it is a bona-fide theft, so that they will no longer have any interest or any desire to do old Luddy harm. . . . And for it to appear real to them, it must appear real to old Luddy himself – do not take any chances there."

Jimmie Dale's eyes narrowed. Yes, it was simple enough now with that pack of hell's wolves guarded for the moment by a locked door, forced to give him warning by breaking the door before they could get out. It was simple enough now to enter old Luddy's room, steal the stones at the revolver point, then make enough disturbance – when he was ready – to set the gang in motion, and, as they rushed in open him, to make his escape with the stones to the roof through Luddy's room. That was simple enough – there was an opening to the roof in Luddy's room, she had said, and there was a ladder kept there in place. On hot nights, it seemed, the old man used to go up there and sleep on the roof – not now, of course. It was too late in the year for that – but the opening in the roof was there, and the ladder remained there, too.

Yes, it was simple enough now. And the next morning the papers would rave with execrations against the Gray Seal – for the robbery of the life savings of a poor, defenseless old man, for committing as vile and pitiful a crime as had ever stirred New York! Even Carruthers, of the *Morning News-Argus,* would be moved to bitter attack. Good old Carruthers – who little thought that the Gray Seal was his old college pal, his present most intimate friend, Jimmie Dale! And afterward – after the next morning? Well, that, at least, had never been in doubt. Old Luddy could be made to leave New York, and, once away, with the Skeeter and his gang robbed of incentive to pay any further attention to him, the stones could be secretly returned to the old man. And it would to the public, to the police, be just another of the Gray Seal's crimes – that was all!

Jimmie Dale had reached old Luddy's door. The Gray Seal? Oh, yes, they would know it was the Gray Seal – the insignia was familiar enough; familiar to the crooks of the underworld, who held it in awe; familiar to the police, to whom it was an added barb of ridicule. He was placing it now, that insignia, a diamond-shaped, gray paper seal, on the panel of the door; and now, a black silk mask adjusted over his face, Jimmie Dale bent to insert the little steel instrument in the lock – a pitiful, paltry thing, a cheap lock, to fingers that could play so intimately with twirling knobs and dials, masters of the intricate mechanism of vaults and safes!

And then, about to open the door, a sort of sudden dismay fell upon him. He had not thought of that – somehow, it had not occurred to him! *What was it they were waiting for?* Why had they not struck at once, as, when he had first entered the house, he had supposed they would do? What was it? Why was it? Was old Luddy out? Were they waiting for his return – or what?

The door, without sound, moved gradually under his hand. A faint odor assailed his nostrils! It was dark, very dark. Across the room, in a direct line, was the doorway of the inner room – she had explained that in her letter. It was slow progress to cross that room without sound, in silence – it was a snail's movement – for fear that even a muscle might crack.

And now he stood in the inner doorway. It was dark here, too – and yet, how bizarre, a star seemed to twinkle through the very roof of the room itself! The odour was pungent now. There was a long-drawn sigh – then a low, indescribable sound of movement. *Somebody, apart from Old Luddy, was in the room!*

It swept, the full consciousness of it, upon Jimmie Dale in an instantaneous flash. Chloroform; the open scuttle in the roof; the waiting of those others – all fused into a compact logical whole. They had loosened the scuttle during the day, probably when old Luddy was away — one of them had crept down there now to chloroform the old man into insensibility — the others would complete the ghastly work presently by stringing their victim up to the ceiling — and it would be suicide, for, long before morning came, long before the old man would be discovered, the fumes of the chloroform would be gone.

It seemed like a cold hand, deathlike, clutching at his heart. Was he too late, after all! Chloroform alone could — kill! To the right, just a little to the right — he must make no mistake — his ear placed the sound! He whipped his hands from the side pockets of his coat — the ray of his flashlight cut across the room and fell upon an aged face upon a bed, upon a hand clutching a wad of cloth, the cloth pressed horribly against the nose and mouth of the upturned face — and then, roaring in the stillness, spitting a vicious lane of fire that paralleled the flashlight's ray, came the tongue flame of his automatic.

There was a yell, a scream, that echoed out, reverberated, and went racketing through the house, and Jimmie Dale leaped forward — over a table, sending it crashing to the floor. The man had reeled back against the wall, clutching at a shattered wrist, staring into the flashlight's eye, white-faced, jaw dropped, lips working in mingled pain and fear.

"Harve Thoms — you, eh?" gritted Jimmie Dale.

A cunning look swept the distorted face. Here, apparently, was only one man — there were pals, three of them, only a few yards away.

"You ain't got nothing on me!" he snarled, sparring for time. "You police are too damned fresh with your guns!"

"I'll take yours!" snapped Jimmie Dale, and snatched it deftly from the other's pocket. "This ain't any police job, my bucko, and you make a move and I'll drop you for keeps, if what you've got already ain't enough to teach you to keep your hands off jobs that belong to your betters!"

He was working with mad haste as he spoke. One minute at the outside was, perhaps, all he could count upon. Already he had caught the rattle of the locked door down the hall. He lit a match and turned on the gas over the bed — it was the most dangerous thing he could do — he knew that well enough, none knew it better — it was offering himself as a fair mark when the others rushed in, as they would in a moment now — but the Skeeter and his gang and this man here must have no misconception of his purpose, his reason for being there, the same as their own, the theft of the stones — and no misconception as to his *success*.

"Y'ain't the police!" — it came in a choked gasp from the other, as he blinked in the sudden light "Say then — "

"Shut up!" ordered Jimmie Dale curtly. "And mind what I told you about moving!" He leaned over the bed. Old Luddy, though under the influence of the chloroform, was moving restlessly. Thoms had evidently only begun to apply the chloroform – old Luddy was safe! Jimmie Dale ran his hand in under the pillow. "If you ain't swiped them already they ought to be here!" he growled; "and if you have I'll – ah!" A little chamois bag was in his hand. He laughed sneeringly at Thoms, opened the bag, allowed a few stones to trickle into his hand – and then, without stopping to replace them, dashed stones and bag into his pocket. The door along the corridor crashed open.

"What's that?" he gasped out, in well-simulated fright – and sprang for the ladder that led up to the roof.

It had all taken, perhaps, the minute that he had counted on – no more. Noises came from the floors below now, a confusion of them – the shot, the scream had been heard by others, save those who had been in the locked room. And the latter were outside now in the corridor, running to their accomplice's aid.

There was a pause at the outer door – then an oath – and coupled with the oath an exclamation:

"The Gray Seal!"

They had swept a flashlight over the door panel – Jimmie Dale, halfway up the ladder, smiled grimly.

The door opened – there was a rush of feet. The man with the shattered wrist yelled, cursing wildly:

"Here he is – on the ladder! Let him have it! Fill him full of holes!"

Jimmie Dale was in the light – they were in the dark of the outer room. He fired at the threshold, checking their rush – as a hail of bullets chipped and tore at the ladder and spat wickedly against the wall. He swung through to the roof, trying, as he did so, to kick the ladder loose behind him. It was fastened!

The three gunmen jumped into the room – from the roof Jimmie Dale got a glimpse of them below, as he flung himself clear of the opening. Bullets whistled through the aperture – a voice roared up as he gained his feet:

"Come on! After him! The whole place is alive, but this lets us out. We can frame up how we came to be here easy enough. Never mind the old geezer there any more! Get the Gray Seal – the reward that's out for him is worth twice the sparklers, and –"

Jimmie Dale hurled the cover over the scuttle. He could have stood them off from above and kept the ladder clear with his revolver, but the alarm seemed general now — windows were opening, voices were calling to one another — from the windows across the street he must stand out in sharp outline against the sky.

Yes — he was seen now.

A woman's voice, from a top-story window across the street, screamed out, high-pitched in excitement:

"There he is! There he is! On the roof there!"

Jimmie Dale started on the run along the roof. The houses, built wall to wall, flat-roofed, seemed to offer an open course ahead of him — until a lane or an intersecting street should bar his way! But they were not quite all on the same level, though — the wall of the next house rose suddenly breast high in front of him. He flung himself up, regained his feet — and ducked instantly behind a chimney.

The crack of a revolver echoed through the night — a bullet drummed through the air — the Skeeter and his gang were on the roof now, dashing forward, firing as they ran. Two shots from Jimmie Dale's automatic, in quick succession cooled the ardour of their rush — and they broke, black, flitting forms, for the shelter of chimneys, too.

And now the whole neighbourhood seemed awakened. A dull-toned roar, as from some great gulf below, rolled up from the street, a medley of slamming windows, the rush of feet as people poured from the houses, cries, shouts, and yells — and high over all the shrill call of the police-patrol whistle — and the *crack, crack, crack* of the Skeeter's revolver shots — the Skeeter and his hellhounds for once self-appointed allies of the law!

Twice again Jimmie Dale fired — then crouching, running low, he zigzagged his way across the next roof. The bullets followed him — once more his pursuers dashed forward. And again Jimmie Dale, his face set like stone now, his breath coming in hard gasps, dodged behind a chimney, and with his gun checked their rush for the third time.

He glanced about him — and with a growing sense of disaster saw that two houses farther on the stretch of roof appeared to end. There would be a lane or a street there! And in another minute or two, if it were not already the case, others would be following the gunmen to the roof, and then he would be — he caught his breath suddenly in a queer little strangled cry of relief. Just back of him, a few yards away, his eyes made out what, in the darkness, seemed to be a glass skylight.

A dark form sped like a deeper shadow across the black in front of him, making for a chimney nearer by, closing in the range. Jimmie Dale fired — wide. Tight as was the corner he was in, little as was the mercy deserved at his hands, he could not, after all, bring himself to shoot — to kill.

A voice, the Skeeter's, bawled out raucously:

"Rush him all together — from different sides at once!"

A backward leap! Jimmie Dale's boot was crashing glass and frame, stamping at it desperately, making a hole for his body through the skylight. A yell, a chorus of them, answered this — then the crunch of racing feet on the gravel roof. He emptied his revolver, sweeping the darkness with a semicircle of vicious flashes.

It seemed an hour — it was barely the fraction of a second, as he hung by his hands from the side of the skylight frame, his body swinging back and forth in the unknown blackness below. The skylight might be, probably was, directly over the stair well, and open clear to the basement of the house — but it was his only chance. He swung his body well out, let go — and dropped. With the impetus he smashed against a wall, was flung back from it in a sort of rebound, and his hands closed, gripping fiercely, on banisters. It had been the stair well beyond any question of doubt, but his swing had sent him clear of it.

Above, they had not yet reached the skylight. Jimmie Dale snatched a precious moment to listen, as he rose, and found himself, apart from bruises, perhaps unhurt. There was commotion, too, in this house below, the alarm had extended and spread along the block — but the commotion was all in the *front* of the house — the street was the lure.

Jimmie Dale started down the stairs, and in an instant he had gained the landing. In another he had slipped to the rear of the hall — somewhere there, from the hall itself, from one of the rear rooms, there must be an exit to the fire escape. To attempt to leave by the front way was certain capture.

They were yelling, shouting down now through the sky-light above, as Jimmie Dale softly raised the window sash at the rear of the hall. The fire escape was there. Shouts from along the corridor, from the tenement dwellers who had been crowding their neighbours' rooms, craning their necks probably from the front windows, answered the shouts now from the roof and the skylight; doors opened; forms rushed out — but it was dark in the corridor, only a murky yellow at the upper end from the opened doors.

Jimmie Dale slipped through the window to the fire escape, and, working cautiously, silently, but with the speed of a trained athlete, made his way down. At the bottom he dropped from the iron platform into the back yard, ran for the fence and climbed over into a lane on the other side.

And then, as he ran, Jimmie Dale snatched the mask from his face and put it in his pocket. He was safe now. He swept the sweat drops from his forehead with the back of his hand — noticing them for the first time. It had been close — almost as close for him as it had been for old Luddy. And to-morrow the papers would execrate the Gray Seal! He smiled a little wanly.

His breath was still coming hard. Presently they would scour the lane – when they found that their quarry was not in the house. What a racket they were making! The whole district seemed roused like a swarm of angry bees.

He kept on along the lane – and dodged suddenly into a cross street where the two intersected. The clang of a bell dinned discordantly in his ears – a patrol wagon swept by him, racing for the scene of the disturbance – the riot call was out!

Again Jimmie Dale smiled wearily, passing his hand across his eyes.

"I guess," said Jimmie Dale, "I'm pretty near all in. And I guess it's time that Larry the Bat went – home."

And a little later a figure turned from the Bowery and shambled down the cross street, a disreputable figure, with hands plunged deep in his pockets – and a shadow across the roadway suddenly shifted its position as the shambling figure slouched into the black alleyway and entered the tenement's side door.

And Larry the Bat smiled softly to himself – Kline's men were still on guard!

CHAPTER VI

DEVIL'S WORK

(Saturday 9/11/1915 to Sunday 9/12/1915)

A WHITE-GLOVED arm, a voice, and a silvery laugh! Just that—no more! Jimmie Dale, in his favourite seat, an aisle seat some seven or eight rows back from the orchestra, stared at the stage, to all outward appearances absorbed in the last act of the play; inwardly, quite oblivious to the fact that even a play was going on. [39]

A white-gloved arm, a voice, and a silvery laugh! The words had formed themselves into a sort of singsong refrain that, for the last few days, had been running through his head. A strange enough guiding star to mould and dictate every action in his life! And that was all he had ever seen of her, all that he had ever heard of her—except those letters, of course, each of which had outlined the details of some affair for the Gray Seal to execute.

Indeed, it seemed a great length of time now since he had heard from her even in that way, though it was not so many days ago, after all. Perhaps it was the calm, as it were, that, by contrast, had given place to the strenuous months and weeks just past. The storm raised by the newspapers at the theft of Old Luddy's diamonds had subsided into sporadic diatribes aimed at the police; Kline, of the secret service, had finally admitted defeat, and a shadow no longer skulked day and night at the entrance to the Sanctuary—and Larry the Bat bore the government indorsement, so to speak, of being no more suspicious a character than that of a disreputable, but harmless, dope fiend of the underworld.

Larry the Bat! The Gray Seal! Jimmie Dale the millionaire! What if it were ever known that that strange three were one! What if--

---

[39] There's something curious about Dale going to the theater by himself here. Elsewhere in this novel we're told he is the "matrimonial target of exclusive drawing-rooms" so a companion would have been easy enough to come by. Yet here he is alone. Jimmie regularly rides the subway, he eats at unpretentious restaurants, and his best friend works for a living so perhaps it's safe to assume Dale has mixed feelings about his own social class.

Jimmie Dale smiled whimsically. A burst of applause echoed through the house, the orchestra was playing, the lights were on, seats banged, there was the bustle of the rising audience, the play was at an end – and for the life of him he could not have remembered a single line of the last act!

The aisle at his elbow was already crowded with people on their way out. Jimmie Dale stooped down mechanically to reach for his hat beneath his seat – and the next instant he was standing up, staring wildly into the faces around him.

It had fallen at his feet – a white envelope. Hers! It was in his hand now, those slim, tapering, wonderfully sensitive fingers of Jimmie Dale, that were an "open sesame" to locks and safes, subconsciously telegraphing to his mind the fact that the texture of the paper – was hers. Hers! And she must be one of those around him – one of those crowding either the row of seats in front or behind, or one of those just passing in the aisle. It had fallen at his feet as he had stooped over for his hat – but from just exactly what direction he could not tell. His eyes, eagerly, hungrily, critically, swept face after face. Which one was hers? What irony! She, whom he would have given his life to know, for whom indeed he risked his life every hour of the twenty-four, was close to him now, within reach – and as far removed as though a thousand miles separated them. She was there – but he could not recognise a face that he had never seen!

With an effort, he choked back the bitter, impotent laugh that rose to his lips. They were talking, laughing around him. Her *voice* – yes, he had once heard that, and that he would recognise again. He strained to catch, to individualise the tone sounds that floated in a medley about him. It was useless – of course – every effort that he had ever made to find her had been useless. She was too clever, far too clever for that – she, too, would know that he could and would recognise her voice where he could recognise nothing else.

And then, suddenly, he realised that he was attracting attention.

Level stares from the women returned his gaze, and they edged away a little from his vicinity as they passed, their escorts crowding somewhat belligerently into their places. Others, in the same row of seats as his own, were impatiently waiting to get by him. With a muttered apology, Jimmie Dale raised the seat of his chair, allowing these latter to pass him – and then, slipping the letter into his pocketbook, he snatched up his hat from the seat rack.

There was still a chance. Knowing he was there, she would be on her guard; but in the lobby, among the crowd and unaware of his presence, there was the possibility that, if he could reach the entrance ahead of her, she, too, might be talking and laughing as she left the theatre. Just a single word, just a tone – that was all he asked.

The row of seats at whose end he stood was empty now, and, instead of stepping into the thronged aisle, he made his way across to the opposite side of the theatre. Here, the far aisle was less crowded, and in a minute he had gained the foyer, confident that he was now in advance of her. The next moment he was lost in a jam of people in the lobby.

He moved slowly now, very slowly – allowing those behind to press by him on the way to the entrance. A babel of voices rose about him, as, tight-packed, the mass of people jostled, elbowed, and pushed good-naturedly. It was a voice now, her voice, that he was listening for; but, though it seemed that every faculty was strained and intent upon that one effort, his eyes, too, had in no degree relaxed their vigilance – and once, half grimly, half sardonically, he smiled to himself. There would be an unexpected aftermath to this exodus of expensively gowned and bejewelled women with their prosperous, well-groomed escorts! There was the Wowzer over there – sleek, dapper, squirming in and out of the throng with the agility and stealth of a cat. As Larry the Bat he had met the Wowzer many times, as indeed he had met and was acquainted with most of the elite of the underworld. The Wowzer, beyond a shadow of doubt, in his own profession stood upon a plane entirely by himself – among those qualified to speak, no one yet had ever questioned the Wowzer's claim to the distinction of being the most dexterous and finished "poke getter" in the United States!

The crowd thinned in the lobby, thinned down to the last few belated stragglers, who passed him as he still loitered in the entrance; and then Jimmie Dale, with a shrug of his shoulders that was a great deal more philosophical than the maddening sense of chagrin and disappointment that burned within him, stepped out to the pavement and headed down Broadway. After all, he had known it in his heart of hearts all the time – it had always been the same – it was only one more occasion added to the innumerable ones that had gone before in which she had eluded him!

And now – there was the letter! Automatically he quickened his steps a little. It was useless, futile, profitless, for the moment, at least, to disturb himself over his failure – there was the letter! His lips parted in a strange, half-serious, half-speculative smile. The letter – that was paramount now. What new venture did the night hold in store for him? What sudden emergency was the Gray Seal called upon to face this time – what role, unrehearsed, without warning, must he play? What story of grim, desperate rascality would the papers credit him with when daylight came? Or would they carry in screaming headlines the announcement that the Gray Seal was caged and caught at last, and in three-inch type tell the world that the Gray Seal was — Jimmie Dale!

A block down, he turned from Broadway out of the theatre crowds that streamed in both directions past him. The letter! Almost feverishly now he was seeking an opportunity to open and read it unobserved; an eagerness upon him that mingled exhilaration at the lure of danger with a sense of premonition that, irritably, inevitably was with him at moments such as these. It seemed, it always seemed, that, with an unopened letter of hers in his possession, it was as though he were about to open a page in the Book of Fate and read, as it were, a pronouncement upon himself that might mean life or death.

He hurried on. People still passed by him — too many. And then a cafe, just ahead, making a corner, gave him the opportunity that he sought. Away from the entrance, on the side street, the brilliant lights from the windows shone out on a comparatively deserted pavement. There was ample light to read by, even as far away from the window as the curb, and Jimmie Dale, with an approving nod, turned the corner and walked along a few steps until opposite the farthest window — but, as he halted here at the edge of the street, he glanced quickly behind him at a man whom he had just passed. The other had paused at the corner and was staring down the street. Jimmie Dale instantly and nonchalantly produced his cigarette case, selected a cigarette, and fastidiously tapped its end on his thumb nail.

"Inspector Burton in plain clothes," he observed musingly to himself. "I wonder if it's just a fluke — or something else? We'll see."

Jimmie Dale took a box of matches from his pocket. The first would not light. The second broke, and, with an exclamation of annoyance, he flung it away. The third was making a fitful effort at life, as another man emerged hastily from the café's side door, hurried to the corner, joined the man who was still loitering there, and both together disappeared at a rapid pace down the street.

Jimmie Dale whistled softly to himself. The second man was even better known than the first; there was not a crook in New York but would side-step Lannigan of headquarters, and do it with amazing celerity — if he could!

"Something up! But it's not my hunt!" muttered Jimmie Dale; then, with a shrug of his shoulders: "Queer the way those headquarters chaps fascinate and give me a thrill every time I see them, even if I haven't a ghost of a reason for imagining that — "

The sentence was never finished. Jimmie Dale's face was gray. The street seemed to rock about him — and he stared, like a man stricken, white to the lips, ahead of him. *The letter was gone!* His hand, wriggling from his empty pocket, swept away the sweat beads that were bursting from his forehead. It had come at last — the pitcher had gone once too often to the well!

Numbed for an instant, his brain cleared now, working with lightning speed, leaping from premise to conclusion. The crush in the theatre lobby — the pushing, the jostling, the close contact — the Wowzer, the slickest, cleverest pickpocket in the United States! For a moment he could have laughed aloud in a sort of ghastly, defiant mockery — he himself had predicted an unexpected aftermath, had he not!

Aftermath! It was — the *end!* An hour, two hours, and New York would be metamorphosed into a seething caldron of humanity bubbling with the news. It seemed that he could hear the screams of the newsboys now shouting their extras; it seemed that he could see the people, roused to frenzy, swarming in excited crowds, snatching at the papers; he seemed to hear the mob's shouts swell in execration, in exultation — it seemed as though all around him had gone mad. The mystery of the Gray Seal was solved! It was Jimmie Dale, Jimmie Dale, Jimmie, Dale, the millionaire, the lion of society — and there was ignominy for an honoured name, and shame and disaster and convict stripes and sullen penitentiary walls — or death! A felon's death — the chair!

He was running now, his hands clenched at his sides; his mind, working subconsciously, urging him onward in a blind, as yet unrealised, objectless way. And then gradually impulse gave way to calmer reason, and he slowed his pace to a quick, less noticeable walk. The Wowzer! That was it! There was yet a chance — the Wowzer! A merciless rage, cold, deadly, settled upon him. It was the Wowzer who had stolen his pocketbook, and with it the letter. There could be no doubt of that. Well, there would be a reckoning at least before the end!

He was in a downtown subway train now — the roar in his ears in consonance, it seemed, with the turmoil in his brain. But now, too, he was Jimmie Dale again; and, apart from the slightly outthrust jaw, the tight-closed lips, impassive, debonair, composed.

There was yet a chance. As Larry the Bat he knew every den and lair below the dead line, and he knew, too, the Wowzer's favourite haunts. There was yet a chance, only one in a thousand, it was true, almost too pitiful to be depended upon — but yet a chance. The Wowzer had probably not worked alone, and he and his pal, or pals, would certainly not remain uptown either to examine or divide their spoils — they would wait until they were safe somewhere in one of their hell holes on the East Side. If he could find the Wowzer, reach the man *before the letter was opened* — Jimmie Dale's lips grew tighter. *That* was the chance! If he failed in that — Jimmie

Dale's lips drooped downward in grim curves at the corners. A chance! Already the Wowzer had at least a half hour's lead, and, worse still, there was no telling which one of a dozen places the man might have chosen to retreat to with his loot.

Time passed. His mind obsessed, Jimmie Dale's physical acts were almost wholly mechanical. It was perhaps fifteen minutes since he had discovered the loss of the letter, and he was walking now through the heart of the Bowery. Exactly how he had got there he could not have told; he had only a vague realisation that, following an intuitive sense of direction, he had lost not a second of time in making his way downtown.

And now he found himself hesitating at the corner of a cross street. Two blocks east was that dark, narrow alleyway, that side door that made the entrance to the Sanctuary. It would be safer, a hundred times safer, to go there, change his clothes and his personality, and emerge again as Larry the Bat — infinitely safer in that role to explore the dens of the underworld, many of them indeed unknown and undreamed of by the police themselves, than to trust himself there in well-cut, fashionable tweeds — but that would take time. Time! When, with every second, the one chance he had, desperate as that already was, was slipping away from him. No; what was apparently the greater risk at least held out the only hope.

He went on again — his brain incessantly at work. At the worst, there was one mitigating factor in it all. He had no need to think of her. Whatever the ruin and disaster that faced him in the next few hours, she in any case was safe. There was no clew to *her* identity in the letter; and where he, for months on end, with even more to work upon, had failed at every turn to trace her, there was little fear that any one else would have any better success. She was safe. As for himself — that was different. The Gray Seal would be referred to in the letter, there would be the outline, the data for the "crime" she had planned for that night; and the letter, though unaddressed, being found in his pocketbook, where cards and notes and a dozen different things among its contents proclaimed him Jimmie Dale, needed no further evidence as to its ownership nor the identity of the Gray Seal.

Jimmie Dale's fingers crept inside his vest and fumbled there for a moment — and a diamond stud, extracted from his shirt front, glistened sportively in the necktie that was now tucked jauntily in at one side of his shirt bosom. He had reached the Blue Dragon, one of Wowzer's usual hang outs, and, swerving from the sidewalk, entered the place. There was wild tumult within — a constant storm of applause, derision, and hilarity that was hurled from the tables around the room at the turkey-trotting, tango-writhing couples on the somewhat restricted space of polished hardwood flooring in the centre. Jimmie Dale swaggered down the room, a cigar tilted up at an angle between his teeth, his soft felt hat a little rakishly on one side of his head and well over his nose.

At the end of the room, at the bar, Jimmie Dale leaned toward the barkeeper and talked out of the corner of his mouth. There were private rooms upstairs, and he jerked his head surreptitiously ceilingward.

"Say, is de Wowzer up dere?" he inquired in a cautious whisper.

The man behind the bar, well known to Jimmie Dale as one of the Wowzer's particular pals, favoured him with a blank stare.

"Never heard of de guy!" he announced brusquely. "Wot's yours?"

"Gimme a mug of suds," said Jimmie Dale, reaching for a match. He puffed at his cigar, blew out the match, and, after a moment, flung the charred end away — but on his hand, as, palm outward, he raised it to take his glass, the match had traced a small black cross.

The barkeeper put down the beer he had just drawn, wiped his hand hurriedly, and with sudden enthusiasm thrust it across the bar.

"Glad to know youse, cull!" [40] he exclaimed. "Wot's de lay?"

Jimmie Dale smiled.

"Nix!" said Jimmie Dale. "I just blew in from Chicago. Used to know de Wowzer dere. He said dis place was on de level, an' I could always find him here, dat's all."

"Sure, youse can!" returned the barkeeper heartily. "Only he ain't here now. He beat it about fifteen minutes ago, him an' Dago Jim. I guess youse'll find him at Chang's, I heard him an' Dago say dey was goin' dere. Know de place?"

Jimmie Dale shook his head.

"I ain't much wise to New York," he explained.

"Aw, dat's easy," whispered the barkeeper. "Go down to Chatham Square, an' den any guy'll show youse Chang Foo's." He winked confidentially. "I guess youse won't bump yer head none gettin' around inside."

Jimmie Dale nodded, grinned back, emptied his glass, and dug for a coin.

"Forget it!" observed the barkeeper cordially. "Dis is on me. Any friend of de Wowzer's gets de glad hand here any time."

---

[40] Possibly short for cullion which was a (vulgar) Old French term for a fellow thief. Packard spoke the language fluently.

"T'anks!" said Jimmie Dale gratefully, as he turned away. "So long, then — see youse later."

Chang Foo's! Jimmie Dale's face set even a little harder than it had before, as he swung on again down the Bowery. Yes; he knew Chang Foo's — too well. Underground Chinatown — where a man's life was worth the price of an opium pill — or less! Mechanically his hand slipped into his pocket and closed over the automatic that nestled there. Once in — where he had to go — and the chances were even, just even, that was all, that he would ever get out. Again he was tempted to return to the Sanctuary and make the attempt as Larry the Bat. Larry the Bat was well enough known to enter Chang Foo's unquestioned, and — but again he shook his head and went on. There was not time. The Wowzer and his pal — it was Dago Jim it seemed — had evidently been drinking and loitering their way downtown from the theatre, and he had gained that much on them; but by now they would be smugly tucked away somewhere in that maze of dens below the ground, and at that moment probably were gloating over the biggest night's haul they had ever made in their lives!

And if they were! What then? Once they knew the contents of that letter — what then? Buy them off for a larger amount than the many thousands offered for the capture of the Gray Seal? Jimmie Dale gritted his teeth. That meant blackmail from them all his life, an intolerable existence, impossible, a hell on earth — the slave, at the beck and call of two of the worst criminals in New York! The moisture oozed again to Jimmie Dale's forehead. God, if he could get that letter before it was opened — before they *knew!* If he could only get the chance to fight for it — against *any* odds! Life! Life was a pitiful consideration against the alternative that faced him now!

From the Blue Dragon to Chang Foo's was not far; and Jimmie Dale covered the distance in well under five minutes. Chang Foo's was just a tea merchant's shop, innocuous and innocent enough in its appearance, blandly so indeed, and that was all — outwardly; but Jimmie Dale, as he reached his destination, experienced the first sensation of uplift he had known that night, and this from what, apparently, did not in the least seem like a contributing cause.

"Luck! The blessed luck of it!" he muttered grimly, as he surveyed the sight-seeing car drawn up at the curb, and watched the passengers crowding out of it to the ground. "It wouldn't have been as easy to fool old Chang as it was that fellow back at the Dragon — and, besides, if I can work it, there's a better chance this way of getting out alive."

The guide was marshalling his "gapers" — some two dozen in all, men and women. Jimmie Dale unostentatiously fell in at the rear; and, the guide leading, the little crowd passed into the tea merchant's shop. Chang

Foo, a wizened, wrinkled-faced little Celestial, oily, suave, greeted them with profuse bows, chattering the while volubly in Chinese.

The guide made the introduction with an all-embracing sweep of his hand.

"Chang Foo—ladies and gentlemen," he announced; then held up his hand for silence. "Ladies and gentlemen," he said impressively, "this is one of the most notorious, if not *the* most notorious dive in Chinatown, and it is only through special arrangement with the authorities and at great expense that the company is able exclusively to gain an entree here for its patrons. You will see here the real life of the Chinese, and in half an hour you will get what few would get in a lifetime spent in China itself. You will see the Chinese children dance and perform; the Chinese women at their household tasks; the joss, the shrine of his hallowed ancestors, at which Chang Foo here worships; and you will enter the most famous opium den in the United States. Now, if you will all keep close together, we will make a start."

In spite of his desperate situation, Jimmie Dale smiled a little whimsically. Yes; they would see it all—*upstairs!* The same old bunk dished out night after night at so much a head—and the nervous little schoolma'am of uncertain age, who fidgeted now beside him, would go back somewhere down in Maine and shiver while she related her "wider experiences" in tremulous whispers into the shocked ears of envious other maiden ladies of equally uncertain age. The same old bunk—and a profitable one for Chang Foo for more reasons than one. It was dust in the eyes of the police. The police smiled knowingly at mention of Chang Foo. Who should know, if they didn't, that it was all harmless fake, all bunk! And so it was—*upstairs!*

They were passing out of the shop now, bowed out through a side door by the obsequious and oily Chang Foo. And now they massed again in a sort of little hallway—and Chang Foo, closing the door upon Jimmie Dale, who was the last in the line, shuffled back behind the counter in his shop to resume his guard duty over customers of quite another ilk. With the door closed, it was dark, pitch dark. And this, too, like everything else connected with Chang Foo's establishment, for more reasons than one—for effect—and for security. Nervous little twitters began to emanate from the women—the guide's voice rose reassuringly:

"Keep close together, ladies and gentlemen. We are going upstairs now to—"

Jimmie Dale hugged back against the wall, sidled along it, and like a shadow slipped down to the end of the hall. The scuffling of two dozen pairs of feet mounting the creaky staircase drowned the slight sound as he cautiously opened a door; the darkness lay black, impenetrable, along the hall. And then, as cautiously as he had opened it, he closed the door behind him, and stood for an instant listening at the head of a ladder-like stairway, his automatic in his hand now. It was familiar ground to Larry the Bat. The steps led down to a cellar; and diagonally across from the foot of the steps was an opening, ingeniously hidden by a heterogeneous collection of odds and ends, boxes, cases, and rubbish from the pseudo tea shop above; a low opening in the wall to a passage that led on through the cellars of perhaps half a dozen adjoining houses, each of which latter was leased, in one name or another – by Chang Foo.

Jimmie Dale crept down the steps, and in another moment had gained the farther side of the cellar; then, skirting around the ruck of cases, he stooped suddenly and passed in through the opening in the wall. And now he halted once more. He was straining his eyes down a long, narrow passage, whose blackness was accentuated rather than relieved by curious wavering, gossamer threads of yellow light that showed here and there from under makeshift thresholds, from doors slightly ajar. Faint noises came to him, a muffled, intermittent clink of coin, a low, continuous, droning hum of voices; the sickly sweet smell of opium pricked at his nostrils.

Jimmie Dale's face set rigidly. It was the resort, not only of the most depraved Chinese element, but of the worst "white" thugs that made New York their headquarters – here, in the succession of cellars, roughly partitioned off to make a dozen rooms on either side of the passage, dope fiends sucked at the drug, and Chinese gamblers spent the greater part of their lives; here, murder was hatched and played too often to its hellish end; here, the scum of the underworld sought refuge from the police to the profit of Chang Foo; and here, somewhere, in one of these rooms, was – the Wowzer.

The Wowzer! Jimmie Dale stole forward silently, without a sound, swiftly – pausing only to listen for a second's space at the doors as he passed. From this one came that clink of coin; from another that jabber of Chinese; from still another that overpowering stench of opium – and once, iron-nerved as he was, a cold thrill passed over him. Let this lair of hell's wolves, so intent now on their own affairs, be once roused, as they certainly must be roused before he could hope to finish the Wowzer, and his chances of escape were –

He straightened suddenly, alert, tense, strained. Voices, raised in a furious quarrel, came from a door just beyond him on the other side of the passage, where a film of light streamed out through a cracked panel – it was the Wowzer and Dago Jim! And drunk, both of them – and both in a blind fury!

It happened quick then, almost instantaneously it seemed to Jimmie Dale. He was crouched now close against the door, his eye to the crack in the panel. There was only one figure in sight — Dago Jim — standing beside a table on which burned a lamp, the table top littered with watches, purses, and small chatelaine bags. [41] The man was lurching unsteadily on his feet, a vicious sneer of triumph on his face, waving tauntingly an open letter and Jimmie Dale's pocket-book in his hands — waving them presumably in the face of the Wowzer, whom, from the restrictions of the crack, Jimmie Dale could not see. He was conscious of a sickening sense of disaster. His hope against hope had been in vain — the letter had been opened and read — *the identity of the Gray Seal was solved.*

Dago Jim's voice roared out, hoarse, blasphemous, in drunken rage:

"De Gray Seal — see! Youse betcher life I knows! I been waitin' fer somet'ing like dis, damn youse! Youse been stallin' on me fer a year every time it came to a divvy. Youse've got a pocketful now youse snitched to-night dat youse are tryin' to do me out of. Well, keep 'em" — he shoved his face forward. "I keeps dis — see! Keep 'em Wowzer, youse cross-eyed — "

"Everyt'ing I pinched to-night's on de table dere wid wot youse pinched yerself," cut in the Wowzer, in a sullen, threatening growl.

"Youse lie, an' youse knows it!" retorted Dago Jim. "Youse have given me de short end every time we've pulled a deal!"

"Dat letter's mine, youse — " bawled the Wowzer furiously.

"Why didn't youse open it an' read it, den, instead of lettin' me do it to keep me busy while youse short-changed me?" sneered Dago Jim. "Youse t'ought it was some sweet billy-doo, eh? Well, t'anks, Wowzer — dat's wot it is! Say," he mocked, "dere's a guy'll cash a t'ousand century notes fer dis, an' if he don't — say, dere's *some* reward out fer the Gray Seal! Wouldn't youse like to know who it is? Well, when I'm ridin' in me private buzz wagon, Wowzer, youse stick around an' mabbe I'll tell youse — an' mabbe I won't!"

"By God" — the Wowzer's voice rose in a scream — "youse hand over dat letter!"

"Youse go to — "

Red, lurid red, a stream of flame seemed to cut across Jimmie Dale's line of vision, came the roar of a revolver shot — and like a madman Jimmie Dale flung his body at the door. Rickety at best, it crashed inward, half wrenched from its hinges, precipitating him inside. He recovered himself

---

[41] Such bags were suspended from the waistband by a cord or chain.

and leaped forward. The room was swirling with blue eddies of smoke; Dago Jim, hands flung up, still grasping letter and pocketbook, pawed at the air—and plunged with a sagging lurch face downward to the floor. There was a yell and an oath from the Wowzer—the crack of another revolver shot, the hum of the bullet past Jimmie Dale's ear, the scorch of the tongue flame in his face, and he was upon the other.

Screeching profanity, the Wowzer grappled; and, for an instant, the two men rocked, reeled, and swayed in each other's embrace; then, both men losing their balance, they shot suddenly backward, the Wowzer, undermost, striking his head against the table's edge—and men, table, and lamp crashed downward in a heap to the floor.

It had been no more, at most, than a matter of seconds since Jimmie Dale had hurled himself into the room; and now, with a gurgling sigh, the Wowzer's arms, that had been wound around Jimmie Dale's back and shoulders, relaxed, and, from the blow on his head the man, lay back inert and stunned. And then it seemed to Jimmie Dale as though pandemonium, unreality, and chaos at the touch of some devil's hand reigned around him. It was dark—no, not dark—a spurt of flame was leaping along the line of trickling oil from the broken lamp on the floor. It threw into ghastly relief the sprawled form of Dago Jim. Outside, from along the passageway, came a confused jangle of commotion— whispering voices, shuffling feet, the swish of Chinese garments. And the room itself began to spring into weird, flickering shadows, that mounted and crept up the walls with the spreading fire.

There was not a second to lose before the room would be swarming with that rush from the passageway—and there was still the letter, the pocketbook! The table had fallen half over Dago Jim—Jimmie Dale pushed it aside, tore the crushed letter and the pocketbook from the man's hands—and felt, with a grim, horrible sort of anxiety, for the other's heartbeat, for the verdict that meant life or death to himself. There was no sign of life—the man was dead.

Jimmie Dale was on his feet now. A face, another, and another showed in the doorway—the Wowzer was regaining his senses, stumbling to his knees. There was one chance—just one—to take those crowding figures by surprise. And with a yell of "Fire!" Jimmie Dale sprang for the doorway.

They gave way before his rush, tumbling back in their surprise against the opposite wall; and, turning, Jimmie Dale raced down the passageway. Doors were opening everywhere now, forms were pushing out into the semi-darkness—only to duck hastily back again, as Jimmie Dale's automatic barked and spat a running fire of warning ahead of him. And then, behind, the Wowzer's voice shrieked out:

"Soak him! Kill de guy! He's croaked Dago Jim! Put a hole in him, de —
"

Yells, a chorus of them, took up the refrain — then the rush of following feet — and the passageway seemed to racket as though a Gatling gun were in play with the fusillade of revolver shots. But Jimmie Dale was at the opening now — and, like a base runner plunging for the bag, he flung himself in a low dive through and into the open cellar beyond. He was on his feet, over the boxes, and dashing up the stairs in a second. The door above opened as he reached the top — Jimmie Dale's right hand shot out with clubbed revolver — and with a grunt Chang Foo went down before the blow and the headlong rush. The next instant Jimmie Dale had sprung through the tea shop and was out on the street.

A minute, two minutes more, and Chinatown would be in an uproar — Chang Foo would see to that — and the Wowzer would prod him on. The danger was far from over yet. And then, as he ran, Jimmie Dale gave a little gasp of relief. Just ahead, drawn up at the curb, stood a taxicab — waiting, probably, for a private slumming party. Jimmie Dale put on a spurt, reached it, and wrenched the door open.

"Quick!" he flung at the startled chauffeur. "The nearest subway station — there's a ten-spot in it for you! Quick man — *quick!* Here they come!"

A crowd of Chinese, pouring like angry hornets from Chang Foo's shop, came yelling down the street — and the taxi took the corner on two wheels — and Jimmie Dale, panting, choking for his breath like a man spent, sank back against the cushions.

But five minutes later it was quite another Jimmie Dale, composed, nonchalant, imperturbable, who entered an up-town subway train, and, choosing a seat alone near the centre of the car, which at that hour of night in the downtown district was almost deserted, took the crushed letter from his pocket. For a moment he made no attempt to read it, his dark eyes, now that he was free from observation, full of troubled retrospect, fixed on the window at his side. It was not a pleasant thought that it had cost a man his life, nor yet that that life was also the price of his own freedom. True, if there were two men in the city of New York whose crimes merited neither sympathy nor mercy, those two men were the Wowzer and Dago Jim — but yet, after all, it was a human life, and, even if his own had been in the balance, thank God it had been through no act of his that Dago Jim had gone out! The Wowzer, cute and cunning, had been quick enough to say so to clear himself, but — Jimmie Dale smiled a little now — neither the Wowzer, nor Chang Foo, nor Chinatown would ever be in a position to recognise their uninvited guest!

Jimmie Dale's eyes shifted to the letter speculatively, gravely. It seemed as though the night had already held a year of happenings, and the night was not over yet — there was the letter! It had already cost one life; was it to cost another — or what?

It began as it always did. He read it through once, in amazement; a second time, with a flush of bitter anger creeping to his cheeks; and a third time, curiously memorising, as it were, snatches of it here and there.

"DEAR PHILANTHROPIC CROOK: Robbery of Hudson-Mercantile National Bank — trusted employee is ex-convict, bad police record, served term in Sing Sing three years ago — known to police as Bookkeeper Bob, real name is Robert Moyne, lives at — — Street, Harlem — Inspector Burton and Lannigan of headquarters trailing him now — robbery not yet made public — "

There was a great deal more — four sheets of closely written data.

With an exclamation almost of dismay, Jimmie Dale pulled out his watch. So that was what Burton and Lannigan were up to! And he had actually run into them! Lord, the irony of it! The — And then Jimmie Dale stared at the dial of his watch incredulously. It was still but barely midnight! It seemed impossible that since leaving the theatre at a few minutes before eleven, he had lived through but a single hour!

Jimmie Dale's fingers began to pluck at the letter, tearing it into pieces, tearing the pieces over and over again into tiny shreds. The train stopped at station after station, people got on and off — Jimmie Dale's hat was over his eyes, and his eyes were glued again to the window. Had Bookkeeper Bob returned to his flat in Harlem with the detectives at his heels — or were Burton and Lannigan still trailing the man downtown somewhere around the cafés? If the former, the theft of the letter and its incident loss of time had been an irreparable disaster; if the latter — well, who knew! The risk was the Gray Seal's!

At One Hundred and Twenty-Fifth Street Jimmie Dale left the train; and, at the end of a sharp four minutes' walk, during which he had dodged in and out from street to street, stopped on a corner to survey the block ahead of him. It was a block devoted exclusively to flats and apartment houses, and, apart from a few belated pedestrians, was deserted. Jimmie Dale strolled leisurely down one side, crossed the street at the end of the block, and strolled leisurely back on the other side — there was no sign of either Burton or Lannigan. It was a fairly safe presumption then that Bookkeeper Bob had not returned yet, or one of the detectives at least would have been shadowing the house.

Jimmie Dale, smiling a little grimly, retraced his steps again, and turned deliberately into a doorway – whose number he had noted as he had passed a moment or so before. So, after all, there was time yet! This was the house. "Number eighteen," she had said in her letter. "A flat – three stories – Moyne lives on ground floor."

Jimmie Dale leaned against the vestibule door – there was a faint click – a little steel instrument was withdrawn from the lock – and Jimmie Dale stepped into the hall, where a gas jet, turned down, burned dimly.

The door of the ground-floor apartment was at his right, Jimmie Dale reached up and turned off the light. Again those slim, tapering, wonderfully sensitive fingers worked with the little steel instrument, this time in the lock of the apartment door – again there was that almost inaudible click – and then cautiously, inch by inch, the door opened under his hand. He peered inside – down a hallway lighted, if it could be called lighted at all, by a subdued glow from two open doors that gave upon it – peered intently, listening intently, as he drew a black silk mask from his pocket and slipped it over his face. And then, silent as a shadow in his movements, the door left just ajar behind him, he stole down the carpeted hallway.

Opposite the first of the open doorways Jimmie Dale paused – a curiously hard expression creeping over his face, his lips beginning to droop ominously downward at the corners. It was a little sitting room, cheaply but tastefully furnished, and a young woman, Bookkeeper Bob's wife evidently, and evidently sitting up for her husband, had fallen sound asleep in a chair, her head pillowed on her arms that were outstretched across the table. For a moment Jimmie Dale held there, his eyes on the scene – and the next moment, his hand curved into a clenched fist, he had passed on and entered the adjoining room.

It was a child's bedroom. A night lamp burned on a table beside the bed, and the soft rays seemed to play and linger in caress on the tousled golden hair of a little girl of perhaps two years of age – and something seemed to choke suddenly in Jimmie Dale's throat – the sweet, innocent little face, upturned to his, was smiling at him as she slept.

Jimmie Dale turned away his head – his eyelashes wet under his mask. *"Beneath the mattress of the child's bed,"* the letter had said. His face like stone, his lips a thin line now, Jimmie Dale's hand reached deftly in without disturbing the child and took out a package – and then another. He straightened up, a bundle of crisp new hundred-dollar notes in each hand – and on the top of one, slipped under the elastic band that held the bills together, an unsealed envelope. He drew out the latter, and opened it – it was a second-class steamship passage to Vera Cruz, made out in a fictitious name, of course, to John Davies, the booking for next day's sailing. From the ticket, from the stolen money, Jimmie Dale's eyes lifted to rest again on the little golden head, the smiling lips—and then, dropping the packages into his pockets, his own lips moving queerly, he turned abruptly to the door.

"My God, the shame of it!" he whispered to himself.

He crept down the corridor, past the open door of the room where the young woman still sat fast asleep, and, his mask in his pocket again, stepped softly into the vestibule, and from there to the street.

Jimmie Dale hurried now, spurred on it seemed by a hot, insensate fury that raged within him—there was still one other call to make that night— still those remaining and minute details in the latter part of her letter, grim and ugly in their portent!

It was close upon one o'clock in the morning when Jimmie Dale stopped again—this time before a fashionable dwelling just off Central Park. And here, for perhaps the space of a minute, he surveyed the house from the sidewalk—watching, with a sort of speculative satisfaction, a man's shadow that passed constantly to and fro across the drawn blinds of one of the lower windows. The rest of the house was in darkness.

"Yes," said Jimmie Dale, nodding his head, "I rather thought so. The servants will have retired hours ago. It's safe enough."

He ran quickly up the steps and rang the bell. A door opened almost instantly, sending a faint glow into the hall from the lighted room; a hurried step crossed the hall—and the outer door was thrown back.

"Well, what is it?" demanded a voice brusquely.

It was quite dark, too dark for either to distinguish the other's features—and Jimmie Dale's hat was drawn far down over his eyes.

"I want to see Mr. Thomas H. Carling, cashier of the Hudson-Mercantile National Bank—it's very important," said Jimmie Dale earnestly.

"I am Mr. Carling," replied the other. "What is it?"

Jimmie Dale leaned forward.

"From headquarters—with a report," he said, in a low tone.

"Ah!" exclaimed the bank official sharply. "Well, it's about time! I've been waiting up for it—though I expected you would telephone rather than this. Come in!"

"Thank you," said Jimmie Dale courteously—and stepped into the hall.

The other closed the front door. "The servants are in bed, of course," he explained, as he led the way toward the lighted room. "This way, please."

Behind the other, across the hall, Jimmie Dale followed and close at Carling's heels entered the room, which was fitted up, quite evidently regardless of cost, as a combination library and study. Carling, in a somewhat pompous fashion, walked straight ahead toward the carved-mahogany flat-topped desk, and, as he reached it, waved his hand.

"Take a chair," he said, over his shoulder – and then, turning in the act of dropping into his own chair, grasped suddenly at the edge of the desk instead, and, with a low, startled cry, stared across the room.

Jimmie Dale was leaning back against the door that was closed now behind him – and on Jimmie Dale's face was a black silk mask.

For an instant neither man spoke nor moved; then Carling, spare-built, dapper in evening clothes, edged back from the desk and laughed a little uncertainly.

"Quite neat! I compliment you! From headquarters with a report, I think you said?"

"Which I neglected to add," said Jimmie Dale, "was to be made in private."

Carling, as though to put as much distance between them as possible, continued to edge back across the room – but his small black eyes, black now to the pupils themselves, never left Jimmie Dale's face.

"In private, eh?" – he seemed to be sparring for time, as he smiled. "In private! You've a strange method of securing privacy, haven't you? A bit melodramatic, isn't it? Perhaps you'll be good enough to tell me who you are?"

Jimmie Dale smiled indulgently.

"My mask is only for effect," he said. "My name is – Smith."

"Yes," said Carling. "I am very stupid. Thank you. I –" he had reached the other side of the room now – and with a quick, sudden movement jerked his hand to the dial of the safe that stood against the wall.

But Jimmie Dale was quicker – without shifting his position, his automatic, whipped from his pocket, held a disconcerting bead on Carling's forehead.

"Please don't do that," said Jimmie Dale softly. "It's rather a good make, that safe. I dare say it would take me half an hour to open it. I was rather curious to know whether it was locked or not."

Carling's hand dropped to his side.

"So!" he sneered. "That's it, is it! The ordinary variety of sneak thief!" His voice was rising gradually. "Well, sir, let me tell you that – "

"Mr. Carling," said Jimmie Dale, in a low, even tone, "unless you moderate your voice some one in the house might hear you – I am quite well aware of that. But if that happens, if any one enters this room, if you make a move to touch a button, or in any other way attempt to attract attention, I'll drop you where you stand!" His hand, behind his back, extracted the key from the door lock, held it up for the other to see, then dropped it into his pocket – and his voice, cold before, rang peremptorily now. "Come back to the desk and sit down in that chair!" he ordered.

For a moment Carling hesitated; then, with a half-muttered oath, obeyed.

Jimmie Dale moved over, and stood in front of Carling on the other side of the desk – and stared silently at the immaculate, fashionably groomed figure before him.

Under the prolonged gaze, Carling's composure, in a measure at least, seemed to forsake him. He began to drum nervously with his fingers on the desk, and shift uneasily in his chair.

And then, from first one pocket and then the other, Jimmie Dale took the two packages of banknotes, and, still without a word, pushed them across the desk until they lay under the other's eyes.

Carling's fingers stopped their drumming, slid to the desk edge, tightened there, and a whiteness crept into his face. Then, with an effort, he jerked himself erect in his chair.

"What's this?" he demanded hoarsely.

"About ten thousand dollars, I should say," said Jimmie Dale slowly. "I haven't counted it. Your bank was robbed this evening at closing time, I understand?"

"Yes!" Carling's voice was excited now, the colour back in his face. "But you – how – do you mean that you are returning the money to the bank?"

"Exactly," said Jimmie Dale.

Carling was once more the pompous bank official. He leaned back and surveyed Jimmie Dale critically with his little black eyes.

"Ah, quite so!" he observed. "That accounts for the mask. But I am still a little in the dark. Under the circumstances, it is quite impossible that you should have stolen the money yourself, and – "

"I didn't," said Jimmie Dale. "I found it hidden in the home of one of your employees."

"You found it – *where?*"

"In Moyne's home — up in Harlem."

"Moyne, eh?" Carling was alert, quick now, jerking out his words. "How did you come to get into this, then? His pal? Double-crossing him, eh? I suppose you want a reward — we'll attend to that, of course. You're wiser than you know, my man. That's what we suspected. We've had the detectives trailing Moyne all evening." He reached forward over the desk for the telephone. "I'll telephone headquarters to make the arrest at once."

"Just a minute," interposed Jimmie Dale gravely. "I want you to listen to a little story first."

"A story! What has a story got to do with this?" snapped Carling.

"The man has got a home," said Jimmie Dale softly. "A home, and a wife — and a little baby girl."

"Oh, that's the game then, eh? You want to plead for him?" Carling flung out gruffly. "Well, he should have thought of all that before! It's quite useless for you to bring it up. The man has had his chance already — a better chance than any one with his record ever had before. We took him into the bank knowing that he was an ex-convict, but believing that we could make an honest man of him — and this is the result."

"And yet—"

"*No!*" said Carling icily.

"You refuse — absolutely?" Jimmie Dale's voice had a lingering, wistful note in it.

"I refuse!" said Carling bluntly. "I won't have anything to do with it."

There was just an instant's silence; and then, with a strange, slow, creeping motion, as a panther creeps when about to spring, Jimmie Dale projected his body across the desk — far across it toward the other. And the muscles of his jaw were quivering, his words rasping, choked with the sweep of fury that, held back so long, broke now in a passionate surge.

"And shall I tell you why you won't? Your bank was robbed to-night of one hundred thousand dollars. There are ten thousand here. *The other ninety thousand are in your safe!*"

"You lie!" Ashen to the lips, Carling had risen in his chair. "You lie!" he cried. "Do you hear! You lie! I tell you, you lie!"

Jimmie Dale's lips parted ominously.

"Sit down!" he gritted between his teeth.

The white in Carling's face had turned to gray, his lips were working — mechanically he sank down again in his chair.

Jimmie Dale still leaned over the desk, resting his weight on his right elbow, the automatic in his right hand covering Carling.

"You cur!" whispered Jimmie Dale. "There's just one reason, only one, that keeps me from putting a bullet through you while you sit there. We'll get to that in a moment. There is that little story first — shall I tell it to you now? For the past four years, and God knows how many before that, you've gone the pace. The lavishness of this bachelor establishment of yours is common talk in New York — far in excess of a bank cashier's salary. But you were supposed to be a wealthy man in your own right; and so, in reality you were — once. But you went through your fortune two years ago. Counted a model citizen, an upright man, an honour to the community — what were you, Carling? What are you? Shall I tell you? Roué, gambler, leading a double life of the fastest kind. You did it cleverly, Carling; hid it well — but your game is up. To-night, for instance, you are at the end of your tether, swamped with debts, exposure threatening you at any moment. Why don't you tell me again that I lie — Carling?"

But now the man made no answer. He had sunk a little deeper in his chair — a dawning look of terror in the eyes that held, fascinated, on Jimmie Dale.

"You cur!" said Jimmie Dale again. "You cur, with your devil's work! A year ago you saw this night coming — when you must have money, or face ruin and exposure. You saw it then, a year ago, the day that Moyne, concealing nothing of his prison record, applied through friends for a position in the bank. Your co-officials were opposed to his appointment, but you, do you remember how you pleaded to give the man his chance — and in your hellish ingenuity saw your way then out of the trap! An ex-convict from Sing Sing! It was enough, wasn't it? What chance had he!" Jimmie Dale paused, his left hand clenched until the skin formed whitish knobs over the knuckles.

Carling's tongue sought his lips, made a circuit of them — and he tried to speak, but his voice was an incoherent muttering.

"I'll not waste words," said Jimmie Dale, in his grim monotone. "I'm not sure enough myself — that I could keep my hands off you much longer. The actual details of how you stole the money to-day do not matter — *now*. A little later perhaps in court — but not now. You were the last to leave the bank, but before leaving you pretended to discover the theft of a hundred thousand dollars — that, done up in a paper parcel, was even then reposing in your desk. You brought the parcel home, put it in that safe there — and notified the president of the bank by telephone from here of the robbery, suggesting that police headquarters be advised at once. He told you to go ahead and act as you saw best. You notified the police, speciously directing suspicion to — the ex-convict in the bank's employ. You knew Moyne was dining out to-night, you knew where — and at a hint from you the police took up the trail. A little later in the evening, you took these two packages of banknotes from the rest, and with this steamship ticket – which you obtained yesterday while out at lunch by sending a district messenger boy with the money and instructions in a sealed envelope to purchase for you – you went up to the Moynes' flat in Harlem for the purpose of secreting them somewhere there. You pretended to be much disappointed at finding Moyne out – you had just come for a little social visit, to get better acquainted with the home life of your employees! Mrs. Moyne was genuinely pleased and grateful. She took you in to see their little girl, who was already asleep in bed. She left you there for a moment to answer the door – and you – you" – Jimmie Dale's voice choked again – "you blot on God's earth, you slipped the money and ticket under the child's mattress!"

Carling came forward with a lurch in his chair – and his hands went out, pawing in a wild, pleading fashion over Jimmie Dale's arm.

Jimmie Dale flung him away.

"You were safe enough," he rasped on. "The police could only construe your visit to Moyne's flat as zeal on behalf of the bank. And it was safer, much more circumspect on your part, not to order the flat searched at once, but only as a last resort, as it were, after you had led the police to trail him all evening and still remain without a clew – and besides, of course, not until you had planted the evidence that was to damn him and wreck his life and home! You were even generous in the amount you deprived yourself of out of the hundred thousand dollars – for less would have been enough. Caught with ten thousand dollars of the bank's money and a steamship ticket made out in a fictitious name, it was prima-facie evidence that he had done the job and had the balance somewhere. What would his denials, his protestations of innocence count for? He was an ex-convict, a hardened criminal caught red-handed with a portion of the proceeds of robbery – he had succeeded in hiding the remainder of it too cleverly, that was all."

Carling's face was ghastly. His hands went out again – again his tongue moistened his dry lips. He whispered:

"Isn't – isn't there some – some way we can fix this?"

And then Jimmie Dale laughed – not pleasantly.

"Yes, there's a way, Carling," he said grimly. "That's why I'm here." He picked up a sheet of writing paper and pushed it across the desk – then a pen, which he dipped into the inkstand, and extended to the other. "The way you'll fix it will be to write out a confession exonerating Moyne."

Carling shrank back into his chair, his head huddling into his shoulders.

"No!" he cried. "I won't—I can't—my God!—I—I—*won't!"*

The automatic in Jimmie Dale's hand edged forward the fraction of an inch.

"I have not used this—yet. You understand now why—don't you?" he said under his breath.

"No, no!" Carling pushed away the pen. "I'm ruined—ruined as it is. But this would mean the penitentiary, too—"

"Where you tried to send an innocent man in your place, you hound; where you—"

"Some other way—some other way!" Carling was babbling. "Let me out of this—for God's sake, let me out of this!"

"Carling," said Jimmie Dale hoarsely, "I stood beside a little bed to-night and looked at a baby girl—a little baby girl with golden hair, who smiled as she slept."

Carling shivered, and passed a shaking hand across his face.

"Take this pen," said Jimmie Dale monotonously; "or—*this!"*

The automatic lifted until the muzzle was on a line with Carling's eyes.

Carling's hand reached out, still shaking, and took the pen; and his body, dragged limply forward, hung over the desk. The pen spluttered on the paper—a bead of sweat spurting from the man's forehead dropped to the sheet.

There was silence in the room. A minute passed—another. Carling's pen travelled haltingly across the paper then, with a queer, low cry as he signed his name, he dropped the pen from his fingers, and, rising unsteadily from his chair, stumbled away from the desk toward a couch across the room.

An instant Jimmie Dale watched the other, then he picked up the sheet of paper. It was a miserable document, miserably scrawled:

"I guess it's all up. I guess I knew it would be some day. Moyne hadn't anything to do with it. I stole the money myself from the bank to-night. I guess it's all up.

"THOMAS H. CARLING."

From the paper, Jimmie Dale's eyes shifted to the figure by the couch—and the paper fluttered suddenly from his fingers to the desk. Carling was reeling, clutching at his throat—a small glass vial rolled upon the carpet. And then, even as Jimmie Dale sprang forward, the other pitched head long over the couch—and in a moment it was over.

Presently Jimmie Dale picked up the vial — and dropped it back on the floor again. There was no label on it, but it needed none — the strong, penetrating odor of bitter almonds was telltale evidence enough. It was prussic, or hydrocyanic acid, probably the most deadly poison and the swiftest in its action that was known to science — Carling had provided against that "some day" in his confession!

For a little space, motionless, Jimmie Dale stood looking down at the silent, outstretched form — then he walked slowly back to the desk, and slowly, deliberately picked up the signed confession and the steamship ticket. He held them an instant, staring at them, then methodically began to tear them into little pieces, a strange, tired smile hovering on his lips. The man was dead now — there would be disgrace enough for some one to bear, a mother perhaps — who knew! And there was another way now — since the man was dead.

Jimmie Dale put the pieces in his pocket, went to the safe, opened it, and took out a parcel, locked the safe carefully, and carried the parcel to the desk. He opened it there. Inside were nearly two dozen little packages of hundred-dollar bills. The other two packages that he had brought with him he added to the rest. From his pocket he took out the thin metal insignia case, and with the tiny tweezers lifted up one of the gray-coloured, diamond-shaped paper seals. He moistened the adhesive side, and, still holding it by the tweezers, dropped it on his handkerchief and pressed the seal down on the face of the topmost package of banknotes. He tied the parcel up then, and, picking up the pen, addressed it in printed characters:

HUDSON-MERCANTILE NATIONAL BANK,
NEW YORK CITY.

"District messenger — some way — in the morning," he murmured.

Jimmie Dale slipped his mask into his pocket, and, with the parcel under his arm, stepped to the door and unlocked it. He paused for an instant on the threshold for a single, quick, comprehensive glance around the room — then passed on out into the street.

At the corner he stopped to light a cigarette — and the flame of the match spurting up disclosed a face that was worn and haggard. He threw the match away, smiled a little wearily — and went on.

The Gray Seal had committed another "crime."

CHAPTER VII

THE THIEF

(Friday 9/17/1915 to Saturday 9/18/1915)

CHOOSING between the snowy napery, the sparkling glass and silver, the cozy, shaded table-lamps, the famous French chef of the ultra-exclusive St. James Club, his own home on Riverside Drive where a dinner fit for an epicure and served by Jason, that most perfect of butlers, awaited him, and Marlianne's, Jimmie Dale, driving in alone in his touring car from an afternoon's golf, had chosen—Marlianne's.

Marlianne's, if such a thing as Bohemianism, or, rather, a concrete expression of it exists, was Bohemian. A two-piece string orchestra played valiantly to the accompaniment of a hoarse-throated piano; and between courses the diners took up the refrain—and, as it was always between courses with some one, the place was a bedlam of noisy riot. Nevertheless, it was Marlianne's—and Jimmie Dale liked Marlianne's. He had dined there many times before, as he had just dined in the person of Jimmie Dale, the millionaire, his high-priced imported car at the curb of the shabby street outside—and he had dined there, disreputable in attire, seedy in appearance, with the police yelping at his heels, as Larry the Bat. In either character Marlianne's had welcomed him with equal courtesy to its spotted linen and most excellent table-d'hôte with *vin ordinaire*—for fifty cents.

And now, in the act of reaching into his pocket for the change to pay his bill, Jimmie Dale seemed suddenly to experience some difficulty in finding what he sought, and his fingers went fumbling from one pocket to another. Two men at the table in front of him were talking—their voices, over a momentary lull in violin squeaks, talk, laughter, singing, and the clatter of dishes, reached him:

"Carling commit suicide! Not on your life! No; of course he didn't! It was that cursed Gray Seal croaked him, just as sure as you sit in that chair!"

The other grunted. "Yes; but what'd the Gray Seal want to pinch a hundred thousand out of the bank for, and then give it back again the next morning?"

"What's he done a hundred other things for to cover up the real object of what he's after?" retorted the first speaker, with a short, vicious laugh;

then, with a thump of his fist on the table: "The man's a devil, a fiend, and anywhere else but New York he'd have been caught and sent to the chair where he belongs long ago, and –"

A burst of ragtime drowned out the man's words. Jimmie Dale placed a fifty-cent piece and a tip beside it on his dinner check, pushed back his chair, and rose from the table. There was a half-tolerantly satirical, half-angry glint in his dark, steady eyes. It was not only the police who yelped at his heels, but every man, woman, and child in the city. The man had not voiced his own sentiments – he had voiced the sentiments of New York! And it was quite on the cards that if he, Jimmie Dale, were ever caught his destination would not even be the death cell and the chair at Sing Sing – his fellow citizens had reached a pitch where they would be quite capable of literally tearing him to pieces if they ever got their hands on him!

And yet there were a few, a very few, a handful out of five millions, who sometimes remembered perhaps to thank God that the Gray Seal lived – that was his reward. That – and *she,* whose mysterious letters prompted and impelled his, the Gray Seal's, acts! She – nameless, fascinating in her brilliant resourcefulness, amazing in her power, a woman whose life was bound up with his and yet held apart from him in the most inexplicable, absorbing way; a woman he had never seen, save for her gloved arm in the limousine that night, who at one unexpected moment projected a dazzling, impersonal existence across his path, and the next, leaving him battling for his life where greed and passion and crime swirled about him, was gone!

Jimmie Dale threaded the small, crowded rooms – the interior of Marlianne's had never been altered from the days when the place had been a family residence of some pretension – and, reaching the hall, received his hat from the frowsy-looking boy in attendance. He passed outside, and, at the top of the steps, paused as he took his cigarette case from his pocket. It was nearly a week since Carling, the cashier of the Hudson-Mercantile National Bank, had been found dead in his home, a bottle that had contained hydrocyanic acid on the floor beside him; nearly a week since Bookkeeper Bob, unaware that he had ever been under temporary suspicion for the robbery of the bank, had, equally unknown to himself, been cleared of any complicity in that affair – and yet, as witness the conversation of a moment ago, it was still the topic of New York, still the vital issue that filled the maw of the newspapers with ravings, threats, and execrations against the Gray Seal, snarling virulently the while at the police for the latter's ineptitude, inefficiency, and impotence!

Jimmie Dale closed his cigarette case with a snap that was almost human in its irony, dropped it back into his pocket, and lighted a match –

but the flame was arrested halfway to the tip of his cigarette, as his eyes fixed suddenly and curiously on a woman's form hurrying down the street. She had turned the corner before he took his eyes from her, and the match between his fingers had gone out. Not that there was anything very strange in a woman walking, or even half running, along the street; nor that there was anything particularly attractive or unusual about her, and if there had been the street was too dark for him to have distinguished it. It was not that—it was the fact that she had neither passed by the house on whose steps he stood, nor come out of any of the adjoining houses. It was as though she had suddenly and miraculously appeared out of thin air, and taken form on a sidewalk a little way down from Marlianne's.

"That's queer!" commented Jimmie Dale to himself. "However—" He took out another match, lighted his cigarette, jerked the match stub away from him, and, with a lift of his shoulders, went down the steps.

He crossed the pavement, walked around the front of his machine, since the steering wheel was on the side next to the curb, and, with his hand out to open the car door—stopped. Some one had been tampering with it—it was not quite closed. There was no mistake. Jimmie Dale made no mistakes of that kind, a man whose life hung a dozen times a day on little things could not afford to make them. He had closed it firmly, even with a bang, when he had got out.

Instantly suspicious, he wrenched the door wide open, switched on the light under the hood, and, with a sharp exclamation, bent quickly forward. A glove, a woman's glove, a white glove lay on the floor of the car. Jimmie Dale's pulse leaped suddenly into fierce, pounding beats. It was *hers!* He *knew* that intuitively—knew it as he knew that he breathed. And that woman he had so leisurely watched as she had disappeared from sight was, must have been—she!

He sprang from the car with a jump, his first impulse to dash after her—and checked himself, laughing a little bitterly. It was too late for that now—he had already let his chance slip through his fingers. Around the corner was Sixth Avenue, surface cars, the elevated, taxicabs, a multitude of people, any one of a hundred ways in which she could, and would, already have discounted pursuit from him—and, besides, he would not even have been able to recognise her if he saw her!

Jimmie Dale's smile was mirthless as he turned back to the car, and picked up the glove. Why had she dropped it there? It could not have been intentional. Why had—he began to tear suddenly at the glove's little finger, and in another second, kneeling on the car's step, his shoulders inside, he was holding a ring close under the little electric bulb.

It was a gold seal ring, a small, dainty thing that bore a crest: a bell, surmounted by a bishop's mitre – the bell, quaint in design, harking the imagination back to some old-time belfry tower. And underneath, in the scroll – a motto. It was a full minute before Jimmie Dale could decipher it, for the lettering was minute and the words, of course, reversed. It was in French: *Sonnez le Tocsin.* [42]

He straightened up, the glove and ring in his hand, a puzzled expression on his face. It was strange! Had she, after all, dropped the glove there intentionally; had she at last let down the barriers just a little between them, and given him this little intimate sign that she –

And then Jimmie Dale laughed abruptly, self-mockingly. He was only trying to deceive himself, to argue himself into believing what, with heart and soul, he wanted to believe. It was not like her – and neither was it so! His eyes had fixed on the seat beside the wheel. He had not used the lap rug all that day, he couldn't use a rug and drive, he had left it folded and hanging on the rack in the tonneau – it was now neatly folded and reposing on the front seat!

"Yes," said Jimmie Dale, a sort of self-pity in his tones, "I might have known."

He lifted the rug. Beneath it on the leather seat lay a white envelope. Her letter! The letter that never came save with the plan of some grim, desperate work outlined ahead – the call to arms for the Gray Seal. *Sonnez le Tocsin!* Ring the Tocsin! Sound the alarm! The Tocsin! The words were running through his brain. A strange motto on that crest – that seemed so strangely apt! The Tocsin! Never once in all the times that he had heard from her, never once in the years that had gone since that initial letter of hers had struck its first warning note, had any communication from her been but to sound again a new alarm – the Tocsin! The Tocsin – the word seemed to visualise her, to give her a concrete form and being, to breathe her very personality.

"The Tocsin!" – Jimmie Dale whispered the word softly, a little wistfully. "Yes; I shall call you that – the Tocsin!"

He folded the glove very carefully, placed it with the ring in his pocketbook, picked up the letter – and, with a sharp exclamation, turned it quickly over in his fingers, then bent hurriedly with it to the light.

---

[42] Tocsin is pronounced, by a French speaker at least, as TOOK-san. This ring was probably fashioned in or after 1611 because that's when the French spelling for tocsin was finalized.

Strange things were happening that night! For the first time, the letter was not even *sealed!* That was not like her, either! What did it mean? Quick, alert now, anxious even, he pulled the double, folded sheets from the envelope, glanced rapidly through them—and, after a moment, a smile, whimsical, came slowly to his lips.

It was quite plain now—all of it. The glove, the ring, and the unsealed letter—and the postscript held the secret; or, rather, what had been intended for a postscript did, for it comprised only a few words, ending abruptly, unfinished: "Look in the cupboard at the rear of the room. The man with the red wig is—" That was all, and the words, written in ink, were badly blurred, as though the paper had been hastily folded before the ink was dry.

It was quite plain; and, in view of the real explanation of it all, eminently characteristic of her. With the letter already written, she had come there, meaning to place it on the seat and cover it with the rug, as, indeed, she had done; then, deciding to add the postscript, and because she would attract less attention that way than in any other, she had climbed into the car as though it belonged to her, and had seated herself there to write it. She would have been hurried in her movements, of course, and in pulling off her glove to use the fountain pen the ring had come with it. The rest was obvious. She had but just begun to write when he had appeared on the steps. She had slipped instantly down to the floor of the car, probably dropping the glove from her lap, hastily inclosed the letter in the envelope which she had no time to seal, thrust the envelope under the rug, and, forgetting her glove and fearful of risking his attention by attempting to close the door firmly, had stolen along the body of the car, only to be noticed by him too late—when she was well down the street!

And at that latter thought, once more chagrin seized Jimmie Dale—then he turned impulsively to the letter. All this was extraneous, apart—for another time, when every moment was not a priceless asset as it very probably was now.

"Dear Philanthropic Crook"—it always began that way, never any other way. He read on more and more intently, crouched there close to the light on the floor of his car, lips thinning as he proceeded—read it to the end, absorbing, memorising it—and then the abortive postscript:

"Look in the cupboard at the rear of the room. The man with the red wig is—"

For an instant, as mechanically he tore the letter into little shreds, he held there hesitant—and the next, slamming the door tight, he flung himself into the seat behind the wheel, and the big, sixty-horse-power, self-starting machine was roaring down the street.

The Tocsin! There was a grim smile on Jimmie Dale's lips now. The alarm! Yes, it was always an alarm, quick, sudden, an emergency to face on the instant – plans, decisions to be made with no time to ponder them, with only that one fact to consider, staggering enough in itself, that a mistake meant disaster and ruin to some one else, and to himself, if the courts were merciful where he had little hope for mercy, the penitentiary for life!

And now to-night again, as it almost always was when these mysterious letters came, every moment of inaction was piling up the odds against him. And, too, the same problem confronted him. How, in what way, in what role, must he play the night's game to its end? As Larry the Bat?

The car was speeding forward. He was heading down Broadway now, lower Broadway, that stretched before him, deserted like some dark, narrow canyon where, far below, like towering walls, the buildings closed together and seemed to converge into some black, impassable barrier. The street lights flashed by him; a patrolman stopped the swinging of his night-stick, and turned to gaze at the car that rushed by at a rate perilously near to contempt of speed laws; street cars passed at indifferent intervals; pedestrians were few and far between – it was the lower Broadway of night.

Larry the Bat? Jimmie Dale shook his head impatiently over the steering wheel. No; that would not do. It would be well enough for this young Burton, perhaps, but not for old Isaac, the East Side fence – for Isaac knew him in the character of Larry the Bat. His quick, keen brain, weaving, eliminating, devising, scheming, discarded that idea. The final coup of the night, as yet but sensed in an indefinite, unshaped way, if enacted in the person of Larry the Bat would therefore stamp Larry the Bat and the Gray Seal as one – a contretemps but little less fatal, in view of old Isaac, than to bracket the Gray Seal and Jimmie Dale! Larry the Bat was not a character to be assumed with impunity, nor one to jeopardize – it was a bulwark of safety, at it were, to which more than once he owed escape from capture and discovery.

He lifted his shoulders with a sudden jerk of decision as the car swerved to the left and headed for the East Side. There was only one alternative then – the black silk mask that folded into such tiny compass, and that, together with an automatic and the curious, thin metal case that looked so like a cigarette case, was always in his pocket for an emergency!

The car turned again, and, approaching its destination, Jimmie Dale slowed down the speed perceptibly. It was a strange case, not a pleasant one – and the raw edges where they showed were ugly in their nakedness.

153

Old Isaac Pelina, young Burton, and Maddon – K. Wilmington Maddon, the wall-paper magnate! Curious, that of the three he should already know two – old Isaac and Maddon! Everybody in the East Side, every denizen of the underworld, and many who posed on a far higher plane knew old Isaac – fence to the most select clientele of thieves in New York, unscrupulous, hand in glove with any rascality or crime that promised profit, a money lender, a Shylock without even a Shylock's humanity as a saving grace! Yes; as Larry the Bat he knew old Isaac, and he knew him not only personally but by firsthand reputation – he had heard the man cursed in blasphemous, whole-souled abandon by more than one crook who was in the old fence's toils. They dealt with him, the crooks, while they swore to "get" him because he was "safe," but – Jimmie Dale's lips parted in a mirthless smile – some day old Isaac would be found in that spiders' den of his back of the dingy loan office with a knife in his heart or a bullet through his head! And K. Wilmington Maddon – Jimmie Dale's smile grew whimsical – he had known Maddon quite intimately for years, had even dined with him at the St. James Club only a few nights before. Maddon was a man in his own "set" – and Maddon, interfered with, was likely to prove none too tractable a customer to handle. And young Burton, the letter had said, was Maddon's private and confidential secretary. Jimmie Dale's lips thinned again. Well, Burton's acquaintance was still to be made! It was a curious trio – and it was dirty work, more raw than cunning, more devilish than ingenious; blackmail in its most hellish form; the stake, at the least calculation, a cool half million. A heavy price for a single slip in a man's life!

He brought the car abruptly to a halt at the edge of the curb, and sprang out to the ground. He was in front of "The Budapest" restaurant, a garish establishment, most popular of all resorts for the moment on the East Side, where Fifth Avenue, in the fond belief that it was seeing the real thing in "seamy" life, engaged its table a week in advance. Jimmie Dale pushed a bill into the door attendant's hand, accompanied by an injunction to keep an eye on the machine, and entered the cafe.

But for a sort of tinselled ostentation the place might well have been the Marlianne's that he had just left – it was crowded and riot was at its height; a stringed orchestra in Hungarian costume played what purported to be Hungarian airs; shouts, laughter, clatter of dishes, and thump of steins added to the din. He made his way between the close-packed tables to the stairs, and descended to the lower floor. Here, if anything, the confusion was greater than above; but here, too, was an exit through to the rear street – and a moment later he was sauntering past the front of an unkempt little pawnshop, closed for the night, over whose door, in the murk of a distant street lamp, three balls hung in sagging disarray, tawny with age, and across whose dirty, unwashed windows, letters missing, ran the legend:

IS AC PELINA

Pawn brok r

The pawnshop made the corner of a very dark and narrow lane — and, with a quick glance around him to assure himself that he was unobserved, Jimmie Dale stepped into the alleyway, and, lost instantly in the blacker shadows, stole along by the wall of the pawnshop. Old Isaac's business was not all done through the front door.

And then suddenly Jimmie Dale shrank still closer against the wall. Was it intuition, premonition — or reality? There seemed an uncanny feeling of *presence* around him, as though perhaps he were watched, as though others beside himself were in the lane. Yes; ahead of him a shadow moved — he could just barely distinguish it now that his eyes had grown accustomed to the darkness. It, like himself, was close against the wall, and now it slunk noiselessly down the length of the lane until he lost sight of it. *And what was that?* He strained his ears to listen. It seemed like a window being opened or closed, cautiously, stealthily, the fraction of an inch at a time. And then he located the sound — it came from the other side of the lane and very nearly opposite to where, on the second floor, a dull, yellow glow shone out from old Isaac's private den in the rear of the pawnshop's office.

Jimmie Dale's brows were gathered in sharp furrows. There was evidently something afoot to-night of which the Tocsin had *not* sounded the alarm. And then the frown relaxed, and he smiled a little. Miraculous as was the means through which she obtained the knowledge that was the basis of their strange partnership, it was no more miraculous than her unerring accuracy in the minutest details. The Tocsin had never failed him yet. It was possible that something was afoot around him, quite probable, indeed, since he was in the most vicious part of the city, in the heart of gangland; but whatever it might be, it was certainly extraneous to his mission or she would have mentioned it.

The lane was empty now, he was quite sure of that — and there was no further sound from the window opposite. He started forward once more — only to halt again for the second time as abruptly as before, squeezing if possible even more closely against the wall. Some one had turned into the lane from the sidewalk, and, walking hurriedly, choosing with evident precaution the exact centre of the alleyway, came toward him.

The man passed, his hurried stride a half run; and, a few feet beyond, halted at old Isaac's side door. From somewhere inside the old building Jimmie Dale's ears caught the faint ringing of an electric bell; a long ring, followed in quick succession by three short ones – then the repeated clicking of a latch, as though pulled by a cord from above, and the man passed in through the door, closing it behind him.

Jimmie Dale nodded to himself in the darkness. It was a spring lock; the signal was one long ring and three short ones – the Tocsin had not missed even those small details. Also, Burton was late for his appointment, for that must have been Burton – business such as old Isaac had in hand that night would have permitted the entrance of no other visitor but K. Wilmington Maddon's private secretary.

He moved down the lane to the door, and tried it softly. It was locked, of course. The slim, tapering, sensitive fingers, whose tips were eyes and ears to Jimmie Dale, felt over the lock – and a slender little steel instrument slipped into the keyhole. A moment more and the catch was released, and the door, under his hand, began to open. With it ajar, he paused, his eyes searching intently up and down the lane. There was nothing, no sign of any one, no moving shadows now. His gaze shifted to the window opposite. Directly facing it now, with the dull reflection upon it from the lighted window of old Isaac's den above his head, he could make out that it was open – but that was all.

Once more he smiled – a little tolerantly at himself this time. Some one had been in the lane; some one had opened the window of his or her room in that tenement house across from him – surely there was nothing surprising, unnatural, or even out of the commonplace in that. He had been a little bit on edge himself, perhaps, and the sudden movement of that shadow, unexpected, had startled him for the moment, as, in all probability, the opening of the window had startled the skulking figure itself into action.

The door was open now. He stepped noiselessly inside, and closed it noiselessly behind him. He was in a narrow hall, where a few yards away, a light shone down a stairway at right angles to the hall itself.

"Rear door of pawnshop opens into hall, and exactly opposite very short flight of stairs leading directly to doorway of Isaac's den above. Ramshackle old place, low ceilings. Isaac, when sitting in his den, can look down, and, by means of a transom over the rear door of the shop, see the customers as they enter from the street, while he also keeps an eye on his assistant. Latter always locks up and leaves promptly at six o'clock – " Jimmie Dale was subconsciously repeating to himself snatches from the Tocsin's letter, which, as subconsciously in reading, he had memorised almost word for word.

And now voices reached him — one, excited, nervous, as though the speaker were labouring under mental strain that bordered closely on the hysterical; the other, curiously mingling a querulousness with an attempt to pacify, but dominantly contemptuous, sneering, cold.

Jimmie Dale moved along the hall — very slowly — without a sound — testing each step before he threw his body weight from one leg to the other. He reached the foot of the stairs. The Tocsin had been right; it was a very short flight. He counted the steps — there were eight. Above, facing him, a door was open. The voices were louder now. It was a sordid-looking room, what he could see of it, poverty-stricken in its appearance, intentionally so probably for effect, with no attempt whatever at furnishing. He could see through the doorway to the window that opened on the alleyway, or, rather, just glimpse the top of the window at an angle across the room — that and a bare stretch of floor. The two men were not in the line of vision.

Burton's voice — it was unquestionably Burton speaking — came to Jimmie Dale now distinctly.

"No, I didn't! I tell you, I didn't! I — I hadn't the nerve."

Jimmie Dale slipped his black silk mask over his face; and with extreme caution, on hands and knees, began to climb the stairs.

"So!" It was old Isaac now, in a half purr, half sneer. "And I was so sure, my young friend, that you had. I was so sure that you were not such a fool. Yes; I could even have sworn that they were in your pocket now — what? It is too bad — too bad! It is not a pleasant thing to think of, that little chair up the river in its horrible little room where —"

"For God's sake, Isaac — not that! Do you hear — not that! My God, I didn't mean to — I didn't know what I was doing!"

Jimmie Dale crept up another step, another, and another. There was silence for a moment in the room; then Burton again, hoarse-voiced:

"Isaac, I'll make good to you some other way. I swear I will — I swear it! If I'm caught at this I'll — I'll get fifteen years for it."

"And which would you rather have?" Jimmie Dale could picture the oily smirk, the shrug of his shoulders, the outthrust hands, palms upward, elbows in at the hips, the fingers curved and wide apart — "fifteen years, or what you get — for murder? Eh, my friend, you have thought of that — eh? It is a very little price I ask — yes?"

"Damn you!" Burton's voice was shrill, then dropped to a half sob. "No, no, Isaac, I didn't mean that. Only, for God's sake be merciful! It is not only the risk of the penitentiary; it's more than that. I — I tried to play white all my life, and until that cursed night there's no man living could say I haven't. You know that—you know that, Isaac. I tell you I couldn't do it this afternoon—I tell you I couldn't. I tried to and—and I couldn't."

Jimmie Dale was lying flat on the little landing now, peering into the room. Back a short distance from the doorway, a repulsive-looking little man in unkempt clothes and soiled linen, with yellowish-skinned, parchment face, out of which small black eyes shone cunningly and shrewdly, sat at a bare deal table in a rickety chair; facing him across the table stood a young man of not more than twenty-five, clean cut, well dressed, but whose face was unnaturally white now, and whose hand, as he extended it in a pleading gesture toward the other, trembled visibly. Jimmie Dale's hand made its way quietly to his side pocket and extracted his automatic.

Old Isaac humped his shoulders, and leered at his visitor.

"We talk a great deal, my young friend. What is the use? A bargain is a bargain. A few rubies in exchange for your life. A few rubies and my mouth is shut. Otherwise"—he humped his shoulders again. "Well?"

Burton drew back, swept his hand in a dazed way across his eyes—and laughed out suddenly in bitter mirth.

"A few rubies!" he cried. "The most magnificent stones on this side of the water—a *few* rubies! It's been Maddon's life hobby. Every child in New York knows that! A few—yes, there's only a few—but those few are worth a fortune. He trusts me, the man has been like a father to me, and—"

"So you are the very last to be suspected," observed old Isaac suavely. "Have I not told you that? There is nothing to fear. Did we not arrange everything so nicely—eh, my young friend? See, it was to-night that Maddon gives a little reception to his friends, and did you not say that the rubies would be taken from the safe-deposit vault this afternoon since his friends always clamoured to see them as a very fitting conclusion to an evening's entertainment? And did you not say that you very naturally had access to the safe in the library where you worked, and that he would not notice they were gone until he came to look for them some time this evening? I think you said all that. And what suspicion let alone proof, would attach itself to you? You were out of the room once when he, too, was absent for perhaps half an hour. It is very simple. In that half hour, some one, somehow, abstracted them. Certainly it was not you. You see how little I ask—and I pay well, do I not? And so I gave you until to-night. Three days have gone, and I have said nothing, and the body has not been found—eh? But to-night—eh—it was understood! The rubies—or the chair."

Burton's lips moved, but it was a moment before he could speak.

"You wouldn't dare!" he whispered thickly. "You wouldn't dare! I'd tell the story of — of what you tried to make me do, and they'd send you up for it."

Old Isaac shrugged with pitying contempt.

"Is it, after all, a fool I am dealing with!" he sneered. "And I — what should I say? That you had stolen the stones from your employer and offered them as a bribe to silence me, and that I had refused. The very act of handing you over to the police would prove the truth of what I said and rob you of even a chance of leniency — *for that other thing.* Is it not so — eh? And why did I not hand you over at once three nights ago? Believe me, my young friend, I should have a very good reason ready, a dozen, if necessary, if it came to that. But we are borrowing trouble, are we not? We shall not come to that — eh?"

For a moment it seemed to Jimmie Dale, as he watched, that Burton would hurl himself upon the other. White to the lips, the muscles of his face twitching, Burton clenched his fists and leaned over the table — and then, with sudden revulsion of emotion, he drew back once more, and once more came that choked sob:

"You'll pay for this, Isaac — your turn will come for this!"

"I have been threatened very often," snapped the other contemptuously. "Bah, what are threats! I laugh at them — as I always will." Then, with a quick change of front, his voice a sudden snarl: "Well, we have talked enough. You have your choice. The stones or — eh? And it is to-night — *now!*"

The old pawnbroker sprawled back in his chair, a cunning leer on his vicious face, a gleam of triumph, greed, in the beady, ratlike eyes that never wavered from the other. Burton, moisture oozing from his forehead, stood there, hesitant, staring back at old Isaac, half in a fascinated gaze, half as though trying to read some sign of weakness in the bestial countenance that confronted him. And then, very slowly, in an automatic, machine-like way, his hand groped into the inside pocket of his vest — and old Isaac cackled out in derision.

"So! You thought you could bluff me, eh — you thought you could fool old Isaac! Bah! I read you like a book! Did I not tell you a while back that you had them in your pocket? I know your kind, my young friend; I know your kind very well indeed — it is my business. You would not have dared to come here to-night without the price. So! You took them this afternoon as we agreed. Yes, yes; you did well. You will not regret it. And now let me see them" — his voice rose eagerly — "let me see them now, my young friend."

"Yes, I took them." Burton spoke listlessly. "God help me!"

Old Isaac, quivering, excited, like a different creature now, sprang from his chair, and, as Burton drew a long, flat, leather case from his pocket, snatched it from the other's hand. His fingers in their rapacious haste could not at first manipulate the catch, and then finally, with the case open, he bent over the table feverishly. The light reflected back as from some living mass of crimson fire, now shading darkly, now glowing into wondrous, colourful transparency as he moved the case to and fro with jerky motions of his hands – and he was babbling, crooning to himself like one possessed.

"Ah, the little beauties! Ah, the pretty little things! Yes, yes; these are the ones! This is the great Aracon – see, see, the six-sided prism terminated by the six-sided pyramid. But it must be cut – it must be cut to sell it, eh? Ah, it is too bad – too bad! And this, this one here, I know them all, this is – "

But his sentence was never finished – it was Jimmie Dale, on his feet now, leaning against the jamb of the door, his automatic covering the two men at the table, who spoke.

"Quite so, Isaac," he said coolly; "you know them all! Quite so, Isaac – but be good enough to *drop* them!"

The case fell from Isaac's hand, the flush on his cheeks died to a sickly pallor, and, his mouth half open, he stood like a man turned to stone, his hands with curved fingers still outstretched over the table, over the crimson gems that, spilled from the case, lay scattered now on the tabletop. Burton neither spoke nor moved – a little whiter, the misery in his face almost apathetic, he moistened his lips with the tip of his tongue.

Jimmie Dale walked across the room, halted at the end of the table, and surveyed the two men grimly. And then, while one hand with revolver extended rested easily on the table, the other gathered up the stones, placed them in the case, and, the case in his pocket, Jimmie Dale's lips parted in an uninviting smile.

"I guess I'm in luck to-night, eh, Isaac?" he drawled. "Between you and your young friend, as I believe you call him, it would appear as though I had fallen on my feet. That Aracon's worth – what would you say? – a hundred, two hundred thousand alone, eh? A very famous stone, that – had your eye on it for quite a time, Isaac, you miserable blood leech, eh?"

Isaac did not answer; but, while he still held back from the table, he seemed to be regaining a little of his composure – burglars of whatever sort were no novelty to him – and was staring fixedly at Jimmie Dale.

"Can't place me – though there's not many in the profession you don't know? Is that it?" inquired Jimmie Dale softly. "Well, don't try, Isaac; it's hardly worth your while. *I've* got the stones now, and – "

"Wait! Wait! Listen!" It was Burton, speaking for the first time, his words coming in a quick, nervous rush. "Listen! You don't –"

"Hold your tongue!" cried old Isaac, with sudden fierceness. "You are a fool!" He leaned toward Jimmie Dale, a crafty smile on his face, quite in control of himself once more. "Don't listen to him – listen to me. You're right. I can't place you, and it doesn't make any difference" – he took a step forward – "but –"

"Not too close, Isaac!" snapped Jimmie Dale sharply. "I know *you!*"

"So!" ejaculated old Isaac, rubbing his hands together. "So! That is good! That is what I want. Listen, we will make a bargain. We are birds of a feather, eh? All thieves, eh? You've got the drop on us who did all the work, but you'll give us our share – eh? Listen! You couldn't get rid of those stones alone. You know that; you're not so green at the game, eh? You'd have to go to some one. You know me; you know old Isaac, you say. Well, then, you know there isn't another man in New York could dispose of those rubies and play *safe* doing it except me. I'll make a good bargain with you."

"Isaac," said Jimmie Dale pensively, "you've made a good many 'good' bargains. I wonder when you'll make your last! There's more than one looking for 'interest' on those bargains in a pretty grim sort of way."

"Bah!" ejaculated old Isaac. "It is an old story. They are all alike. I am afraid of none of them. I hold them all like – *that!*" His hand opened and closed like a taloned claw.

"And you'd add me to the lot, eh?" said Jimmie Dale. He lifted the revolver, its muzzle on old Isaac, examined the mechanism thoughtfully, and lowered it again. "Very well, I'll make a bargain with you – providing it is agreeable to your young friend here."

"Ah!" exclaimed old Isaac shrilly. "So! That is good! It is done then." He chuckled hoarsely. "Any bargain I make he will agree to. Is it not so?" He fixed his eyes on Burton. "Well, is it not so? Speak up! Say –"

He stopped – the words cut short off on his lips. It came without warning – a crash, a pound on the door below – another.

Burton shrank back against the wall.

"My God! The police!" he gasped. "Maddon's found out! We're – we're caught!"

Jimmie Dale's eyes, on old Isaac, narrowed. The pounding in the alleyway grew louder, more insistent. And then his first suspicion passed – it was no "game" of Isaac's. Crafty though the old fox was, the other's surprise and agitation was too genuine to be questioned.

Still the pounding continued—some one was kicking viciously at the door, and banging a tattoo on the panels with his fists.

Old Isaac's clawlike hands doubled suddenly.

"It is some drunken sot," he snarled out, "that knows no better than to come here and rouse the whole neighbourhood! It is true, in a moment we will have the police running in from the street. But wait—wait—I'll teach the fool a lesson!" He dashed around the table, ran for the window, wrenched the catch up, flung the window open, and, snarling again, leaned out—and instantly the knocking ceased.

And instantly then, with a sharp cry, as the whole ghastly meaning of it swept upon him, Jimmie sprang after the other—too late! Came the roar of a revolver shot, a stream of flame cutting the darkness of the alleyway from the window in the house opposite—and, without a sound, old Isaac crumpled up, hung limply for a moment over the sill, and slid in a heap to the floor.

On his hands and knees, protected from the possibility of another bullet by the height of the sill, Jimmie Dale, quick in every movement now, dragged the inert form toward the table away from the window, and bent hurriedly over the other. A minute perhaps he stayed there—and then rose slowly.

Burton, horror-stricken, unmanned, beside himself, was hanging, clutching with both hands at the table edge.

"He's dead," said Jimmie Dale laconically.

Burton flung out his hands.

"Dead!" he whispered hoarsely. "I—I think I'm going mad. Three days of hell—and now this. We'd—we'd better get out of here quick—they'll get us if—"

Jimmie Dale's hand fell with a tight grip on Burton's shoulder.

"There won't be any more shots fired—pull yourself together!"

Burton stared at him in a demented way.

"What's—what's it mean?" he stammered.

"It means that I didn't put two and two together," said Jimmie Dale a little bitterly. "It means that there's a dozen crooks been dancing old Isaac's tune for a long time—and that some of them have got him at last."

Burton reached out suddenly and clutched Jimmie Dale's arm.

"Then I'm safe!" He mumbled the words, but there was dawning hope, relief in his white face. "Safe! I'm safe—if you'll only give me back those stones. Give them back to me, for God's sake give them back to me! You don't know—you don't understand. I stole them because—because he made me—because I—it was the only chance I had. Oh, my God, you don't know what the last three days have been! Give them back to me, won't you – won't you? You – you don't know!"

"Don't lose your nerve!" said Jimmie Dale sharply. "Sit down!" He pushed the other into the chair. "There's no one will disturb us here for some time at least. What is it that I don't know? That three nights ago you were in a gambling hell, Sagosto's, to be exact, one of the most disreputable in New York – and you went there on the invitation of a stray acquaintance, a man named Perley – shall I describe him for you? A short, slim-built man, black eyes, red hair, beard, and – "

"*You* know that!" The misery, the hopelessness was back in Burton's face again – and suddenly he bent over the table and buried his head in his outflung arms.

There was silence for a moment. Tight-lipped, Jimmie Dale's eyes travelled from Burton's shaking shoulders to the motionless form on the floor. Then he spoke again:

"You're a bit of a rounder, Burton, but I think you've had a lesson that will last you all your life. You were half-drunk when you and Perley began to hobnob over a downtown bar. He said he'd show you some real life, and you went with him to Sagosto's. He gave you a revolver before you went in, and told you the place wasn't safe for an unarmed man. He introduced you to Sagosto, the proprietor, and you were shown to a back room. You drank quite a little there. You and Perley were alone, throwing dice. You got into a quarrel. Perley tried to draw his revolver. You were quicker. You drew the one he had given you – and fired. He fell to the floor – you saw the blood gush from his breast just above the heart – he was dead. In a panic you rushed from the place and out into the street. I don't think you went home that night."

Burton raised his head, showing his haggard face.

"I guess it's no use," he said dully. "If you know, others must. I thought only Isaac and Sagosto knew. Why haven't I been arrested? I wish to God I had – I wouldn't have had to-day to answer for."

"I am not through yet," said Jimmie Dale gravely. "The next day old Isaac here sent for you. He said Sagosto had told him of the murder, and had offered to dispose of the corpse and keep his mouth shut for fifty thousand dollars – that no one in his place knew of it except himself. Isaac, for his share, wanted considerably more. You told him you had no such sums, that you had no money. He told you how you could get it – you had access to Maddon's safe, you were Maddon's confidential secretary, fully in your employer's trust, the last man on earth to be suspected – and there were Maddon's famous, priceless rubies."

Jimmie Dale paused. Burton made no answer.

"And so," said Jimmie Dale presently, "to save yourself from the death penalty you took them."

"Yes," said Burton, scarcely above his breath. "Are you an officer? If you are, take me, have done with it! Only for Heaven's sake end it! If you're not—"

Jimmie Dale was not listening. "The cupboard at the rear of the room," she had said. He walked across to it now, opened it, and, after a little search, found a small bundle. He returned with it in his hand, and, kneeling beside the dead man on the floor, his back to Burton, untied it, took out a red wig and beard, and slipped them on to old Isaac's head and face.

"I wonder," he said grimly, as he stood up, "if you ever saw this man before?"

"My God—*Perley!*" With a wild cry, Burton was on his feet, straining forward like a man crazed.

"Yes," said Jimmie Dale, "Perley! Sort of an ironic justice in his end as far as you are concerned, isn't there? I think we'll leave him like that—as Perley. It will provide the police with an interesting little problem—which they will never solve, and—*steady!*"

Burton was rocking on his feet, the tears were streaming down his face. He lurched heavily—and Jimmie Dale caught him, and pushed him back into the chair again.

"I thought—I thought there was blood on my hands," said Burton brokenly; "that—that I had taken a man's life. It was horrible, horrible! I've lived through three days that I thought would drive me mad, while I—I tried to do my work, and—and talk to people, just as if nothing had happened. And every one that spoke to me seemed so carefree and happy, and I would have sold my soul to have changed places with them." He stared at the form on the floor, and shivered suddenly. "It—it was like that I saw him last!" he whispered. "But—but I do not understand."

Jimmie Dale smiled a little wearily.

"It was simple enough," he said. "Old Isaac had had his eyes on those rubies for a long time. The easiest way of getting them was through you. The revolver he gave you before you entered Sagosto's was loaded with blank cartridges, the blood you saw was the old, old trick—a punctured bladder of red pigment concealed under the vest."

"Let us get out of here!" Burton shuddered again. "Let us get out of here—at once—now. If we're found here, we'll be accused of—*that!*"

"There is no hurry," Jimmie Dale answered quietly. "I have told you that no one is liable to come here to-night—and whoever did this certainly will not raise an alarm. And besides, there is still the matter of the rubies – Burton."

"Yes," said Burton, with a quick intake of his breath.

"Yes – the rubies – what are you going to do with them? I – I had forgotten them. You'll –" He stopped, stared at Jimmie Dale, and burst into a miserable laugh. "I'm a fool, a blind fool!" he moaned. "It does not matter what you do with them. I forgot Sagosto. When they find Isaac here, Sagosto will either tell his story, which will be enough to convict me of this night's work, the *real* murder, even though I'm innocent; or else he'll blackmail me just as Isaac did."

Jimmie Dale shook his head.

"You are doing Isaac's cunning an injustice," he said grimly. "Sagosto was only a tool, one of many that old Isaac had in his power – and, for that matter, as likely as any one else to have had a hand in Isaac's murder to-night. Sagosto saw you once when Isaac brought you into his place – not because Isaac wanted Sagosto to see you, but because he wanted *you* to see Sagosto. Do you understand? It would make the story that Sagosto came to him with the tale of the murder the next day ring true. Sagosto, however, did not go to old Isaac the next day to tell about any fake murder – naturally. Sagosto would not know you again from Adam – neither does he know anything about the rubies, nor what old Isaac's ulterior motives were. He was paid for his share in the game in old Isaac's usual manner of payment probably – by a threat of exposure for some old-time offence, that Isaac held over him, if he didn't keep his mouth shut."

Burton's hand brushed his eyes.

"Yes," he muttered. "Yes – I see it now."

Jimmie Dale stooped down, picked up the paper from the floor in which the wig and beard had been wrapped, walked back with it, and replaced it in the cupboard. And then, with his back to Burton again, he took the case of gems from his pocket, opened it, and laid it on the cupboard shelf. Also from his pocket came that thin metal case, and from the case, with a pair of tweezers that obviated the possibility of telltale finger prints, a gray, diamond-shaped piece of paper, adhesive on one side that, cursed by the distracted authorities in every police headquarters on both sides of the Atlantic, and raved at by a virulent press whose printed reproductions had made it familiar in every household in the land – was the insignia of the Gray Seal. He moistened the adhesive side, dropped it from the tweezers to his handkerchief, and pressed it down firmly on the inside of the cover of the jewel case. He put both cases back in his pockets, and returned to Burton.

"Burton," he said a little sharply, "while I was outside that doorway there, I heard you beg old Isaac to let you keep the rubies, and three times already you have asked the same of me. What would you do with them if I gave them back to you?"

Burton did not reply for a moment – he was gazing at the masked face in a half-eager, half-doubtful way.

"You – you mean you will give them back!" he burst out finally.

"Answer my question," prompted Jimmie Dale.

"Do with them?" Burton repeated slowly. "Why, I've told you. They'd go back to Mr. Maddon – I'd take them back."

"Would you?" Jimmie Dale's voice was quizzical.

A puzzled expression came to Burton's face.

"I don't know what you mean by that," he said. "Of course, I would!"

"How?" asked Jimmie Dale. "Do you know the combination of Mr. Maddon's safe?"

"No," said Burton

"And the safe would be locked, wouldn't it?"

"Yes."

"Quite so," said Jimmie Dale musingly. "Then, granted that Mr. Maddon has not already discovered the theft, how would you replace the stones before he does discover it? And if he already knows that they are gone, how would you get them back into his hands?"

"Yes, I know," Burton answered a little listlessly. "I've thought of that. There's only one way – to take them back to him myself, and make a clean breast of it, and – " He hesitated.

"And tell him you stole them," supplied Jimmie Dale.

Burton nodded his head. "Yes," he said.

"And then?" prodded Jimmie Dale. "What will Maddon do? From what I've heard of him, he's not a man to trifle with, nor a man to take an overly complacent view of things – not the man whose philosophy is 'all's well that ends well.'"

"What does it matter?" Burton's voice was low. "It isn't that so much. I'm ready for that. It's the fact that he trusted me implicitly, and I – well, I played the fool, or I'd never have got into a mess like this."

For an instant Jimmie Dale looked at the other searchingly, and then, smiling strangely, he shook his head.

"There's a better way than that, Burton," he said quietly.

"I think, as I said before, you've had a lesson to-night that will last you all your life. I'm going to give you another chance—with Maddon. Here are the stones." He reached into his pocket and laid the case on the table.

But now Burton made no effort to take the case—his eyes, in that puzzled way again, were on Jimmie Dale.

"A better way?" he repeated tensely. "What do you mean? What way?"

"Well, say at the expense of another man's reputation—of mine," suggested Jimmie Dale, with his whimsical smile. "You need only say that a man came to you this evening, told you that he stole these rubies from Mr. Maddon during the afternoon, and asked you, as Mr. Maddon's private secretary, to restore them with his compliments to their owner."

A slow flush of disappointment, deepening to one of anger dyed Burton's cheeks.

"Are you trying to make a fool of me?" he cried out. "Go to Maddon with a childish tale like that! There's no man living would believe such a cock-and-bull story!"

"No?" inquired Jimmie Dale softly. "And yet I am inclined to think there are a good many—that even Maddon would, hard-headed as he is. You might say that when the man handed you the case you thought it was some practical joke being foisted on you, until you opened the case"— Jimmie Dale pushed it a little farther across the table, and Burton, mechanically, his eyes still on Jimmie Dale, loosened the catch with his thumb nail—"until you opened the case, saw the rubies, and-"

"The Gray Seal!" Burton had snatched the case toward him, and was straining his eyes at the inside cover. "You—the Gray Seal!"

"Well?" said Jimmie Dale whimsically.

Motionless, the case held open in his hands, Burton stood there.

"The Gray Seal!" he whispered. Then, with a catch in his voice: "You mean this? You mean to let me have these back—you mean—you mean all you've said? For God's sake, don't play with me—the Gray Seal, the most notorious criminal in the country, to give back a fortune like this! You—you—"

"Dog with a bad name," said Jimmie Dale, with a wry smile; then, a little gruffly: "Put it in your pocket!"

Slowly, almost as though he expected the case to be snatched back from him the next instant, Burton obeyed.

"I don't understand—I *can't* understand!" he murmured. "They say that you—and yet I believe you now—you've saved me from a ruined life

to-night. The Gray Seal! If – if every one knew what you had done, they –
"

"But every one won't," Jimmie Dale broke in bluntly, "Who is to tell them? You? You couldn't very well, when you come to think of it – could you? Well, who knows, perhaps there have been others like you!"

"You mean," said Burton excitedly, "you mean that all these crimes of yours that have seemed without motive, that have been so inexplicable, have really been like to-night to –"

"I don't mean anything at all," interposed Jimmie Dale a little hurriedly. "Nothing, Burton – except that there is still one little thing more to do to bolster up that 'childish' story of mine – and then get out of here." He glanced sharply, critically around the room, his eyes resting for a moment at the last on the form on the floor. Then tersely: "I am going to turn out the light – we will have to pass the window to get to the door, and we will invite no chances. Are you ready?"

"No; not yet," said Burton eagerly. "I haven't said what I'd like to say to you, what I –"

"Walk straight to the door," said Jimmie Dale curtly. There was the click of an electric-light switch, and the room was in darkness. "Now, no noise!" he instructed.

And Burton, perforce, made his way across the room – and at the door Jimmie Dale joined him and led him down the short flight of stairs. At the bottom, he opened the door leading into the rear of the pawnshop itself, and, bidding Burton follow, entered.

"We can't risk even a match; it could be seen from the street," he said brusquely, as he fumbled around for a moment in the darkness. "Ah – here it is!" He lifted a telephone receiver from its hook, and gave a number.

Burton caught him quickly by the arm.

"Good Lord, man, what are you doing?" he protested anxiously. "That's Mr. Maddon's house!"

"So I believe," said Jimmie Dale complacently. "Hello! Is Mr. Maddon there? . . . I beg pardon? . . . Personally, yes, if you please."

There was a moment's wait. Burton's hand was still nervously clutching at Jimmie Dale's sleeve. Then:

"Mr. Maddon?" asked Jimmie Dale pleasantly. "Yes? . . . I am very sorry to trouble you, but I called you up to inquire if you were aware that your rubies, and among them your Aracon, had been stolen? . . . I beg pardon! . . . Rubies – yes. . . . You weren't. . . . Oh, no, I am quite in my right mind; if you will take the trouble to open your safe you will find they are gone – shall I hold the line while you investigate? . . . What? . . . Don't shout, please – and stand a little farther away from the mouthpiece." Jimmie Dale's tone was one of insolent composure now. "There is really no use in getting excited. . . . I beg pardon? . . . Certainly, this is the Gray Seal speaking. . . . What?" Jimmie Dale's voice grew plaintive, "I really can't make out a word when you yell like that. . . . Yes. . . . I had occasion to use them this afternoon, and I took the liberty of borrowing them temporarily – are you still there, Mr. Maddon? . . . Oh, quite so! Yes, I hear you *now.* . . . No, that is all, only I am returning them through your private secretary, a very estimable young man, though I fear somewhat excitable and shaky, who is on his way to you with them now. . . . *What's that you say?* You repeat that," snapped Jimmie Dale suddenly, icily, "and I'll take them from under your nose again before morning! . . . Ah! That is better! Good-night – Mr. Maddon."

Jimmie Dale hung up the receiver and shoved Burton toward the door.

"Now then, Burton, we'll get out of here – and the sooner you reach Fifth Avenue and Mr. Maddon's house the better. No; not that way!" They had reached the hall, and Burton had turned toward the side door that opened on the alleyway. "Whoever they were who settled their last account with Isaac may still be watching. They've nothing against any one else, but they know some one was in here at the time, and, if the police are clever enough ever to get on their track, they might find it very convenient to be able to say *who* was in the room when Isaac was murdered – there's nothing to show, since Isaac so obligingly opened the window for them, that the shot was fired *through* the window and not from the inside of the room. And even if they have already taken to their heels" – Jimmie Dale was leading Burton up the stairs again as he talked – "it might prove exceedingly inconvenient for us if some passer-by should happen to recollect that he saw two men of our general appearance leaving the premises. Now keep close – and follow me."

They passed the door of Isaac's den, turned down a narrow corridor that led to the rear of the house – Jimmie Dale guiding unerringly, working from the mental map of the house that the Tocsin had drawn for him – descended another short flight of stairs that gave on the kitchen, crossed the kitchen, and Jimmie Dale opened a back door. He paused here for a moment to listen; then, cautioning Burton to be silent, moved on again across a small back yard and through a gate into a lane that ran at right angles to the alleyway by which both had entered the house – and, a minute later, they were crouched against a building, a half block away, where the lane intersected the cross street.

Here Jimmie Dale peered out cautiously. There was no one in sight. He touched Burton's shoulder, and pointed down the street.

"That's your way, Burton — mine's the other. Hurry while you've got the chance. Good-night."

Burton's hand reached out, caught Jimmie Dale's, and wrung it.

"God bless you!" he said huskily. "I —"

And Jimmie Dale pushed him out on to the street.

Burton's steps receded down the sidewalk. Jimmie Dale still crouched against the wall. The steps grew fainter in the distance and died finally away. Jimmie Dale straightened up, slipped the mask from his face to his pocket, stepped out on the street — and five minutes later was passing through the noisy bedlam of the Hungarian restaurant on his way to the front door and his car.

"*Sonnez le Tocsin*," Jimmie Dale was saying softly to himself. "I wonder what she'll do when she finds I've got the ring?"

CHAPTER VIII

THE MAN HIGHER UP

(Tuesday 9/28/1915 to Saturday 9/29/1915)

THE Tocsin! By neither act, sign, nor word had she evidenced the slightest interest in that ring—and yet she must know, she certainly must know that it was now in his possession. Jimmie Dale was disappointed. Somehow, he had counted more than he had cared to admit on developments from that ring.

He pulled a little viciously at his cigarette, as he stared out of the St. James Club window. That was how long ago? Ten days? Yes; this would be the eleventh. Eleven days now and no word from her—eleven days since that night at old Isaac's, since she had last called him, the Gray Seal, to arms. It was a long while—so long a while even that what had come to be his prerogative in the newspapers, the front page with three-inch type recounting some new exploit of that mysterious criminal the Gray Seal, was being usurped. The papers were howling now about what they, for the lack of a better term, were pleased to call a wave of crime that had inundated New York, and of which, for once, the Gray Seal was not the storm centre, but rather, for the moment, forgotten.

He drew back from the window, and, settling himself again in the big leather lounging chair, resumed the perusal of the evening paper. His eye fell on what was common to every edition now, a crime editorial—and the paper crackled suddenly under the long, slim, tapering fingers, so carefully nurtured, whose sensitive tips a hundred times had made mockery of the human ingenuity squandered on the intricate mechanism of safes and vaults. No; he was wrong—the Gray Seal had not been forgotten.

"We should not be surprised," wrote the editor virulently, "to discover at the bottom of these abominable atrocities that the guiding spirit, in fact, was the Gray Seal—they are quite worthy even of his diabolical disregard for the laws of God and man."

Jimmie Dale's lips straightened ominously, and an angry glint crept into his dark, steady eyes. There was nothing then, nothing too vile that, in the public's eyes, could not logically be associated with the Gray Seal— even this! A series of the most cold-blooded, callous murders and robberies, the work, on the face of it, of a well-organized band of thugs, brutal, insensate, little better than fiends, though clever enough so far to have evaded capture, clever enough, indeed, to have kept the police still staggering and gasping after a clew for one murder — while another was in the very act of being committed! The Gray Seal! What exquisite irony! And yet, after all, the papers were not wholly to blame for what they said; he had invited much of it. Seeming crimes of the Gray Seal had apparently been genuine beyond any question of doubt, as he had intended them to appear, as in the very essence of their purpose they had to be.

Yes; he had invited much — he and she together — the Tocsin and himself. He, Jimmie Dale, millionaire, clubman, whose name for generations in New York had been the family pride, was "wanted" as the Gray Seal for so many "crimes" that he had lost track of them himself — but from any one of which, let the identity of the Gray Seal be once solved, there was and could be no escape! What exquisite irony — yet full, too, of the most deadly consequences!

Once more Jimmie Dale's eyes sought the paper, and this time scanned the headlines of the first page:

BRUTAL MURDER OF MILL PAYMASTER.
THE CRIME WAVE STILL AT ITS HEIGHT.
HERMAN ROESSLE FOUND DEAD NEAR HIS CAR.
ASSASSINS ESCAPE WITH $20,000.

Jimmie Dale read on — and as he read there came again that angry set to his lips. The details were not pleasant. Herman Roessle, the paymaster of the Martindale-Kensington Mills, whose plant was on the Hudson, had gone that morning in his runabout to the nearest town, three miles away, for the monthly pay roll; had secured the money from the bank, a sum of twenty-odd thousand dollars; and had started back with it for the mill. At first, it being broad daylight and a well-frequented road, his nonappearance caused no apprehension; but as early afternoon came and there was still no sign of Roessle the mill management took alarm. Discovering that he had left the bank for the return journey at a few minutes before eleven, and that nothing had been seen of him at his home, the police were notified. Followed then several hours of fruitless search, until finally, with the whole countryside aroused and the efforts of the police augmented by private search parties, the car was found in a thicket at the edge of a crossroad some four miles back from the river, and, a little way from the car, the body of Roessle, dead, the man's head crushed in where it had been fiendishly battered by some blunt, heavy object. There was no clew — no one could be found who had seen the car on the crossroad — the murderer, or murderers, and the twenty-odd thousand dollars in cash had disappeared leaving no trace behind.

There were several columns of this, which Jimmie Dale skimmed through quickly; but at the end he stared for a long time at the last paragraph. Somehow, strange, to relate, the paper had neglected to turn its "sob" artist loose, and the few words, added almost as though they were an afterthought, for once rang true and full of pathos in their very simplicity — at the Roessle home, where Mrs. Roessle was prostrated, two little tots of five and seven, too young to understand, had gravely received the reporter and told him that some bad man had hurt their daddy.

"Mr. Dale, sir!"

Jimmie Dale lowered his paper. A club attendant was standing before him, respectfully extending a silver card tray. From the man, Jimmie Dale's eyes fixed on a white envelope on the tray. One glance was enough — it was *hers*, that letter. The Tocsin again! His brain seemed suddenly to be afire, and he could feel his pulse quicken, the blood begin to pound in fierce throbs at his heart. Life and death lay in that white, innocent-looking, unaddressed envelope, danger, peril — it was always life and death, for those were the stakes for which the Tocsin played. But, master of many things, Jimmie Dale was most of all master of himself. Not a muscle of his face moved. He reached nonchalantly for the letter.

"Thank you," said Jimmie Dale.

The man bowed and started away. Jimmie Dale laid the envelope on the arm of the lounging chair. The man had reached the door when Jimmie Dale stopped him.

"Oh, by the way," said Jimmie Dale languidly, "where did this come from?"

"Your chauffeur, sir," replied the other. "Your chauffeur gave it to the hall porter a moment ago, sir."

"Thank you," said Jimmie Dale again.

The door closed.

Jimmie Dale glanced around the room. It was the caution of habit, that glance; the habit of years in which his life had hung on little things. He was alone in one of the club's private library rooms. He picked up the envelope, tore it open, took out the folded sheets inside, and began to read. At the first words he leaned forward, suddenly tense in his chair. He read on, turning the pages hurriedly, incredulity, amazement, and, finally, a strange menace mirroring itself in turn upon his face.

He stood up — the letter in his hand.

"My God!" whispered Jimmie Dale.

It was a call to arms such as the Gray Seal had never received before — such as the Tocsin had never made before. And if it were true it — True! He laughed aloud a little gratingly. True! Had the Tocsin, astounding, unbelievable, mystifying as were the means by which she acquired her knowledge not only of this, but of countless other affairs, ever by so much as the smallest detail been astray. If it were true!

He pulled out his watch. It was half-past nine. Benson, his chauffeur, had sent the letter into the club. Benson had been waiting outside there ever since dinner. Jimmie Dale, for the first time since the first communication that he had ever received from the Tocsin, did not immediately destroy her letter now. He slipped it into his pocket — and stepped quickly from the room.

In the cloakroom downstairs he secured his hat and overcoat, and, though it was a warm evening, put on the latter since he was in evening clothes, then walked leisurely out of the club.

At the curb, Benson, the chauffeur, sprang from his seat, and, touching his cap, opened the door of a luxurious limousine.

Jimmie Dale shook his head.

"I shall not keep you waiting any longer, Benson," he said. "You may take the car home, and put it up. I shall probably be late to-night."

"Very good, sir," replied the chauffeur.

"You sent in a letter a moment or so ago, Benson?" observed Jimmie Dale casually, opening his cigarette case.

"Yes, sir," said Benson. "I hope I didn't do wrong, sir. He said it was important, and that you were to have it at once."

"He?" Jimmie Dale was lighting his cigarette now.

"A boy, sir," Benson amplified. "I couldn't get anything out of him. He just said he'd been told to give it to me, and tell me to see that you got it at once. I hope, sir, I haven't—"

"Not at all, Benson," said Jimmie Dale pleasantly. "It's quite all right. Good-night, Benson."

"Good-night, sir," Benson answered, climbing back to his seat.

There was a queer little smile on Jimmie Dale's lips, as he watched the great car swing around in the street and glide noiselessly away — a queer little smile that still held there even after he himself had started briskly along the avenue in a downtown direction. It was invariably the same, always the same — the letters came unexpectedly, when least looked for, now by this means, now by that, but always in a manner that precluded the slightest possibility of tracing them to their source. Was there anything, in his intimate surroundings, in his intimate life, that she did not know about him—who knew absolutely nothing about her! Benson, for instance—that the man was absolutely trustworthy—or else she would never for an instant have risked the letter in his possession. Was there anything that she did not—yes, one thing—she did not know him in the role he was going to play to-night. That at least was one thing that surely she did not know about him; the role in which, many times, for weeks on end, he had devoted himself body and soul in an attempt to solve the mystery with which she surrounded herself; the role, too, that often enough had been a bulwark of safety to him when hard pressed by the police; the role out of which he had so carefully, so painstakingly created a now recognised and well-known character of the underworld—the role of Larry the Bat.

Jimmie Dale turned from Fifth Avenue into Broadway, continued on down Broadway, across to the Bowery, kept along the Bowery for several more blocks—and finally headed east into the dimly lighted cross street on which the Sanctuary was located.

And now Jimmie Dale became cautious in his movements. As he approached the black alleyway that flanked the miserable tenement, he glanced sharply behind and about him; and, at the alleyway itself, without pause, but with a curious lightning-like side step, no longer Jimmie Dale now, but the Gray Seal, he disappeared from the street, and was lost in the deep shadows of the building.

In a moment he was at the side door, listening for any sound from within—none had ever seen or met the lodger or the first floor either ascending or descending, except in the familiar character of Larry the Bat. He opened the door, closed it behind him, and in the utter blackness went noiselessly up the stairs—stairs so rickety that it seemed a mouse's tread alone would have set them creaking. There seemed an art in the play of Jimmie Dale's every muscle; in the movements, lithe, balanced, quick, absolutely silent. On the first landing he stopped before another door, there was the faint click of a key turning in the lock; and then this door, too, closed behind him. Sounded the faint click of the key as it turned again, and Jimmie Dale drew a long breath, stepped across the room to assure himself that the window blind was down, and lighted the gas jet.

A yellow, murky flame spurted up, pitifully weak, almost as though it were ashamed of its disreputable surroundings. Dirt, disorder, squalour, the evidence of low living testified eloquently enough to any one, the police, for instance, in times past inquisitive until they were fatuously content with the belief that they knew the occupant for what he was, that the place was quite in keeping with its tenant, a mute prototype, as it were, of Larry the Bat, the dope fiend.

For a little space, Jimmie Dale, immaculate in his evening clothes, stood in the centre of the miserable room, his dark eyes, keen, alert, critical, sweeping comprehensively over every object about him – the position of a chair, of a cracked drinking glass on the broken-legged table, of an old coat thrown with apparent carelessness on the floor at the foot of the bed, of a broken bottle that had innocently strewn some sort of white powder close to the threshold, inviting unwary foot tracks across the floor. And then, taking out the Tocsin's letter, he laid it upon the table, placed what money he had in his pockets beside it, and began rapidly to remove his clothes. The Sanctuary had not been invaded since his last visit there.

He turned back the oilcloth in the far corner of the room, took up the piece of loose flooring, which, however, strangely enough, fitted so closely as to give no sign of its existence even should it inadvertently, by some curious visitor again be trod upon; and from the aperture beneath lifted out a bundle of clothes and a small box.

Undressed now, he carefully folded the clothes he had taken off, laid them under the flooring, and began to dress again, his wardrobe supplied by the bundle he had taken out in exchange – an old pair of shoes, the laces broken; mismated socks; patched trousers, frayed at the bottoms; a soiled shirt, collarless, open at the neck. Attired to his satisfaction, he placed the box upon the table, propped up a cracked mirror, sat down in front of it, and, with a deft, artist's touch, began to apply stain to his hands, wrists, neck, throat, and face – but the hardness, the grim menace that now grew into the dominant characteristic of his features was not due to the stain alone.

"Dear Philanthropic Crook" – his eyes were on the Tocsin's letter that lay before him. He read on – for once, even to Jimmie Dale's keen, facile mind, a first reading had failed to convey the full significance of what she had written. It was too amazing, almost beyond belief – the series of crimes, rampant for the past few weeks, at which the community had stood aghast, the brutal murder of Roessle but a few hours old, lay bare before his eyes. It was all there, all of it, the details, the hellish cleverness, the personnel even of the thugs, all, everything – except the proof.

"Get him, Jimmie – the man higher up. Get him, Jimmie – before another pays forfeit with his life" – the words seemed to leap out at him from the white page in red, dancing lines – "Get him – Jimmie – the man higher up."

Jimmie Dale finished the second reading of the letter, read it again for the third time, then tore it into tiny fragments. His fingers delved into the box again, and the transformation of Jimmie Dale, member of New York's most exclusive social set, into a low, vicious-featured denizen of the underworld went on – a little wax applied skilfully behind the ears, in the nostrils and under the upper lip.

It was all there – all except the proof. And the proof – he laughed aloud suddenly, unpleasantly. There seemed something sardonic in it; ay, more than that, all that was grim in irony. The proof, in Stangeist's own writing, sworn to before witnesses in the presence of a notary, the text of the document, of course, unknown to both witnesses and notary, evidence, absolute and final, that would be admitted in any court, for Stangeist was a lawyer, and would see to that, was in Stangeist's own safe, for Stangeist's own protection – Stangeist, who was himself the head and brains of this murder gang – Stangeist, who was the man higher up!

It was amazing, without parallel in the history of crime – and yet ingenious, clever, full of the craft and cunning that had built up the shyster lawyer's reputation below the dead line.

Jimmie Dale's lips were curiously thin now. So it was Stangeist! A Doctor Jekyll and Mr. Hyde with a vengeance! He knew Stangeist – not personally; not by the reputation Stangeist held, low even as that was, among his brother members of the profession; but as the man was known for what he really was among the crooks and criminals of the underworld, where, in that strange underground exchange, whispered confidences passed between those whose common enemy was the law, where Larry the Bat himself was trusted in the innermost circles.

Stangeist was a power in the Bad Lands. There were few among that unholy community that Stangeist, at one time or another, in one way or another, had not rescued from the clutches of the law, resorting to any trick or cunning, but with perjury, that he could handle like the master of it that he was, employed as the most common weapon of defence for his clients – provided he were paid well enough for it. The man had become more than the attorney for the crime world – he had become part of it. Cunning, shrewd, crafty, conscienceless, cold-blooded – that was Stangeist.

The form and features of the man pictured themselves in Jimmie Dale's mind – the six-foot muscular frame, that was invariably clothed in attire of the most fashionable cut; the thin lips with their oily, plausible smile, the straight black hair that straggled into pin point, little black eyes, the dark face with its high cheek bones, which, with the pronounced aquiline nose and the persistent rumour that he was a quarter caste, had led the underworld, prejudiced always in favour of a "monaker," to dub the man the "Indian Chief."

Jimmie Dale laughed again – still unpleasantly. So Stangeist had taken the plunge at last and branched out into a wider field, had he? Well, there was nothing surprising in that—except that he had not done it before! The irony of it lay in the fact that at last he had been *too* clever, overstepped himself in his own cleverness, that was all. It was Australian Ike, The Mope, and Clarie Deane that Stangeist had gathered around him, the Tocsin had said—and there were none worse in Larry the Bat's wide range of acquaintanceship than those three. Stangeist had made himself master of Australian Ike, The Mope, and Clarie Deane—and he had driven them a little too hard on the division of the spoils—and laughed at them, and cracked the whip much after the fashion that the trainer in the cage handles the growling beasts around him.

A dozen of the crimes that had appalled and staggered New York they had committed under his leadership; and then, it seemed, they had quarrelled furiously, the three pitted against Stangeist, threatening him, demanding a more equitable share of the proceeds. None was better aware than Stangeist that threats from men of their calibre were likely to result in a grim aftermath—and Stangeist, yesterday, the Tocsin said, had answered them as no other man than Stangeist would either have thought of or have dared to do. One by one, at separate times, covering the other with a revolver, Stangeist had permitted them to read a document that was addressed to the district attorney. It was a confession, complete in every detail, of every crime the four together had committed, implicating Stangeist as fully and unreservedly as it did the other three. It required no commentary! If anything happened to Stangeist, a stab in the dark, for instance, a bullet from some dark alleyway, a blackjack deftly wielded, as only Australian Ike, The Mope or Clarie Deane knew how to wield it—the document automatically became a *death sentence* for Australian Ike, The Mope, and Clarie Deane!

It was very simple—and, evidently, it had been effective, as witness the renewal of their operations in the murder of Roessle that afternoon. Fear and avarice had both probably played their part; fear of the man who would with such consummate nerve fling his life into the balance to turn the tables upon them, while he jeered at them; avarice that prompted them to get what they could out of Stangeist's brains and leadership, and to be satisfied with what they *could* get—since they could get no more!

Satisfied? Jimmie Dale shook his head. No; that was hardly the word—cowed, perhaps, for the moment, would be better. But afterward, with a document like that in existence, when they would never be safe for an instant—well, beasts in the cages had been known to get the better of the man with the whip, and beasts were gentle things compared with Australian Ike, The Mope, and Clarie Deane! Some day they would reverse the tables on the Indian Chief—if they could. And if they couldn't it would not be for the lack of trying.

There would be another act in that drama of the House Divided before the curtain fell! And there would be a sort of grim, poetic justice in it, a temptation almost to let the play work itself out to its own inevitable conclusion, only – Jimmie Dale, the final touches given to his features, stood up, and his hands clenched suddenly, fiercely – it was not just the man higher up alone, there were the other three as well, the whole four of them, all of them, crimes without number at their door, brutal, fiendish acts, damnable outrages, murder to answer for, with which the public now was beginning to connect the name of the Gray Seal! The Gray Seal!

Jimmie Dale's hands, whose delicate fingers were artfully grimed and blackened now beneath the nails, clenched still tighter – and then, with a quick shrug of his shoulders, a thinning of the firmly compressed lips, he picked up the coat from where it lay upon the floor, put it on, put the money that was on the table in his pocket, and replaced the box under the flooring.

In quick succession, from the same hiding place, an automatic, a black silk mask, an electric flashlight, that thin metal box like a cigarette case, and a half dozen vicious-looking little blued-steel burglar's tools were stowed away in his pockets, the flooring carefully replaced, the oilcloth spread back again; and then, pulling a slouch hat well down over his eyes, he reached up to turn off the gas.

For an instant his hand held there, while his eyes, sweeping around the apartment, took in every single detail about him in that same alert, comprehensive way as when he had entered – then the room was in darkness, and the Gray Seal, as Larry the Bat, a shuffling, unkempt creature of the underworld, alias Jimmie Dale, the lionised of clubs, the matrimonial target of exclusive drawing-rooms, closed the door of the Sanctuary behind him, shuffled down the stairs, shuffled out into the lane, and shuffled along the street toward the Bowery.

A policeman on the corner accosted him familiarly. [43]

"Hello, Larry!" grinned the officer.

"'Ello!" returned Jimmie Dale affably through the side of his mouth. "Fine night, ain't it?" – and shuffled on along the street.

And now Jimmie Dale began to hurry – still with that shuffling tread, but covering the ground nevertheless with amazing celerity. He had lost no time since receiving the Tocsin's letter, it was true, but, for all that, it was now after ten o'clock. Stangeist's house was "dark" that evening, she

---

[43] I believe the Sanctuary was located in the 15th Precinct which had its station house at 321 East 5th Street. It was renamed the 9th Precinct in 1929. The station house façade has appeared in several television series including *The Naked City*, *Kojak*, and *NYPD Blue*.

had said, meaning that the occupants, Stangeist as well as whatever servants there might be, for Stangeist had no family, were out – the servants in town for a theatre or picture show probably – and Stangeist himself as yet not back, presumably from that Roessle affair. The stub of an old cigar, unlighted, shifted with a sudden, savage twist of the lips from one side of Jimmie Dale's mouth to the other. There was need for haste. There was no telling when Stangeist might get back – as for the servants, that did not matter so much; servants in suburban homes had a marked affinity for "last trains!"

Jimmie Dale boarded a cross-town car, effected a transfer, and in a quarter of an hour after leaving the Sanctuary was huddled, an inoffensive heap, like a tired-out workingman, in a corner seat of a Long Island train. From here, there was only a short run ahead of him, and, twenty minutes later, descending from the train at Forest Hills, he had passed through the more thickly settled portion of the little place, and was walking briskly out along the country road.

Stangeist's house lay, approximately, a mile and a half from the station, quite by itself, and set well back from the road. Jimmie Dale could have found it with his eyes blindfolded – the Tocsin's directions had lacked none of their usual explicit minuteness. The road was quite deserted. Jimmie Dale met no one. Even in the houses that he passed the lights were in nearly every instance already out.

Something, merciless in its rage, swept suddenly over Jimmie Dale, as, unbidden, of its own volition, the last paragraph he had read in that evening's paper began to repeat itself over and over again in his mind. The two little kiddies – it seemed as though he could see them standing there – and from Jimmie Dale's lips, not given to profanity, there came a bitter oath. It might possibly be that, even if he were successful in what was before him to-night, the authors of the Roessle murder would never be known. That confession of Stangeist's was written prior to what had happened that afternoon, and there would be no mention, naturally, of Roessle. And, for a moment, that seemed to Jimmie Dale the one thing paramount to all others, the one thing that was vital; then he shook his head, and laughed out shortly. After all, it did not matter – whether Stangeist and the blood wolves he had gathered around him paid the penalty specifically for one particular crime or for another could make little difference – they would *pay,* just as surely, just as certainly, once that paper was in his possession!

Jimmie Dale was counting the houses as he passed – they were more infrequent now, farther apart. Stangeist was no fool – not the fool that he would appear to be for keeping a document like that, once he had had the temerity to execute it, in his own safe; for, in a day or two, the Tocsin had hinted at this, after holding it over the heads of Australian Ike, The Mope, and Clarie Deane again to drive the force of it a little deeper home, he would undoubtedly destroy it — and the *supposition* that it was still in existence would have equally the same effect on the minds of the other three! Stangeist was certainly alive to the peril that he ran with such a thing in his possession, only the peril had not appealed to him as imminent either from the three thugs with whom he had allied himself, or, much less, from any one else, that was all.

Jimmie Dale halted by a low, ornamental stone fence, some three feet high, and stood there for a moment, glancing about him. This was Stangeist's house — he could just make out the building as it loomed up a shadowy, irregular shape, perhaps two hundred yards back from the fence. The house was quite dark, not a light showed in any window. Jimmie Dale sat down casually on the fence, looked carefully again up and down the road — then, swinging his legs over, quick now in every action, he dropped to the other side, and stole silently across the grass to the rear of the house.

Here he stopped again, reached up to a window that was about on a level with his shoulders, and tested its fastenings. The window — it was the window of Stangeist's private sanctum, according to the plan in her letter — was securely locked. Jimmie Dale's hands went into his pocket — and the black silk mask was slipped over his face. He listened intently — then a little steel instrument began to gnaw like a rat.

A minute passed — two of them. Again Jimmie Dale listened. There was not a sound save the night sounds — the light breeze whispering through the branches of the trees; the far-off rumble of a train; the whir of insects; the hoarse croaking of a frog from some near-by creek or pond. The window sash was raised an inch, another, and gradually to the top. Like a shadow, Jimmie Dale pulled himself up to the sill, and, poised there, his hand parted the heavy portières that hung within. It was too dark to distinguish even a single object in the room. He lowered himself to the floor, and slipped cautiously between the portières.

From somewhere in the house, a clock began to strike. Jimmie Dale counted the strokes. Eleven o'clock. It was getting late — *too* late! Stangeist was likely to be back at any moment. The flashlight, in Jimmie Dale's hand now, circled the room with its little round white ray, lingering an instant in a queer, inquisitive sort of way here and there on this object and that — and went out. Jimmie Dale nodded — the flat desk in the centre of the floor, the safe in the corner by the rear wall, the position of everything in the room, even to the chairs, was photographed on his mind.

He stepped from the portières to the safe, and the flashlight played again—this time reflecting back from the glistening nickelled knobs. Jimmie Dale's lips tightened. It was a small safe, almost ludicrously small; but to such height as the art of safe design had been carried, that design was embodied in the one before him.

"Type K-four-two-eight-Colby," muttered Jimmie Dale. "A nasty little beggar—and it's eleven o'clock now! I'd use 'soup' for once, if it weren't that it would put Stangeist wise, and give him a chance to make his getaway before the district attorney got the nippers on the four of them."

The light went out. Jimmie Dale dropped to his knees; and, while his left hand passed swiftly, tentatively over dials and handle, he rubbed the fingers of his right hand rapidly to and fro over the carpet. Wonderful finger tips were those of Jimmie Dale, sensitive to an abnormal degree; and now, tingling with the friction, the nerves throbbing at the skin surface, they closed in a light, delicate touch upon the knob of the dial—and Jimmie Dale's ear pressed close against the face of the safe.

Time passed. The silence grew heavy—seemed to palpitate through the room. Then a deep breath, half like a sigh, half like a fluttering sob as of a strong man taxed to the uttermost of his endurance, came from Jimmie Dale, and his left hand swept away the sweat beads that had spurted to his forehead.

"Eight—thirteen—twenty-two," whispered Jimmie Dale.

There was a click, a low metallic thud as the bolts slid back, and the door swung open.

And now the flashlight again, searching the mechanism of the inner door—then darkness once more.

Five minutes, ten minutes went by. The clock struck again—and the single stroke seemed to boom out through the house in a weird, raucous, threatening note, and seemed to linger, throbbing in the air.

The inner door was open—the flashlight's ray was flooding a nest of pigeonholes and little drawers. The pigeonholes were crammed with papers, as, presumably, too, were the drawers. Jimmie Dale sucked in his breath. He had already been there well over half an hour—every minute now, every second was counting against him, and to search that mass of papers before Stangeist returned was—

"Ah!"—it came in a fierce little ejaculation from Jimmie Dale. From the centre pigeonhole, almost the first paper he had touched, he drew a long, sealed envelope and at a single swift glance had read the inscription upon it, written in longhand:

TO THE DISTRICT ATTORNEY,

NEW YORK CITY.

Important.   *Urgent.*

The words in the corners were underscored three times.

Swiftly, deftly, Jimmie Dale's fingers rolled the rounded end of one of his collection of little steel instruments under the flap of the envelope, turned the flap back, and drew out the folded document inside. There were four sheets of legal foolscap, neatly fastened together at the top left-hand corner with green tape. He opened them out, read a few words here and there, and turned the pages hurriedly over to scrutinise the last one — and nodded grimly. Three witnesses had testified to the signature of Stangeist, and a notary's seal, accompanied by the usual legal formula, was duly affixed.

Jimmie Dale slipped the document into his pocket, and, with the envelope in his hand, moved to the desk. He opened first one drawer and then another, and finally discovering a pile of blank foolscap, took out four sheets, folded them, and placed them in the envelope, sealing the flap of the latter again. That it did not seal very well now brought a quizzical twitch to Jimmie Dale's lips. Sealed or unsealed, perhaps, it made little difference; but, for all that, he was not through with it yet. Apart from bringing the four to justice, there was, after all, a chance to vindicate the Gray Seal in this matter at least, and repudiate the newspaper theory which the public, to whom the Gray Seal was already a monster of iniquity, would seize upon with avidity.

There was no further need of light now. Jimmie Dale replaced the flashlight in his pocket, took out the thin, metal case, opened it, and with the tiny pair of tweezers that likewise nestled there, lifted out one of the gray, diamond-shaped paper seals. There was no question but that, once under arrest, Stangeist's effects would be immediately and thoroughly searched by the authorities! Jimmie Dale's smile from quizzical became ironic. It would afford the police another little, bewildering reminder of the Gray Seal, and give Carruthers, good old Carruthers of the *Morning News-Argus,* so innocently ignorant that the Gray Seal was his old college pal, yet the one editor of them all who was not forever barking and yelping at the Gray Seal's heels, a chance to vindicate himself a little, too! Jimmie Dale moistened the adhesive side of the gray seal, and, still mindful of tell-tale finger prints, laid it with the tweezers on the flap of the envelope, and pressed it firmly into place with his elbow.

And then, suddenly, every faculty instantly on the alert, he snatched up the envelope from the desk, and listened. Was it imagination, a trick of nerves, or — no, there it was again! — a footfall on the gravel walk at the front of the house. The sound became louder, clearer — two footfalls instead of one. It was Stangeist, and somebody was with him.

In an instant Jimmie Dale was across the room and kneeling again before the safe. His fingers were flying now. The envelope shot back into the pigeonhole from which he had taken it — the inner door of the safe closed silently and swiftly.

A dry chuckle came from Jimmie Dale's lips. It was just like fiction, just precisely time enough to have accomplished what he had come for before he was interrupted, not a second more or less, the villain foiled at the psychological moment! The key was rattling in the front door now — they were in the hall — he could hear Stangeist's voice — there came a dull glow from the hallway, following the click of an electric-light switch. The outer door of the safe swung shut, the bolts slid into place, the dial whirled under Jimmie Dale's fingers. It was only a step to the portières, the open window — and escape. He straightened up, stepped back, the portières closed behind him — and the chuckle died on Jimmie Dale's lips.

He was trapped — caught without so much as a corner in which to turn! Stangeist was even then coming into the room — and *outside,* darkly outlined, two forms stood just beneath the window. Instinctively, quick as a flash, Jimmie Dale crouched below the sill. Who were they? What did it mean? Questions swept in swift sequence through his brain. Had they seen him? It would be very dark against the background of the portières, but yet if they were watching — he drew a breath of relief. He had not been seen. Their voices reached him in low, guarded whispers.

"Say, youse, Ike, pipe it! Dere's a window open in the snitch's room. Come on, we'll get in dere. It'll make the hair stand up on the back of his neck fer a starter."

"Aw, ferget it!" replied another voice. "Can the tee-ayter stunt! Clarie leaves the front door unfastened, don't he? An' dey'll be in dere in a minute now. Wotcher want ter do? Crab the game? He might hear us an' fix Clarie before we had a chanst, the skinny old fox! An' dere's the light now — see! Beat it on yer toes fer the front of the house!"

The room was flooded with light. Through the portières, that Jimmie Dale parted by the barest fraction of an inch, he could see Stangeist and another man, a thick-set, ugly-faced-looking customer — Clarie Deane, according to that brief, whispered colloquy that he had heard outside. He looked again through the window. The two dark forms had disappeared now, but they had disappeared just a few seconds too late — with the two other men now in the room, and one of them so close that Jimmie Dale could almost have reached out and touched him, it was impossible to get through the window without being detected, when the slightest sound would attract instant attention and equally instant suspicion. It was a chance to be taken only as a last resort.

Jimmie Dale's face grew hard, as his fingers closed around his automatic and drew the weapon from his pocket. It was all plain enough. That last act in the drama which he had speculatively anticipated was being staged with little loss of time – and in a grim sort of way the thought flashed across his mind that, perilous as his own position was, Stangeist at that moment was in even greater peril than himself. Australian Ike, The Mope, and Clarie Deane, given the chance, and they seemed to have made that chance now, were not likely to deal in half measures – Clarie Deane had dropped into a chair beside the desk; and The Mope and Australian Ike were creeping around to the front door!

The parting in the portières widened a little more, a very little more, slowly, imperceptibly, until Jimmie Dale, by the simple expedient of moving his head, could obtain an unobstructed view of the entire room.

Stangeist tossed a bag he had been carrying on the desk, pulled up a chair opposite to Clarie Deane, and sat down. Both men were side face to Jimmie Dale.

"You tell the boys," said Stangeist abruptly, "to fade away after this for a while. Things are getting too hot. And you tell The Mope I dock him five hundred for that extra crunch on Roessle's skull. That sort of thing isn't necessary. That's the kind of stunt that gets the public sore – the man was dead enough as it was. See?"

"Sure!" Clarie Deane's ejaculation was a grunt.

Stangeist opened the bag, and dumped the contents on the desk – pile after pile of banknotes, the pay roll of the Martindale-Kensington Mills.

"Some haul!" observed Clarie Deane, with a hoarse chuckle. "The papers said over twenty thousand."

"You can't always believe what the papers say," returned Stangeist curtly; and, taking a scribbling pad from the desk, began to check up the packages.

Clarie Deane's cigar had gone out. He rolled the short stub in his mouth, and leaned forward.

The bills were evidently just as they had been delivered to the murdered paymaster at the bank, done up with little narrow paper bands in packages of one hundred notes each, save for a small bundle of loose bills which latter, with the rolls of silver, Stangeist swept to one side of the desk.

Package by package, Stangeist went on jotting the amounts down on the pad.

"Nix!" growled Clarie Deane suddenly. "Cut that out! Them's fivers in that wad. Make that five hundred instead of one – I'm onter yer!"

"Mistake," said Stangeist suavely, changing the figures with his pencil. "You're pretty wide awake for this time of night, aren't you, Clarie?"

"Oh, I dunno!" responded Clarie Deane gruffly. "Not so very!"

Stangeist, finished with the packages, picked up the loose bills, and, with a short laugh, tossed them into the bag and followed them with the rolls of silver. He pushed the bag toward Clarie Deane.

"That's a little extra for you," he said. "The trouble with you fellows is that you don't know when you're well off – but the sooner you find it out the better, unless you want another lesson like yesterday." He made the addition on the pad. "Fifteen thousand, eight hundred dollars," he announced softly. "That's seven thousand, nine hundred for the three of you to divide, less five hundred from The Mope."

Clarie Deane's eyes narrowed. His hands were on his knees, hidden by the desk.

"There's more'n twenty there," he said sullenly – and drew a match across the under edge of the desk with a long, crackling noise.

Stangeist's face lost its suavity, a snarl curled his lips; but, about to reply, he sprang suddenly to his feet instead, his head turned sharply toward the door.

"What's that!" he said hoarsely. "It's not the servants, they wouldn't dare to –"

Stangeist's words ended in a gulp. He was staring into the muzzle of a heavy-calibered revolver that Clarie Deane had jerked up from under the desk.

"You sit down, or I'll blow your block off!" said Clarie Deane, with a sudden leer.

It happened then almost before Jimmie Dale could grasp the details; before even Clarie Deane himself could interfere. The door burst open, two men rushed in – and one, with a bound, flung himself at Stangeist. The man's hand, grasping a clubbed revolver, rose in the air, descended on Stangeist's head – and Stangeist went down in a limp heap, crashed into the chair, and slid from the chair with a thud to the floor.

There was an oath from Clarie Deane. He jumped from his seat, and with a violent shove sent the man reeling half across the room.

"Blast you, Mope!" he snarled. "You're too blamed fly! D'ye wanter queer the whole biz?"

"Aw, wot's the matter wid youse!" The Mope, purple-faced with rage, little black eyes glittering, mouth working under a flattened nose that some previous encounter had broken and bent over the side of his face, advanced belligerently.

Australian Ike, who had entered the room with him, pulled him back.

"Ferget it!" he flung out. "Clarie's dealin' the deck. Ferget it!"

The Mope glared from one to the other; then shook his fist at Stangeist on the floor.

"Youse two make me sick!" he sneered. "Wot's the use of waitin' all night? We was to bump him off, anyway, wasn't we? Dat's wot youse said yerselves, 'cause wot was ter stop him writin' out another paper if we didn't fix him fer keeps?"

"That's all right," rejoined Clarie Deane; "but that's the second act, you bonehead, see! We ain't got the paper yet, have we? Say, take a look at that safe! It's easier ter scare him inter openin' it than ter crack it, ain't it?"

Jimmie Dale, from his crouched position, began to rise to his feet slowly, making but the slightest movement at a time, cautious of the least sound. His lips were like a thin line, his fingers tightly pressed over the automatic in his hand. There was not room for him between the portières and the window; and, do what he could, the hangings bulged a little. Let one of the three notice that, or inadvertently brush against the portières, and his life would not be worth an instant's purchase.

They were lifting Stangeist up now, propping him up in the chair. Stangeist moaned, opened his eyes, stared in a dazed way at the three faces that leered into his, then dawning intelligence came, and his face, that had been white before, took on a pasty, grayish pallor.

"You – the three of you!" he mumbled. "What's this mean?"

And then Clarie Deane laughed in a low, brutal way.

"Wot d'ye think it means? We want that paper, an' we want it damn quick – see! D'ye think we was goin' ter stand fer havin' a trip ter Sing Sing an' the wire chair danglin' over our heads!"

Stangeist closed his eyes. When he opened them again, something of the old-time craftiness was in his face.

"Well, what are you going to do about it?" he inquired, almost sharply. "You know what will happen to you, if anything happens to me."

"Don't youse kid yerself!" retorted Clarie Deane. "D'ye think we're fools? This ain't like it was yesterday – see! We *gets* the paper this time – so there won't nothin' happen to us. You come across with it blasted quick now, or The Mope'll give you another on the bean that'll put you to sleep fer keeps!"

187

The blood was running down Stangeist's face. He wiped it away from his eyes.

"It's not here," he said innocently. "It's in my box in the safety-deposit vaults."

"Aw," blurted out Australian Ike, pushing suddenly forward, "youse can't work dat crawl on —"

"Cut it out, Ike!" snapped Clarie Dane. "I'm runnin' this! So it's in the vaults, eh?" He shoved his face toward Stangeist's.

"Yes," said Stangeist easily. "You see — I was looking for something like this."

Clarie Deane's fist clenched.

"You lie!" he choked. "The Mope, here, was the last of us you showed the paper to yesterday afternoon, an' the vaults was closed then — an' you ain't been there to-day, 'cause you've been watched. That's why we fixed it fer to-night after the divvy that you've just tried ter do us on again, 'cause we knew you had it here."

"I tell you, it's not here," said Stangeist evenly.

"You lie!" said Clarie Deane again. "It's in that safe. The Mope heard you tell the girl in yer office that if anything happened to you she was ter wise up the district attorney that there was a paper in your safe at home fer him that was important. Now then, you beat it over ter that safe, an' open it up — we'll give you a minute ter do it in."

"The paper's not there, I tell you," said Stangeist once more.

"That's all right," submitted Clarie Deane grimly. "There's a quarter of that minute gone."

"I won't!" Stangeist flashed out violently.

"That's all right," repeated Clarie Deane. "There's half of that minute gone."

Jimmie Dale's eyes, in a fascinated sort of way, were on Stangeist. The man's face was twitching now, moisture began to ooze from his forehead, as the callous brutality of the scowling faces seemed to get him — and then he lurched suddenly forward in his chair.

"My God!" he cried out, a ring of terror in his voice "What do you mean to do? You'll pay for it! They'll get you! The servants will be back in a minute."

"Two skirts!" jeered Clarie Deane. "We ain't goin' ter run away from them. If they comes before we goes, we'll fix 'em. That minute's up!"

Stangeist licked his lips with his tongue.

"Suppose — suppose I refuse?" he said hoarsely.

"You can suit yerself," said Clarie Deane, with a vicious grin. "We know the paper's there, an' we gets it before we leaves here — see? You can take yer choice. Either you goes over ter the safe an' opens it yerself, or else" — he paused and produced a small bottle from his pocket — "this is nitro-glycerin', an' we opens it fer you with this. Only if we does the job we does it proper. We ties you up and sets you against the door of the safe before we touches off the 'soup,' an' mabbe if yer a good guesser you can guess the rest."

There was a short, raucous guffaw from The Mope.

Stangeist turned a drawn face toward the man, stared at him, and stared in a miserable way at the other two in turn. He licked his lips again — none was in a better position than himself to know that there would be neither scruples nor hesitancy to interfere with carrying out the threat.

"Suppose," he said, trying to keep his voice steady, "suppose I open the safe — what then — afterward?"

"We ain't got the safe open yet," countered Clarie Deane uncompromisingly. "An' we ain't got no more time ter fool over it, either. You get a move on before I counts five, or The Mope an' Ike ties you up! One — "

Stangeist staggered to his feet, wiped the blood out of his eyes for the second time, and, with lips working, went unsteadily across the room to the safe.

He knelt before it, and began to manipulate the dial; while the others crowded around behind him. The Mope was fingering his revolver again club fashion. Australian Ike's elbow just grazed the portières, and Jimmie Dale flattened himself against the window, holding his breath — a smile on his lips that was mirthless, deadly, cold. The end was not far off now; and then — *what?*

Stangeist had the outer door of the safe open now — and now the inner door swung back. He reached in his hand to the pigeonhole, drew out the envelope — and with a sudden, wild cry, reeled to his feet.

"My God!" he screamed out. "What's — what's this!"

Clarie Deane snatched the envelope from him.

"The Gray Seal!" — the words came with a jerk from his lips. He ripped the envelope open frantically — and like a man stunned gazed at the four blank sheets, while the colour left his face. *"It's gone!"* he cried out hoarsely.

"Gone!" There was a burst of oaths from Australian Ike. "Gone! Den we're nipped — de lot of us!"

The Mope's face was like a maniac's as he whirled on Stangeist.

"Sure!" he croaked. "But youse gets yers first, youse – "

With a cry, Stangeist, to elude the blow, ducked blindly backward – into the portières – and with a rip and tear the hangings were wrenched apart.

It came instantaneously – a yell of mingled surprise and fury from the three – the crash and spit of Jimmie Dale's revolver as he fired one shot at the floor to stop their rush – then he flung himself at the window, through it, and dropped sprawling to the ground.

A stream of flame cut the darkness above him, a bullet whistled by his head – another – and another. He was on his feet, quick as a cat, and running close alongside of the wall of the house. He heard a thud behind him, still another, and yet a third – they were dropping through the window after him. Came another shot, an angry hum of the bullet closer than before – then the pound of racing feet.

Jimmie Dale swung around the corner of the house, running at top speed. Something that was like a hot iron suddenly burned and seared along the side of his head just above the ear. He reeled, staggered, recovered himself, and dashed on. It nauseated him, that stinging in his head, and all at once seemed to be draining his strength away. The shouts, the shots, the running feet became like a curious buzzing in his ears. It seemed strange that they should have hit him, that he should be wounded! If he could only reach the low stone wall by the road, he could at least make a fight for his life on the other side!

Red streaks swam before Jimmie Dale's eyes. The wall was such a long way off – a yard or two was a very long way more to go – the weakness seemed to be creeping up now even to numb his brain. No, here was the wall – they hadn't hit him again – he laughed in a demented way – and rolled his body over, and fell to the other side.

"Jimmie!"

The cry seemed to reach some inner consciousness, revive him, send the blood whipping through his veins. That voice! It was her – hers! The Tocsin! There was an automobile, engine racing, standing there in the road. He won to his feet – dark, rushing forms were almost at the wall. He fired – once – twice – fired again – and turned, staggering for the car.

"Jimmie! Jimmie – quick!"

Panting, gasping, he half fell into the tonneau. The car leaped forward, yells filled the air – but only one thing was dominant in Jimmie Dale's reeling brain now. He pulled himself up to his feet, and leaned over the back of the seat, reaching for the slim figure that was bent over the wheel.

"It's you – you at last!" he cried. "Your face – let me see your face!"

A bullet split the back panel of the car – little spurting flames were dancing out from the roadway behind.

"Are you mad!" she shouted back at him. "Let me steer – do you want them to hit me!"

"No-o," said Jimmie Dale, in a queer singsong sort of way, and his head seemed to spin dizzily around. "No – I guess – " He choked. "The paper – it's in – my pocket" – and he went down unconscious on the floor of the car.

When he recovered his senses he was lying on a couch in a plainly furnished room, and a man, a stranger, red, jovial-faced, farmerish looking, was bending over him.

"Where am I?" he demanded finally, propping himself up on his elbow.

"You're all right," replied the man. "She said you'd come around in a little while."

"Who said so?" inquired Jimmie Dale.

"She did. The woman who brought you here about five minutes ago. She said she ran you down with her car."

"Oh!" said Jimmie Dale. He felt his head – it was bandaged, and it was bandaged, he was quite sure, with a piece of torn underskirt. He looked at the man again. "You haven't told me yet where I am."

"Long Island," the other answered. "My name's Hanson. I keep a bit of a truck garden here."

"Oh," said Jimmie Dale again.

The man crossed the room, picked up an envelope from the table, and came back to Jimmie Dale.

"She said to give you this as soon as you got your senses, and asked us to put you up for a while, as long as you wanted to stay, and paid us for it, too. She's all right, she is. You don't want to hold the accident up against her, she was mighty sorry about it. And now I'll go and see if the old lady's got your room ready while you're readin' your letter."

The man left the room.

Jimmie Dale sat up on the couch, and tore the envelope open. The note, scrawled in pencil, began abruptly:

"You were quite a problem. I couldn't take you *home* – could I?

couldn't take you to what you call the Sanctuary could I? [44] I couldn't take you to a hospital, nor call in a doctor — the stain you use wouldn't stand it. [45] But, thank God! I know it's only a flesh wound, and you are all right where you are for the day or two that you must keep quiet and take care of yourself. By the time you read this the paper will be on the way to the proper hands, and by morning the four where they should be. There were a few articles in your clothes I thought it better to take charge of in case — well, in case of accident."

Jimmie Dale tore the note up, and smiled wryly at the door. He felt in his pockets. Mask, revolver, burglar's tools, and the thin metal insignia case were gone.

"And I had the sublime optimism," murmured Jimmie Dale, "to spend months trying to find her as Larry the Bat!"

---

[44] Dale is too preoccupied to notice right now but the Tocsin should *not* know what he calls his secret identity-changing hideout. Whether as himself or as Larry the Bat he wouldn't have ever mentioned it to anyone else. Apparently while unconscious here he was speaking aloud.

[45] The implication being that Tocsin has access to better makeup materials.

CHAPTER IX

TWO CROOKS AND A KNAVE

(Thursday 10/7/1915 to Friday 10/8/1915)

 THE bullet wound along the side of his head and just above his ear would have been a very awkward thing indeed, in more ways than one, for Jimmie Dale, the millionaire, to have explained at his club, in his social set, or even to his servants, and of these latter to Jason the Solicitous in particular; but for Jimmie Dale as Larry the Bat it was a matter of little moment. There was none to question Larry the Bat, save in a most casual and indifferent way; and a bandage of any description, primarily and above all one that he could arrange himself, with only himself to take note of the incongruous hues of skin where the stain, the grease paint, and the make-up was washed off, would excite little attention in that world where daily affrays were common-place happenings, and a wound, for whatever reason, had long since lost the tang of novelty. Why then should it arouse even a passing interest if Larry the Bat, credited as the most confirmed of dope fiends, should have fallen down the dark, rickety stairs of the tenement in one of his orgies, and, in the expressive language of the Bad Lands, cracked his bean!

And so Jimmie Dale had been forced to maintain the role of Larry the Bat for a far longer period than he had anticipated when, ten days before, he had assumed it for the night's work that had so nearly resulted fatally for himself, though it had placed Roessle's murderers behind the bars. For, the next day, unwilling to court the risk of remaining in that neighbourhood, he had left Hanson's, the farmer's, house on Long Island where the Tocsin had carried him in an unconscious state, telephoned Jason that he had been unexpectedly called out of town for a few days, and returned to the Sanctuary in New York. And here, to his grim dismay, he had found the underworld in a state of furious, angry unrest, like a nest of hornets, stirred up, seeking to wreak vengeance on an unseen assailant.

For years, as the Gray Seal, Jimmie Dale had lived with the slogan of the police, "The Gray Seal dead or alive – but the Gray Seal!" sounding in his ears; with the newspapers screaming their diatribes, arousing the people against him, nagging the authorities into sleepless, frenzied efforts to trap him; with a price upon his head that was large enough to make a man, not too pretentious, rich for life – but in the underworld, until then, the name of the Gray Seal had been one to conjure with, for the underworld had sworn by the unknown master criminal, and had spoken his name with a reverence that was none the less genuine even if pungently tainted with unholiness. But now it was different. Up and down through the Bad Lands, in gambling hells, in vicious resorts, in the hiding places where thugs and crooks burrowed themselves away from the daylight, through the heart and the outskirts of the underworld travelled the fiat, whispered out of mouths crooked to one side – *death to the Gray Seal!*

Gangland differences were forgotten in the larger issue of the common weal. The gang spirit became the spirit of a united whole, and the crime fraternity buzzed and hummed poisonously, spurred on by hatred, thirst for revenge, fear, and, perhaps most potent of all, a hideous suspicion now of each other.

The underworld had received a shock at which it stood aghast, and which, with its terrifying possibilities, struck consternation into the soul of every individual of that brotherhood whose bond was crime, who was already "wanted" for some offence or other, whether it ranged from murder in the first degree to some petty piece of sneak thievery. Stangeist, the Indian chief, the lawyer whose cunning brain had stood as a rampart between the underworld and a prison cell, was himself now in the Tombs with the certainty of the electric chair before him; and with him, the same fate equally assured, were Australian Ike, The Mope, and Clarie Deane! Aristocrats of the Bad Lands, peers of that inglorious realm were those four – and the blow had fallen with stunning force, a blow that in itself would have been enough to have stirred the underworld to its depths. But that was not all – from the cells in the Tombs, from the four came the word, and passed from mouth to mouth in that strange underground exchange until all had heard it, that the Gray Seal had *"squealed."* The Gray Seal who, though unknown, they had counted the most eminent among themselves, had squealed! Who was the Gray Seal? If he had held the secrets of Stangeist and his band, what else might he not know? Who else might not fall next? The Gray Seal had become a snitch, a menace, a source of danger that stalked among them like a ghastly spectre. Who was the Gray Seal? None knew.

"Death to the Gray Seal! Run him to earth!" went the whisper from lip to lip; and with the whisper men stared uncertainly into each other's faces, fearful that the one to whom they spoke might even be – the Gray Seal!

Jimmie Dale's lips twisted queerly as he looked around him at the squalid appointments of the Sanctuary. The police were bad enough, the papers were worse; but this was a still graver peril. With every denizen of the underworld below the dead line suspicious of each other, their lives, the penitentiary, or a prison sentence the stakes against which each one played, the role of Larry the Bat, clever as was the make-up and disguise, was fraught now more than ever before with danger and peril. It seemed as though slowly the net was beginning at last to tighten around him.

The murky, yellow flame of the gas jet flickered suddenly, as though in acquiescence with the quick, impulsive shrug of Jimmie Dale's shoulders – and Jimmie Dale, bending to peer into the cracked mirror that was propped up on the broken-legged table, knotted his dress tie almost fastidiously. The hair, if just a trifle too long, covered the scar on his head now, the wound no longer required a bandage, and Larry the Bat, for the time being at least, had disappeared. Across the foot of the bed, neatly folded, lay his dress coat and overcoat, but little creased for all that they had lain in that hiding-place under the flooring since the night when, hurrying from the club, he had placed them there to assume instead the tatters of Larry the Bat. It was Jimmie Dale in his own person again who stood there now in Larry the Bat's disreputable den, an incongruous figure enough against the background of his miserable surroundings, in perfect-fitting shoes and trousers, the broad expanse of spotless white shirt bosom glistening even in the poverty-stricken flare from the single, sputtering gas jet.

Jimmie Dale took the watch from his pocket that had not been wound for many days, wound it mechanically, set it by guesswork – it was not far from eight o'clock – and replaced it in his pocket. Carefully then, one at a time, he examined his fingers, long, slim, sensitive, tapering fingers, magical masters of safes and locks and vaults of the most intricate and modern mechanism – no single trace of grime remained, they were metamorphosed hands from the filthy paws of Larry the Bat. He nodded in satisfaction; and picked up the mirror for a final inspection of himself, that, this time, did not miss a single line in his face or neck. Again Jimmie Dale nodded. As though he had vanished into thin air, as though he had never existed, not a trace of Larry the Bat remained – except the heap of rags upon the floor, the battered slouch hat, the frayed trousers, the patched boots with their broken laces, the mismated socks, the grimy flannel shirt, and the old coat that he had just discarded.

The mirror was replaced on the table; and, pushing the heap of clothes before him with his foot, Jimmie Dale knelt down in the corner of the room where the oilcloth had been turned up and the loose planking of the floor removed, and began to pack the articles away in the hole. Jimmie Dale rolled the trousers of Larry the Bat into a compact little bundle, and stuffed them under the flooring. The gas jet seemed to blink again in a sort of confidential approval, as though the secret lay inviolate between itself and Jimmie Dale. Through the closed window, shade tightly drawn, came, low and muffled, the sound of distant life from the Bowery, a few blocks away. The gas jet, suffering from air somewhere within the pipes, hissed angrily, the yellow flame died to a little blue, forked spurt – and Jimmie Dale was on his feet, his face suddenly hard and white as marble.

Some one was knocking at the door!

For the fraction of a second Jimmie Dale stood motionless. Found as Jimmie Dale in the den of Larry the Bat, and the consequences required no effort of the imagination to picture them; police or denizen of the underworld who was knocking there, it was all the same, the method of death would be a little different, that was all – one legalised, the other not. Jimmie Dale, Larry the Bat, the Gray Seal, once uncovered, could expect as much quarter as would be given to a cornered rat. His eyes swept the room with a swift, critical glance – evidences of Larry the Bat, the clothes, were still about, even if he in the person of Jimmie Dale, alone damning enough, were not standing there himself. And he was even weaponless – the Tocsin had taken the revolver from his pocket, together with those other telltale articles, the mask, the flashlight, the little blued-steel tools, before she had intrusted him that night, wounded and unconscious, to Hanson's care.

Jimmie Dale slipped his feet out of his low evening pumps, snatched up the old coat and hat from the pile, put them on, and, without a sound, reached the gas jet and turned it off. A second had gone by – no more – the knocking still sounded insistently on the door. It was dark now, perfectly black. He started across the room, his tread absolutely silent as the trained muscles, relaxing, threw the body weight gradually upon one foot before the next step was taken. It was like a shadow, a little blacker in outline than the surrounding blackness, stealing across the floor.

Halfway to the door he paused. The knocking had ceased. He listened intently. It was not repeated. Instead, his ear caught a guarded step retreating outside in the hall. Jimmie Dale drew a breath of relief. He went on again to the door, still listening. Was it a trap – that step outside?

At the door now, tense, alert, he lowered his ear to the keyhole. There came the faintest creak from the stairs. Jimmie Dale's brows gathered. It was strange! The knocking had not lasted long. Whoever it was was going away – but it required the utmost caution to descend those stairs, rickety and tumble-down as they were, with no more sound than that! Why such caution? Why not a more determined and prolonged effort at his door – the visitor had been easily satisfied that Larry the Bat was not within. *Too* easily satisfied! Jimmie Dale turned the key noiselessly in the lock. He opened the door cautiously – half inch – an inch, there was no sound of footsteps now. Occasionally a lodger moved about on the floor above; occasionally from somewhere in the tenement came the murmur of voices as from behind closed doors—that was all. All else was silence and darkness now.

The door, on its well-oiled hinges, swung wide open. Jimmie Dale thrust out his head into the hall—and something fell upon the threshold with a little thud—but for a moment Jimmie Dale did not move. Listening, trying to pierce the darkness, he was as still as the silence around him; then he stooped and groped along the threshold. His hand closed upon what seemed like a small box wrapped in paper. He picked it up, closed and locked the door again, and retreated back across the room. It was strange—unpleasantly strange—a box propped stealthily against the door so that it would fall to the threshold when the door was opened! And why the stealth? What did it mean? Had the underworld with its thousand eyes and ears already succeeded in a few days where the police had failed signally for years—had they sent him this, whatever it was, as some grim token that they had run Larry the Bat to earth? He shook his head. No; gangland struck more swiftly, with less finesse than that—the "cat-and-mouse" act was never one it favoured, for the mouse had been known to get away.

Jimmie Dale lighted the gas again, and turned the package over in his hands. It was, as he had surmised, a small cardboard box; and it was wrapped in plain paper and tied with a string. He untied the string, and still suspicious, as a man is suspicious in the knowledge that he is stalked by peril at every turn, removed the wrapper a little gingerly. It was still without sign or marking upon it, just an ordinary cardboard box. He lifted off the cover, and, with a short, sudden laugh, stared, a little out of countenance, at the contents.

On the top lay a white, unaddressed envelope. *Hers!* Beneath—he emptied the box on the table—his black silk mask, his automatic revolver, the kit of fine, small blued-steel burglar's tools, his pocket flashlight, and the thin metal insignia case. The Tocsin! Impulsively Jimmie Dale turned toward the door—and stopped. His shoulders lifted in a shrug that, meant to be philosophical, was far from philosophical. He could not, dared not venture far through the tenement dressed as he was; and even if he could there were three exits to the Sanctuary, a fact that now for the first time was not wholly a source of unmixed satisfaction to him; and besides—she was gone!

Jimmie Dale opened the letter, a grim smile playing on his lips. He had forgotten for the moment that the illusion he had cherished for years in the belief that she did not know Larry the Bat as an alias of Jimmie Dale was no more than—an illusion. Well, it had been a piece of consummate egotism on his part, that was all. But, after all, what did it matter? He had had his innings, tried in the role of Larry the Bat to solve her identity, devoted weeks on end to the attempt – and failed. Some day, perhaps, his turn would come; some day, perhaps, she would no longer be able to elude him, unless – the letter crackled suddenly in his fingers – unless the house that they had built on such strange and perilous foundations crashed at some moment, without an instant's warning, in disaster and ruin to the ground. Who knew but that this letter now, another call to the Gray Seal to act, another peril invited, would be the *last?* There must be an end some day; luck and nerve had their limitations – it had almost ended last week!

"Dear Philanthropic Crook" – it was the same inevitable beginning. "You are well enough again, aren't you, Jimmie? – I am sending these little things back to you, for you will need them to-night." – Jimmie Dale read on, muttering snatches of the letter aloud: "Michael Breen prospecting in Alaska – map of location of rich mining claim – Hamvert, his former partner, had previously fleeced him of fifteen thousand dollars – his share of a deal together – Breen was always a very poor man – Breen later struck a claim alone; but, taking sick, came back home – died on arrival in New York after giving map to his wife – wife in very needy circumstances – lives with little daughter of seven in New Rochelle – works out by the day at Henry Mittel's house on the Sound near-by – wife intrusted map for safe-keeping and advice to Mittel – Hamvert after map – telephone wires cut – room one hundred and forty-eight, corner, right, first floor, Palais-Metropole Hotel, unoccupied – connecting doors – quarter past nine to-night – the Weasel – Mittel's house later – the police – look out for both the Weasel and the police, Jimmie – "

There was more, several pages of it, explanations, specific details down to a minute description of the locality and plan of the house on the Sound. Jimmie Dale, too intent now to mutter, read on silently. At the end he shuffled the sheets a little abstractedly, as his face hardened. Then his fingers began to tear the letter into little shreds, tearing it over and over again, tearing the shreds into tiny particles. He had not been far wrong. From what the night promised now, this might well be the last letter. Who knew? There would be need of all the wit and luck and nerve to-night that the Gray Seal had ever had before.

With a jerk, Jimmie Dale roused himself from the momentary reverie into which he had fallen; and, all action now, stuffed the torn pieces of the letter into his trousers pocket to be disposed of later in the street; took off the old coat and slouch hat again, and resumed the disposal of Larry the Bat's effects under the flooring.

This accomplished, he replaced the planking and oilcloth, stood up, put on his dress coat and light overcoat, and, from the table, stowed the black silk mask, the automatic, the little kit of tools, the flashlight, and the thin metal case away in his pockets.

Jimmie Dale raised his hand to the gas fixture, circled the room with a glance that missed no single detail—then the light went out, the door closed behind him, locked, a dark shadow crept silently down the stairs, out through the side door into the alleyway, along the alleyway close to the wall of the tenement where it was blackest, and, satisfied that for the moment there were no passers-by, emerged on the street, walking leisurely toward the Bowery.

Once well away from the Sanctuary, however, Jimmie Dale quickened his steps; and twenty minutes later, having stopped but once to telephone to his home on Riverside Drive for his touring car, he was briskly mounting the steps of the St. James Club on Fifth Avenue. Another twenty minutes after that, and he had dismissed Benson, his chauffeur, and, at the wheel of his big, powerful machine, was speeding uptown for the Palais-Metropole Hotel.

It was twelve minutes after nine when he drew up at the curb in front of the side entrance of the hotel—his watch, set by guesswork, had been a little slow, and he had corrected it at the club. He was replacing the watch in his pocket as he sauntered around the corner, and passed in through the main entrance to the big lobby.

Jimmie Dale avoided the elevators—it was only one flight up, and elevator boys on occasions had been known to be observant. At the top of the first landing, a long, wide, heavily carpeted corridor was before him. "Number one hundred and forty-eight, the corner room on the right," the Tocsin had said. Jimmie Dale walked nonchalantly along—past No. 148. At the lower end of the hall a group of people were gathered around the elevator doors; halfway down the corridor a bell boy came out of a room and went ahead of Jimmie Dale.

And then Jimmie Dale stopped suddenly, and began to retrace his steps. The group had entered the elevator, the bell boy had disappeared around the farther end of the hall into the wing of the hotel—the corridor was empty. In a moment he was standing before the door of No. 148; in another, under the persuasion of a little steel instrument, deftly manipulated by Jimmie Dale's slim, tapering fingers, the lock clicked back, the door opened, and he stepped inside, closing and locking the door again behind him.

It was already a quarter past nine, but no one was as yet in the connecting room—the fanlight next door had been dark as he passed. His flashlight swept about him, located the connecting door – and went out. He moved to the door, tried it, and found it locked. Again the little steel instrument came into play, released the lock, and Jimmie Dale opened the door. Again the flashlight winked. The door opened into a bathroom that, obviously, at will, was either common to the two rooms or could, by the simple expedient of locking one door or the other, be used by one of the rooms alone. In the present instance, the occupant of the adjoining apartment had taken "a room with a bath."

Jimmie Dale passed through the bathroom to the opposite door. This was already three-quarters open, and swung outward into the bedroom, near the lower end of the room by the window. Through the crack of the door by the hinges, Jimmie Dale flashed his light, testing the radius of vision, pushed the door a few inches wider open, tested it again with the flashlight – and retreated back into No. 148, closing the door on his side until it was just ajar.

He stood there then silently waiting. It was Hamvert's room next door, and Hamvert and the Weasel were already late. A step sounded outside in the corridor. Jimmie Dale straightened intently. The step passed on down the hallway and died away. A false alarm! Jimmie Dale smiled whimsically. It was a strange adventure this that confronted him, quite the strangest in a way that the Tocsin had ever planned – and the night lay before him full of peril in its extraordinary complications. To win the hand he must block Hamvert and the Weasel without allowing them an inkling that his interference was anything more than, say, the luck of a hotel sneak thief at most. The Weasel was a dangerous man, one of the slickest second-story workers in the country, with safe cracking as one of his favourite pursuits, a man most earnestly desired by the police, provided the latter could catch him "with the goods." As for Hamvert, he did not know Hamvert, who was a stranger in New York, except that Hamvert had fleeced a man named Michael Breen out of his share in a claim they had had together when Breen had first gone to Alaska to try his luck, and now, having discovered that Breen, when prospecting alone somewhere in the interior a month or so ago, had found a rich vein and had made a map or diagram of its location, he, Hamvert, had followed the other to New York for the purpose of getting it by hook or crook. Breen's "find" had been too late; taken sick, he had never worked his claim, had barely got back home before he died, and only in time to hand his wife the strange legacy of a roughly scrawled little piece of paper, and – Jimmie Dale straightened up alertly once more. Steps again – and this time coming from the direction of the elevator; then voices; then the opening of the door of the next room; then a voice, distinctly audible:

"Pull up a chair, and we'll get down to business. You're late, as it is.

We haven't any time to waste, if we're going to wash pay-dirt to-night."

"Aw, dat's all right!" responded another voice – quite evidently the Weasel's. "Don't youse worry – de game's cinched to a fadeaway."

There was the sound of chairs being moved across the floor. Jimmie Dale slipped the black silk mask over his face, opened the door on his side of the bathroom cautiously, and, without a sound, stepped into the bathroom that was lighted now, of course, by the light streaming in through the partially opened door of Hamvert's room. The two were talking earnestly now in lower tones. Jimmie Dale only caught a word here and there – his faculties for the moment were concentrated on traversing the bathroom silently. He reached the farther door, crouched there, peered through the crack – and the old whimsical smile flickered across his lips again.

The Palais-Metropole was high class and exclusive, and the Weasel for once looked quite the gentleman, and, for all his sharp, ferret face, not entirely out of keeping with his surroundings – else he would never have got farther than the lobby. The other was a short, thickset, heavy-jowled man, with a great shock of sandy hair, and small black eyes that looked furtively out from overhanging, bushy eyebrows.

"Well," Hamvert was saying, "the details are your concern. What I want is results. We won't waste time. You're to be back here by daylight – only see that there's no come-back."

"Leave it to me!" returned the Weasel, with assurance. "How's dere goin' ter be any come-back? Mittel keeps it in his safe, don't he? Well, gentlemen's houses has been robbed before – an' dis job'll be a good one. De geographfy stunt youse wants gets pinched wid de rest, dat's all. It disappears – see? Who's ter know youse gets yer claws on it? It's just lost in de shuffle."

"Right!" agreed Hamvert briskly – and from his inside pocket produced a package of crisp new bills, yellow-backs, [46] and evidently of large denominations. "Half down and half on delivery – that's our deal."

"Dat's wot!" assented the Weasel curtly.

Hamvert began to count the bills.

Jimmie Dale's hand stole into his pocket, and came out with his handkerchief and the thin metal insignia case. From the latter, with its little pair of tweezers, he took out one of the adhesive gray seals. His eyes warily on the two men, he dropped the seal on his handkerchief, restored

---

46 Paper currency redeemable for gold coins.

the thin metal case to his pocket—and in its stead the blue-black ugly muzzle of his automatic peeped from between his fingers.

"Five thousand down," said Hamvert, pushing a pile of notes across the table, and tucking the remainder back into his pocket; "and the other five's here for you when you get back with the map. Ordinarily, I wouldn't pay a penny in advance, but since you want it that way and the map's no good to you while the rest of the long green is, I—" He swallowed his words with a startled gulp, clutched hastily at the money on the table, and began to struggle up from his chair to his feet.

With a swift, noiseless side-step through the open door, Jimmie Dale was standing in the room.

Jimmie Dale's tones were conversational. "Don't get up," said Jimmie Dale coolly. "And take your hand off that money!"

The Weasel, whose back had been to the door, squirmed around in his chair—and in his turn stared into the muzzle of Jimmie Dale's revolver, while his jaw dropped and sagged.

"Good-evening, Weasel," observed Jimmie Dale casually. "I seem to be in luck to-night. I got into that room next door, but an empty room is slim picking. And then it seemed to me I heard some one in here mention five thousand dollars twice, which makes ten thousand, and which happens to be just exactly the sum I need at the present moment—if I can't get any more! I haven't the honour of your wealthy friend's acquaintance, but I am really charmed to meet him. You—er—understand, both of you, that the slightest sound might prove extremely embarrassing."

Hamvert's face was white, and he stirred uneasily in his chair; but into the Weasel's face, the first shock of surprised dismay past, came a dull, angry red, and into the eyes a vicious gleam—and suddenly he laughed shortly.

"Why, youse damned fool," jeered the Weasel, "d'youse t'ink youse can get away wid dat! Say, take it from me, youse are a piker! Say, youse make me tired. Wot d'youse t'ink youse are? D'youse t'ink dis is a tee-ayter, an' dat youse are a cheap-skate actor strollin' acrost de stage? Aw, beat it, youse make me sick! Why, say, youse pinch dat money, an' youse have got de same chanst of gettin' outer dis hotel as a guy has of breakin' outer Sing Sing! By de time youse gets five feet from de door of dis room we has de whole works on yer neck."

"Do you think so, Weasel?" inquired Jimmie Dale politely. He carried his handkerchief to his mouth to cloak a cough—and his tongue touched the adhesive side of the little diamond-shaped gray seal. Hand and handkerchief came back to the table, and Jimmie Dale leaned his weight carelessly upon it, while the automatic in his right hand still covered the two men. "Do you think so, Weasel?" he repeated softly. "Well, perhaps you are right; and yet; somehow, I am inclined to disagree with you. Let me see, Weasel—it was Tuesday night, two nights ago; wasn't it, that a trifling break in Maiden Lane at Thorold and Sons disturbed the police? It was a three-year job for even a first offender, ten for one already on nodding terms with the police and fifteen to twenty for—well, say, for a man like you, Weasel—*if he were caught!* Am I making myself quite plain?"

The colour in the Weasel's cheeks faded a little—his eyes were holding in sudden fascination upon Jimmie Dale.

"I see that I am," observed Jimmie Dale pleasantly. "I said, 'if he were caught,' you will remember. I am going to leave this room in a moment, Weasel, and leave it entirely to your discretion as to whether you will think it wise or not to stir from that chair for ten minutes after I shut the door. And now"—Jimmie Dale nonchalantly replaced his handkerchief in his pocket, nonchalantly followed it with the banknotes which he picked up from the table—and smiled.

With a gasp, both men had strained forward, and were staring, wild-eyed, at the gray seal stuck between them on the tabletop.

"The Gray Seal!" whispered the Weasel, and his tongue circled his lips.

Jimmie Dale shrugged his shoulders.

"That *was* a bit theatrical, Weasel," he said apologetically; "and yet not wholly unnecessary. You will recall Stangeist, The Mope, Australian Ike, and Clarie Deane, and can draw your own inference as to what might happen in the Thorold affair if you should be so ill-advised as to force my hand. Permit me"—the slim, deft fingers, like a streak of lightning, were inside Hamvert's coat pocket and out again with the remainder of the banknotes—and Jimmie Dale was backing for the door—not the door of the bathroom by which he had entered, but the door of the room itself that opened on the corridor. There he stopped, and his hand swept around behind his back and turned the key in the locked door. He nodded at the two men, whose faces were working with incongruously mingled expressions of impotent rage, bewilderment, fear, and fury—and opened the door a little. "Ten minutes, Weasel," he said gently. "I trust you will not have to use heroic measures to restrain your friend for that length of time, though if it is necessary I should advise you for your own sake to resort almost—to murder. I wish you good evening, gentlemen."

The door opened farther; Jimmie Dale, still facing inward, slipped between it and the jamb, whipped the mask from his face, closed the door softly, stepped briskly but without any appearance of haste along the corridor to the stairs, descended the stairs, mingled with a crowd in the lobby for an instant, walked, seemingly a part of it, with a group of ladies and gentlemen down the hall to the side entrance, passed out—and a moment later, after drawing on a linen dust coat which he took from under the seat, and exchanging his hat for a tweed cap, the car glided from the curb and was lost in a press of traffic around the corner.

Jimmie Dale laughed a little harshly to himself. So far, so good—but the game was not ended yet for all the crackle of the crisp notes in his pocket. There was still the map, still the robbery at Mittel's house—the ten-thousand-dollar "theft" would not in any way change that, and it was a question of time now to forestall any move the Weasel might make.

Through the city Jimmie Dale alternately dodged, spurted, and dragged his way, fuming with impatience; but once out on the country roads and headed toward New Rochelle, the big machine, speed limits thrown to the winds, roared through the night—a gray streak of road jumping under the powerful lamps; a village, a town, a cluster of lights flashing by him, the steady purr of his sixty-horse-power engines; the gray thread of open road again.

It was just eleven o'clock when Jimmie Dale, the road to himself for the moment at a spot a little beyond New Rochelle, extinguished his lights, and very carefully ran his car off the road, backing it in behind a small clump of trees. He tossed the linen dust coat back into the car, and set off toward where, a little distance away, the slap of waves from the stiff breeze that was blowing indicated the shore line of the Sound. There was no moon, and, while it was not particularly dark, objects and surroundings at best were blurred and indistinct; but that, after all, was a matter of little concern to Jimmie Dale—the first house beyond was Mittel's. He reached the water's edge and kept along the shore. There should be a little wharf, she had said. Yes; there it was—and there, too, was a gleam of light from the house itself.

Jimmie Dale began to make an accurate mental note of his surroundings. From the little wharf on which he now stood, a path led straight to the house, bisecting what appeared to be a lawn, trees to the right, the house to the left. At the wharf, beside him, two motor boats were moored, one on each side. Jimmie Dale glanced at them, and, suddenly attracted by the familiar appearance of one, inspected it a little more closely. His momentarily awakened interest passed as he nodded his head. It had caught his attention, that was all—it was the same type and design, quite a popular make, of which there were hundreds around New York, as the one he had bought that year as a tender for his yacht.

He moved forward now toward the house, the rear of which faced him—the light that flooded the lawn came from a side window. Jimmie Dale was figuring the time and distance from New York as he crept cautiously along. How quickly could the Weasel make the journey? The

Weasel would undoubtedly come, and if there was a convenient train it might prove a close race – but in his own favour was the fact that it would probably take the Weasel quite some little time to recover his equilibrium from his encounter with the Gray Seal in the Palais-Metropole, also the further fact that, from the Weasel's viewpoint, there was no desperate need of haste. Jimmie Dale crossed the lawn, and edged along in the shadows of the house to where the light streamed out from what now proved to be open French windows. It was a fair presumption that he would have an hour to the good on the Weasel.

The sill was little more than a couple of feet from the ground, and, from a crouched position on his knees below the window, Jimmie Dale raised himself slowly and peered guardedly inside. The room was empty. He listened a moment – the black silk mask was on his face again – and with a quick, agile, silent spring he was in the room.

And then, in the centre of the room, Jimmie Dale stood motionless, staring around him, an expression, ironical, sardonic, creeping into his face. *The robbery had already been committed!* At the lower end of the room everything was in confusion; the door of a safe swung wide, the drawers of a desk had been wrenched out, even a liqueur stand, on which were well-filled decanters, had been broken open, and the contents of safe and desk, the thief's discards as it were, littered the floor in all directions.

For an instant Jimmie Dale, his eyes narrowed ominously, surveyed the scene; then, with a sort of professional instinct aroused, he stepped forward to examine the safe – and suddenly darted behind the desk instead. Steps sounded in the hall. The door opened – a voice reached him:

"The master said I was to shut the windows, and I haven't dast to go in. And he'll be back with the police in a minute now. Come on in with me, Minnie."

"Lord!" exclaimed another voice. "Ain't it a good thing the missus is away. She'd have highsteericks!"

Steps came somewhat hesitantly across the floor – from behind the desk, Jimmie Dale could see that it was a maid, accompanied by a big, rawboned woman, sleeves rolled to the elbows over brawny arms, presumably the Mittel's cook.

The maid closed the French windows, there were no others in the room, and bolted them; and, having gained a little confidence, gazed about her.

"My, but wasn't he cute!" she ejaculated. "Cut the telephone wires, he did. And ain't he made an awful mess! But the master said we wasn't to touch nothing till the police saw it."

"And to think of it happening in *our* house!" observed the cook heavily, her hands on her hips, her arms akimbo. "It'll all be in the papers, and mabbe they'll put our pictures in, too."

"I won't get over it as long as I live!" declared the maid. "The yell Mr. Mittel gave when he came downstairs and put his head in here, and then him shouting and using the most terrible language into the telephone, and then finding the wires cut. And me following him downstairs half dead with fright. And he shouts at me. 'Bella,' he shouts, 'shut those windows, but don't you touch a thing in that room. I'm going for the police.' And then he rushes out of the house."

"I was going to bed," said the cook, picking up her cue for what was probably the twentieth rehearsal of the scene, "when I heard Mr. Mittel yell, and — Lord, Bella, there he is now!"

Jimmie Dale's hands clenched. He, too, had caught the scuffle of footsteps, those of three or four men at least, on the front porch. There was one way, only one, of escape — through the French windows! It was a matter of seconds only before Mittel, with the police at his heels, would be in the room — and Jimmie Dale sprang to his feet. There was a wild scream of terror from the maid, echoed by another from the cook — and, still screaming, both women fled for the door.

"Mr. Mittel! Mr. Mittel!" shrieked the maid — she had flung herself out into the hall. "He's — he's back again!"

Jimmie Dale was at the French windows, tearing at the bolts. They stuck. Shouts came from the front entryway. He wrenched viciously at the fastenings. They gave now. The windows flew open. He glanced over his shoulder. A man, Mittel presumably, since he was the only one not in uniform, was springing into the room. There was a blur of forms and brass buttons behind Mittel — and Jimmie Dale leaped to the lawn, speeding across it like a deer.

But quick as he ran, Jimmie Dale's brain was quicker, pointing the single chance that seemed open to him. The motor boat! It seemed like a God-given piece of luck that he had noticed it was like his own; there would be no blind, and that meant fatal, blunders in the dark over its mechanism, and he could start it up in a moment — just the time to cast her off, that was all he needed.

The shouts swelled behind him. Jimmie Dale was running for his life. He flung a glance backward. One form — Mittel, he was certain — was perhaps a hundred yards in the rear. The others were just emerging from the French windows — grotesque, leaping things they looked, in the light that streamed out behind them from the room.

Jimmie Dale's feet pounded the planking of the wharf. He stooped and snatched at the mooring line. Mittel was almost at the wharf. It seemed an age, a year to Jimmie Dale before the line was clear. Shouts rang still louder across the lawn—the police, racing in a pack, were more than halfway from the house. He flung the line into the boat, sprang in after it—and Mittel, looming over him, grasped at the boat's gunwhale.

Both men were panting from their exertions.

"Let go!" snarled Jimmie Dale between clenched teeth.

Mittel's answer was a hoarse, gasping shout to the police to hurry — and then Mittel reeled back, measuring his length upon the wharf from a blow with a boat hook full across the face, driven with a sudden, untamed savagery that seemed for the moment to have mastered Jimmie Dale.

There was no time—not a second—not the fraction of a second. Desperately, frantically he shoved the boat clear of the wharf. Once — twice—three times he turned the engine over without success—and then the boat leaped forward. Jimmie Dale snatched the mask from his face, and jumped for the steering wheel. The police were rushing out along the wharf. He could just faintly discern Mittel now — the man was staggering about, his hands clapped to his face. A peremptory order to halt, coupled with a threat to fire, rang out sharply—and Jimmie Dale flung himself flat in the bottom of the boat. The wharf edge seemed to open in little, crackling jets of flame, came the roar of reports like a miniature battery in action, then the *flop, flop, flop,* as the lead tore up the water around him, the duller thud as a bullet buried its nose in the boat's side, and the curious rip and squeak as a splinter flew. Then Mittel's voice, high-pitched, as though in pain:

"Can't any of you run a motor boat? He's got me bad, I'm afraid. That other one there is twice as fast."

"Sure!" another voice responded promptly. "And if that's right, he's run his head into a trap. Cast loose, there, MacVeay, and pile in, all of you! You go back to the house, Mr. Mittel, and fix yourself up. We'll get him!"

Jimmie Dale's lips thinned. It was true! If the other boat had any speed at all, it was only a question of time before he would be overtaken. The only point at issue was how much time. It was dark—that was in his favour—but it was not so dark but that a boat could be distinguished on the water for quite a distance, for a longer distance than he could hope to put between them. There was no chance of eluding the police that way! The keen, facile brain that had saved the Gray Seal a hundred times before was weaving, planning, discarding, eliminating, scheming a way out— with death, ruin, disaster the price of failure. His eyes swept the dim, irregular outline of the shore. To his right, in the opposite direction from where he had left his car, and perhaps a mile ahead, as well as he could judge, the land seemed to run out into a point. Jimmie Dale headed for it instantly. If he could reach it with a little lead to the good, there was a chance! It would take, say, six minutes, granting the boat a speed of ten miles an hour – and she could do that. The others could hardly overtake him in that time – they hadn't got started yet. He could hear them still shouting and talking at the wharf. And Mittel's "twice as fast" was undoubtedly an exaggeration, anyhow.

A minute more passed, another – and then, astern, Jimmie Dale caught the racket from the exhaust of a high-powered engine, and a white streak seemed to shoot out upon the surface of the water from where, obscured now, he placed the wharf. A quarter-mile lead, roughly four hundred yards; yes, he had as much as that – but that, too, was very little.

He bent over his engine, coaxing it, nursing it to its highest efficiency; his eyes strained now upon the point ahead, now upon his pursuers behind. He was running with the wind, thank Heaven! or the small boat would have had a further handicap – it was rolling up quite a sea.

The steering gear, he found, was corded along the side of the boat, permitting its manipulation from almost any position, and, abruptly now, Jimmie Dale left the engine to rummage through the little locker in the stern of the boat. But as he rummaged, his eyes held speculatively on the boat astern. She was gaining unquestionably, steadily, but not as fast as he had feared. He would still have a hundred yards' lead, at least, abreast the point – and, he was smiling grimly now, a hundred yards there meant life to the Gray Seal! The locker was full of a heterogeneous collection of odds and ends – a suit of oilskins, tools, tins, and cans of various sizes and descriptions. Jimmie Dale emptied the contents, some sort of powder, of a small, round tin box overboard, and from his pocket took out the banknotes, crammed them into the box, crammed his watch in on top of them, and screwed the cover on tightly. His fingers were flying now. A long strip torn from the trousers' leg of the oilskins was wrapped again and again around the box – and the box was stuffed into his pocket.

The flash of a revolver shot cut the blackness behind him, then another, and another. They were firing in a continuous stream again. It was fairly long range, but there was always the chance of a stray bullet finding its mark. Jimmie Dale, crouching low, made his way to the bow of the boat again.

The point was looming almost abreast now. He edged in nearer, to hug it as closely as he dared risk the depth of the water. Behind, remorselessly, the other boat was steadily closing the gap; and the shots were not all wild – one struck, with a curious singing sound, on some piece of metal a foot from his elbow. Closer to the shore, running now parallel with the head of the point, Jimmie Dale again edged in the boat, his jaws, clamped, working in little twitches.

And then suddenly, with a swift, appraising glance behind him, he swerved the boat from her course and headed for the shore – not directly, but diagonally across the little bay that, on the farther side of the point, had now opened out before him. He was close in with the edge of the point, ten yards from it, sweeping past it – the point itself came between the two boats, hiding them from each other – and Jimmie Dale, with a long spring, dove from the boat's side to the water.

The momentum from the boat as he sank robbed him for an instant of all control over himself, and he twisted, doubled up, and rolled over and over beneath the water – but the next moment his head was above the surface again, and he was striking out swiftly for the shore. It was only a few yards – but in a few *seconds* the pursuing boat, too, would have rounded the point. His feet touched bottom. It was haste now, nothing else, that counted. The drum of the racing engines, the crackling roar of the exhaust from the oncoming boat was in his ears. He flung himself upon the shore and down behind a rock. Around the point, past him, tore the police boat, dark forms standing clustered in the bow – and then a sudden shout:

"There she is! See her? She's heading into the bay for the shore!"

Jimmie Dale's lips relaxed. There was no doubt that they had sighted their quarry again – a perfect fusillade of revolver shots directed at the now empty boat was quite sufficient proof of that! With something that was almost a chuckle, Jimmie Dale straightened up from behind the rock and began to run back along the shore. The little motor boat would have grounded long before they overtook her, and, thinking naturally enough, that he had leaped ashore from her, they would go thrashing through the woods and fields searching for him!

It was a longer way back by the shore, a good deal longer; now over rough, rocky stretches where he stumbled in the darkness, now through marshy, sodden ground where he sank as in a quagmire time and again over his ankles. It was even longer than he had counted on, and time, with the Weasel on one hand and the return of the police on the other, was a factor to be reckoned with again, as, a half hour later, Jimmie Dale stole across the lawn of Mittel's house for the second time that night, and for the second time crouched beneath the open French windows.

Masked again, the water still dripping from what were once immaculate evening clothes but which now sagged limply about him, his collar a pasty string around his neck, the mud and dirt splashed to his knees, Jimmie Dale was a disreputable and incongruous-looking object as he crouched there, shivering uncomfortably from his immersion in spite of his exertions. Inside the room, Mittel passed the windows, pacing the floor, one side of his face badly cut and bruised from the blow with the boat hook – and as he passed, his back turned for an instant, Jimmie Dale stepped into the room.

Mittel whirled at the sound, and, with a suppressed cry, instinctively drew back – Jimmie Dale's automatic was dangling carelessly in his right hand.

"I am afraid I am a trifle melodramatic," observed Jimmie Dale apologetically, surveying his own bedraggled person; "but I assure you it is neither intentional nor for effect. As it is, I was afraid I would be late. Pardon me if I take the liberty of helping myself; one gets a chill in wet clothes so easily" – he passed to the liqueur stand, poured out a generous portion from one of the decanters, and tossed it off.

Mittel neither spoke nor moved. Stupefaction, surprise, and a very obvious regard for Jimmie Dale's revolver mingled themselves in a helpless expression on his face.

Jimmie Dale set down his glass and pointed to a chair in front of the desk.

"Sit down, Mr. Mittel," he invited pleasantly. "It will be quite apparent to you that I have not time to prolong our interview unnecessarily, in view of the possible return of the police at any moment, but you might as well be comfortable. You will pardon me again if I take another liberty" – he crossed the room, turned the key in the lock of the door leading into the hall, and returned to the desk. "Sit down, Mr. Mittel!" he repeated, a sudden rasp in his voice.

Mittel, none too graciously, now seated himself.

"Look here, my fine fellow," he burst out, "you're carrying things with a pretty high hand, aren't you? You seem to have eluded the police for the moment, somehow, but let me tell you I – "

"No," interrupted Jimmie Dale softly, "let *me* tell you – all there is to be told." He leaned over the desk and stared rudely at the bruise on Mittel's face. "Rather a nasty crack, that," he remarked.

Mittel's fists clenched, and an angry flush swept his cheeks.

"I'd have made it a good deal harder," said Jimmie Dale, with sudden insolence, "if I hadn't been afraid of putting you out of business and so precluding the possibility of this little meeting. Now then" – the revolver swung upward and held steadily on a line with Mittel's eyes – "I'll trouble you for the diagram of that Alaskan claim that belongs to Mrs. Michael Breen!"

Mittel, staring fascinated into the little, round, black muzzle of the automatic, edged back in his chair.

"So—so that's what you're after, is it?" he jerked out. "Well"—he laughed unnaturally and waved his hand at the disarray of the room—"it's been stolen already."

"I know that," said Jimmie Dale grimly. "By—*you!*"

"Me!" Mittel started up in his chair, a whiteness creeping into his face. "Me! I—I—"

"Sit down!" Jimmie Dale's voice rang out ominously cold. "I haven't any time to spare. You can appreciate that. But even if the police return before that map is in my possession, they will still be *too late* as far as you are concerned. Do you understand? Furthermore, if I am caught—you are ruined. Let me make it quite plain that I know the details of your little game. You are a curb broker, Mr. Mittel—ostensibly. In reality, you run what is nothing better than an exceedingly profitable bucket shop. [47] The Weasel has been a customer and also a stool for you for years. How Hamvert met the Weasel is unimportant—he came East with the intention of getting in touch with a slick crook to help him—the Weasel is the coincidence, that is all. I quite understand that you have never met Hamvert, nor Hamvert you, nor that Hamvert was aware that you and the Weasel had anything to do with one another and were playing in together—but that equally is unimportant. When Hamvert engaged the Weasel for ten thousand dollars to get the map from you for him, the Weasel chose the line of least resistance. He knew you, and approached you with an offer to split the money in return for the map. It was not a question of your accepting his offer—it was simply a matter of how you could do it and still protect yourself. The Weasel was well qualified to point the way—a fake robbery of your house would answer the purpose admirably—you could not be held either legally or morally responsible for a document that was placed, unsolicited by you, in your possession, if it were stolen from you."

Mittel's face was ashen, colourless. His hands were opening and shutting with nervous twitches on the top of the desk.

Jimmie Dale's lips curled.

"But"—Jimmie Dale was clipping off his words now viciously—"neither you nor the Weasel were willing to trust the other implicitly—perhaps you know each other too well. You were unwilling to turn over the map until you had received your share of the money, and you were

---

[47] A curb broker is someone not affiliated with the Stock Exchange who sells securities. Those transactions might actually occur out on the street but if the curb broker has an office it would be known as a bucket shop.

equally unwilling to turn it over until you were *safe;* that is, until you had engineered your fake robbery even to the point of notifying the police that it had been committed; the Weasel, on the other hand, had some scruples about parting with any of the money without getting the map in one hand before he let go of the banknotes with the other. It was very simply arranged, however, and to your mutual satisfaction. While you robbed your own house this evening, he was to get half the money in advance from Hamvert, giving Hamvert to understand that *he* had planned to commit the robbery himself to-night. He was to come out here then, receive the map from you in exchange for your share of the money, return to Hamvert with the map, and receive in turn his own share. I might say that Hamvert actually paid down the advance – and it was perhaps unfortunate for you that you paid such scrupulous attention to details as to cut your own telephone wires! I had not, of course, an exact knowledge of the hour or minute in which you proposed to stage your little play here. The object of my first visit a little while ago was to forestall your turning the diagram over to the Weasel. Circumstances favoured you for the moment. I am back again, however, for the same purpose – the map!"

Mittel, in a cowed way, was huddled back in his chair. He smiled miserably at Jimmie Dale.

"*Quick!*" Jimmie Dale flung out the word in a sharp, peremptory bark. "Do you need to be told that the *cartridges* are dry?"

Mittel's hand, trembling, went into his pocket and produced an envelope.

"Open it!" commanded Jimmie Dale. "And lay it on the desk, so that I can read it – I am too wet to touch it."

Mittel obeyed – like a dog that has been whipped.

A glance at the paper, and Jimmie Dale's eyes lifted again – to sweep the floor of the room. He pointed to a pile of books and documents in one corner that had been thrown out of the safe.

"Go over there and pick up that check book!" he ordered tersely.

"What for?" Mittel made feeble protest.

"Never mind what for!" snapped Jimmie Dale. "Go and get it – and *hurry!*"

Once more Mittel obeyed – and dropped the book hesitantly on the desk.

Jimmie Dale stared silently, insolently, contemptuously at the other.

Mittel stirred uneasily, sat down, shifted his feet, and his fingers fumbled aimlessly over the top of the desk.

"Compared with you," said Jimmie Dale, in a low voice, "the Weasel, ay, and Hamvert, too, crooks though they are, are gentlemen! Michael Breen, as he died, told his wife to take that paper to some one she could trust, who would help her and tell her what to do; and, knowing no one to go to, but because she scrubbed your floors and therefore thought you were a fine gentleman, she came timidly to you, and trusted you – you cur!"

Jimmie Dale laughed suddenly – not pleasantly. Mittel shivered.

"Hamvert and Breen were partners out there in Alaska when Breen first went out," said Jimmie Dale slowly, pulling the tin can wrapped in oilskin from his pocket. "Hamvert swindled Breen out of the one strike he made, and Mrs. Breen and her little girl back here were reduced to poverty. The amount of that swindle was, I understand, fifteen thousand dollars. I have ten of it here, contributed by the Weasel and Hamvert; and you will, I think, recognise therein a certain element of poetic justice – but I am still short five thousand dollars."

Jimmie Dale removed the cover from the tin can. Mittel gazed at the contents numbly.

"You perhaps did not hear me?" prompted Jimmie Dale coldly. "I am still short five thousand dollars."

Mittel circled his lips with the tip of his tongue.

"What do you want?" he whispered hoarsely.

"The balance of the amount." There was an ominous quiet in Jimmie Dale's voice. "A check payable to Mrs. Michael Breen for five thousand dollars."

"I – I haven't got that much in the bank," Mittel fenced, stammering.

"No? Then I should advise you to see that you have by ten o'clock to-morrow morning!" returned Jimmie Dale curtly. "Make out that check!"

Mittel hesitated. The revolver edged insistently a little farther across the desk – and Mittel, picking up a pen, wrote feverishly. He tore the check from its stub, and, with a snarl, pushed it toward Jimmie Dale.

"Fold it!" instructed Jimmie Dale, in the same curt tones. "And fold that diagram with it. Put them both in this box. Thank you!" He wrapped the oilskin around the box again, and returned the box to his pocket. And again with that insolent, contemptuous stare, he surveyed the man at the desk – then he backed to the French windows. "It might be as well to remind you, Mittel," he cautioned sternly, "that if for any reason this check is not honoured, whether through lack of funds or an attempt by you to stop payment, you'll be in a cell in the Tombs to-morrow for this night's work – that is quite understood, isn't it?"

Mittel was on his feet—sweat glistened on his forehead.

"My God!" he cried out shrilly. "Who are you?"

And Jimmie Dale smiled and stepped out on the lawn.

"Ask the Weasel," said Jimmie Dale—and the next instant, lost in the shadows of the house, was running for his car.

CHAPTER X

THE ALIBI

(Saturday 10/9/1915 to Sunday 10/10/1915)

D EATH *to the Gray Seal!"* — through the underworld, in dens and dives that sheltered from the law the vultures that preyed upon society, prompted by self-fear, by secret dread, by reason of their very inability to carry out their purpose, the whispered sentence grew daily more venomous, more insistent. *"The Gray Seal, dead or alive – but the Gray Seal!"* It was the "standing orders" of the police. Railed at by a populace who angrily demanded at its hands this criminal of criminals, mocked at and threatened by a virulent press, stung to madness by the knowledge of its own impotence, flaunted impudently to its face by this mysterious Gray Seal to whose door the law laid a hundred crimes, for whom the bars of a death cell in Sing Sing was the certain goal could he but be caught, the police, to a man, was like an uncaged beast that, flicked to the raw by some unseen assailant and murderous in its fury, was crouched to strike. Grim paradox – a common bond that linked the hands of the law with those that outraged it!

Death to the Gray Seal! Was it, at last, the beginning of the end? Jimmie Dale, as Larry the Bat, unkempt, disreputable in appearance, supposed dope fiend, a figure familiar to every denizen below the dead line, skulked along the narrow, ill-lighted street of the East Side that, on the corner ahead, boasted the notorious resort to which Bristol Bob had paid the doubtful, if appropriate, compliment of giving his name. From under the rim of his battered hat, Jimmie Dale's eyes, veiled by half-closed, well-simulated drug-laden lids, missed no detail either of his surroundings or pertaining to the passers-by. Though already late in the evening, half-naked children played in the gutters; hawkers of multitudinous commodities cried their wares under gasoline banjo torches affixed to their pushcarts; shawled women of half a dozen races, and men equally cosmopolitan, loitered at the curb, or blocked the pavement, or brushed by him. Now a man passed him, flinging a greeting from the corner of his mouth; now another, always without movement of the lips – and Jimmie Dale answered them – from the corner of his mouth.

But while his eyes were alert, his mind was only subconsciously attune to his surroundings. Was it indeed the beginning of the end? Some day, he had told himself often enough, the end must come. Was it coming now, surely, with a sort of grim implacability – when it was too late to escape! Slowly, but inexorably, even his personal freedom of action was narrowing, being limited, and, ironically enough, through the very conditions he had himself created as an avenue of escape.

It was not only the police now; it was, far more to be feared, the underworld as well. In the old days, the role of Larry the Bat had been assumed at intervals, at his own discretion, when, in a corner, he had no other way of escape; now it was forced upon him almost daily. The character of Larry the Bat could no longer be discarded at will. He had flung down the gauntlet to the underworld when, as the Gray Seal, he had closed the prison doors behind Stangeist, The Mope, Australian Ike, and Clarie Deane, and the underworld had picked the gauntlet up. Betrayed, as they believed, by the one who, though unknown to them; they had counted the greatest among themselves, and each one fearful that his own betrayal might come next, every crook, every thug in the Bad Lands now eyed his oldest pal with suspicion and distrust, and each was a self-constituted sleuth, with the prod of self-preservation behind him, sworn to the accomplishment of that unhallowed slogan – death to the Gray Seal. Almost daily now he must show himself as Larry the Bat in some gathering of the underworld – a prolonged absence from his haunts was not merely to invite certain suspicion, where all were suspicious of each other, it was to invite certain disaster. He had now either to carry the role like a little old man of the sea upon his back, or renounce it forever. And the latter course he dared not even consider – the Sanctuary was still the Sanctuary, and the role of Larry the Bat was still a refuge, the trump card in the lone hand he played.

He reached the corner, pushed open the door of Bristol Bob's, and shuffled in. The place was a glare of light, a hideous riot of noise. On a polished section of the floor in the centre, a turkey trot was in full swing; laughter and shouting vied raucously with an impossible orchestra.

Jimmie Dale slowly made the circuit of the room past the tables, that, ranged around the sides, were packed with occupants who thumped their glasses in tempo with the music and clamoured at the rushing waiters for replenishment. A dozen, two dozen, men and women greeted him. Jimmie Dale indifferently returned their salutes. What a galaxy of crooks – the cream of the underworld! His eyes, under half-closed lids, swept the faces – lags, dips, gatmen, yeggs, mob stormers, murderers, petty sneak thieves, stalls, hangers-on – they were all there. [48] He knew them all; he was known to all.

He shuffled on to the far end of the room, his leer a little arrogant, a certain arrogance, too, in the tilt of his battered hat. He also was quite a celebrity in that gathering – Larry the Bat was of the aristocracy and the elite of gangland. Well, the show was over; he had stalked across the stage, performed for his audience – and in another hour now, free until he must repeat the same performance the next day in some other equally notorious dive, he would be sitting in for a rubber of bridge at that most exclusive of all clubs, the St. James, where none might enter save only those whose names were vouched for in the highest and most select circles, and where for partners he would possibly have a justice of the supreme court, or mayhap an eminent divine! He looked suddenly around him, as though startled. It always startled him, that comparison. There was something too stupendous to be simply ironical in the incongruity of it. If – if he were ever run to earth!

His eyes met those of a heavy-built, coarse-featured man, the chewed end of a cigar in his mouth, who stepped from behind the bar, carrying a tin tray with two full glasses upon it. It was Bristol Bob, ex-pugilist, the proprietor.

"How're you, Larry?" grunted the man, with what he meant to be a smile.

Jimmie Dale was standing in the doorway of a passage that prefaced a rear exit to the lane. He moved aside to allow the other to pass.

"'Ello, Bristol," he returned dispassionately.

Bristol Bob went on along down the passage, and Jimmie Dale shuffled slowly after him. He had intended to leave the place by the rear door – it obviated the possibility of an undesirable acquaintance joining company with him if he went out by the main entrance. But now his eyes were fixed on the proprietor's back with a sort of speculative curiosity. There was a private room off the passage, with a window on the lane; but they must be favoured customers indeed that Bristol Bob would condescend to serve personally – any one who knew Bristol Bob knew that.

Jimmie Dale slowed his shuffling gait, then quickened it again. Bristol Bob opened the door and passed into the private room – the door was just closing as Jimmie Dale shuffled by. He had had only a glance inside – but

---

[48] Lag is slang for a convict, a dip is a pickpocket, a gatman an armed criminal, a yegg is a robber, a stormer is a successful gambler, and a stall a pickpocket's assistant.

it was enough. They were favoured customers indeed! It was no wonder that Bristol Bob himself was on the job! Two men were in the room: Lannigan of headquarters, rated the smartest plain-clothes man in the country – and, across the table from Lannigan, Whitey Mack, [49] as clever, finished and daring a crook as was to be found in the Bad Lands, whose particular "line" was diamonds, or, in the vernacular of his ilk, "white stones," that had earned him the sobriquet of "Whitey." Lannigan of headquarters, Whitey Mack of the underworld, sworn enemies those two – in secret session! Bristol Bob might well play the part of outer guard. If a choice few of those outside in the dance hall could get a glimpse into that private room it would be "good-night" to Whitey Mack.

Jimmie Dale's eyes were narrowed a little as he shuffled on down the passage. Lannigan and Whitey Mack with their heads together! What was the game? There was nothing in common between the two men. Lannigan, it was well known, could not be "reached." Whitey Mack, with his ingenious cleverness, coupled with a cold-blooded fearlessness that had made him an object of unholy awe and respect in the eyes of the underworld, was a thorn that was sore beyond measure in the side of the police. Certainly, it was no ordinary thing that had brought these two together; especially, since, with the unrest and suspicion that was bubbling and seething below the dead line, and with which there was none more intimate than Whitey Mack, Whitey Mack was inviting a risk in "making up" with the police that could only be accounted for by some urgent and vital incentive.

Jimmie Dale pushed open the door that gave on the lane. Behind him, Bristol Bob closed the door of the private room and retreated back along the passage. Jimmie Dale stepped out into the lane – and instinctively his eyes sought the window of the private room. The shade was drawn, only a yellow murk filtered out into the black, unlighted lane, but suddenly he started noiselessly toward it. The window was open a bare inch or so at the bottom!

The sill was just shoulder high, and, placing his ear to the opening, he flattened himself against the wall. He could not see inside, for the shade was drawn well to the bottom; but he could hear as distinctly as though he were at the table beside the two men – and at the first words, the loose, disjointed frame of Larry the Bat seemed to tauten curiously and strain forward lithe and tense.

"This Gray Seal dope listens good, Whitey; but, coming from you, I'm leery. You've got to show me."

"Don't you want him?" There was a nasty laugh from Whitey Mack.

---

[49] **Apparently no connection to Whitie Burns of Chapter Four.**

"You *bet* I want him!" returned the headquarters man with a suppressed savagery that left no doubt as to his earnestness. "I want him fast enough, but –"

"Then, blast him, so do I!" Whitey Mack rapped out with a vicious snarl. "So does every guy in the fleet down here. We got it in for him. You get that, don't you? He's got Stangeist and his gang steered for the electric chair now; he put a crimp in the Weasel the other night – get that? He's like a blasted wizard with what he knows. And who'll he deal the icy mitt to next? Me – damn him – me, for all I know!"

"That's all right," observed Lannigan coolly. "I'm not questioning your sincerity for a minute; I know all about that; but that doesn't land the Gray Seal. I'll work with you if you've anything to offer, but we've had enough 'tips' and 'information' handed us at headquarters in the last few years to make us a trifle skeptical. Show me what you've got, Whitey?"

"Show you!" echoed Whitey Mack passionately. "Sure, I'll show you! That's what I'm going to do – show you. I'll show you the Gray Seal! I ain't handing you any tips. *I've found out who the Gray Seal is!*"

There was a tense silence. It seemed to Jimmie Dale as though cold fingers were clutching at his heart, stifling its beat – then the blood came bursting to his forehead. He could not see into the room, but that silence was eloquent. It seemed as though he could picture the two men – Lannigan leaning suddenly forward – Lannigan and Whitey Mack staring tensely into each other's eyes.

"You – *what!*" It came low and grim from Lannigan.

"That's what!" asserted Whitey Mack bluntly. "You heard me! That's what I said! I know who the Gray Seal is – and I'm the only guy that's wise to him. Am I letting you in right?"

"You're sure?" demanded Lannigan hoarsely. "You're sure? Who is he, then?"

There was a half laugh, half snarl from Whitey Mack.

"Oh, no, you don't!" he growled. "Nix on that! What do you take me for – a fool? You beat it out of here and round him up – eh – while I suck my thumbs? Say, forget it! Do you think I'm doing this because I love you? Why, blame you, you've been aching for a year to put the bracelets on me yourself! Say, wake up! I'm in on this myself."

Again that silence. Then Lannigan spoke slowly, in a puzzled way.

"I don't get you, Whitey," he said. "What do you mean?" Then, a little sharply: "You're quite right; you've got some reputation yourself, and you're badly 'wanted' if we could get the 'goods' on you. If you're trying to plant something, look out for yourself, or –"

"Can that!" snapped Whitey Mack threateningly. "Can that sort of spiel right now — or quit! I ain't telling you his name — yet. *But I'll take you to him to-night* — and you and me nabs him together. Is that straight enough goods for you?"

"Don't get sore," said Lannigan, more pacifically. "Yes, if you'll do that it's good enough for any man. But lay your cards on the table face up, Whitey — I want to see what you opened the pot on."

"You've seen 'em," Whitey Mack answered ungraciously. "I've told you already. The Gray Seal goes out for keeps — curse him for a snitch! If I bumped him off, or wised up any of the guys to it, and we was caught, we'd get the juice for it even if it was the Gray Seal, wouldn't we? Well, what's the use! If one of you dicks get him, he gets bumped off just the same, only regular, up in the wire parlour at Sing Sing. I ain't looking for that kind of trouble when I can duck it. See?"

"Sure," said Lannigan.

"Besides, and moreover," continued Whitey Mack, "there's *some* reward hung out for him that I'm figuring to horn in on. I'd swipe it all myself, don't you make any mistake about that, and you'd never get a look-in, only, sore as the mob is on the Gray Seal, it ain't healthy for any guy around these parts to get the reputation of being a snitch, no matter who he snitches on. Bump him off — sure! Snitching — well, you get the idea, eh? I'm ducking that too. Get me?"

"I get you," said Lannigan, with a short, pleased laugh.

"Well, then," announced Whitey Mack, "here's my proposition, and it's my turn to hand out the 'look-out-for-your-self' dope. I'm busting the game wide open for you to play, but you throw me down, and" — his voice sank into a sullen snarl again — "you can take it from me, I'll get you for it!"

"All right," responded Lannigan soberly. "Let's hear it. If I agree to it, I'll stick to it."

"I believe you," said Whitey Mack curtly. "That's why I picked you out for the medal they'll pin on you for this. And here's getting down to tacks! I'll lead you to the Gray Seal to-night and help you nab him and stay with you to the finish, but there's to be nobody but you and me on the job. When it's done I fade away, and nobody's to know I snitched, and no questions asked as to how I found out about the Gray Seal. I ain't looking for any of the glory — you can fix that up to suit yourself. The cash is different — you come across with half the reward the day they pay it."

"You'll get it!" There was savage elation in Lannigan's voice, the emphatic smash of a fist on the table. "You're on, Whitey. And if we get the Gray Seal to-night, I'll do better by you than that."

"We'll get him!" said Whitey Mack, with a vicious oath. "And – "

Jimmie Dale crouched suddenly low down, close against the wall. The crunch of a footstep sounded from the end of the lane. Some one had turned in from the cross street, some fifty yards away, and was heading evidently for the back entrance to Bristol Bob's. Jimmie Dale edged noiselessly, cautiously back past the doorway, kept on, pressed close against the wall, and finally paused. He had not been seen. The back door of Bristol Bob's opened and closed. The man had gone in.

For a moment Jimmie Dale stood hesitant. There was a wild surging in his brain, something like a myriad batteries of trip hammers seemed to be pounding at his temples. Then, almost blindly, he kept on down the lane in the same direction in which he had started to retreat – as well one cross street as another.

He turned into the cross street, went along it – and presently emerged into the full tide of the Bowery. It was garishly lighted; people swarmed about him. Subconsciously, there were crowded sidewalks; subconsciously, he was on the Bowery – that was all.

Ruin, disaster, peril faced him – faced him, and staggered him with the suddenness of the shock. Was it true? No; it could not be true! It was a bluff – Whitey Mack was bluffing. Jimmie Dale's lips grew thin in a mirthless smile as he shook his head. Neither Whitey Mack nor any other man would dare to bluff like that. It was too straight, too open-handed, Whitey Mack had laid his cards too plainly on the table. Whitey Mack's words rang in his ears: "I'll *lead* you to the Gray Seal to-night and help you nab him and stay with you to the finish." The man meant what he said, meant what he said, too, about the "finish" of the Gray Seal; not a man in the Bad Lands but meant – death to the Gray Seal! But how, by what means, when, where had Whitey Mack got his information? "I'm the only one that's wise," Whitey Mack had said. It seemed impossible. It *was* impossible! Whitey Mack was sincere enough probably in what he had said, but the man simply could not know. Whitey Mack could only have spotted some one that, for some reason or other, he *imagined* was the Gray Seal. That was it – must be it! Whitey Mack had made a mistake. What clew could he have obtained to –

Over the unwashed face of Larry the Bat a gray pallor spread slowly. His fingers were plucking at the frayed edge of his inside vest pocket. The dark eyes seemed to turn coal-black. A laugh, like the laugh of one damned, rose to his lips, and was choked back. It was gone! *Gone!* That thin metal case, like a cigarette case, that, between the little sheets of oil paper, held those diamond-shaped, gray-coloured, adhesive seals, the insignia of the Gray Seal – was gone! Clew! It seemed as though there were an overpowering nausea upon him. *Clew!* That little case was not a clew—it was a death warrant!

His hands clenched fiercely. If he could only think for a moment! The lining of his pocket had given away. The case had dropped out. But there was nothing about the case to identify any one as the Gray Seal unless it were found in one's actual possession. Therefore Whitey Mack, to have solved his identity, must have seen him drop the case. There could be no question about that. It was equally obvious then that Whitey Mack would know the Gray Seal as Larry the Bat. Did he also know him as Jimmie Dale? Yes, or no? It was a vital question. His life hung on it.

That keen, facile brain, numbed for the moment, was beginning to work with lightning speed. It was four o'clock that afternoon when he had assumed the character of Larry the Bat—some time between four o'clock and the present, it was now well after eleven, the case had dropped from his pocket. There had been ample time then for Whitey Mack to have made that appointment with Lannigan—and ample time to have made a surreptitious visit to the Sanctuary. Had Whitey Mack gone there? Had Whitey Mack found that hiding place in the flooring under the oilcloth? Had Whitey Mack discovered that the Gray Seal was not only Larry the Bat—but Jimmie Dale?

Jimmie Dale swept his hand across his forehead. It was damp from little clinging beads of moisture. Should he go to the Sanctuary and change—become Jimmie Dale again? Was it the safest thing to do—or the most dangerous? Even if Whitey Mack had been there and discovered the dual personality of Larry the Bat, how would he, Jimmie Dale, know it? The man would have been crafty enough to have left no sign behind him. Was it to the Sanctuary that Whitey Mack meant to lead Lannigan that evening—or did Whitey Mack know him as Jimmie Dale, and to make it the more sensational, plan to carry out the coup, say, at the St. James Club? Whitey Mack and Lannigan were still at Bristol Bob's; he had probably time, if he so elected, to reach the Sanctuary, change, and get away again. But every minute was priceless now. What should he do? Run from the city as he was for cover—or take the gambler's chance? Whitey Mack knew him as Larry the Bat—it was not certain that Whitey Mack knew him as Jimmie Dale.

He had halted, absorbed, in front of a moving-picture theatre. Great placards, at first but a blur of colour, suddenly forced themselves in concrete form upon his consciousness. Letters a foot high leaped out at him: "THE DOUBLE LIFE." [50] There was the picture of a banker in his

---

[50] There was a play with that title in 1906 but no such movie can be identified.

private office hastily secreting a forged paper as the hero in the guise of a clerk entered; the companion picture was the banker in convict stripes staring out from behind the barred doors of a cell. There seemed a ghastly augury in the coincidence. Why should a thing like that be thrust upon him to shake his nerve when he needed nerve now more than he had ever needed it in his life before?

He raised his hand to jerk aimlessly at the brim of his hat, dropped his hand abruptly to his side again, and started quickly, hurriedly away through the throng around him. A sort of savagery had swept upon him. In a flash he had made his decision. He would take the gambler's chance! And afterward – Jimmie Dale's lips were like a thin, straight line – it was Whitey Mack's life or his own! Whitey Mack had said he was the only one that was wise – and Whitey Mack had not told Lannigan yet, wouldn't tell Lannigan until the show-down. If he, Jimmie Dale, got to the Sanctuary, became Jimmie Dale and got away again, even if Whitey Mack knew him as Jimmie Dale, there was still a chance. It was his life or Whitey Mack's – Whitey Mack, with his lean-jawed, clean-shaven wolf's face! If he could get Whitey Mack before the other was ready to tell Lannigan! Surely he had the right of self-preservation! Surely his life was as valuable as Whitey Mack's, as valuable as a man's who, as those in the secrets of the underworld knew well enough, had blood upon his hands, who lived by crime, who was a menace to the community! Had he not the right to preserve his own life at the expense of one such as that? He had never taken life – the thought was abhorrent! But was there any other way in event of Whitey Mack knowing him as Jimmie Dale? His back was against the wall; he was trapped; certain death, and, worse, dishonour stared him in the face. Lannigan and Whitey Mack would be together – the odds would be two to one against him – and he had no quarrel with Lannigan – somehow he must let Lannigan out of it.

The other side of the street was less crowded. He crossed over, and, still with the shuffling tread that dozens around him knew as the characteristic gait of Larry the Bat, but covering the ground with amazing celerity, he hurried along. It was only at the end of the block, that cross street from the Bowery that led to the Sanctuary. How much time had he? He turned the corner into the darker cross street. Whitey Mack would have learned from Bristol Bob that Larry the Bat had just been there; that is, that Larry the Bat was not at the Sanctuary. Whitey Mack would probably be in no hurry – he and Lannigan might wait until later, until Whitey Mack should be satisfied that Larry the Bat had gone home. It was the line of least resistance; they would not attempt to scour the city for him. They might even wait in that private room at Bristol Bob's until they decided that it was time to sally out. He might perhaps still find them there when he got back; at any rate, from there he must pick up their trail again. On the other hand – all this was but supposition – they might make at once for the Sanctuary to lie in wait for him. In any case there was need, desperate need, for haste.

He glanced sharply around him; and, by the side of the tenement house now that bordered on the alleyway, with a curious, swift, gliding motion, he seemed to blend into the shadow and darkness. It was the Sanctuary, that room on the first floor of the tenement, the tenement that had three entrances, three exits – a passageway through to the saloon on the next street that abutted on the rear, the usual front door, and the side door in the alleyway. Gone was the shuffling gait. Quick, alert, he ran, crouching, bent down, along the alleyway, reached the side door, opened it stealthily, closed it behind him with equal caution, and, in the dark entry, stood motionless, listening intently.

There was no sound. He began to mount the rickety, dilapidated stairs; and, where it seemed that the lightest tread must make them creak out in blatant protest, his trained muscles, delicately compensating his body weight, carried him upward with a silence that was almost uncanny. There was need of silence, as there was need of haste. He was not so sure now of the time at his disposal – that he had even reached the Sanctuary *first*. How long had he loitered in that half-dazed way on the Bowery? He did not know – perhaps longer than he had imagined. There was the possibility that Whitey Mack and Lannigan were already above, waiting for him; but, even if they were not already there and he got away before they came, it was imperative that no one should know that Larry the Bat had come and gone.

He reached the landing, and paused again, his right hand, with a vicious muzzle of his automatic peeping now from between his fingers, thrown a little forward. It was black, utterly black, around him. Again that stealthy, catlike tread – and his ear was at the keyhole of the Sanctuary door. A full minute, priceless though it was, passed; then, satisfied that the room was empty, he drew his head back from the keyhole, and those slim, tapering fingers, that in their tips seemed to embody all the human senses, felt over the lock. Apparently it had been undisturbed; but that was no proof that Whitey Mack had not been there after finding the metal case. Whitey Mack was known to be clever with a lock – clever enough for that, anyhow.

He slipped in the key, turned it, and, on hinges that were always oiled, silently pushed the door open and stepped across the threshold. He closed the door until it was just ajar, that any sound might reach him from without – and, whipping off his coat, began to undress swiftly.

There was no light. He dared not use the gas; it might be seen from the alleyway. He was moving now quickly, surely, silently here and there. It was like some weird spectre figure, a little blacker than the surrounding darkness, flitting about the room. The oilcloth in the corner was turned back, the loose flooring lifted, the clothes of Jimmie Dale taken out, the rags of Larry the Bat put in. The minutes flew by. It was not the change of clothing that took long—it was the eradication of Larry the Bat's make-up from his face, throat, neck, wrists, and hands. Occasionally his head was turned in a tense, listening attitude; but always the fingers were busy, working with swift deftness.

It was done at last. Larry the Bat had vanished, and in his place stood Jimmie Dale, the young millionaire, the social lion of New York, immaculate in well-tailored tweeds. He stooped to the hole in the flooring, and, his fingers going unerringly to their hiding place, took out a black silk mask and an electric flashlight—his automatic was already in his possession. His lips parted grimly. Who knew what part a flashlight might not play—and he would need the mask for Lannigan's benefit, even if it did not disguise him from Whitey Mack. Had he left any telltale evidence of his visit? It was almost worth the risk of a light to make sure. He hesitated, then shook his head, and, stooping again, carefully replaced the flooring and laid the oilcloth over it—he dared not show a light at any cost.

But now even more caution than before was necessary. At times, the lodgers had naturally enough seen their fellow lodger, Larry the Bat, enter and leave the tenement—none had ever seen Jimmie Dale either leave or enter. He stole across the room to the door, halted to assure himself that the hall was empty, slipped out into the hall, and locked the door behind him. Again that trained, long-practiced, silent tread upon the stairs. It seemed as though an hour passed before he reached the bottom, and his brain was shrieking at him to hurry, hurry, *hurry!* The entryway at last, the door, the alleyway, a long breath of relief—and he was on the cross street.

A step, two, he took in the direction of the Bowery—and he was bending down as though to tie his shoe, his automatic, from his side pocket, concealed in his hand. *Was that some one there?* He could have sworn he saw a shadow-like form start out from behind the steps of the house on the opposite side of the street as he had emerged from the alleyway. In his bent posture, without seemingly turning his head, his eyes swept sharply up and down the other side of the ill-lighted street. Nothing! There was not even a pedestrian in sight on the block from there to the Bowery.

Jimmie Dale straightened up nonchalantly, and stooped almost instantly again, as though the lace were still proving refractory. Again that sharp, searching glance. Again—nothing! He went forward now in apparent unconcern; but his right hand, instead of being buried in his coat pocket, swung easily at his side.

It was strange! His ineffective ruse to the contrary, he was certain that he had not been mistaken. Was it Whitey Mack? Was the question answered? Was the Gray Seal known, too, as Jimmie Dale? Were they trailing him now, with the climax to come at the club, at his own palatial home, wherever the surroundings would best lend themselves to assuaging that inordinate thirst for the sensational that was so essentially a characteristic of the confirmed criminal? What a headline in the morning's papers it would make!

At the corner he loitered by the curb to light a cigarette—still not a soul in sight on either side of the street behind him, except a couple of Italians who had just passed by. Strange again! The intuition, if it were only intuition, was still strong. He swung abruptly on his heel, mingled with the passers-by on the Bowery, walked a rapid half dozen steps until the building hid the cross street, then ran across the road to the opposite side of the Bowery, and, in a crowd now, came back to the corner. He crossed from curb to curb slowly, sheltered by a fringe of people that, however, in no way obstructed his view down the side street. And then Jimmie Dale shrugged his shoulders. He had evidently been mistaken, after all. He was overexcited; his nerves were raw—that, perhaps, was the solution. Meanwhile, every minute was counting, if Whitey Mack and Lannigan should still be at Bristol Bob's.

He kept on down the Bowery, hurrying with growing impatience through the crowds that massed in front of various places of amusement. He had not intended to come along the Bowery, and, except for what had occurred, would have taken a less frequented street. He would turn off at the next block.

He was in front of that moving-picture theatre again. "THE DOUBLE LIFE"—his eyes were attracted involuntarily to the lurid, overdone display. It seemed to threaten him; it seemed to dangle before him a premonition as it were, of what the morning held in store; but now, too, it seemed to feed into flame that smouldering fury that possessed him. His life—or Whitey Mack's! Men, women, and the children who turned night into day in that quarter of the city were clustered thick around the signs, hiving like bees to the bald sensationalism. Almost savagely he began to force his way through the crowd—and the next instant, like a man stunned, had stopped in his tracks. His fingers had closed in a fierce, spasmodic clutch over an envelope that had been thrust suddenly into his hand.

"Jimmie!" from somewhere came a low, quick voice. "Jimmie, it is half-past eleven now—*hurry.*"

He whirled, scanning wildly this face, then that. It was her voice—*her* voice! The Tocsin! The sensitive fingers were telegraphing to his brain, as they always did, that the texture of the envelope, too, was hers. Her voice; yes, anywhere, out of a thousand voices, he would distinguish hers—but her face, he had never seen that. Which, out of all the crowd around him, was hers? Surely he could tell her by her dress; she would be different; her personality alone must single her out. She—

"Say, have youse got de pip, or do youse t'ink youse owns de earth!" a man flung at him, heaving and pushing to get by.

With a start, though he scarcely heard the man, Jimmie Dale moved on. His brain was afire. All the irony of the world seemed massed in a sudden, overwhelming attack upon him. It was useless—intuitively he had known it was useless from the instant he had heard her voice. It was always the same—always! For years she had eluded him like that, come upon him without warning and disappeared, but leaving always that tangible proof of her existence—a letter, the call of the Gray Seal to arms. But to-night it was as it had never been before. It was not alone baffled chagrin now, not alone the longing, the wild desire to see her face, to look into her eyes—it was life and death. She had come at the very moment when she, perhaps alone of all the world, could have pointed the way out, when life, liberty, everything that was common to them both was at stake, in deadly peril—and she had gone, ignorant of it all, leaving him staggered by the very possibility of the succour that was held up before his eyes only to be snatched away without power of his to grasp it. His intuition had not been at fault—he had made no mistake in that shadow across the street from the Sanctuary. It had been the Tocsin. He had been followed; and it was she who had followed him, until, in a crowd, she had seized the opportunity of a moment ago. Though ultimately, perhaps, it changed nothing, it was a relief in a way to know that it was she, not Whitey Mack, who had been lurking there; but her persistent, incomprehensible determination to preserve the mystery with which she surrounded herself was like now to cost them both a ghastly price. If he could only have had one word with her—just one word!

The letter in his hand crackled under his clenched fist. He stared at it in a half-blind, half-bitter way. The call of the Gray Seal to arms! Another coup, with its incident danger and peril, that she had planned for him to execute! He could have laughed aloud at the inhuman mockery of it. The call of the Gray Seal to arms—*now!* When with every faculty drained to its last resource, cornered, trapped, he was fighting for his very existence!

"Jimmie, it is half-past eleven now — *hurry!*" The words were jangling discordantly in his brain.

And now he laughed outright, mirthlessly. A young girl hanging on her escort's arm, passing, glanced at him and giggled. It was a different Jimmie Dale for the moment. For once his immobility had forsaken him. He laughed again — a sort of unnatural, desperate indifference to everything falling upon him. What did it matter, the moment or two it would take to read the letter? He looked around him. He was on the corner in front of the Palace Saloon, and, turning abruptly, he stepped in through the swinging doors. As Larry the Bat, he knew the place well. At the rear of the barroom and along the side of the wall were some half dozen little stalls, partitioned off from each other. Several of these were unoccupied, and he chose the one farthest from the entrance. It was private enough; no one would disturb him.

From the aproned individual who presented himself he ordered a drink. The man returned in a moment, and Jimmie Dale tossed a coin on the table, bidding the other keep the change. He wanted no drink; the transaction was wholly perfunctory. The waiter was gone; he pushed the glass away from him, and tore the envelope open.

A single sheet, closely written on both sides of the paper, was in his hand. It was her writing; there was no mistaking that, but every word, every line bore evidence of frantic haste. Even that customary formula, "dear philanthropic crook," that had prefaced every line she had ever written him before, had been omitted. His eyes traversed the first few lines with that strange indifference that had settled upon him. What, after all, did it matter what it was; he could do nothing — not even save himself probably. And then, with a little start, he read the lines over again, muttering snatches from them.

". . . Max Diestricht — diamonds — the Ross-Logan stones — wedding — sliding panel in wall of workshop — end of the room near window — ten boards to the right from side wall — press small knot in the wood in the centre of the tenth board — to-night . . ."

It brought a sudden thrill of excitement to Jimmie Dale that, impossible as he would have believed it an instant ago, for the moment overshadowed the realisation of his own peril. A robbery such as that, if it were ever accomplished, would stir the country from end to end; it would set New York by the ears; it would loose the police in full cry like a pack of bloodhounds with their leashes slipped. The society columns of the newspapers had been busy for months featuring the coming marriage of the Ross-Logans' daughter to one of the country's young merchant princes. The combined fortunes of the two families would make the young couple the richest in America. The prospective groom's wedding gift was to be a diamond necklace of perfectly matched, large stones that would eclipse anything of the kind in the country. Europe, the foreign markets, had been literally combed and ransacked to supply the gems. The stones had arrived in New York the day before, the duty on them alone amounting to over fifty thousand dollars. All this had appeared in the papers.

Jimmie Dale's brows drew together in a frown. On just exactly what percentage the duty was figured he did not know; but it was high enough on the basis of fifty thousand dollars to assume safely that the assessed value of the stones was not less than four times that amount. Two hundred thousand dollars – laid down, a quarter of a million! Well, why not? In more than one quarter diamonds were ranked as the soundest kind of an investment. Furthermore, through personal acquaintance with the "high contracting parties," who were in his own set, he knew it to be true.

He shrugged his shoulders. The papers, too, had thrown the limelight on Max Diestricht, who, though for quite a time the fashion in the social world, had, up to the present, been comparatively unknown to the average New Yorker. His own knowledge of Max Diestricht went deeper than the superficial biography furnished by the newspapers – the old Hollander had done more than one piece of exquisite jewelry work for him. The old fellow was a character that beggared description, eccentric to the point of extravagance, and deaf as a post; but, in craftmanship, a modern Cellini. He employed no workmen, lived alone over his shop on one of the lower streets between Fifth and Sixth Avenues near Washington Square – and possessed a splendid contempt for such protective contrivances as safes and vaults. If his prospective patrons expostulated on this score before intrusting him with their valuables, they were at liberty to take their work elsewhere. It was Max Diestricht who honoured you by accepting the commission; not you who honoured Max Diestricht by intrusting him with it. "Of what use is it to me, a safe!" he would exclaim. "It hides nothing; it only says, 'I am inside; do not look farther; come and get me!' Yes? It is to explode with the nitro-glycerin – *pouf!* – and I am deaf and I hear nothing. It is a foolishness, that" – he had a habit of prodding at one with a levelled fore-finger – "every night somewhere they are robbed, and have I been robbed? *Hein,* tell me that; have I been robbed?"

It was true. In ten years, though at times having stones and precious metal aggregating large amounts deposited with him by his customers, Max Diestricht had never lost so much as the gold filings. There was a queer smile on Jimmie Dale's lips now. The knot in the tenth board was significant! Max Diestricht was scrupulously honest, a genius in originality and conception of design, a master in the perfection and delicacy of his finished work – he had been commissioned to design and set the Ross-Logan necklace.

The brain works quickly. All this and more had flashed almost instantaneously through Jimmie Dale's mind. His eyes fell to the letter again, and he read on. Halfway through, a sudden whiteness blanched his face, and, following it, a surging tide of red that mounted to his temples. It dazed him; it seemed to rob him for the moment of the power of coherent thought. He was wrong; he had not read aright. It was incredible, dare-devil beyond belief – and yet in its very audacity lay success. He finished the letter, read it once more – and his fingers mechanically began to tear it into little shreds. His brain was in a whirl, a vortex of conflicting emotions. Had Whitey Mack and Lannigan left Bristol Bob's yet? Where were they now? Was there time for – *this?* He was staring at the little torn scraps of paper in his hand. He thrust them suddenly into his pocket, and jerked out his watch. It was nearly midnight. The broad, muscular shoulders seemed to square back curiously, the jaws to clamp a little, the face to harden and grow cold until it was like stone. With a swift movement he emptied his glass into the cuspidor, set the glass back on the table, and stepped out from the stall. His destination was Max Diestricht's.

The Palace Saloon was near the upper end of the Bowery, and, failing a taxicab, of which none was in sight, his quickest method was to walk, and he started briskly forward. It was not far; and it was barely ten minutes from the time he had left the Palace Saloon when he swung through Washington Square to Fifth Avenue, and, a moment later, turned from that thoroughfare, heading west toward Sixth Avenue, along one of those streets which, with the city's northward trend, had quite lost any distinctive identity, and from being once a modestly fashionable residential section had now become a conglomerate potpourri of small tradesmen's stores, shops and apartments of the poorer class. He knew Max Diestricht's – he could well have done without the aid of the arc lamp which, even if dimly, indicated that low, almost tumble-down, two-story structure tucked away between the taller buildings on either side that almost engulfed it. It was late. The street was quiet. The shops and stores had long since been closed, Max Diestricht's among them – the old Hollanders' name in painted white letters stood out against the background of a darkened workshop window. In the story above, the lights, too, were out; Max Diestricht was probably fast asleep – and he was stone deaf!

A glance up and down the street, and Jimmie Dale was standing, or, rather, leaning against Max Diestricht's door. There was no one to see, and if there were, what was there to attract attention to a man standing nonchalantly for a moment in a doorway? It was only for a moment. Those master fingers of Jimmie Dale were working surely, swiftly, silently. A little steel instrument that was never out of his possession was in the lock and out again. The door opened, closed; he drew the black silk mask from his pocket and slipped it over his face. Immediately in front of him the stairs led upward; immediately to his right was the door into the shop – the modest street entrance was common to both.

The door into the workshop was not locked. He opened it, stepped inside, and closed it quietly behind him. The place was in blackness. He stood for a moment silent, straining his ears to catch the slightest sound, reconstructing the plan of his surroundings in his mind as he remembered it. It was a narrow, oblong room, running the entire depth of the building, a very long room, blank walls on either side, a window in the middle of the rear wall that gave on a back yard, and from the back yard there was access to the lane; also, as he remembered the place, it was a riot of disorder, with workbenches and odds and ends strewn without system or reason in every direction – one had need of care to negotiate it in the dark. He took his flashlight from his pocket, and, preliminary to a more intimate acquaintance with the interior, glanced out through the front window near which he stood – and, with a suppressed cry, shrank back instinctively against the wall.

Two men were crossing the street, heading directly for the shop door. The arc lamp lighted up their faces. *It was Inspector Lannigan of headquarters and Whitey Mack!* The quick intake of Jimmie Dale's breath was sucked through clenched teeth. They were close on his heels then – far closer than he had imagined. It would take Whitey Mack scarcely any longer to open that front door than it had taken him. Close on his heels! His face was rigid. He could hear them now at the door. The flashlight in his hand winked down the length of the room. If was a dangerous thing to do, but it was still more dangerous to stumble into some object and make a noise. He darted forward, circuiting a workbench, a stool, a small hand forge. Again the flashlight gleamed. Against the side wall, near the rear, was another workbench, with a sort of coarse canvas curtain hanging part way down in front of it, evidently to protect such things as might be stored away beneath it from dust, and Jimmie Dale sprang for it, whipped back the canvas, and crawled underneath. He was not an instant too soon. As the canvas fell back into place, the shop door opened, closed, and the two men had stepped inside.

Whitey Mack's voice, in a low whisper though it was, seemed to echo raucously through the shop.

"Mabbe we'll have a sweet wait, but I got the straight dope on this. He's going to make a try for Dutchy's sparklers to-night. We'll let him go the limit, and we don't either of us make a move till he's pinched them, and then we get him with the goods on him. He can't get away; he hasn't a hope! There's only two ways of getting in here or getting out – this door and window here, and a window that's down there at the back. You guard this, and I'll take care of the other end. Savvy?"

"Right!" Lannigan answered grimly. "Go ahead!"

There was the sound of footsteps moving forward, then a vicious bump, the scraping of some object along the floor, and a muffled curse from Whitey Mack.

"Use your flashlight!" advised the inspector, in a guarded voice.

"I haven't got one, damn it !" growled Whitey Mack. "It's all right. I'll get along."

Again the steps, but more warily now, as though the man were cautiously feeling ahead of him for possible obstacles. Jimmie Dale for a moment held his breath. He could have reached out and touched the man as the other passed. Whitey Mack went on until he had taken up a position against the rear wall. Jimmie Dale heard him as he brushed against it.

Then silence fell. He was between them now. Stretched full length on the floor, Jimmie Dale raised the lower portion of the canvas away from in front of his face. He could see nothing; the place was in Stygian blackness; but it had been close and stifling, and, at least, it gave him more air.

The minutes dragged by – each more interminable than the one that had gone before. Not a movement, not a sound, and then, through the stillness, very faint at first, came the regular, repressed breathing of Whitey Mack, who was much the nearer of the two men. And, once noticeable, almost imperceptible as it was it seemed to pervade the room and fill it with a strange, ominous resonance that rose and fell until the blackness palpitated with it.

Slowly, very slowly, Jimmie Dale's hand crept into his pocket – and crept out again with his automatic. He lay motionless once more. Time in any concrete sense ceased to exist. Fancied shapes began to assume form in the darkness. By the door, Lannigan stirred uneasily, shifting his position slightly.

Was it hours – was it only minutes? It seemed to ring through the nerve-racking stillness like the shriek of a hurtling shell – and it was only a whisper.

"Watch yourself, Lannigan," whispered Whitey Mack. "He's coming now through the yard! Don't move till I start something. Let him get his paws on the sparklers."

Silence again. And then a low rasping at the window, like the gnawing of a rat; then, inch by inch, the sash was lifted. There was the sound as of a body forcing its way over the sill cautiously, then a step upon the floor inside, another, and still another. The figure of a man loomed up suddenly against the glow of a flashlight as he threw the round, white ray inquisitively here and there over the rear wall. And now he appeared to

be counting the boards. One, two, three – ten. His hand ran up and down the tenth board. Again and again he repeated the operation, and something like the snarl of a baited beast echoed through the room. He half turned to snatch at something in his pocket, and the light for a moment showed a black-bearded, lowering face, partially hidden by a peaked cap that was pulled far down over his eyes.

There was the rip and tear of rending wood, as a steel jimmy, in lieu of the spring the man evidently could not find, bit in between the boards, a muttered oath of satisfaction, and a portion of the wall slid back, disclosing what looked like a metal-lined cupboard. He reached in, seized one of a dozen little boxes, and wrenched off the cover. A blue, scintillating gleam seemed to leap out to meet the white ray of the flashlight. The man chuckled hoarsely, and began to cram the rest of the boxes into his pockets.

Jimmie Dale stirred. On hands and knees he was creeping now from beneath the workbench. Something caught and tore behind him – the canvas curtain. And at the sound, with a sharp cry, the man at the wall whirled, the light went out, and he sprang toward the window. Jimmie Dale gained his feet and leaped forward. A revolver shot cut a lane of fire through the blackness; and, above the roar of the report, Whitey Mack's voice in a fierce yell:

"It's all right, Lannigan! I got him! No – *hell!*" There was a terrific crash of breaking glass. "He's got away!"

"Not yet, he hasn't!" gritted Jimmie Dale between his teeth, and his clubbed revolver swung crashing to the head of a dark form in front of him.

There was a half sigh, half moan. The form slid limply to the floor. Lannigan was floundering down the shop, leaping obstacles in a mad rush, his flashlight picking out the way.

Jimmie Dale stepped swiftly backward, and his hand groped out for the droplight, over the end of the bench, that he had knocked against in his own rush. His fingers clutched it – and the lower end of the shop was flooded with light. Except for his felt hat that lay a little distance away, there was no sign of Whitey Mack; the huddled form of the man, who but a moment since had chuckled as he pocketed old Max Diestricht's gems, lay sprawled, inert, upon the floor, and Lannigan was staring into the muzzle of Jimmie Dale's automatic.

"Drop that gun, Lannigan!" said Jimmie Dale coolly. "And I'll trouble you not to make a noise; it might attract attention from the street; there's been too much already. *Drop that gun!"*

The revolver clattered from Lannigan's hand to the floor. A step forward, and Jimmie Dale's toe sent it spinning under a bench. Another step, and, his revolver still covering the other, he had whipped a pair of handcuffs from the officer's side pocket.

Lannigan, as though the thought had never occurred to him, offered no resistance. He was staring in a dazed sort of way back and forth from Jimmie Dale to the man on the floor.

"What's this mean?" he burst out suddenly, "Where's — "

"Your wrist, please!" requested Jimmie Dale pleasantly. "No — the left one. Thank you" — as the handcuff snapped shut. "Now go over there and sit down on the floor beside that fellow. *Quick!"* Jimmie Dale's voice rasped suddenly, imperatively.

Still bewildered, but a little sullen now, Lannigan obeyed.

Jimmie Dale stooped quickly, and snapped the other link of the handcuff over the unconscious man's right wrist.

Jimmie Dale smiled.

"That's the approved way of taking your man, isn't it? Left wrist to the prisoner's right. He's only stunned; he'll be around in a moment. Know him?"

Lannigan shook his head.

"Take a good look at him," invited Jimmie Dale. "You ought to know most of them in the business."

Lannigan bent over a little closer, and then, with an amazed cry, his free hand shot forward and tore away the other's beard.

It was Whitey Mack!

"My God!" gasped Lannigan.

"Quite so!" said Jimmie Dale evenly. "You'll find the diamonds in his pockets, and, excuse me" — his fingers were running through Whitey Mack's clothes — "ah, here it is" — the thin metal case was in his hand — "a little article that belongs to me, and whose loss, I am free to admit, caused me considerable concern until I was informed that he had only found it without having the slightest idea as to whom it belonged. It made quite a difference!" He had opened the case carelessly before Lannigan's eyes. "'The Gray Seal!' I'll say it for you," said Jimmie Dale whimsically. "This is what probably put the idea into his head, after first, in some way, having discovered old Max Diestricht's hiding place; and, if I had given him time enough, he would probably have stuck one of these seals, in clumsy imitation of that little eccentricity of mine, on the wall over there to stamp the job as genuine. You begin to get it, don't you Lannigan? Pretty sure-fire as an alibi, eh? And he'd have got away with it, too, as far as you were concerned. He had only to fire that shot, smash the window, tuck his false beard, mustache, and peaked cap into his pocket, put on his own hat that you see there on the floor — and yell that the man had escaped. He'd help you chase the thief, too! Rather neat, don't you think, Lannigan? And worth the risk, too, considering the howl that would go up at the theft of those stones, and that, known as the slickest diamond thief in the country, he would be the first to be suspected — except that the police themselves, in the person of Inspector Lannigan of headquarters, would be prepared to prove a perfectly good alibi for him."

Lannigan's head was thrust forward; his eyes, hard, were riveted on Whitey Mack.

"My God!" he said again under his breath. Then fiercely: "He'll get his for this!"

It was a moment before Jimmie Dale spoke; he was musingly examining the automatic in his hand.

"I am going now, Lannigan," he observed quietly. "I require, say, fifteen minutes in which to effect my escape. It is, of course, obvious that an alarm raised by you might prove extremely awkward, but a piece of canvas from that bench there, together with a bit of string, would make a most effective gag. I prefer, however, not to submit you to that indignity. Instead, I offer you the alternative of giving me your word to remain quietly where you are for — fifteen minutes."

Lannigan hesitated.

Jimmie Dale smiled.

"I agree," said Lannigan shortly.

Jimmie Dale stepped back. The electric-light switch clicked. The place was in darkness. There was a moment, two, of utter stillness; then softly, from the front end of the shop, a whisper:

"If I were you, Lannigan, I'd take that gun from Whitey's pocket before he comes round and beats you to it."

And the door had closed silently behind Jimmie Dale.

CHAPTER XI

THE STOOL-PIGEON

(Monday 10/11/1915 to Tuesday 10/12/1915)

IN the subway, ten minutes before, a freckled-faced messenger boy had squeezed himself into a seat beside Jimmie Dale, yanked a dime novel from a refractory pocket, and, blissfully lost to all the world, had buried his head in its pages. Jimmie Dale's glance at the youngster had equally, perforce, embraced the lurid title of the thriller, "Dicing with Death," [51] so imperturbably thrust under his nose. At the time, he had smiled indulgently; but now, as he left the subway and headed for his home on Riverside Drive, the words not only refused to be ignored, but had resolved themselves into a curiously persistent refrain in his mind. They were exactly what they purported to be, dime-novelish, of the deepest hue of yellow, melodramatic in the extreme; but also, to him now, they were grimly apt and premonitorily appropriate. "Dicing with Death" — there was not an hour, not a moment in the day, when he was not literally dicing with death; when, with the underworld and the police allied against him, a single false move would lose him the throw that left death the winner!

The risk of the dual life enforced upon him grew daily greater, and in the end there must be the reckoning. He would have been a madman to have shut his eyes in the face of what was obvious — but it was worth it all, and in his soul he knew that he would not have had it otherwise even now. To-night, to-morrow, the day after, would come another letter from the Tocsin, and there would be another "crime" of the Gray Seal's blazoned in the press — would that be the last affair, or would there be another — or to-night, to-morrow, the day after, would he be trapped before even one more letter came!

He shrugged his shoulders, as he ran up the steps of his house. Those were the stakes that he himself had laid on the table to wager upon the game, he had no quarrel there; but if only, before the end came, or even with the end itself, he could find — *her!*

---

[51] The Frank L. Packard short story in the June 1915 issue of London-based *Cassell's Magazine of Fiction* is called 'Dicing with Death.' It was probably the United Kingdom version of this chapter.

With his latchkey he let himself into the spacious, richly furnished, well-lighted reception hall, and, crossing this, went up the broad staircase, his steps noiseless on the heavy carpet. Below, faintly, he could hear some of the servants – they evidently had not heard him close the door behind him. Discipline was relaxed somewhat, it was quite apparent, with Jason, that peer of butlers, away. Jason, poor chap, was in the hospital. Typhoid, they had thought it at first, though it had turned out to be some milder form of infection. He would be back in a few days now; but meanwhile he missed the old man sorely from the house.

He reached the landing, and, turning, went along the hall to the door of his own particular den, opened the door, closed it behind him – and in an instant the keen, agile brain, trained to the little things that never escaped it, that daily held his life in the balance, was alert. The room was unusually dark, even for night-time. It was as though the window shades had been closely drawn – a thing Jason never did. But then Jason wasn't there! Jimmie Dale, smiling then a little quizzically at himself, reached up for the electric-light switch beside the door, pressed it – and, his finger still on the button, whipped his automatic from his pocket with his other hand. *The room was still in darkness.*

The smile on Jimmie Dale's lips was gone, for his lips now had closed together in a tight, drawn line. The lights in the rest of the house, as witness the reception hall, were in order. This was no *accident!* Silent, motionless, he stood there, listening. Was he trapped at last – in his own house! By whom? The police? The thugs of the underworld? It made little difference – the end would differ only in the method by which it was attained! What was that! Was there a slight stir, a movement at the lower end of the room – or was it his imagination? His hand fell from the electric-light switch to the doorknob behind his back. Slowly, without a sound, it began to turn under his slim, tapering fingers, whose deft, sensitive touch had made him known and feared as the master cracksman of them all; and, as noiselessly, the door began to open.

It was like a duel – a duel of silence. What was the intruder, whoever he might be, waiting for? The abortive click of the electric-light switch, to say nothing of the opening of the door when he had entered, was evidence enough that he was there. Was the other trying to place him exactly through the darkness to make sure of his attack! The door was open now. And suddenly Jimmie Dale laughed easily aloud – and on the instant shifted his position.

"Well?" inquired Jimmie Dale coolly from the other side of the threshold.

It seemed like a long-drawn sigh fluttering through the room, a gasp of relief—and then the blood was pounding madly at his temples, and he was back in the room again, the door closed once more behind him.

"Oh, Jimmie—why didn't you speak? I had to be sure that it was you."

It was her voice! *Hers! The Tocsin! Here!* She was here—here in his house!

"You!" he cried. "You—here!" He was pressing the electric-light switch frantically, again and again.

Her voice came out of the darkness from across the room:

"Why are you doing that, Jimmie? You know already that I have turned off the lights."

"At the sockets—of course!" He laughed out the words almost hysterically. "Your face—I have never seen your face, you know." He was moving quickly toward the reading lamp on his desk.

There was a quick, hurried swish of garments, and she was blocking his way.

"No," she said, in a low voice; "you must not light that lamp."

He laughed again, shortly, fiercely now. She was close to him, his hands reached out for her, touched her, and thrilling at the touch, swept her toward him.

"Jimmie—Jimmie—are you mad!" she breathed.

Mad! Yes—he was mad with the wildest, most passionate exhilaration he had ever known. He found his voice with an effort.

"These months and years that I have tried until my soul was sick to find you!" he cried out. "And you are here now! Your face—I must see your face!"

She had wrenched herself away from him. He could hear her breath coming sharply in little gasps. He groped his way onward toward the desk.

"*Wait!*"—her tones seemed to ring suddenly vibrant through the room. "Wait, before you touch that lamp! I—I put you on your honour not to light it."

He stopped abruptly.

"My—honour?" he repeated mechanically.

"Yes! I came here to-night because there was no other way. No other way—do you understand? I came, trusting to your honour not to take advantage of the conditions that forced me to do this. I had no fear that I was wrong—I have no fear now. You will not light that lamp, and you will not make any attempt to prevent my going away as I came—unknown. Is there any question about it, Jimmie? I am in *your* house."

"You don't know what you are saying!" he burst out wildly. "I've risked my life for a chance like this again and again; I've gone through hell, living in squalour for a month on end as Larry the Bat in the hope that I might discover who you are – and do you think I'll let anything stop me now! I tell you, no – a thousand times no!"

She made no answer. There was only her low, quick breathing coming from somewhere near him. He made another step toward the lamp – and stopped.

"I tell you, no!" he said again, and took another step forward – and stopped once more.

Still she made no answer. A minute passed – another. His hand lifted and swept across his forehead in an agitated way. Still silence. She neither moved nor spoke. His hand dropped slowly to his side. There was a queer, twisted smile upon his lips.

"You win!" he said hoarsely.

"Thank you, Jimmie," she said simply.

"And your name, who you are" – he was speaking, but he did not seem to recognise his own voice – "the hundred other things I've sworn I'd make you explain when I found you, are all taboo as well, I suppose!"

"Yes," she said.

He laughed bitterly.

"Don't you know," he cried out, "that between the police and the underworld, our house of cards is likely to collapse at any minute – that they are hunting the Gray Seal day and night! Is it to be always like this – that I am never to know – until it is too late!"

She came toward him out of the darkness impulsively.

"They will never get you, Jimmie," she said, in a suppressed voice. "And some day, I promise you now, you shall have your reward for to-night. You shall know – everything."

"When?" The word came from him with fierce eagerness.

"I do not know," she answered gently. "Soon, perhaps – perhaps sooner than either of us imagine."

"And by that you mean – what?" he asked, and his hand reached out for her again through the blackness.

This time she did not draw away. There was an instant's hesitation; then she spoke again hurriedly, a note of anxiety in her voice.

"You are beginning all over again, aren't you, Jimmie? And I have told you that to-night I can explain nothing. And, besides, it is what has brought me here that counts now, and every moment is of – "

"Yes. I know," he interposed; "but, then, at least you will tell me one thing: Why did you come to-night, instead of sending me a letter as you always have before?"

"Because it is different to-night than it ever was before," she replied earnestly. "Because there is something in what has happened that I cannot explain myself; because there is danger, and where I could not see clearly I feared a trap, and so I dared not send what, in a letter, could at best be only vague and incomplete details. Do you see?"

"Yes," said Jimmie Dale—but he was only listening in an abstracted way. If he could only see that face, so close to his! He had yearned for that with all his soul for years now! And she was here, standing beside him, and his hand was upon her arm; and here, in his own den, in his own house, he was listening to another call to arms for the Gray Seal from her own lips! Honour! Was he but a poor, quixotic fool! He had only to step to the desk and switch on the light! Why should—he steadied himself with a jerk, and drew away his hand. She was in *his* house. "Go on," he said tersely.

"Do you know, or did you ever hear of old Luther Doyle?" she asked.

"No," said Jimmie Dale.

"Do you know a man, then, named Connie Myers?"

Connie Myers! Who in the Bad Lands did not know Connie Myers, who boasted of the half dozen prison sentences already to his credit? Yes; he knew Connie Myers! But, strangely enough, it was not in the Bad Lands or as Larry the Bat that he knew the man, or that the other knew him—it was as Jimmie Dale. Connie Myers had introduced himself one night several years ago with a blackjack that had just missed its mark as the man had jumped out from a dark alleyway on the East Side, and he, Jimmie Dale, had thrashed the other to within an inch of his life. He had reason to know Connie Myers—and Connie Myers had reason to remember him!

"Yes," he said, with a grim smile; "I know Connie Myers."

"And the tenement across the street from where you live as Larry the Bat—that, of course, you know." He leaned toward her wonderingly now.

"Of course!" he ejaculated. "Naturally!"

"Listen, then, Jimmie!" She was speaking quickly now. "It is a strange story. This Luther Doyle was already over fifty, when, some eight or nine years ago, his parents died within a few months of each other, and he inherited somewhere in the neighbourhood of a hundred thousand dollars; but the man, though harmless enough, was mildly insane, half-witted, queer, and the old couple, on account of their son's mental defects, took care to leave the money securely invested, and so that he could only touch the interest. During these eight or nine years he has lived by himself in the same old family house where he had lived with his parents, in a lonely spot near Pelham. And he has lived in a most frugal, even miserly, manner. His income could not have been less than six thousand dollars a year, and his expenditures could not have been more than six hundred. His dementia, ironically enough from the day that he came into his fortune, took the form of a most pitiable and abject fear that he would die in poverty, misery, and want; and so, year after year, cashing his checks as fast as he got them, never trusting the bank with a penny, he kept hiding away somewhere in his house every cent he could scrape and save from his income — which to-day must amount, at a minimum calculation, to fifty thousand dollars."

"And," observed Jimmie Dale quietly. "Connie Myers robbed him of it, and —"

"No!" Her voice was quivering with passion, as she caught up his words. "Twice in the last month Connie Myers *tried* to rob him, but the money was too securely hidden. Twice he broke into Doyle's house when the old man was out, but on both occasions was unsuccessful in his search, and was interrupted and forced to make his escape on account of Doyle's return. To-night, an hour ago, in an empty room on the second floor of that tenement, in the room facing the landing, old Luther Doyle was *murdered!*"

There was silence for an instant. Her hand had closed in a tight pressure on his arm. The darkness seemed to add a sort of ghastly significance to her words.

"In God's name, how do you know all this?" he demanded wildly. "How do you know all these things?

"Does that matter now?" she answered tensely. "You will know that when you know the rest. Oh, don't you understand, Jimmie, there is not a moment to lose now? It was easy to lure a half-witted creature like that anywhere; it was Connie Myers who lured him to the tenement and murdered him there — but from that point, Jimmie, I am not sure of our ground. I do not know whether Connie Myers is alone in this or not; but I do know that he is going to Doyle's house again to-night to make another search for the money. There is no question but that old Doyle was murdered to give Connie Myers and his accomplices, if there are any, a chance to tear the house inside out to find the money, to give them the whole night to work in without interruption if necessary — but Doyle dead in his own house could have interfered no more with them than Doyle dead in that tenement! Why was he lured to the tenement by Connie Myers when he could much more easily have been put out of the way in his own house? Jimmie, there is something behind this, something more that you must find out. There may be others in this besides Connie Myers, I do not know; but there is something here that I am afraid of. Jimmie, you must get that man, you must get the others if there are others, and you must stop them from getting the money in that house to-night! Do you understand now why I have come here? I could not explain in a letter; I do not quite seem to be explaining now. It would seem as though there were no need for the Gray Seal – that simply the police should be notified. But I *know,* Jimmie, call it intuition, what you will, I know that there is need for us, for you to-night – that behind all this is a tragedy, deeper, blacker, than even the brutal, cold-blooded murder that is already done."

Her voice, in its passionate earnestness, died away; and an anger, cold, grim, remorseless, settled upon Jimmie Dale – settled as it always settled upon him at her call to arms. His brain was already at work in its quick, instant way, probing, sifting, planning. She was right! It was strange, it was more than strange that, with the added risk, the danger, the difficulty, the man should have been brought miles to be done away with in that tenement! Why? Connie Myers took form before him – the coarse features, the tawny hair that straggled across the low forehead, the shifty eyes that were an indeterminate colour between brown and gray, the thin lips that seemed to draw in and give the jaw a protruding, belligerent effect. And Connie Myers knew him as Jimmie Dale – it would have to be then as Larry the Bat that the Gray Seal must work. That meant time – to go to the Sanctuary and change.

"The police," he asked suddenly, aloud, "they have not yet discovered the body?"

"Not yet," she replied hurriedly. "And that is still another reason for haste – there is no telling when they will. See – here!" She thrust a paper into his hand. "Here is a plan of old Doyle's house, and directions for finding it. You must get Connie Myers red-handed, you must make him convict himself, for the evidence through which I know him to be guilty can never be used against him. And, Jimmie, be careful – I know I am not wrong, that there is still something more behind all this. And now go, Jimmie, go! There is no time to lose!" She was pushing him across the room toward the door.

Go! The word seemed suddenly to bring dismay. It was she again who was dominant now in his mind. Who knew if to-night, when he was taking his life in his hands again, would not be the last! And she was here now, here beside him – where she might never be again!

She seemed to divine his thoughts, for she spoke again, a strange new note of tenderness in her voice that thrilled him.

"You must never let them get you, Jimmie – for my sake. It will not last much longer—it is near the end—and I shall keep my promise. But go, now, Jimmie—go!"

"Go?" he repeated numbly. "Go? But—but you?"

"I?" She slipped suddenly away from him, retreating back down the room. "I will go—as I came." [52]

"Wait! Listen!" he pleaded.

There was no answer.

She was there—somewhere back there in the darkness still. He stood hesitant at the door. It seemed that every faculty he possessed urged him back there again—to her. Could he let her escape him now when she was so utterly in his power, she who meant everything in his life! And then, like a cold shock, came that other thought—she who had trusted to his honour! With a jerk, his hand swept out, felt for the doorknob, and closed upon it.

"Good-night!" he said heavily, and stepped out into the hall.

It seemed for a while, even after he had gained the street and made his way again to the subway, that nothing was concrete around him, that he was living through some fantastical dream. His head whirled, and he could not think rationally—and then

slowly, little by little, his grip upon himself came back. She had come— and gone! With the roar of the subway in his ears, its raucous note seeming to strike so perfectly in consonance with the turmoil within him, he smiled mirthlessly. After all, it was as it always was! She was gone—and ahead of him lay the chances of the night!

"Dicing with death!" The words, unbidden, came back once more. If they were true before, they were doubly applicable now. It was different to-night from what it had ever been before, as she had said. Usually, to the smallest detail, everything was laid open, clear before him in those astounding letters. To-night, it was vague at best. A man had been murdered. Connie Myers had committed the murder under circumstances that pointed strongly to some hidden motive behind and beyond the mere chance it afforded him to search his victim's house for the hidden cash. What was it?

---

[52] It's reasonable to suppose that the Tocsin herself has some skill at lockpicking – given her demonstrated familiarity with different types of safes - but another possible explanation for how she was able to enter his residence undetected is that she had made a wax impression of Dale's house key when he was unconscious back at the end of Chapter Eight.

Jimmie Dale stared out at the black subway walls. The answer would not come. Station after station passed. At Fourteenth Street he changed from the express to a local, got out at Astor Place, and a few minutes later was walking rapidly down the upper end of the Bowery.

The answer would not come — only the fact itself grew more and more deeply significant. The ghastly, callous fiendishness that lured an old, half-witted man to his death had Jimmie Dale in that grip of cold, merciless anger again, and there was a dull flush now upon his cheeks. Whatever it meant, whatever was behind it, one thing at least was certain — *he would get Connie Myers!*

He was close to the Sanctuary now — it was down the next cross street. He reached the corner and turned it, heading east; but his brisk walk had changed to a nonchalant saunter — there were some people coming toward him. It was the Gray Seal now, alert and cautious. The little group passed by. Ahead, the tenement bordering on the black alleyway loomed up — the Sanctuary, with its three entrances and exits; the home of Larry the Bat. And across from it was that other tenement, that held a new interest for him now, where, in an empty room on the second floor, she had said, old Doyle still lay. Should he go there? He was thinking quickly now, and shook his head. It would take what he did not have to spare — time. It was already ten o'clock; and, granted that Connie Myers had committed the crime only a little over an hour ago, the man by this time would certainly be on his way to Doyle's house near Pelham, if, indeed, he were not already there. No, there was no time to spare — the question resolved itself simply into how long, since he had already searched twice and failed on both occasions, it would take Connie Myers to unearth old Doyle's hiding place for the money.

Jimmie Dale glanced sharply around him, slipped into the alleyway, and, crouching against the tenement wall, moved noiselessly along to the side entrance. A moment more, and he had negotiated the rickety stairs with practiced, soundless tread, was inside the squalid quarters of Larry the Bat, and the door of the Sanctuary was locked and bolted behind him.

Perhaps five minutes passed — and then, where Jimmie Dale, the millionaire, had entered, there emerged Larry the Bat, of the aristocracy and the elite of the Bad Lands. But instead of leaving by the side door and the alleyway, as he had entered, he went along the lower hallway to the front entrance. And here, instinctively, he paused a moment at the top of the steps, as his eyes rested upon the tenement on the opposite side of the street.

It was strange that the crime should have been committed there! Something again seemed to draw him toward that empty room on the second story. He had decided once that he would not go, that there was not time; but, after all, it would not take long, and there was at least the possibility of gaining something more valuable even than time from the scene of the crime itself—there might even be the evidence he wanted there that would disclose the whole of Connie Myers' game.

He went down the steps, and started across the street; but halfway over, he hesitated uncertainly, as a child's cry came petulantly from the doorway. It was dark in the street; and, likewise, it was one of those hot, suffocating evenings when, in the crowded tenements of the poorer class, miserable enough in any case, misery was added to a hundredfold for lack of a single God-given breath of air. These two facts, apparently irrelevant, caused Jimmie Dale to change his mind again. He had not noticed the woman with the baby in her arms, sitting on the doorstep; but now, as he reached the curb, he not only saw, but recognised her—and he swung on down the street toward the Bowery. He could not very well go in without passing her, without being recognised himself—and that was a needless risk.

He smiled a little wanly. Once the crime was discovered, she would not have hesitated long before informing the police that she had seen him enter there! Mrs. Hagan was no friend of his! One could not live as he had lived, as Larry the Bat, and not see something in an intimate way of the pitiful little tragedies of the poor around him; for, bad, tough, and dissolute as the quarter was, all were not degraded there, some were simply—poor. Mrs. Hagan was poor. Her husband was a day labourer, often out of a job—and sometimes he drank. That was how he, Jimmie Dale, or rather, Larry the Bat, had come to earn Mrs. Hagan's enmity. He had found Mike Hagan [53] drunk one night, and in the act of being arrested, and had wheedled the man away from the officer on the promise that he would take Hagan home. And he was Larry the Bat, a dope fiend, a character known to all the neighbourhood, and Mrs. Hagan had laid her husband's condition to *his* influence and companionship! He had taken Mike Hagan home—and Mrs. Hagan had driven Larry the Bat from the door of her miserable one-room lodging in that tenement with the bitter words on her tongue that only a woman can use when shame and grief and anger are breaking her heart.

He shrugged his shoulders, as, back along the Bowery, he retraced his steps, but now, with the hurried shuffle of Larry the Bat where before had been the brisk, athletic stride of Jimmie Dale.

At Astor Place again, he took the subway, this time to the Grand Central Station—and, well within an hour from the time he had left the Sanctuary, including the train journey to Pelham, he was standing in a

---

[53] **Not to be confused with young Bert Hagan from Chapter One.**

clump of trees that fringed a deserted roadway. He had passed but few houses, once he was away from Pelham, and, as well as he could judge, there was none now within a quarter of a mile of him — except this one of old Luther Doyle's that showed up black and shadowy just beyond the trees.

Jimmie Dale's eyes narrowed as he surveyed the place. It was little wonder that, known to have money, an attempt to rob old Doyle should have been made in a place like this! It was even more grimly significant than ever of some deeper meaning that, in its loneliness an ideal place for a murder, the man should have been lured from there for that purpose to a crowded tenement in the city instead! What did it mean? Why had it been done? He shook his head. The answer would not come now any more than it had come before in the subway, or in the train on the way out, when he had set his brain so futilely to solve the problem.

From a survey of the house, Jimmie Dale gave attention to the details of his surroundings: the trees on either side; the open space in front, a distance of fifty yards to the road; the absence of any fence. And then, abruptly, he stole forward. There was no light to be seen anywhere about the house. Was it possible that Connie Myers was not yet there? He shook his head again impatiently. Connie Myers would not have wasted any time — as the Tocsin had said, there was always present the possibility that the crime in that tenement might be discovered at *any* moment. Connie Myers would have lost no time; for, let the discovery be made, let the police identify the body, as they most certainly would, and they would be out here hotfoot. Jimmie Dale stood suddenly still. What did it mean! He had not thought of that before! If old Doyle had been murdered *here,* there would not have been even the possibility of discovery until the morning at the earliest, and Connie Myers would have had all the time he wanted!

What was that sound! A low, muffled tapping, like a succession of hammer blows, came from within the house. Jimmie Dale darted forward, reached the side of the house, and dropped on hands and knees. One question at least was answered — Connie Myers was inside.

The plan that she had given him showed an old-fashioned cellarway, closed by folding trapdoors, that was located a little toward the rear and, in a moment, creeping along, he came upon it. His hands felt over it. It was shut, fastened by a padlock on the outside. Jimmie Dale's lips thinned a little, as he took a small steel instrument from his pocket. Either through inadvertence or by intention, Connie Myers had passed up an almost childishly simple means of entrance into the house! One side of the trapdoor was lifted up silently — and silently closed. Jimmie Dale was in the cellar. The hammering, much more distinct now, heavy, thudding blows, came from a room in the front — the connection between the cellar and the house, as shown on the Tocsin's plan, was through another trapdoor in the floor of the kitchen.

Jimmie Dale's flashlight played on a short, ladderlike stairway, and in an instant he was climbing upward. The sounds from the front of the house continued now without interruption; there was little fear that Connie Myers would hear anything else — even the protesting squeak of the hinges as Jimmie Dale cautiously pushed back the trapdoor in the flooring above his head. An inch, two inches he lifted it; and, his eyes on a level with the opening now, he peered into the room. The kitchen itself was intensely dark; but through an open doorway, well to one side so that he could not see into the room beyond, there struggled a curiously faint, dim glimmer of light. And then Jimmie Dale's form straightened rigidly on the stairs. The blows stopped, and a voice, in a low growl, presumably Connie Myers', reached him.

"Here, take a drive at it from the lower edge!"

There was no answer — save that the blows were resumed again. Jimmie Dale's face had set hard. Connie Myers was not alone in this, then! Well, the odds were a little heavier, *doubled* — that was all! He pushed the trapdoor wide open, swung himself up through the opening to the floor; and the next instant, back a little from the connecting doorway, his body pressed closely against the kitchen wall, he was staring, bewildered and amazed, into the next room.

On the floor, presumably to lessen the chance of any light rays stealing through the tightly drawn window shades, burned a small oil lamp. The place was in utter confusion. The right-hand side of a large fireplace, made of rough, untrimmed stone and cement, and which occupied almost the entire end of the room, was already practically demolished, and the wreckage was littered everywhere; part of the furniture was piled unceremoniously into one corner out of the way; and at the fireplace itself, working with sledge and bar, were two men. One was Connie Myers. An ironical glint crept into Jimmie Dale's eyes. The false beard and mustache the man wore would deceive no one who knew Connie Myers! And that he should be wearing them now, as he knelt holding the bar while the other struck at it, seemed both uncalled for and absurd. The other man, heavily built, roughly dressed, had his back turned, and Jimmie Dale could not see his face.

The puzzled frown on Jimmie Dale's forehead deepened. Somewhere in the masonry of the fireplace, of course, was where old Luther Doyle had hidden his money. That was quite plain enough; and that Connie Myers, in some way or other, had made sure of that fact was equally obvious. But how did old Luther Doyle get his money *in* there from time to time, as he received the interest and dividends whose accumulation, according to the Tocsin, comprised his hoard! And how did he get it *out* again?

"All right, that'll do!" grunted Connie Myers suddenly. "We can pry this one out now. Lend a hand on the bar!"

The other dropped his sledge, turned sideways as he stooped to help Connie Myers, his face came into view — and, with an involuntary start, Jimmie Dale crouched farther back against the wall, as he stared at the other. It was Hagan! Mrs. Hagan's husband! Mike Hagan!

"My God!" whispered Jimmie Dale, under his breath.

So that was it! That the murder had been committed in the tenement was not so strange now! A surge of anger swept Jimmie Dale — and was engulfed in a wave of pity. Somehow, the thin, tired face of Mrs. Hagan had risen before him, and she seemed to be pleading with him to go away, to leave the house, to forget that he had ever been there, to forget what he had seen, what he was seeing now. His hands clenched fiercely. How realistically, how importunately, how pitifully she took form before him! She was on her knees, clasping his knees, imploring him, terrified.

From Jimmie Dale's pocket came the black silk mask. Slowly, almost hesitantly, he fitted it over his face — Mike Hagan knew Larry the Bat. Why should he have pity for Mike Hagan? Had he any for Connie Myers? What right had he to let pity sway him! The man had gone the limit; he was Connie Myers' accomplice — a murderer! But the man was not a hardened, confirmed criminal like Connie Myers. Mike Hagan — a murderer! It would have been unbelievable but for the evidence before his own eyes now. The man had faults, brawled enough, and drank enough to have brought him several times to the notice of the police — but this!

Jimmie Dale's eyes had never left the scene before him. Both men were throwing their weight upon the bar, and the stone that they were trying to dislodge — they were into the heart of the masonry now — seemed to move a little. Connie Myers stood up, and, leaning forward, examined the stone critically at top and bottom, prodding it with the bar. He turned from his examination abruptly, and thrust the bar into Hagan's hands.

"Hold it!" he said tersely. "I'll strike for a turn."

Crouched, on his hands and knees, Hagan inserted the point of the bar into the crevice. Connie Myers picked up the sledge.

"Lower! Bend lower!" he snapped — and swung the sledge.

It seemed to go black for a moment before Jimmie Dale's eyes, seemed to paralyse all action of mind and body. There was a low cry that was more a moan, the clang of the iron bar clattering on the floor, and Mike Hagan had pitched forward on his face, an inert and huddled heap. A half laugh, half snarl purled from Connie Myers' lips, as he snatched a stout piece of cord from his pocket and swiftly knotted the unconscious man's wrists together. Another instant, and, picking up the bar, prying with it again, the loosened stone toppled with a crash into the grate.

It had come sudden as the crack of doom, that blow – too quick, too unexpected for Jimmie Dale to have lifted a finger to prevent it. And now that the first numbed shock of mingled horror and amazement was past, he fought back the quick, fierce impulse to spring out on Connie Myers. Whether the man was killed or only stunned, he could do no good to Mike Hagan now, and there was Connie Myers – he was staring in a fascinated way at Connie Myers. Behind the stone that the other had just dislodged was a large hollow space that had been left in the masonry, and from this now Connie Myers was eagerly collecting handfuls of banknotes that were rolled up into the shape of little cylinders, each one grotesquely tied with a string. The man was feverishly excited, muttering to himself, running from the fireplace to where the table had been pushed aside with the rest of the furniture, dropping the curious little rolls of money on the table, and running back for more. And then, having apparently emptied the receptacle, he wriggled his body over the dismantled fireplace, stuck his head into the opening, and peered upward.

"Kinks in his nut, kinks in his nut!" Connie Myers was muttering. "I'll drop the bar through from the top, mabbe there's some got stuck in the pipe."

He regained his feet, picked up the bar, and ran with it into what was evidently the front hall – then his steps sounded running upstairs.

Like a flash, Jimmie Dale was across the room and at the fireplace. Like Connie Myers, he, too, put his head into the opening; and then, a queer, unpleasant smile on his lips, he bent quickly over the man on the floor. Hagan was no more than stunned, and was even then beginning to show signs of returning consciousness. There was a rattle, a clang, a thud – and the bar, too long to come all the way through, dropped into the opening and stood upright. Connie Myers' footsteps sounded again, returning on the run – and Jimmie Dale was back once more on the other side of the kitchen doorway.

It was all simple enough – once one understood! The same queer smile was still flickering on Jimmie Dale's lips. There was no way to get the money out, except the way Connie Myers had got it out – by digging it out! With the irrational cunning of his mad brain, that had put the money even beyond his own reach, old Doyle had built his fireplace with a hollow some eighteen inches square in a great wall of solid stonework, and from it had run a two-inch pipe up somewhere to the story above; and down this pipe he had dropped his little string-tied cylinders of banknotes, satisfied that his hoard was safe! There seemed something pitifully ironic in the elaborate, insane craftiness of the old man's fear-twisted, demented mind.

And now Connie Myers was back in the room again—and again a puzzled expression settled upon Jimmie Dale's face as he watched the other. For perhaps a minute the man stood by the table sifting the little rolls of money through his fingers gloatingly—then, impulsively, he pushed these to one side, produced a revolver, laid it on the table, and from another pocket took out a little case which, as he opened it, Jimmie Dale could see contained a hypodermic syringe. One more article followed the other two—a letter, which Connie Myers took out of an unsealed envelope. He dropped this suddenly on the table, as Mike Hagan, three feet away on the floor, groaned and sat up.

Hagan's eyes swept, bewildered, confused, around him, questioningly at Connie Myers—and then, resting suddenly on his bound wrists, they narrowed menacingly.

"Damn you, you smashed me with that sledge on *purpose!*" he burst out—and began to struggle to his feet.

With a brutal chuckle, Connie Myers pushed Hagan back and shoved his revolver under the other's nose.

"Sure!" he admitted evenly. "And you keep quiet, or I'll finish you now—instead of letting the police do it!" He laughed out jarringly. "You're under arrest, you know, for the murder of Luther Doyle, and for robbing the poor old nut of his savings in his house here."

Hagan wrenched himself up on his elbow.

"What—what do you mean?" he stammered.

"Oh, don't worry!" said Connie Myers maliciously. "*I'm* not making the arrest, I'd rather the police did that. I'm not mixing up in it, and by and by"—he lifted up the hypodermic for Hagan to see—"I'm going to shoot a little dope into you that'll keep you quiet while I get away myself."

Hagan's face had gone a grayish white—he had caught sight of the money on the table, and his eyes kept shifting back and forth from it to Myers' face.

"Murder!" he said huskily. "There is no murder. I don't know who Doyle is. You said this house was yours—you hired me to come here. You said you were going to tear down the fireplace and build another. You said I could work evenings and earn some extra money."

"Sure, I did!" There was a vicious leer now on Connie Myers' lips. "But you don't think I picked you out by *accident,* do you? Your reputation, my bucko, was just shady enough to satisfy anybody that it wouldn't be beyond you to go the limit. Sure, you murdered Doyle! Listen to this." He took up the letter:

"TO THE POLICE: Luther Doyle was murdered this evening in the tenement at 67 — Street. You'll find his body in a room on the second floor. If you want to know who did it, look in Mike Hagan's room on the floor above. There's a paper stuck under the edge of Hagan's table with a piece of chewing gum, where he hid it. You'll know what it is when you go out and take a look at Doyle's house in Pelham. Yours truly,
A FRIEND."

Mike Hagan did not speak—his lips were twitching, and there was horror creeping into his eyes.

"D'ye get me!" sneered Connie Myers. "Tell your story—who'd believe it! I got you cinched. Twice I tried to get this old dub's coin out here, and couldn't find it. But the second time I found something else—a piece of paper with a drawing of the fireplace on it, and a place in the drawing marked with an X. That was good enough, wasn't it? That's the paper I stuck under your table this afternoon when your wife was out— see? Somebody's got to stand for the job, and if it's somebody else it won't be me—get me! When I had a look at that fireplace I knew I couldn't do the job alone in a week, and I didn't dare blast it with 'soup' for fear of spoiling what was inside. And since I had to have somebody to help me, I thought I might as well let him help me all the way through—and stand for it. I picked you, Mike—that's why I croaked old Doyle in your tenement to-night. I wrote this letter while I was waiting for you to show up at the station to come out here with me, and I'm going to see that the police get it in the next hour. When they find Doyle in the room below yours, and that paper in your room, and the busted fireplace here—I guess they won't look any farther for who did it. And say"—he leaned forward with an ugly grin—"mabbe you think I'm soft to be telling you all this? But don't you fool yourself. You don't know me—you don't know who I am. So tell 'em the *truth!* They won't believe you anyway with evidence like that against you—and the neater the story the more they'll think it shows brains enough on your part to have pulled a job like this!"

"My God!" Hagan was rocking on his knees, beads of sweat were starting out on his forehead. "You wouldn't plant a man like that!" he cried brokenly. "You wouldn't do it, would you? My God—you wouldn't do that!"

Jimmie Dale's face under his mask was white and rigid. There was something primal, elemental in the savagery that was sweeping upon him.

He had it all now — *all!* She had been right — there was need to-night for the Gray Seal. So that was the game, inhuman, hellish, the whole of it, to the last filthy dregs — Connie Myers, to protect himself, was railroading an innocent man to death for the crime that he himself had committed! There was a cold smile on Jimmie Dale's lips now, as he took his automatic from his pocket. No, it wasn't quite all the game — there was still *his* hand to play! He edged forward a little nearer to the door — and halted abruptly, listening. An automobile had stopped outside on the road. Hagan was still pleading in a frenzied way; Connie Myers was callously folding his letter, while he watched the other warily — neither of the men had heard the sound.

And then, quick, almost on the instant, came a rush of feet, a crash upon the front door — an imperative command to open in the name of the law. *The police!* Jimmie Dale's brain was working now with lightning speed. Somehow the police had stumbled upon the crime in that tenement; and, as he had foreseen in such an event, had identified Doyle. But they could not be sure that any one was present here in the house now — they could not see a light any more than he had. He must get Mike Hagan away — must see that Connie Myers did *not* get away. Myers was on his feet now, fear struck in his turn, the letter clutched in a tight-closed fist, his revolver swung out, poised, in the other hand. Hagan, too, was on his feet, and, unheeded now by Connie Myers, was wrenching his wrists apart.

Another crash upon the door — another. Another demand in a harsh voice to open it. Then some one running around to the window at the side of the house — and Jimmie Dale sprang forward.

There was the roar of a report, a blinding flash almost in Jimmie Dale's eyes, as Connie Myers, whirling instantly at his entrance, fired — and missed. It happened quick then, in the space of the ticking of a watch — before Jimmie Dale, flinging himself forward, had reached the man. Like a defiant challenge to their demand it must have seemed to the officers outside, that shot of Connie Myers at Jimmie Dale, for it was answered on the instant by another through the side window. And the shot, fired at random, the interior of the room hidden from the officers outside by the drawn shades, found its mark — and Connie Myers, a bullet in his brain, pitched forward, dead, upon the floor.

"*Quick!*" Jimmie Dale flung at Hagan. "Get that letter out of his hand!" He jumped for the lamp on the floor, extinguished it, and turned again toward Hagan. "Have you got it?" he whispered tensely.

"Yes," said Hagan, in a numbed way.

"This way, then!" Jimmie Dale caught Hagan's arm, and pulled the other across the room and into the kitchen to the trapdoor. "Quick!" he breathed again. "Get down there – quick! And no noise! They don't know how many are in the house. When they find *him* they'll probably be satisfied."

Hagan, stupefied, dazed, obeyed mechanically – and, in an instant, the trapdoor closed behind them, Jimmie Dale was standing beside the other in the cellar.

"Not a sound now!" he cautioned once more.

His flashlight winked, went out, winked again; then held steadily, in curious fascination it seemed, as, in its circuit, the ray fell upon Hagan – *fell upon the torn, ragged edge of a paper in Hagan's hand!* With a suppressed cry, Jimmie Dale snatched it away from the other. It was but a torn *half* of the letter! "The other half! The other half, Hagan – where is it?" he demanded hoarsely.

Hagan, almost in a state of collapse, muttered inaudibly. The crash of a toppling door sounded from above. Jimmie Dale shook the man desperately.

"Where is it?" he repeated fiercely.

"He – he was holding it tight, it – it tore in his hand," Hagan stammered. "Does it make any difference? Oh, let's get out of here, whoever you are – for God's sake let's get out of here!"

Any difference! Jimmie Dale's jaws were clamped like a steel vise. Any difference! The difference between life and death for the man beside him – that was all! He was reading the portion in his hand. It was the last part of the letter, beginning with: "There's a paper stuck under the edge of Hagan's table – " From above, from the floor of the front room now, came the rush and trample of feet. He could not go back for the other half. And any attempt to conceal the fact that Connie Myers had been alone in the house was futile now. They would find the torn letter in the dead man's hand, proof enough that some one else had been there. What was in that part of the letter that was still clutched in that death grip upstairs? A sentence from it, that he had heard Connie Myers read, seemed to burn itself into his brain. *"If you want to know who did it, look in Mike Hagan's room on the floor above."* And then, suddenly, like light through the darkness, came a ray of hope. He pulled Hagan to the cellarway, and stealthily lifted one side of the double trapdoor. There was a chance, desperate enough, one in a thousand – but still a chance!

Voices from the house came plainly now, but there was no one in sight. The police, to a man, were evidently all inside. From the road in front showed the lamp glare of their automobile.

"Run for the car!" Jimmie Dale jerked out from between set teeth – and with Hagan beside him, steadying the man by the arm, dashed across the intervening fifty yards.

They had not been seen. A minute more, and the car, evidently belonging to the local police, for it was headed in the direction of New York, and as though it had come from Pelham, swept down the road, swept around a turn, and Jimmie Dale, with a gasp of relief, straightened up a little from the wheel.

How much time had he? The police must have heard the car; but, equally, occupied as they were, they might well give it no thought other than that it was but another car passing by. There was no telephone in the house; the nearest house was a quarter of a mile away, and that might or might not have a telephone. Could he count on half an hour? He glanced anxiously at the crouched figure beside him. He would have to! It was the only chance. They would telephone the contents of the dead man's half of the letter to the New York police. Could he get to Hagan's room *first!* "Look in Hagan's room," their part of the letter read—but it did not say for *what,* or exactly *where!* If they found nothing, Hagan was safe. Connie Myers' reputation, the fact that he was found in disguise at Doyle's house, was, barring any incriminating evidence, quite enough to let Hagan out. There would only remain in the minds of the police the question of who, beside Connie Myers, had been in old Doyle's house that night? And now Jimmie Dale smiled a little whimsically. Well, perhaps he could answer that—and, if not quite to the satisfaction of the police, at least to the complete vindication of Mike Hagan.

But he could not drive through towns and villages with a mask on his face; and there, ahead now, lights were beginning to show. And more than ever now, with what was before him, it was imperative that Mike Hagan should not recognise Larry the Bat. Jimmie Dale glanced again at Hagan—and slowed down the car. They were on the outskirts of a town, and off to the right he caught the twinkling lights of a street car.

"Hagan," he said sharply, "pull yourself together, and listen to me! If you keep your mouth shut, you've nothing to fear; if you let out a word of what's happened to-night, you'll probably go to the chair for a crime you know nothing about. Do you understand?—keep your mouth shut!"

The car had stopped. Hagan nodded his head.

"All right, then. You get out here, and take a street car into New York," continued Jimmie Dale crisply. "But when you get there, keep away from your home for the next two or three hours. Hang around with some of the boys you know, and if you're asked anything afterward, say you were batting around town all evening. Don't worry—you'll find you're out of this when you read the morning papers. Now get out—hurry!" He pushed Hagan from the car. "I've got to make my own get-away."

Hagan, standing in the road, brushed his hand bewilderingly across his eyes.

"Yes—but you—I—"

"Never mind about that!" Jimmie Dale leaned out, and gripped Hagan's arm impressively. "There's only one thing you've got to think of, or remember. Keep your mouth shut! No matter what happens, keep your mouth shut—if you want to save your neck! Good-night, Hagan!"

The car was racing forward again. It shot streaking through the streets of the town ahead, and, dully, over its own inferno, echoed shouts, cries, and execrations of an outraged populace—then out into the night again, roaring its way toward New York.

He had half an hour—perhaps! It was a good thing Hagan did not know, or had not grasped the significance of that torn letter—the man would have been unmanageable with fear and excitement. It would puzzle Hagan to find no paper stuck under his table when he came to look for it! But that was a minor consideration, that mattered not at all.

Half an hour! On roared the car—towns, black roads, villages, wooded lands were kaleidoscopic in their passing. Half an hour! Had he done it? Had he come anywhere near doing it? He did not know. He was in the city at last—and now he had to moderate his speed; but, by keeping to the less frequented streets, he could still drive at a fast pace. One piece of good fortune had been his—the long motor coat he had found in the car with which to cover the rags of Larry the Bat, and without which he would have been obliged to leave the car somewhere on the outskirts of the city, and to trust, like Mike Hagan, to other and slower means of transportation.

Blocks away from Hagan's tenement, he ran the car into a lane, slipped off the motor coat, and from his pocket whipped out the little metal insignia case—and in another moment a diamond-shaped gray seal was neatly affixed to the black ebony rim of the steering wheel. He smiled ironically. It was necessary, quite necessary that the police should have no doubt as to who had been in Doyle's house with Connie Myers that night, or to whom they had so considerately loaned their automobile!

He was running now—through lanes, dodging down side streets, taking every short cut he knew. Had he beaten the police to Mike Hagan's room? It would be easy then. If they were ahead of him, then, by some means or other, he must still get that paper first.

He was at the tenement now—shuffling leisurely up the steps. The front door was open. He entered, and went up the first flight of stairs, then along the hall, and up the next flight. He had half expected the place to be bustling with excitement over the crime; but the police evidently had kept the affair quiet, for he had seen no one since he had entered. But now, as he began to mount the third flight, he went more slowly – some one was ahead of him. It was very dark – he could not see. The steps above died away. He reached the landing, started along for Hagan's room – and a light blazed suddenly in his face, and a hard, quick grip on his shoulder forced him back against the wall. Then the flashlight wavered, glistened on brass buttons went out, and a voice laughed roughly:

"It's only Larry the Bat!"

"Larry the Bat, eh?" It was another voice, harsh and curt. "What are you doing here?"

He was not first, after all! The telephone message from Pelham – it was almost certainly that – had beaten him! They were ahead of him, just ahead of him, they had only been a few steps ahead of him going up the stairs, just a second ahead of him on their way to Hagan's room! Jimmie Dale was thinking fast now. He must go, too – to Hagan's room with them – somehow – there was no other way – there was Hagan's life at stake.

"Aw, I ain't done nothin'!" he whined. "I was just goin' ter borrow the price of a feed from Mike Hagan – lemme go!"

"Hagan, eh!" snapped the questioner. "Are you a friend of his?"

"Sure, I am!"

The officers whispered for a moment together.

"We'll try it," decided the one who appeared to be in command. "We're in the dark, anyhow, and the thing may be only a steer. Mabbe it'll work – anyway, it won't do any harm." His hand fell heavily on Jimmie Dale's shoulder. "Mrs. Hagan know you?" brusquely.

"Sure she does!" sniffled Larry the Bat.

"Good!" rasped the officer. "Well, we'll make the visit with you. And you do what you're told, or we'll put the screws on you – see? We're after something here, and you've blown the whole game – savvy? You've spilled the gravy – understand?"

In the darkness, Jimmie Dale smiled grimly. It was far more than he had dared to hope for – they were playing into his hands!

"But I don't know 'bout any game," grovelled Larry the Bat piteously.

"Who in hell said you did!" growled the officer. "You're supposed to have snitched the lay to us, that's all – and mind you play your part! Come on!"

It was two doors down the hall to Mike Hagan's room, and there one of the officers, putting his shoulder to the door, burst it open and sprang in. The other shoved Jimmie Dale forward. It was quickly done. The three were in the room. The door was closed again.

Came a cry of terror out of the darkness, a movement as of some one rising up hurriedly in bed; and then Mrs. Hagan's voice:

"What is it! Who is it! Mike!"

The table—it was against the right-hand wall, Jimmie Date remembered. He sidled quickly toward it.

"Strike a light!" ordered the officer in charge.

Jimmie Dale's fingers were feeling under the edge of the table — a quick sweep along it — *nothing!* He stooped, reaching farther in — another sweep of his arm — and his fingers closed on a sheet of paper and a piece of hard gum. In an instant they were in his pocket.

A match crackled and flared up. A lamp was lighted. Larry the Bat sulked sullenly against the wall.

Terror-stricken, wide-eyed, Mrs. Hagan had clutched the child lying beside her to her arms, and was sitting bolt upright in bed.

"Now then, no fuss about it!" said the officer in charge, with brutal directness. "You might as well make a clean breast of Mike's share in that murder downstairs—Larry the Bat, here, has already told us the whole story. Come on, now — out with it!"

"Murder!" — her face went white. "My Mike — *murder!*" She seemed for an instant stunned — and then down the worn, thin, haggard face gushed the tears. "I don't believe it!" she cried. "I don't believe it!"

"Come on now, cut that out!" prodded the officer roughly. "I tell you Larry the Bat, here, has opened everything up wide. You're only making it worse for yourself."

"Him!" She was staring now at Jimmie Dale. "Oh, God!" she cried. "So that's what you are, are you — a stool-pigeon for the cops? Well, whatever you told them, you lie! You're the curse of this neighbourhood, you are, and if my Mike is bad at all, it's you that's helped to make him bad. But murder — you *lie!*"

She had risen slowly from the bed — a gaunt, pitiful figure, pitifully clothed, the black hair, gray-streaked, streaming thinly over her shoulders, still clutching the baby that, too, was crying now.

The officers looked at one another and nodded.

"Guess she's handing it straight — we'll have a look on our own hook," the leader muttered.

She paid no attention to them — she was walking straight to Jimmie Dale.

"It's you, is it," she whispered fiercely through her sobs, "that would bring more shame and ruin here — you that's selling my man's life away with your filthy lies for what they're paying you – it's you, is it, that – " Her voice broke.

There was a frightened, uneasy look in Larry the Bat's eyes, his lips were twitching weakly, he drew far back against the wall – and then, glancing miserably at the officers, as though entreating their permission, began to edge toward the door.

For a moment she watched him, her face white with outrage, her hand clenched at her side – and then she found her voice again.

"Get out of here!" she said, in a choked, strained way pointing to the door. "Get out of here – you dirty skate!"

"Sure!" mumbled Larry the Bat, his eyes on the floor. "Sure!" he mumbled – and the door closed behind him.

PART TWO: THE WOMAN IN THE CASE

(The chapters comprising Part Two of this novel appeared in *People's* from June to August of 1915 under the serial title of "The Lodestone." In the first magazine installment Jimmie Dale refers to the Tocsin as "the lodestone of his life.")

PART TWO: THE WOMAN IN THE CASE [54]

CHAPTER I

BELOW THE DEAD LINE

(Friday 10/15/1915)

Whispering! Always whisperings, low, sibilant, floating errantly from all sides, until they seemed a component part of the drug-laden atmosphere itself. And occasionally another sound: the soft *slap-slap* of loose-slippered feet, the faint rustle of equally loose-fitting garments. And everywhere the sweet, sickish smell of opium. It was Chang Foo's, simply a cellar or two deeper in Chang Foo's than that in which Dago Jim had quarrelled once—and died!

Larry the Bat, vicious-faced, unkempt, disreputable, lay sprawled out on one of the dive's bunks, an opium pipe beside him. But Larry the Bat was not smoking; instead, his ear was pressed closely against the boarding that formed the rather flimsy partition at the side of the bunk. One heard many things in Chang Foo's if one cared to listen—if one could first win one's way through the carefully guarded gateway, that to the uninitiated offered nothing more interesting than the entrance to a Chinese tea-shop, and an uninviting one at that!

Had he been followed in here? He had been shadowed for the last hour; of that, at least, he was certain. Why? By whom? For an hour he had dodged in and out through the dens of the underworld, as only one who was at home there and known to all could do—and at last he had taken refuge in Chang Foo's like a fox burrowing deep into its hole.

Few could find their way into the most infamous opium den in all New York, where not only the poppy ruled as master, but where crime was hatched, ay, and carried to its ghastly consummation, sometimes, as well; and of those few, not one but was of the underworld itself. And it was that fact which held his muscles strained and rigid now under the miserable rags that covered them, and it was that which kept the keen, quick brain alert and active, every faculty keyed up and tense. If it were the police, he

---

[54] **The Prologue to the fifth Gray Seal book,** *Jimmie Dale and the Missing Hour,* **occurs between Parts One and Two of this novel.**

260

had little to fear, for they could not force their way in without warning; but if it were the underworld, he was in imminent peril, and had done little better than run himself into a trap from which there was no escape.

"Death to the Gray Seal!" – he had heard that whispered more than once in this very place. Who knew at what moment the role of Larry the Bat would be uncovered, and the underworld, where now he held so high a place, would be at his throat like a pack of snarling wolves! Who had been shadowing him during the last hour?

Whisperings! Nothing tangible! He could catch no words. Only the never-ending whisperings of gathered groups here and there – and sometimes the clink of coin where some game was in progress.

The curtain before his bunk was drawn suddenly aside – and Larry the Bat's fingers, where his hand was carelessly hidden by his body tightened upon his automatic.

"Smokee some more?"

The fingers relaxed. It was only Sam Wah, one of the attendants.

"Nix!" said Larry the Bat, in a slightly muddled tone. "Got enough."

The curtain fell into place again. Larry the Bat's lips set in a thin smile. Ultimately it made little difference whether it was the police or the underworld! The smile grew thinner. It was the flip of a coin, that was all! With one there was the death house at Sing Sing for the Gray Seal; with the other – well, there were many ways, from a shot or a knife thrust in the open street, to his murder in some hidden dive like this of Chang Foo's, for instance, where he now was – the Gray Seal was responsible for the occupancy of too many penitentiary cells by those of the underworld to look for any other fate!

He raised himself up sharply on his elbow. A shrill, high note, like the scream of a parrakeet, rang out a second time. He tore the curtain aside, and jumped to his feet. All around him, in the twinkling of an eye, Chinamen in fluttering blouses, chattering like magpies, mingled with snarling, cursing whites, were running madly. A voice, prefaced with an oath, bawled out behind him, as he sprang forward and joined the rush:

"Beat it! De cops! Beat it!"

The police! A raid! Was it for *him?* From rooms, an amazing number of them, more forms rushed out, joined, divided, separated, and dashed, some this way, some that, along branching passageways. There had been raids before, the police had begun to change their minds about Chang Foo's, but Chang Foo's was not an easy place to raid. House after house in that quarter of Chinese laundries, of tea shops, of chop-suey joints, opened one into the other through secret passages in the cellars. Larry the Bat plunged down a staircase, and halted in the darkness of a cellar, drawing back against the wall while the flying feet of his fellow fugitives scurried by him.

Was it for *him,* this raid? If not, the police had not a hope of getting him if he kept his head; for back in Chang Foo's proper, which would be quite closed off now, Chang Foo would be blandly submitting to arrest, offering himself as a sort of glorified sacrifice while the police confiscated opium and fan-tan layouts. If the police had no other purpose than that in mind, Chang Foo would simply pay a fine; the next night the place would be in full blast again; and Chang Foo, higher than ever in the confidence of the underworld's aristocracy, would reap his reward – and that would be all there was to it.

But was that all? The raid had followed significantly close upon the heels of his entry into Chang Foo's. Larry the Bat began to move forward again. He dared not follow the others, and, later on, when quiet was restored, issue out into the street from any one of the various houses in which he might temporarily have taken refuge. There was a chance in that, a chance that the police might be more zealous than usual, even if he particularly was not their game – and he could take no chance. Arrest for Larry the Bat, even on suspicion, could have but one conclusion – not a pleasant one – the disclosure that Larry the Bat was not Larry the Bat at all, but Jimmie Dale, the millionaire club-man, and, to complete a fatal triplication, that Larry the Bat and Jimmie Dale was the Gray Seal upon whose head was fixed a price!

All was silence around him now, except that from overhead came occasionally the muffled tread of feet. He felt his way along into a black, narrow passage, emerged into a second cellar, swept the place with a single, circling gleam from a pocket flashlight, passed a stairway that led upward, reached the opposite wall, and, dropping on hands and knees, crawled into what, innocently enough, appeared to be the opening of a coal bin.

He knew Chang Foo's well – as he knew the ins and outs of every den and place he frequented, knew them as a man knows such things when his life at any moment might hang upon his knowledge.

He was in another passage now, and this, in a few steps, brought him to a door. Here he halted, and stood for a full five minutes, absolutely motionless, absolutely still, listening. There was nothing – not a sound. He tried the door cautiously. It was locked. The slim, sensitive, tapering fingers of Jimmie Dale, unrecognisable now in the grimy digits of Larry the Bat, felt tentatively over the lock. To fingers that seemed in their tips to possess all the human senses, that time and again in their delicate touch upon the dial of a safe had mocked at human ingenuity and driven the police into impotent frenzy, this was a pitiful thing. From his pocket came a small steel instrument that was quickly and deftly inserted in the keyhole. There was a click, the door swung open, and Jimmie Dale, alias Larry the Bat, stepped outside into a back yard half a block away from the entrance to Chang Foo's.

Again he listened. There did not appear to be any unusual excitement in the neighbourhood. From open windows above him and from adjoining houses came the ordinary, commonplace sounds of voices talking and laughing, even the queer, weird notes of a Chinese chant. He stole noiselessly across the yard, out into the lane, and made his way rapidly along to the cross street.

In a measure, now, he was safe; but one thing, a very vital thing, remained to be done. It was absolutely necessary that he should know whether he was the quarry that the police had been after in the raid, if it was the police who had been shadowing him all evening. If it was the police, there was but one meaning to it—Larry the Bat was known to be the Gray Seal, and a problem perilous enough in any aspect confronted him. Dare he risk the Sanctuary—for the clothes of Jimmie Dale? Or was it safer to burglarise, as he had once done before, his own mansion on Riverside Drive?

His thoughts were running riot, and he frowned, angry with himself. There was time enough to think of that when he knew that it was the police against whom he had to match his wits.

Well in the shadow of the buildings, he moved swiftly along the side street until he came to the corner of the street on which, halfway down the block, fronted Chang Foo's tea-shop. A glance in that direction, and Jimmie Dale drew a breath of relief. A patrol wagon was backed up to the curb, and a half dozen officers were busy loading it with what was evidently Chang Foo's far from meagre stock of gambling appurtenances; while Chang Foo himself, together with Sam Wah and another attendant, were in the grip of two other officers, waiting possibly for another patrol wagon. There was a crowd, too, but the crowd was at a respectful distance—on the opposite side of the street.

Jimmie Dale still hugged the corner. A man swaggered out from a doorway, quite close to Chang Foo's, and came on along the street. As the other reached the corner, Jimmie Dale sidled forward.

"'Ello, Chick!" he said, out of the corner of his mouth. "Wot's de lay?"

"'Ello, Larry!" returned the other. "Aw, nuthin'! De nutcracker on Chang, dat's all."

"I t'ought mabbe dey was lookin' for some guy dat was in dere," observed Jimmie Dale.

"Nuthin' doin'!" the other answered. "I was in dere meself. De whole mob beat it clean, an' de bulls never batted an eye. Didn't youse pipe me make me get-away outer Shanghai's a minute ago? De bulls never went nowhere except into Chang's. Dere's a new lootenant in de precinct inaugeratin' himself, dat's all. S'long, Larry — I gotta date."

"S'long, Chick!" responded Jimmie Dale — and started slowly back along the cross street.

It was not the police, then, who were interested in his movements! Then who? He shook his head with a little, savage, impotent gesture. One thing was clear: it was too early to risk a return to the Sanctuary and attempt the rehabilitation of Jimmie Dale. If any one was on the hunt for Larry the Bat, the Sanctuary would be the last place to be overlooked.

He turned the next corner, hesitated a moment in front of a garishly lighted dance hall, and finally shuffled in through the door, made his way across the floor, nodding here and there to the elite of gangland, and, with a somewhat arrogant air of proprietorship, sat down at a table in the corner. Little better than a tramp in appearance, certainly the most disreputable-looking object in the place, even the waiter who approached him accorded him a certain curious deference — was not Larry the Bat the most celebrated dope fiend below the dead line?

"Gimme a mug o' suds!" ordered Jimmie Dale, and sprawled royally back in his chair.

Under the rim of his slouch hat, pulled now far over his eyes, he searched the faces around him. If he had been asked to pick the actors for a revel from the scum of the underworld, he could not have improved upon the gathering. There were perhaps a hundred men and women in the room, the majority dancing, and, with the exception of a few sight-seeing slummers, they were men and women whose acquaintance with the police was intimate but not cordial — far from cordial.

Jimmie Dale shrugged his shoulders, and sipped at the glass that had been set before him. It was grimly ironic that he should be, not only there, but actually a factor and a part of the underworld's intimate life! He, Jimmie Dale, a wealthy man, a member of New York's exclusive clubs, [55] a member of New York's most exclusive society! It was inconceivable. He smiled sardonically. Was it? Well, then, it was none the less true. His life unquestionably was one unique, apart from any other man's, but it was, for all that, actual and real.

---

[55] We only ever see Dale at the St. James Club but it's feasible that he had memberships at the Harvard Club and the New York Yacht Club as well. Possibly the Lotos Club too given his artistic abilities.

There had been three years of it now – since *she* had come into his life. Jimmie Dale slouched down a little in his chair. The ice was thin, perilously thin, that he was skating on now. Each letter, with its demand upon him to match his wits against police or underworld, or against both combined, perhaps, made that peril a little greater, a little more imminent – if that were possible, when already his life was almost literally carried, daily, hourly, in his hand. Not that he rebelled against it; it was worth the price that some day he expected he must pay – the price of honour, wealth, a name disgraced, ruin, death. Was he quixotic? Immoderately so? He smiled gravely. Perhaps. But he would do it all over again if the choice were his. There were those who blessed the name of the Gray Seal, as well as those who cursed it. And there was the Tocsin!

Who was she? He did not know, but he knew that he had come to love her, come to care for her, and that she had come to mean everything in life to him. He had never seen her, to know her face. He had never seen her face, but he knew her voice – ay, he had even held her for a moment, the moment of wildest happiness he had ever known, in his arms. That night when he had entered his library, his own particular den in his own house, and in the darkness had found her there – found her finally through no effort of his own, when he had searched so fruitlessly for years to find her, using every resource at his command to find her! And she, because she had come of her own volition, relying upon him, had held him in honour to let her go as she had come – without looking upon her face! Exquisite irony! But she had made him a promise then – that the work of the Gray Seal was nearly over – that soon there would be an end to the mystery that surrounded her – that he should know all – that he should know *her*.

He smiled again, but it was a twisted smile on the mechanically misshapen lips of Larry the Bat. *Nearly* over! Who knew? That "nearly" might be too late! Even tonight he had been shadowed, was skulking even now in this place as a refuge. Who knew? Another hour, and the newsboys might be shrieking their "Uxtra! Uxtra! De Gray Seal caught! De millionaire Jimmie Dale de Jekyll an' Hyde of real life!"

Jimmie Dale straightened up suddenly in his seat. There was a shout, an oath bawled out high above the riot of noise, a chorus of feminine shrieks from across the room. What was the matter with the underworld to-night? He seemed fated to find nothing but centres of disturbance – first a raid at Chang Foo's, and now this. What was the matter here? They were stampeding toward him from the other side of the room. There was the roar of a revolver shot – another. Black Ike! He caught an instant's glimpse of the gunman's distorted face through the crowd. That was it probably – a row over some moll.

And then, as Jimmie Dale lunged up from his chair to his feet to escape the rush, pandemonium itself seemed to break loose. Yells, shots, screams, and oaths filled the air. The crowd surged this way and that. Tables were overturned and sent crashing to the floor. And then came sudden darkness, as some one of the attendants in misguided excitability switched off the lights.

The darkness but served to increase the panic, not allay it. With a savage snap of his jaws, Jimmie Dale swung from his table in the corner with the intention of making his way out by a side door behind him—it was a case of the police again, and the patrolman outside would probably be pulling a riot call by now. And the police—He stopped suddenly, as though he had been struck. An envelope, thrust there out of the darkness, was in his hand; and her voice, *hers,* the Tocsin's, was sounding in his ears:

"Jimmie! Jimmie! I've been trying all evening to catch you! Quick! Get to the Sanctuary and change your clothes. There's not an instant to lose! It's for my sake to-night!"

And then a surging mob was around him on every side, and, pushing, jostling, half lifting him at times from his feet, carried him forward with its rush, and with him in its midst burst through the door and out into the street.

CHAPTER II

THE CALL TO ARMS

(Friday 10/15/1915)

NOT a sound as the key turned in the lock; not a sound as the door swung back on its carefully oiled hinges; not a sound as Larry the Bat slipped like a shadow into the blackness of the room, closing the door behind him again. With a tread as noiseless as a cat's, he was across the room to satisfy himself that the shutters were tightly closed; and then the single gas jet flared up, murky, yellow, illuminating the miserable, squalid room—the Sanctuary—the home of Larry the Bat. There was need for silence, need for caution. In five minutes, ten at the outside, he must emerge again—as Jimmie Dale.

With a smile on his lips that mingled curiously chagrin and self-commiseration, he took the letter from his pocket and tore it open. It was she, then, who had been following him all evening, and, like a blundering idiot, he had wasted precious, perhaps irreparable, hours! What had she meant by "It's for my sake to-night"? The words had been ringing in his ears since the moment she had whispered them in that panic-stricken crowd. Was it not always for her sake that he answered these calls to arms? Was it not always for her sake that he, as the Gray Seal, was—The mental soliloquy came to an abrupt end. He had subconsciously read the first sentence of the letter, and now, with sudden feverish eagerness and excitement, he was reading it to the last word.

"DEAR PHILANTHROPIC CROOK: In an hour after you receive this, if all goes well, you shall know everything—everything. Who I am—yes, and my name. It has been more than three years now, hasn't it? It has been incomprehensible to you, but there has been no other way. I dared not take the chance of discovery by any one; I dared not expose you to the risk of being known by me. Your life would not have been worth a moment's purchase. Oh, Jimmie, am I only making the mystery more mystifying? But to-night, I think, I hope, I pray that it is all at an end: though against me, and against you to-night when you go to help me, is the most powerful and pitiless organisation of criminals that the world has ever known; and the stake we are playing for is a fortune of millions—and my life. And yet somehow I am afraid now, just because the end is so near, and the victory seems so surely won. And so, Jimmie, be careful; use all that wonderful cleverness of yours as you have never used it before, and — But there should be no need for that, it is so simple a thing that I am going to ask you to do. Why am I writing so illogically! Nothing, surely, can possibly happen. This is not like one of my usual letters, is it? I am beside myself to-night with hope, anxiety, fear, and excitement.

"Listen, then, Jimmie: Be at the northeast corner of Sixth Avenue and Waverly Place at exactly half-past ten. A taxicab will drive up, as though you had signalled it in passing, and the chauffeur will say: 'I've another fare, in half an hour, sir, but I can get you most anywhere in that time.' You will be smoking a cigarette. Toss it out into the street, make any reply you like, and get into the cab. Give the chauffeur that little ring of mine with the crest of the bell and belfry and the motto, 'Sonnez le Tocsin,' that you found the night old Isaac Pelina was murdered, and the chauffeur will give you in exchange a sealed packet of papers. He will drive you to your home, and I will telephone to you there.

"I need not tell you to destroy this. Keep the appointment in your proper person—as Jimmie Dale. Carry nothing that might identify you as the Gray Seal if any accident should happen. And, lastly, trust the pseudo chauffeur absolutely."

There was no signature. Her letters were never signed. He stood for a moment staring at the closely written sheets in his hand, a heightened colour in his cheeks, his lips pressed tightly together — and then his fingers automatically began to tear the letter into pieces, and the pieces again into little shreds. To-night! It was to be to-night, the end of all this mystery. To-night was to see the end of this dual life of his, with its constant peril! To-night the Gray Seal was to exit from the stage forever! To-night, a wonderful climax of the years, he was to see *her!*

His blood was quickened now, his heart pounding in a faster beat; a mad elation, a fierce uplift was upon him. He thrust the torn bits of paper into his pocket hurriedly, stepped across the room to the corner, rolled back the oilcloth, and lifted up the loose plank in the flooring, so innocently dustladen, as, more than once, to have eluded the eyes of inquisitive visitors in the shape of police and plainclothes men from headquarters.

From the space beneath he removed a neatly folded pile of clothes, laid these on the bed, and began to undress. He was working rapidly now. Tiny pieces of wax were removed from his nostrils, from under his lips, from behind his ears; water from a cracked pitcher poured into a battered tin basin, and mixed with a few drops of some liquid from a bottle which he procured from its hiding place under the flooring, banished the make-up stain from his face, his neck, his wrists, and hands as if by magic. It was a strange metamorphosis that had taken place—the coarse, brutal-featured, blear-eyed, leering countenance of Larry the Bat was gone, and in its place, clean-cut, square-jawed, clear-eyed, was the face of Jimmie Dale. And where before had slouched a slope-shouldered, misshapen, flabby creature, a broad-shouldered form well over six feet in height now stood erect, and under the clean white skin the muscles of an athlete, like knobs of steel played back and forth with every movement of his body.

In the streaked and broken mirror Jimmie Dale surveyed himself critically, methodically, and, with a nod of satisfaction, hastily donned the fashionably cut suit of tweeds upon the bed. He rummaged then through the ragged garments he had just discarded, transferred to his pockets a roll of bills and his automatic, and paused hesitantly, staring at the thin metal case, like a cigarette case, that he held in the palm of his hand. He shrugged his shoulders a little whimsically; it seemed strange indeed that he was through with that! He snapped it open. Within, between sheets of oil paper, lay the scores of little diamond-shaped, gray-coloured, adhesive paper seals—the insignia of the Gray Seal. Yes, it seemed strange that he was never to use another! He closed the case, gathered up the clothes of Larry the Bat, tucked the case in among them, and shoved the bundle into the hole under the flooring. All these things would have to be destroyed, but there was not time to-night; to-morrow, or the next day, would do for that. What would it be like to live a normal life again, without the menace of danger lurking on every hand, without that grim slogan of the underworld, "Death to the Gray Seal!" or that savage fiat of the police, "The Gray Seal, dead or alive—but the Gray Seal!" forever ringing in his ears? What would it be like, this new life—with her?

The thought was thrilling him again, bringing again that eager, exultant uplift. In an hour, *one* hour, and the barriers of years would be swept away, and she would be in his arms!

"It's for my sake to-night!" His face grew suddenly tense, as the words came back to him. That "hour" wasn't over yet! It was no hysterical exaggeration that had prompted her to call her enemies the most powerful and pitiless organisation of criminals that the world had ever known. It was not the Tocsin's way to exaggerate. The words would be literally true. The very life she had led for the three years that had gone stood out now as a grim proof of her assertion.

Jimmie Dale replaced the flooring, carefully brushed the dust back into the cracks, spread the oilcloth into place, and stood up. Who and what was this organisation? What was between it and the Tocsin? What was this immense fortune that was at stake? And what was this priceless packet that was so crucial, that meant victory now, ay, and her life, too, she had said?

The questions swept upon him in a sort of breathless succession. Why had she not let him play a part in this? True, she had told him why—that she dared not expose him to the risk. Risk! Was there any risk that the Gray Seal had not taken, and at her instance! He did not understand, he smiled a little uncertainly, as he reached up to turn out the gas. There were a good many things that he did not understand about the Tocsin!

The room was in darkness, and with the darkness Jimmie Dale's mind centred on the work immediately before him. To enter the tenement where he was known and had an acknowledged right as Larry the Bat was one thing; for Jimmie Dale to be discovered there was quite another.

He crossed the room, opened the door silently, stood for a moment listening, then stepped out into the black, musty, ill-smelling hallway, closing the door behind him. He stooped and locked it. The querulous cry of a child reached him from somewhere above—a murmur of voices, muffled by closed doors, from everywhere. How many families were housed beneath that sordid roof he had never known, only that there was miserable poverty there as well as vice and crime, only that Larry the Bat, who possessed a room all to himself, was as some lordly and super-being to these fellow tenants who shared theirs with so many that there was not air enough for all to breathe.

He had no doors to pass—his was next to the staircase. He began to descend. They could scream and shriek, those stairs, like aged humans, twisted and rheumatic, at the least ungentle touch. But there was no sound from them now. There seemed something almost uncanny in the silent tread. Stair after stair he descended, his entire weight thrown gradually upon one foot before the other was lifted. The strain upon the muscles, trained and hardened as they were, told. As he moved from the bottom step, he wiped little beads of perspiration from his forehead.

The door, now, that gave on the alleyway! He opened it, slipped outside, darted across the narrow lane, stole along where the shadows of the fence were blackest, paused, listening, as he reached the end of the alleyway, to assure himself that there was no near-by pedestrian—and stepped out into the street.

He kept on along the block, turned into the Bowery, and, under the first lamp, consulted his watch. It was a quarter past ten. He could make it easily in a leisurely walk. He continued on up the Bowery, finally crossed to Broadway, and shortly afterward turned into Waverly Place. At the corner of Fifth Avenue he consulted his watch again—and now he lighted a cigarette. Sixth Avenue was only a block away. At precisely half-past ten, to the second, he halted on the designated corner, smoking nonchalantly.

A taxicab, coincidentally coming from an uptown direction, swung in to the curb.

"Taxi, sir? Yes, sir?" Then, with an admirable mingling of eagerness to secure the fare and a fear that his confession might cause him the loss of it: "I've another fare in half an hour, sir, but I can get you most anywhere in that time."

Jimmie Dale's cigarette was tossed carelessly into the street.

"St. James Club!" he said curtly, and stepped into the cab.

The cab started forward, turned the corner, and headed along Waverly Place toward Broadway. The chauffeur twisted around in his seat in a matter-of-fact way, as though to ask further directions.

"Have you anything for me?" he inquired casually.

It lay where it always lay, that ring, between the folds of that little white glove in his pocketbook. Jimmie Dale took it out now, and handed it silently to the chauffeur.

The other's face changed instantly – composure was gone, and a quick, strained look was in its place.

"I'm afraid I've been watched," he said tersely. "Look behind you, will you, and tell me if you see anything?"

Jimmie Dale glanced backward through the little window in the hood.

"There's another taxi just turned in from Sixth Avenue," he reported the next instant.

"Keep your eye on it!" instructed the chauffeur shortly.

The speed of the cab increased sensibly.

With a curious tightening of his lips, Jimmie Dale settled himself in his seat so that he could watch the cab behind. There was trouble coming, intuitively he sensed that; and, he reflected bitterly, he might have known! It was too marvellous, too wonderful ever to come to pass that this one hour, the thought of which had fired his blood and made him glad beyond any gladness life had ever held for him before, should bring its promised happiness.

"Where's the cab now?" the chauffeur flung back over his shoulder.

They had passed Fifth Avenue, and were nearing Broadway.

"About the same distance behind," Jimmie Dale answered.

"That looks bad!" the chauffeur gritted between his teeth. "We'll have to make sure. I'll run down Lower Broadway."

"If you think we're followed," suggested Jimmie Dale quietly,

271

"why not run uptown and give them the slip somewhere where the traffic is thick? Lower Broadway at this time of night is as empty and deserted as a country road."

The chauffeur's sudden laugh was mirthless.

"My God, you don't know what you are talking about!" he burst out. "If they're following, all hell couldn't throw them off the track. And I've got to know, I've got to be *sure* before I dare make a move to-night. I couldn't tell up in the crowded districts if I was followed, could I? They won't come out into the open until their hands are forced."

The car swerved sharply, rounded the corner, and, speeding up faster and faster, began to tear down Lower Broadway.

"Watch! *Watch!*" cried the chauffeur.

There was no word between them for a moment; then Jimmie Dale spoke crisply:

"It's turned the corner! It's coming this way!"

The taxicab was rocking violently with the speed; silent, empty, Lower Broadway stretched away ahead. Apart from an occasional street car, probably there would be nothing between them and the Battery. Jimmie Dale glanced at his companion's face as a light, flashing by, threw it into relief. It was set and stern, even a little haggard; but, too, there was something else there, something that appealed instantly to Jimmie Dale — a sort of bulldog grit that dominated it.

"If he holds our speed, we'll know!" the chauffeur was shouting now to make himself heard over the roar of the car. "Look again! Where is it now?"

Once more Jimmie Dale looked through the little rear window. The cab had been a block behind them when it had turned the corner, and he watched it now in a sort of grim fascination. There was no possible doubt of it! The two bobbing, bouncing headlights were creeping steadily nearer. And then a sort of unnatural calm settled upon Jimmie Dale, and his hand went mechanically to his pocket to feel his automatic there, as he turned again to the chauffeur.

"If you've got any more speed, you'd better use it!" he said significantly.

The man shot a quick look at him.

"They are following us? You are *sure?*"

"Yes," said Jimmie Dale.

The chauffeur laughed again in that mirthless, savage way.

"Lean over here, where I can talk to you!" he rasped out. "The game's up, as far as I am concerned, I guess! But there's a chance for you. They don't know you in this."

"Give her more speed – or dodge into a cross street!" suggested Jimmie Dale coolly. "They haven't got us yet, by a long way!"

The other shook his head.

"It's not only that cab behind," he answered, through set lips. "You don't know what we're up against. If they're really after us, there's a trap laid in every section of this city – the devils! It's the package they want. Thank God for the presentiment that made me leave it behind! I was going back for it, you understand, if I was satisfied that we weren't followed. Listen! There's a chance for you – there's none for me. That package – remember this! – no one else knows where it is, and it's life and death to the one who sent you here. It's in Box 428 at – My God, *look!* Look there!" he yelled, and, with a wrench at the wheel, sent the taxi lurching and staggering for the car tracks in the centre of the street.

The scene, fast as thought itself, was photographing itself in every detail upon Jimmie Dale's brain. From the cross street ahead, one from each corner, two motor cars had nosed out into Broadway, blocking the road on both sides. And now the car on the left-hand side was moving forward across the tracks to counteract the chauffeur's move, deliberately insuring a collision. There was no chance, no further room to turn, no time to stop – the man driving the other car jumped for safety – they would be into it in an instant.

"Box 428!" Jimmie pleaded fiercely. "Go on, man! Go on! *Finish!*"

"Yes!" cried the chauffeur. "John Johansson, at – "

But Jimmie Dale heard no more. There was the crash of impact as the taxicab plowed into the car that had been so craftily manœuvered in front of it, and Jimmie Dale, lifted from his feet, was hurled violently forward with the shock, and all went black before his eyes.

CHAPTER III

THE CRIME CLUB

(Friday 10/15/1915)

FOR what length of time he had remained unconscious, Jimmie Dale had not the slightest idea. He regained his senses to find himself lying on a couch in a strange room that had a most exquisitely brass-wrought dome light in the ceiling. That was what attracted his attention, because the light hurt his eyes, and his head was already throbbing as though a thousand devils were beating a diabolical tattoo upon it.

He closed his eyes against the light. Where was he? What had happened? Oh, yes, he remembered now! That smash on Lower Broadway! He had been hurt. He moved first one limb and then another tentatively, and was relieved to find that, though his body ached as if it had been severely shaken, and his head was bad, he had apparently escaped without serious injury.

Where was he? In a hospital? His fingers, resting at his side upon the couch, supplied him with the information that it was a very expensive couch, upholstered in finest leather. If he were in a hospital, he would be in a cot.

He opened his eyes again to glance curiously around him. The room was quite in keeping with the artistic lighting fixture and the refined, if expensive, taste that was responsible for the couch. A heavy velvet rug of rich, dark green was bordered by a polished hardwood floor; panellings of dark-green frieze and beautifully grained woodwork made the lower walls; while above, on a background of some soft-toned paper, hung a few, and evidently choice, oil paintings. There was a big, inviting lounging chair; a massive writing table, or more properly, a desk of walnut; and behind the desk, his back half turned, apparently intent upon a book, sat a man in immaculate evening dress.

Jimmie Dale closed his eyes again. There was something reassuring about it all, comfortably reassuring. Though why there should be any occasion for a feeling of reassurance at all, he could not for the moment make out. And then, in a sudden flash, the details of the night came back to him. The Tocsin's letter – the package he was to get – the taxicab – the chauffeur, who was not a chauffeur – the chase – the trap. He lay perfectly still. It was the professional Jimmie Dale now whose brain, in spite of the throbbing, brutally aching head, was at work, keen, alert.

The chauffeur! What had happened to him? Had the man been killed in the auto smash; or, less fortunate than himself, fallen into the hands of those whose power he seemed both to fear and rate so highly? And that package! Box—what was the number?—yes, 428. What did that mean? What box? Where was it? Who was John Johansson? He hadn't heard any more than that; the smash had come then. And lastly, he was back again to the same question he had begun with: Where was he now himself? It looked as though some good Samaritan had picked him up. Who was this gentleman so quietly reading there at the desk?

Jimmie Dale opened his eyes for the third time. How still, how absolutely silent the room was! He studied the man's back speculatively for a moment, then his gaze travelled on past the man to the wall, riveted there, and his fingers, without movement of his arm, pressed against the outside of his coat pocket. He thought as much! His automatic was gone!

Not a muscle of Jimmie Dale's face moved. His eyes shifted to a picture on the wall. *The man was watching him – not reading!* Just above the level of the desk, a small mirror held the couch in focus—but, equally, it held the man in focus, and Jimmie Dale had seen the other's eyes, through a black mask that covered the face to the top of the upper lip, fixed intently upon him.

There was a chill now where before there had been reassurance, something ominous in the very quiet and refinement of the room; and Jimmie Dale smiled inwardly in bitter irony—his good Samaritan wore a mask! His self-congratulations had come too soon. Whatever had happened to the chauffeur, it was evident enough that he himself was caught! What was it the chauffeur had said? Something about a chance through being unknown. Was it to be a battle of wits, then? God, if his head did not ache so frightfully! It was hard to think with the brain half sick with pain.

Those two eyes shining in that mirror! There seemed something horribly spectre-like about it. He did not look again, but he knew they were there. It was like a cat watching a mouse. Why did not the man speak, or move, or do something, and—He turned his head slowly; the man was laughing in a low, amused way.

"You appear to be taken with that picture," observed a pleasant voice. "Perhaps you recognise it from there? It is a Corot." [56]

---

[56] Jean-Baptiste-Camille Corot (1796 to 1875) was a French painter and printmaker. He is mentioned a number of times in the Saga so apparently the artist had some significance for Packard. There is a Rue Corot in Packard's home town of Montreal.

Jimmie Dale, with a well-simulated start, sat up – and, with another quite as well simulated, stared at the masked man. The other had laid down his book, and swung around in his chair to face the couch. Jimmie Dale stood up a little shakily.

"Look here!" he said awkwardly. "I – I don't quite understand. I remember that my taxi got into a smash-up, and I suppose I have to thank you for the assistance you must have rendered me; only, as I say" – he looked in a puzzled way around the room, and in an even more perplexed way at the mask on the other's face – "I must confess I am at a loss to understand quite the meaning of this."

"Suppose that instead of trying to understand you simply accept things as you find them." The voice was soft, but there was a finality in it that its blandness only served to make the more suggestive.

Jimmie Dale drew himself up, and bowed coldly.

"I beg your pardon," he said. "I did not mean to intrude. I have only to thank you again, then, and bid you good-night."

The lips beneath the mask parted slightly in a politely deprecating smile.

"There is no hurry," said the man, a sudden sharpness creeping into his tones. "I am sorry that the rule I apply to you does not work both ways. For instance, I might be quite at a loss to account for your presence in that taxicab."

Jimmie Dale's smile was equally polite, equally deprecating.

"I fail to see how it could be of the slightest possible interest to you," he replied. "However, I have no objection to telling you. I hailed the taxi at the corner of Sixth Avenue and Waverly Place, told the chauffeur to drive me to the St. James Club, and –"

"The St. James Club," broke in the other coldly, "is, I believe, north, not *south* of Waverly Place – and on Broadway not at all."

Jimmie Dale stared at the other for an instant in patient annoyance.

"I am quite well aware of that," he said stiffly. "Nevertheless I told the man to drive me to the St. James Club. We came across Waverly Place, but on reaching Broadway, instead of turning uptown, he suddenly whirled in the other direction and sent the car flying at full speed down Lower Broadway. I shouted at the man. I don't know yet whether he was drunk or crazy or" – Jimmie Dale's eyes fixed disdainfully on the other's mask – "whether there might not, after all, have been method in his madness. I can only say that before we had gone more than two or three blocks, a wild effort on his part to avoid a collision with an auto swinging out from a side street resulted in an even more disastrous smash with another on the other side, and I was knocked senseless."

"'Victim,' I presume, is the idea you desire to convey," observed the other evenly. "You were quite the victim of circumstances, as it were!"

Jimmie Dale's eyebrows lifted slightly.

"It would appear to be fairly obvious, I should say."

"Very clever!" commented the man. "But now suppose we remove the buttons from the foils!" [57] His voice rasped suddenly. "You are quite as well aware as I am that what has happened to-night was not an accident. Nor — in case the possibility may have occurred to you — are the police any the wiser, save for the existence of two wrecked cars on Lower Broadway, and another which escaped, and for which doubtless they are still searching assiduously. The ownership of the taxicab you so inadvertently entered they will have no difficulty in establishing — you, perhaps, however, are in a better position than I am to appreciate the fact that the establishment of its ownership will lead them nowhere. As I understand it, the man who drove you to-night obtained the loan of the cab from one of the company's chauffeur's in return for a hundred-dollar bill. Am I right?"

"In view of what has happened," admitted Jimmie Dale simply, "I should not be surprised."

There was a sort of sardonic admiration in the other's laugh.

"As for the other car," he went on, "I can assure you that its ownership will never be known. When the nearest patrolman rushed up, there were no survivors of the disaster, save those in the third car which he was powerless to stop — which accounts for your presence here. You will admit that I have been quite frank."

"Oh, quite!" said Jimmie Dale, a little wearily. "But would you mind telling me what all this is leading to?"

The man had been leaning forward in his chair, one hand, palm downward, resting lightly on the desk. He shifted his hand now suddenly to the arm of his chair.

"*This!*" he said, and on the desk where his hand had been lay the Tocsin's gold signet ring.

Jimmie Dale's face expressed mild curiosity. He could feel the other's eyes boring into him.

"We were speaking of ownership," said the man, in a low, menacing tone. "I want to know where the woman who owns this ring can be found to-night."

---

[57] A fencing reference, one which Dale will use himself later in the series.

There was no play, no trifling here; the man was in deadly earnest. But it seemed to Jimmie Dale, even with the sense of peril more imminent with every instant, that he could have laughed outright in savage mockery at the irony of the question. Where was she? Even *who* was she? And this was the hour in which he was to have known!

"May I look at it?" he requested calmly.

The other nodded, but his eyes never left Jimmie Dale.

"It will give you an extra moment or so to frame your answer," he said sarcastically.

Jimmie Dale ignored the thrust, picked up the ring, examined it deliberately, and set it back again on the table.

"Since I do not know who owns it," he said, "I cannot answer your question."

"No! Well, then, there is still another matter — a little package that was in the taxicab with you. Where is that?"

"See here!" said Jimmie Dale irritably. "This has gone far enough! I have seen no package, large or small, or of any description whatever. You are evidently mistaking me for some one else. You have only to telephone to the St. James Club." He reached toward his pocket for his cardcase. "My name is —"

"Dale," supplied the other curtly. "Don't bother about the card, Mr. Dale. We have already taken the liberty of searching you." He rose abruptly from his chair. "I am afraid you do not quite realise your position, Mr. Dale," he said, with an ominous smile. "Let me make it clear. I do not wish to be theatrical about this, but we do not temporise here. You will either answer both of those questions to my satisfaction, *or you will never leave this place alive.*"

Jimmie Dale's face hardened. His eyes met the other's steadily.

"Ah, I think I begin to see!" he said caustically. "When I have been thoroughly frightened I shall be offered my freedom at a price. A sort of up-to-date game of holdup! The penalty of being a wealthy man! If you had named your figure to begin with, we would have saved a lot of idle talk, and you would have had my answer the sooner: *Nothing!*"

"Do you know," said the other, in a grimly musing way, "there has always been one man, but only one until now, that I have wished I might add to my present associates. I refer to the so-called Gray Seal. To-night there are two. I pay you the compliment of being the other. But" — he was smiling ominously again — "we are wasting time, Mr. Dale. I am willing to expose my hand to the extent of admitting that the information you are withholding is infinitely more valuable to me than the mere wreaking of reprisal upon you for a refusal to talk. Therefore, if you will answer, I pledge you my word you will be free to leave here within five minutes. If you refuse, you are already aware of the alternative. Well, Mr. Dale?"

Who was this man? Jimmie Dale was studying the other's chin, the lips, the white, even teeth, the jet-black hair. Some day the tables might be turned. Could he recognise again this cool, imperturbable ruffian who so callously threatened him with murder?

"Well, Mr. Dale? I am waiting!"

"I am not a magician," said Jimmie Dale contemptuously. "I could not answer your questions if I wanted to."

The other's hand slid instantly to a row of electric buttons on the desk.

"Very well, Mr. Dale!" he said quietly. "You do not believe, I see, that I would dare to carry my threat into execution; you perhaps even doubt my power. I shall take the trouble to convince you—I imagine it will stimulate your memory."

The door opened. Two men were standing on the threshold, both in evening dress, both masked. The man behind the desk came forward, took Jimmie Dale's arm almost courteously, and led him from the room out into a corridor, where he halted abruptly.

"I want to call your attention first, Mr. Dale, to the fact that as far as you are concerned you neither have now, nor ever will have, any idea whether you are in the heart of New York or fifty miles away from it. Now, listen! Do you hear anything?"

There was nothing. Only the strange silence of that other room was intensified now. There was not a sound; stillness such as it seemed to Jimmie Dale he had never experienced before was around him.

"You may possibly infer from the silence that you are *not* in the city," suggested the other, after a moment's pause. "I leave you to your own conclusions in that respect. The cause, however, of the silence is internal, not external; we had sound-proof principles in mind to a perhaps exaggerated degree when this building was constructed. If you care to do so, you have my permission to shout, say, for help, to your heart's content. We shall make no effort to stop you."

Jimmie Dale shrugged his shoulders. He was staring down a brilliantly lighted, richly carpeted corridor. There were doors on one side, windows on the other, the windows all hung with heavy, closely drawn portières. The corridor was certainly not on the ground floor, but whether it was on the second or third, or even above that again, he had no means of knowing. From appearances, though, the place seemed more like a large, private mansion than anything else.

"Just one word more before we proceed," continued the other. "I do not wish you to labour under any illusion. Here we are frankly criminals.

This is our home. It should have some effect in impressing you with the power and resource at our command, and also with the class of men with whom you are dealing. There is not one among us whose education is not fully equal to your own; not one, indeed, but who is chosen, granting first his criminal tendencies, because he is a specialist in his own particular field – in commerce, in the government diplomatic service, in the professions of law and medicine, in the ranks of pure science. We are bordering on the fantastical, are we not? Dreaming, you will probably say, of the Utopian in crime organisation. Quite so, Mr. Dale. I only ask you to consider the *possibilities* if what I say is true. Now let us proceed. I am going to take you into three rooms – the three whose doors you see ahead of you. You will notice that, including the one you have just left, there are four on this corridor. I do not wish to strain your credulity, or play tricks upon you; so I am going to ask you to fix an approximate idea of the length of the corridor in your mind, as it will perhaps enable you to account more readily for what may appear to be a discrepancy in the corresponding size of the rooms."

One of the men opened the door ahead. Jimmie Dale, at a sign from his conductor, moved forward and entered. Just what he had expected to find he could not have told; his brain was whirling, partly from his aching head, partly from his desperate effort to conceive some way of escape from the peril which, for all his nonchalance, he knew only too well was the gravest he had ever faced; but what he saw was simply a cozily furnished bedroom. There was nothing peculiar about it; nothing out of the way, except perhaps that it was rather narrow.

And then suddenly, rubbing his eyes involuntarily, he was staring in a dazed way before him. The whole right-hand side of the wall was sinking without a sound into the floor, increasing the width of the room by some five or six feet – and in this space was disclosed what appeared to be a sort of chemical laboratory, elaborately equipped, extending the entire length of the room.

"The wall is purely a matter of mechanical construction, operated hydraulically." The man was speaking softly at Jimmie Dale's side. "The room beneath is built to correspond; the base, ceiling, and wall mouldings here do not have to be very ingenious to effect a disguise. I might say, however, that few visitors, other than yourself, have ever seen anything here but a bedroom." He waved his hand toward the retorts, the racks of test tubes, the hundred and one articles that strewed the laboratory bench. "As for this, its purpose is twofold. We, as well, as the police, have often need of analysis. We make it. If we require a drug, a poison, say, we compound it from its various ingredients, or, as the case may be, distil it, perhaps – it is, you will agree, somewhat more difficult to trace to its source if procured that way. And speaking of poisons" – he stepped forward, and lifted a glass-stoppered bottle containing a colourless liquid from a shelf — "in a modest way we have even done some original research work here. This, for instance, is as Utopian from our standpoint as the formation, and personnel of the organisation I have briefly outlined to you. It possesses very essential qualities. It is almost instantaneous in its action, requires a very small quantity, and defies detection even by autopsy." He uncorked the bottle, and dipped in a long glass rod. "Will you watch the experiment?" he invited, with a sort of ghastly pleasantry. "I do not want you to accept anything on trust."

With a start, Jimmie Dale swung around. He had heard no sound, but another man was at his elbow now — and, struggling in the man's hand, was a little white rabbit.

It was over in an instant. A single drop in the rabbit's mouth, and the animal had stiffened out, a lifeless thing.

"It is quite as effective on the human organism," continued the other, "only, instead of one drop, three are required. If I make it ten" — he was carefully measuring the liquid into two wineglasses — "it is only that even you may be satisfied that the quantity is fatal." He filled up the glasses with what was apparently wine of some description, which he poured from a decanter, and held out the glasses in front of him.

And again Jimmie Dale started, again he had heard no one enter, and yet two men had stepped forward from behind him and had taken the glasses from their leader's hands. He glanced around him, counting quickly — they were surely the two who had entered with him from the corridor. No! Including the leader, there were now six men, all in evening dress, all masked, in the room with him.

A wave of the leader's hand, and the two men holding the glasses left the room. The man turned to Jimmie Dale again.

"Shall we proceed to the second room, Mr. Dale?" he asked politely. "I think it is now prepared for us — I do not wish to bore you with a repetition of magical sliding walls."

There was something now that numbed the ache in Jimmie Dale's brain — a sense of some deadly, remorseless thing that seemed to be constantly creeping closer to him, clutching at him — to smother him, to choke him. There was something absolutely fiendish, terrifying, in the veneer of culture around him.

They had entered the second room. This, like the other, was a pseudo-bedroom; but here the movable wall was already down. Ranged along the right-hand side were a great number of cabinets that slid in and out, much after the style and fashion used by clothing dealers to stock and display their wares. These cabinets were now all open, displaying hundreds of costumes of all kinds and descriptions, and evidently complete to the minutest detail. The cabinets were flanked by full-length mirrors at each end of the room, and on little tables before the mirrors was an assortment, that none better than Jimmie Dale himself could appreciate, of make-up accessories.

The man smiled apologetically.

"I am afraid this is rather uninteresting," he said. "I have shown it to you simply that you may understand that we are alive to the importance of detail. Disguise, that is daily vital to us, is an art that depends essentially on detail. I venture to say we could impersonate any character or type or nationality or class in the United States at a moment's notice. But" – he took Jimmie Dale's arm again and conducted him out into the corridor, while the two men who were evidently acting the role of guards followed closely behind – "there is still the third room – here." He halted Jimmie Dale before the door. "I have asked you to answer two questions, Mr. Dale," he said softly. "I ask you now to remember the alternative."

They still stood before the door. There was that uncanny silence again – it seemed to Jimmie Dale to last interminably. Neither of the three men surrounding him moved nor spoke. Then the door before him was opened on an unlighted room, and he was led across the threshold. He heard the door close behind him. The lights came on. And then it seemed as though he could not move, as though he were rooted to the spot – -and the colour ebbed from his face. Three figures were before him: the two men who had carried the glasses from the first room, and the chauffeur who had driven him in the taxicab. The two men still held the glasses – the chauffeur was bound hand and foot in a chair. One of the glasses was *empty*; the other was still significantly full.

Jimmie Dale, with a violent effort at self-control, leaned forward.

The man in the chair was dead. [58]

---

[58] In the beginning of this novel Jimmie Dale attributes his decision to become the Gray Seal to his "restless, adventurous spirit." He readily admits his goal was to "set the police by the ears" and "puzzle them to the verge of madness." Amateur psychologists can propose that the NYPD was made a proxy target for the unconscious anger Dale felt toward his father, the industrialist who kept Jimmie from "the artistic pursuits" he preferred, but undeniably the Gray Seal's exploits would have drawn away police resources best devoted to combatting true threats to public safety. If Dale ever realized that then the thought is unrecorded by Mr. Packard, but there was still a price to be paid for his "criminal" career. As Robert Sampson has written "It is reasonable to think that he (Packard) deliberately planned the redemption of Jimmie Dale as the foundation of the series." {Yesterday's Faces Volume One, Glory Figures, page 152}.

CHAPTER IV

THE INNOCENT BYSTANDER

(Friday 10/15/1915 to Saturday 10/16/1915)

THERE was not a sound. That stillness, weird, unnerving, that permeated, as it were, everywhere through that mysterious house, was, if that were possible, accentuated now. The four masked men in evening dress, five including their leader, for the man who had appeared in that other room with the rabbit was not here, were as silent, as motionless, as the dead man who was lashed there in the chair. And to Jimmie Dale it seemed at first as though his brain, stunned and stupefied at the shock, refused its functions, and left him groping blindly, vaguely, with only a sort of dull, subconscious realisation of menace and a deadly peril, imminent, hanging over him.

He tried to rouse himself mentally, to prod his brain to action, to pit it in a fight for life against these self-confessed criminals and murderers with their mask of culture, who surrounded him now. Was there a way out? What was it the Tocsin had said — "the most powerful and pitiless organisation of criminals the world has ever known — the stake a fortune of millions — her life!" There had, indeed, been no overemphasis in the words she had used! They had taken pains themselves to make that ominously clear, these men! Every detail of the strange house, with its luxurious furnishings, its cleverly contrived appointments, breathed a horribly suggestive degree of power, a deadly purpose, and an organisation swayed by a master mind; and, grim evidence of the merciless, inexorable length to which they would go, was the ghastly white face of the dead chauffeur, bound hand and foot, in the chair before him!

That *empty* glass in the hand of one of the men! He could not take his eyes from it — except as his eyes were drawn magnetically to that *full* glass in the hand of one of the others. What height of sardonic irony! He was to drink that other glass, to die because he refused to answer questions that for years, with every resource at his command, risking his liberty, his wealth, his name, his life, with everything that he cared for thrown into the scales, he had struggled to solve — and failed!

And then the leader spoke.

"Mr. Dale," he said, with cold significance, "I regret to admit that your pseudo taxicab driver was so ill-advised as to refuse to answer the *same* questions that I have put to you."

Five to one! That was the only way out — and it was hopeless. It was the only way out, because, convinced that he could answer those questions if he wanted to, these men were in deadly earnest; it was hopeless, because they were — five to one! And probably there were as many more, twice or three times as many more within call. But what did it matter how many more there were! He could fight until he was overpowered, that was all he could do, and the five could accomplish that. Still, if he could knock the full glass out of that man's hand, and gain the door, then perhaps — he turned quickly, as the door opened. It was as though they had read his thoughts. A number of men were grouped outside in the corridor, then the door closed again with a cordon ranged against it inside the room; and at the same instant his arms and wrists were caught in a powerful grasp by the two men immediately behind him, who all along had enacted the role of guards.

Again the leader spoke.

"I will repeat the questions," he said sharply. "Where is the woman whose ring was found on that man there in the chair? And where is the package that you two men had with you in the taxicab to-night?"

Jimmie Dale glanced from the tall, straight, immaculately clothed figure of the speaker, from the threatening smile on the set lips that just showed under the edge of the mask, to the dead man in the chair. He had faced the prospect of death before many times, but it had come with the heat of passion accompanying it, it had come quickly, abruptly, with every faculty called into action to combat it, without time to dwell upon it, to sift, weigh, or measure its meaning, and if there had been fear it had been subordinate to other emotions. But it was different now. He could not, of course, answer those questions; nor, he was doggedly conscious, would he have answered them if he could — and there was no middle course.

Death, within the next few moments, stared him in the face; and it seemed curiously irrelevant that, in a sort of unnatural calmness, he should be attempting to analyse his feelings and emotions concerning it. All his life it had seemed to him that the acme of human mental torture was the cell of a condemned criminal, with the horror of its hopelessness, with the time to dwell upon it; and that the acme of that torture itself must be that awful moment immediately preceding execution, when anticipation at last was to merge into soul-sickening reality.

Strange that thought should come! Strange that he should be framing a brain picture of such a scene, vivid, minute in detail! No — not strange. He was picturing himself. The analogy was not perfect, it was true, he had not had the months, weeks, days and hours of suspense; but it was perfect enough to bring home to him with appalling force the realisation of his position. He was standing as a condemned man might stand in those last, final moments, those moments which he had imagined must be the most terrible that could exist in life; but that dismay of soul, the horror, the terror were not his — there was, instead, a smouldering fury, a passionate amazement that it was his own life that was threatened. It seemed impossible that it could be his voice that was speaking now in such quiet, measured tones.

"Is it worth while, will it convince you now, any more than before, to repeat that there is some mistake here? I am no more able to answer your questions than you are yourselves. I never saw that man in the chair there in my life until the moment that I hailed him in his cab to-night. I do not know who the woman is to whom that ring belongs, much less do I know where she is. And if there was a package of any sort in the taxicab, as you state, I never saw it."

The lips under the mask curved into a lupine smile.

"Think well, Mr. Dale!" The man's voice was low, menacing. "Ethically, if you so choose to consider it, your refusal may be the act of a brave man; practically, it is the act of — a fool. Now — your answer!"

"I have answered you," said Jimmie Dale — and, relaxing the muscles in his arms, let them hang limply for an instant in the grip of the two men behind him. "I have no other answer."

It was only a sign, a motion of the leader's hand — but with it, quick as a lightning flash, Jimmie Dale was in action. The limp arms tautened into steel as he wrenched them loose, and, whirling around, he whipped his fist to the chin of one of the two guards.

In an instant, with the blow, as the man staggered backward, the room was in pandemonium. There was a rush from the door, and two, three, four leaping forms hurled themselves upon Jimmie Dale. He shook them off — and they came again. There was no chance ultimately, he knew that; it was only the elemental within him that rose in fierce revolt at the thought of tame submission, that bade him sell his life as dearly as he could. Panting, gasping for breath, dragging them by sheer strength as they clung to him, he got his back to the wall, fighting with the savage fury and abandon of a wild cat.

But it could not last. Where one man went down before him, two remorselessly appeared — the room seemed filled with men — they poured in through the door — he laughed at them in a half-demented way — more and more of them came — there was no play for his arms, no room to fight — they seemed so close around him, so many of them upon him, that he could not breathe — and he was bending, being crushed down as by an intolerable weight. And then his feet were jerked from beneath him, he crashed to the floor, and, in another moment, bound hand and foot, he was tied into a chair beside that other chair whose grim occupant sat in such ghastly apathy of the scene.

The room cleared instantly of all but the original five. His head was drawn suddenly, violently backward, and clamped in that position; and a metal instrument, forced into his mouth, while his lips bled in their resistance, pried jaws apart and held them open.

"One drop!" the leader ordered curtly.

The man with the full glass bent over him, and dipped a glass rod into the liquid. The drop glistened a ruby red on the end of the rod – and fell with a sharp, acrid, burning sensation upon Jimmie Dale's tongue.

For a moment Jimmie Dale's animation, mental and physical, seemed swept away from him in, as it were, a hiatus of hideous suspense. What was it to be like this passing? Why did it not act at once, as it had acted on the rabbit they had showed him in the other room? Yes, he remembered! It took more than one drop for a man; and besides, this was diluted. One drop had no effect on a man; it required – Good God, *one drop even of this was enough?* He strained forward in the chair until the sweat in great beads sprang from his forehead, strained and fought and tore at his bonds in a paroxysm of madness to free himself while there still remained a little strength. There was something filming before his eyes, a numbed feeling was creeping through his limbs, robbing them, sapping them of their vitality and power. He felt himself slipping away into a state of utter weakness, and his brain began to grow confused.

A voice seemed to float in the air near him: "For the last time – will you answer?"

With a supreme effort, Jimmie Dale strove to rally his tottering senses. Did they not understand the stupendous mockery of their questions? Did they not understand that he did not know? He had told them so – perhaps he had better tell them so again.

"I–" He tried to speak, and found the words thick upon his tongue. "I – do not – know."

The glass itself was thrust abruptly between his lips. Some of the contents spilled and trickled upon his chin, and then a flood of it, burning, fiery, poured down his throat. A flood of it – and it needed but *three* drops and there had been *ten* in the glass!

So this was death – a hazy, nebulous thing! There was no pain. It was like – like – nothingness. And out of the nothingness *she* came. Strange that she should come! Alone she had fought these fiends and outwitted them for – how long was it? Three years! She would be more than ever alone now. Pray God she did not finally fall into their clutches!

How it burned now, that fatal draught they had forced down his throat, and how it gripped at him and seemed to eat and bore its way into the very tissues! It was the end, and — no! It was *stimulating* him! Strength seemed to be returning to his limbs; it seemed as though he were being carried, as though the bonds about him were being loosened; and now his brain seemed to be growing clearer.

He roused up with a startled exclamation. He was back in the same room in which he had first returned to consciousness after the accident. He was on the same couch. The same masked figure was at the same desk. Had he been dreaming? Was this then only some horrible, ghastly nightmare through which he had passed?

No, it had been real enough; his clothes, rent and torn, and the blood upon his hands, where the skin had been scraped from his knuckles in the fight, bore evidence to that. He must then have lost consciousness for a while, though it seemed to him that at no moment, hazy, irrational though his brain might have been, had he become entirely oblivious to what was taking place around him. And yet it must have been so!

The eyes from behind the mask were fixed steadily upon him, and below the mask there was the hard, unpleasant set to the lips that Jimmie Dale had grown accustomed to expect.

The man spoke abruptly.

"That you find yourself alive, Mr. Dale," he said grimly, "is no confession of weakness upon the part of those with whom you have had to deal here. To bear witness to that there is one who is not alive, as you have seen. That man we knew. With you it was somewhat different. Your presence in the taxicab was only suspicious. There was always the possibility that you might be one of those ubiquitous 'innocent bystanders.' Your name, your position, the improbability that you could have anything in common with — shall we say, the matter that so deeply interests us? — was all in your favour. However, presumption and probability are the tools of fools. We do not depend upon them — we apply the test. And having applied the test, we are convinced that you have told the truth — that is all."

He rose from his chair brusquely. "I shall not apologise to you for what has happened. I doubt very much if you are in a frame of mind to accept anything of the sort. I imagine, rather, that you are promising yourself that we shall pay, and pay dearly, for this — that, among other things, we shall answer for the murder of that man in the other room. All this will be quite within your province, Mr. Dale — and quite fruitless. To-morrow morning the story that you are preparing to tell now would sound incredible even in your own ears; furthermore, as we shall take pains to see that you leave this place with as little knowledge of its location as you obtained when you arrived, your story, even if believed, would do little service to you and less harm to us. I think of nothing more, Mr. Dale, except – " There was a whimsical smile on the lips now. "Ah, yes, the matter of your clothes. We can, and shall be glad to make reparation to you to the slight extent of offering you a new suit before you go."

Jimmie Dale scowled. Sick, shaken, and weak as he was, the cool, imperturbable impudence of the man was fast growing unbearable.

The man laughed. "I am sure you will not refuse, Mr. Dale – since we insist. The condition of the clothes you have on at present might – I say 'might' – in a measure support your story with some degree of tangible evidence. It is not at all likely, of course; but we prefer to discount even so remote a possibility. When you have changed, you will be motored back to your home. I bid you good-night, Mr. Dale."

Jimmie Dale rubbed his eyes. The man was gone – through a door at the rear of the desk, a door that he had not noticed before, that was not even in evidence now, that was simply a movable section of the wall panelling – and for an instant Jimmie Dale experienced a sense of sickening impotence. It was as though he stood defenceless, unarmed, and utterly at the mercy of some venomous power that could crush what it would remorselessly and at will in its might.

The place was a veritable maze, a lair of hellish cleverness. He had no illusions now, he laboured under no false estimate of either the ingenuity or the resources of this inhuman nest of vultures to whom murder was no more than a matter of detail. And it was against these men that henceforth he was to match his wits! There could be no truce, no armistice. It was their lives, or hers, or his! Well, he was alive now, the first round was over, and so far he had won. His brows furrowed suddenly. Had he? He was not so sure, after all. He was conscious of a disquieting, premonitory intuition that, in some way which he could not explain, the honours were not entirely his.

He was apparently – the "apparently" was a mental reservation – quite alone in the room. He got up from the couch and walked shakily across the floor to the desk. A revolver lay invitingly upon the blotting pad. It was his own, the one they had taken from him after the accident. Jimmie Dale picked it up, examined it – and smiled a little sarcastically at himself for his trouble. It was unloaded, of course. He was twirling it in his hand, as a man, masked as every one in the house was masked, and carrying a neatly folded suit over his arm, entered from the corridor.

"The car is ready as soon as you are dressed," announced the other briefly. He laid the clothes upon the couch – and settled himself significantly in a chair.

Jimmie Dale hesitated. Then, with a shrug of his shoulders, recrossed the room, and began to remove his torn garments. What was the use! They would certainly have their own way in the end. It wasn't worth another fight, and there was nothing to be gained by a refusal except to offer a sop to his own exasperation.

He dressed quickly, in what proved to be an exceedingly well-fitting suit; and finally turned tentatively to the man in the chair.

The other stood up, and produced a heavy black silk scarf.

"If you have no objections," he said curtly, "I'll tie this over your eyes."

Again Jimmie Dale shrugged his shoulders.

"I am glad enough to get out on any conditions," he answered caustically.

"'Fortunate' would be the better word," rejoined the other meaningly – and, deftly knotting the scarf, led Jimmie Dale blindfolded from the room.

CHAPTER V

ON GUARD

(Saturday 10/16/1915)

WAS he in the city? In a suburban town? On a country road? It seemed childishly absurd that he could not at least differentiate to that extent; and yet, from the moment he had been placed in the automobile in which he now found himself, he was forced to admit that he could not tell. He had started out with the belief that, knowing New York and its surroundings as minutely as he knew them, it would be impossible, do what they would to prevent it, that at the end of the journey he should be without a clew, and a very good clew at that, to the location of what he now called, appropriately enough it seemed, the Crime Club.

But he had never ridden blindfolded in a car before! He could see absolutely nothing. And if that increased or accentuated his sense of hearing, it helped little—the roar of the racing car beat upon his eardrums the more heavily, that was all. He could tell, of course, the nature of the roadbed. They were running on an asphalt road, that was obvious enough; but city streets and suburban streets and hundreds of miles of country road around New York were of asphalt!

Traffic? He was quite sure, for he had strained his ears in an effort to detect it, that there was little or no traffic; but then, it must be one or two o'clock in the morning, and at that hour the city streets, certainly those that would be chosen by these men, would be quite as deserted as any country road! And as for a sense of direction, he had none whatever— even if the car had not been persistently swerving and changing its course every little while. If he had been able to form even an approximate idea of the compass direction in which they had started, he might possibly have been able in a general way to counteract this further effort of theirs to confuse him; but without the initial direction he was essentially befogged.

With these conclusions finally thrust home upon him, Jimmie Dale philosophically subordinated the matter in his mind, and, leaning back, composed himself as comfortably as he could upon his seat. There was a man beside him, and he could feel the legs of two men on the seat facing him. These, with the driver, would make four. He was still well guarded! The car itself was a closed car—not hooded, the sense of touch told him— therefore a limousine of some description. These facts, in a sense inconsequential, were absorbed subconsciously; and then Jimmie Dale's brain, remorselessly active, in spite of the pain from his throbbing head, was at work again.

It seemed as though a year had passed since, in the early evening, as Larry the Bat, he had burrowed so ironically for refuge in Chang Foo's den — from her! It seemed like some mocking unreality, some visionary dream that, so short a while before, he had read those words of hers that had sent the blood coursing and leaping through his veins in mad exultation at the thought that the culmination of the years had come, that all he longed for, hoped for, that all his soul cried out for was to be his — "in an hour." An *hour* — and he was to have seen her, the woman whose face he had never seen, the woman whom he loved! And the hour instead, the hours since then, had brought a nightmare of events so incredible as to seem but phantoms of the imagination.

Phantoms! He sat up suddenly with a jerk. The face of the dead chauffeur, the limp form lashed in that chair, the horrible picture in its entirety, every detail standing out in ghastly relief, took form before him. God knew there was no phantom there!

The man beside him, at the sudden start, lifted a hand and felt hurriedly over the bandage across Jimmie Dale's eyes.

Jimmie Dale was scarcely conscious of the act. With that face before him, with the scene re-enacting itself in his mind again, had come another thought, staggering him for a moment with the new menace that it brought. He had had neither time nor opportunity to think before; it had been all horror, all shock when he had entered that room. But now, like an inspiration, he saw it all from another angle. There was a glaring fallacy in the game these men had played for his benefit to-night — a fallacy which they had counted on glossing over, as it had, indeed, been glossed over, by the sudden shock with which they had forced that scene upon him; or, failing in that, they had counted on the fact that his, or any other man's nerve would have failed when it came to open defiance based on a supposition which might, after all, be wrong, and, being wrong, meant death.

But it was not supposition. Either he was right now, or these men were childish, immature fools — and, whatever else they might be, they were not that! *Not a single drop of poison had passed the chauffeur's lips.* The man had not been murdered in that room. He had not, in a sense, been murdered at all. The man, absolutely, unquestionably, without a loophole for doubt, had either been killed outright in the automobile accident, or had died immediately afterward, probably without regaining consciousness, certainly without supplying any of the information that was so determinedly sought.

Yes, he saw it now! Their backs were against the wall, they were at their wits' end, these men! The knowledge that the chauffeur possessed, that they *knew* he possessed, was evidently life and death to them. To kill the man before they had wormed out of him what they wanted to know, or, at least, until, by holding him a prisoner, they had exhausted every means at their command to make him speak, was the last thing they would do!

Jimmie Dale sat for a long time quite motionless. The car was speeding at a terrific rate along a straight stretch of road. He could almost have sworn, guided by some intuitive sense, that they were in the country. Well, even if it were so, what did that prove! They might have started *from* New York itself — only to return to it when they had satisfied themselves that he was sufficiently duped. Or they might have started legitimately from outside New York, and be going toward the city now. Since the ultimate destination was New York, and they had made no attempt to hide that from him, it was useless to speculate — for at best it could be only speculation. He had decided that once before! The man at his side felt again over the scarf to see that it was in place.

Curiously now Jimmie Dale recalled the inward monitor that had warned him the honours had not all been his in this first round with the Crime Club to-night. If they had deliberately murdered the chauffeur because of a refusal to answer, they would equally have done the same to him. Fool that he had been not to have seen that before! And yet would it have made any difference? He shook his head. He could not have acted to any better advantage than he had done. He could not — his lips curled in grim derision — have been any more convincing.

Convincing! It was all clear enough now! If the chauffeur had suffered death rather than talk, even admitting the fact that they had more grounds for suspecting the chauffeur's complicity, would his, Jimmie Dale's, mere denial, his choice, too, of death, have been any the more convincing, or have saved his life where it had not saved the other's? A certain added respect for these men, against whom, until the end now, his victory or theirs, he realised he was fighting for his life, came over him as he recognised the touch of a master hand. They did not know where to find the Tocsin; the package that she had said was vital to them was still beyond their reach; the chauffeur was dead; and he, Jimmie Dale, alone remained — a clew that they had still to prove valid or invalid it was true, but the only clew in their possession. And, gaining nothing from him by a show of force, to throw him off his guard, they had let him go — meaning him to believe they were convinced he knew nothing, and that the episode, the adventure of the night, was, as far as they were concerned, ended, finished, and done with!

Time passed, a very long time, as he sat there. It might have been an hour—he could only hazard a guess. Not one of the men in the car had spoken a word. But to Jimmie Dale, the car itself, the ride, its duration, these three strange companions, were for the time being extraneous. Even that sick giddiness in his head had, at least temporarily, gone from him.

And so, all unsuspectingly, he was to lead them to the Tocsin and fall into the trap himself! His hands, thrust deep in his pockets, were tightly clenched. They were clever enough, ingenious enough, powerful enough to watch him henceforth at every turn—and from now on, day and night, they were to be reckoned with. Suppose that in some way, as it might well have happened, for it was now vitally necessary that she should communicate with him and he with her, he had played blindly into their hands, and through him she should have fallen into their power! It brought a sickening chill, a sort of hideous panic to Jimmie Dale—and then fury, anger, in a torrent, surged upon him, and there came a merciless desire to crush, to strangle, to stamp out this inhuman band of criminals that, with intolerable effrontery to the laws of God and man, were so elaborately and scientifically equipped for their monstrous purposes!

And then Jimmie Dale, in the darkness, smiled again grimly as the leader's reference to the Gray Seal recurred to him. Well, perhaps, who knew, they would have reason more than they dreamed of to wish the Gray Seal enrolled in their own ranks! It was strange, curious! He had thought all that was ended. Only a few short hours before he had hidden away all, everything that was incident to the life of the Gray Seal, the clothes of Larry the Bat, that little metal case with the gray-coloured, adhesive seals, a dozen other things, believing that it only remained for him to return and destroy them at his leisure as a finishing touch to the Gray Seal's career—and now, instead, he was face to face with the gravest and most dangerous problem that she had ever called upon him to undertake!

Well, at least, the odds were not all in the Crime Club's favour. Where they now certainly believed him to be entirely off his guard, he was thoroughly on his guard; and where they might suspect him, watch him, they would suspect and watch only the character, the person of Jimmie Dale, and count not at all upon either Larry the Bat or—the Gray Seal.

A sort of savage elation fell upon Jimmie Dale. His brain, that had been stagnant, confused, physically sick with pain and suffering, was working now with its old-time vigour and ease, mapping, planning, scheming the way ahead. To strike, and strike quickly—to strike *first*! It must be his move next—not theirs! And he must act to-night at once, the moment he was given this pretence to liberty that they had in store for him, before they had an opportunity of closing down around him with a network of spies that he could not elude. By morning, Jimmie Dale would be Larry the Bat, and inhabiting the Sanctuary again. And a tip to Jason, his old butler, to the effect, say, that he had gone away for a trip, would account for his disappearance satisfactorily enough; it would not necessarily arouse their suspicions when they eventually discovered he was gone, for against that was always the possible, and quite likely presumption that, where they had succeeded in nothing else, they had at least succeeded in frightening him thoroughly and to the extent of imbuing him with a hasty desire to put a safe distance between himself and them.

And now, with his mind made up to his course of action, an intense impatience to put his plan into effect, an irritation at the useless twistings and turnings of the car that had latterly become more frequent, took hold upon him. How much longer was this to last! They must have been fully an hour and a half on the road already, and — ah, the car was stopping now!

He straightened up in his seat as the machine came to a halt — but the man at his side laid a restraining hand upon him. The car door opened, and one of the men got out. Jimmie Dale caught an indistinct murmur of voices from without, then the man returned to his seat, and the car went on again.

Another half hour passed, that, curbing his irritation and impatience, was filled with the conjectures and questions that anew came crowding in upon his mind. Why had the car made that stop? It was rather curious. It was certainly a prearranged meeting place. Why? And these clothes that he now wore — why had they made him change? His own had not been very badly torn. The reason given him was, on the face of it now, in view of what he now knew, mere pretence. What was the ulterior motive behind that pretence? What did this package, that had already cost a man his life to-night, contain? Who was the chauffeur? What was this death feud between the Tocsin and these men? Did she know where the Crime Club was? Who and where was John Johansson? What was this box that was numbered 428? Could she supply the links that would forge the chain into an unbroken whole?

And then for the second time the car slowed down — and this time the man on the seat beside Jimmie Dale reached up and untied the scarf.

"You get out here," said the man tersely.

CHAPTER VI

THE TRAP

(Saturday 10/16/1915)

HAD it not been for the stop the car had previously made, for the possibility that he might have obtained a glimpse outside when the door had been opened, the scarf over his eyes would have been superfluous; for now, with it removed, he could scarcely distinguish the forms of the three men around him, since the window curtains of the car were tightly drawn. Nor was he given the opportunity to do more, even had it been possible. The car stopped, the door was opened, he was pushed toward it—and even as he reached the ground, the door was closed behind him, and the car was speeding on again. But where he could not see before, it took now but a glance to obtain his bearings—he was standing on a corner on Riverside Drive, within a few doors of his own house.

Jimmie Dale stood still for a moment, watching the car as it disappeared rapidly up the Drive. And with a sort of grim facetiousness his brain began to correlate time and distance. Where had he come from? Where was this Crime Club? They had been, as nearly as he could estimate, two hours in making the journey; and, as nearly as he could estimate, in their turnings and twistings had covered at least twice the distance that would be represented by a direct route. Granting, then, an average speed of forty miles an hour, which was overgenerous to be on the safe side, and the fact that they certainly had not crossed the Hudson, which now lay before him, flanking the Drive, the Crime Club was somewhere within the area of a semicircle, whose centre was the corner on which he now stood, and whose radius was forty miles—*or forty yards!* He forced a laugh. It was just that, no more, no less—he was as likely to have started on his ride from within a biscuit throw of where he now stood, as to have started on it from miles away!

But—he aroused himself with a start—he was wasting time! It must be very late, near morning, and he would have need for every moment that was left between now and daylight. He turned, walked quickly to his house, mounted the steps, and with his latch-key—they had at least permitted him to retain the contents of his pockets when they had forced him to change his clothes—opened the front door softly, and, stepping inside, closed the door as silently as he had opened it.

He paused for an instant to listen. There was not a sound. The servants, naturally, would have been in bed hours ago. Even old Jason — Jimmie Dale smiled, half whimsically, half affectionately — whose paternal custom it was to sit up for his Master Jim, who, as he was fond of saying, he had dandled as a baby on his knee, had evidently given it up as a bad job on this occasion and had turned in himself. Jason, however, had left the light burning here in the big reception hall.

Jimmie Dale stepped to the switch and turned off the light; then stood hesitant in the darkness. Was there anything to be gained by rousing Jason now and telling him what he intended to do — to instruct him to answer any inquiries by the statement that "Mr. Dale had gone away for a trip"? He could trust Jason; Jason already knew much — more than one of those mysterious letters of the Tocsin's had passed through Jason's hands.

Jimmie Dale shook his head. No; he could communicate with Jason from downtown in the morning. He had half expected to find Jason up, and, in that case, would have taken the other, as far as necessary, into his confidence; but it was not a matter that pressed for the moment. He could get into touch with Jason at any time readily enough. Was there anything else before he went? He would not be able to get back as easily as he got out! Money! He shook his head again — a little grimly this time. He had been caught once before as Larry the Bat without funds! There was plenty of money now hidden in the Sanctuary, enough for any emergency, enough to last him indefinitely.

He stepped forward along the hall, his tread noiseless on the rich, heavy rug, passed into the rear of the house, descended the back stairs, and reached the cellar. It was below the level of the ground, of course; but a narrow window here, though quite large enough to permit of egress, gave on the driveway at the side of the house that led to the garage in the rear.

Cautiously now, for the cement flooring was, in the stillness, little less than a sounding board, Jimmie Dale reached the wall and felt along it to the window, the lower edge of whose sill was just slightly below the level of his shoulder. It opened inward, if he remembered correctly. His fingers were feeling for the fastenings. It was too dark to see a thing. He muttered in annoyance. Where were the fastenings! At the sides, or at the bottom? His hand began to make a circuit of the sill — and then suddenly, with a low, sharp cry, he leaned forward!

What did this mean? Wires! No wires had ever been there before! His fingers were working now with feverish haste, telegraphing their message to his brain. The wires ran through the sill close to the corner of the wall — tiny fragments of wood, as from an auger, were still on the sill — and here was a small particle of wire insulation that, those sensitive finger tips proclaimed, was *fresh.*

A cold thrill ran through Jimmie Dale; and there came again that sickening sense of impotency in the face of the malignant, devilish cunning arrayed against him, that once before he had experienced, that night. He had thought to forestall them – and he had been forestalled himself! This could only have been done – they had had no interest in him before then – while they held him at the Crime Club, while he was spending that two hours in the car! Was that why they had taken so long in coming? Was that why the car had stopped that time – that those with him might be told that the work here had been completed, and he need no longer be kept away?

He edged away from the window, and, as cautiously as he had come, retraced his steps across the cellar and up the stairs – and then, the possibility of being heard from without gone, he broke into a run. There was no need to wonder long what those wires meant. They could mean only one of two things – and the Crime Club would have little concern in his electric light! *They had tapped his telephone.* The mains, he knew, ran into the cellar from the underground service in the street. He was racing like a madman now. How long ago, how many hours ago, had they done that! Great Scott, *she* was to have telephoned! Had she done so? Was the game, all, everything, she herself, at their mercy already? If she had telephoned, Jason would have left a message on his desk – he would look there first – afterward he would waken Jason.

He gained the door of his den on the first landing, a room that ran the entire length of one side of the house from front to rear, burst in, switched on the light – -and stood stock-still in amazement.

"Jason!" he cried out.

The old butler, fully dressed, rubbing and blinking his eyes at the light, and with a startled cry, rose up from the depths of a lounging chair.

"Jason!" exclaimed Jimmie Dale again.

"I beg pardon, sir, Master Jim," stammered the man. "I – I must have fallen asleep, sir."

"Jason, what are you doing here?" Jimmie Dale demanded sharply.

"Well, sir," said Jason, still fumbling for his words, "it – it was the telephone, sir."

"The – *telephone!*"

"Yes, sir. A woman, begging your pardon, Master Jim, a lady, sir, has been telephoning every hour or so, and she – "

"*Yes!*" Jimmie Dale had jumped across the room and had caught the other fiercely by the shoulder. "Yes – yes! What did she say? *Quick,* man!"

"Good Lord, Master Jim!" faltered Jason. "I – she – "

"Jason," said Jimmie Dale, suddenly as cold as ice, "what did she say? Think, man! Every word!"

"She didn't say anything, Master Jim. Nothing at all, sir – except to keep asking each time if she could speak to you."

"Nothing else, Jason?"

"No, sir."

"You are *sure?*"

"I'm sure, Master Jim. Not another thing but that, sir, just as I've told you."

"Thank God!" said Jimmie Dale, in a low voice.

"Yes, sir," said Jason mechanically.

"How long ago was it since she telephoned last?" asked Jimmie Dale quickly.

"Well, sir, I couldn't rightly say. You see, as I said, Master Jim, I must have gone to sleep, but – "

They were staring tensely into each other's face. The telephone on the desk was ringing vibrantly, clamourously, through the stillness of the room.

Jason, white, frightened, bewildered, touched his lips with the tip of his tongue.

"That'll be her again, sir," he said hoarsely.

"Wait!" said Jimmie Dale tersely.

He was trying to think, to think faster than he had ever thought before. He could not tell Jason to say that he had not yet come in – *they* knew he was in, it would be but showing his hand to that "some one" who would be listening now on the wire. He dared not speak to her, or, above all, allow her to expose herself by a single inadvertent word. He dared not speak to her – and she was here now, calling him! He could not speak to her – and it was life and death almost that she should know what had happened; life and death almost for both of them that he should know all and everything she could tell him. True, it would take but a minute to run to the cellar and cut those wires, while Jason held her on the pretence of calling him, Jimmie Dale, to the 'phone; only a minute to cut those wires – and in so doing advertise to these fiends the fact that he had discovered their trick; admit, as though in so many words, that their suspicions of him were justified; lay himself open to some new move that he could not hope to foresee; and, paramount to all else, rob her and himself of this master trump the Crime Club had placed in his hands, by means of which there was a chance that he could hoist them with their own petard!

The telephone rang again – imperatively, persistently.

"Listen, Jason." Jimmie Dale was speaking rapidly, earnestly. "Say that I've come in and have gone to bed – in a vile humour. That you told me a lady had been calling, but that I said if she called again I wasn't to be disturbed if it was the Queen of Sheba herself – that I wouldn't answer any 'phone to-night for anybody. Do you understand? No argument with her – just that. Now, answer!"

Jason lifted the receiver from the hook.

"Yes – hello!" he said. "Yes, ma'am, Mr. Dale has come in, but he has retired. . . . Yes, I told him; but, begging your pardon, ma'am, he was in what I might say was a bit of a temper, and said he wasn't to be disturbed by any one."

Jimmie Dale snatched the receiver from Jason, and put it to his own ear.

"Kindly tell Mr. Dale that unless he comes to the 'phone now," a feminine voice, her voice, in well-simulated indignation, was saying, "it will be a very long day before I shall trouble myself to – "

Jimmie Dale clapped his hand firmly over the mouthpiece of the instrument. Thank God for that clever brain of hers! She understood!

"Repeat what you said before, Jason," he instructed hurriedly. "Then say 'Good-night.'"

He removed his hand from the mouthpiece.

"It's quite useless, ma'am," said Jason apologetically. "In the rare temper he was in, he wouldn't come, to use his own words, ma'am, not for the Queen of Sheba herself, ma'am. Good-night, ma'am."

Jimmie Dale hung the receiver back on the hook – and with his hand flirted away a bead of moisture that had sprung to his forehead.

"Good Lord, Master Jim, what's wrong, sir? What's happened, sir? And – and those clothes, Master Jim, sir! They aren't the ones you went out in, sir – they aren't yours at all, sir!" Jason ventured anxiously.

"Jason," said Jimmie Dale, "switch off the light, and go to the front window and look out. Keep well behind the curtains. Don't show yourself. Tell me if you see anything."

"Yes, sir," said Jason obediently.

The light went out. Jimmie Dale moved to the rear of the room – to the window overlooking the garage and yard.

"I don't see anything, sir," Jason called.

"Watch!" Jimmie Dale answered.

A minute passed – two – three. Jimmie Dale was staring down into the black of the yard. She understood! She knew, of course, before she 'phoned that something had gone wrong to-night. She knew that only peril of the gravest moment would have kept him from the 'phone – and her. She knew now, as a logical conclusion, that it was dangerous to attempt to communicate with him at his home. Those wires! Where did they lead to? Not far away – that would be almost a mechanical impossibility. Was it into the Crime Club itself – near at hand? Or the basement, say, of that apartment house across the driveway? Or – where?

And then Jimmie Dale spoke again:

"Do you see anything, Jason?"

"I'm not sure, sir," Jason answered hesitantly. "I thought I saw a man move behind a tree out there across the road a minute ago, sir. Yes, sir – there he is again!"

There was a thin, mirthless smile on Jimmie Dale's lips.

Below, in the shadow of the garage, a dark form, like a deeper shadow, stirred – and was still again.

"What time is it, Jason?" Jimmie Dale asked presently.

"It'll be about half-past four, sir."

"Go to bed, Jason."

"Yes, sir; but" – Jason's voice, low, troubled, came through the darkness from the upper end of the room – "Master Jim, sir, I – "

"Go to bed, Jason – and not a word of this."

"Yes, sir. Good-night, Master Jim."

"Good-night, Jason."

Jimmie Dale groped his way to the big lounging chair in which he had found Jason asleep, and flung himself into it. They had struck quickly, these ingenious, dress-suited murderers of the Crime Club! The house was already watched, would be watched now untiringly, unceasingly; not a movement of his henceforth but would be under their eyes!

His hands, resting on the arms of the chair, closed slowly until they became tight-clenched, knotted fists. What was he to do? It was not only the Crime Club, it was not only the Tocsin and her peril – there was the underworld snapping and snarling at his heels, there was the police, dogged and sullen, ever on the trail of the Gray Seal! His life, even before this, in his fight against the underworld and the police, had depended upon his freedom of action – and now, at one and the same time, that freedom was cut away from beneath his feet, as it were, and a third foe, equally as deadly as the others, was added to the list!

For months, to preserve and sustain the character of Larry the Bat, he had been forced to assume the role almost daily; for, in that sordid empire below the dead line, whose one common bond and aim was the Gray Seal's death, where suspicion, one of the other, was rampant and extravagant, where each might be the one against whom all swore their vengeance, Larry the Bat could not mysteriously disappear from his accustomed haunts without inviting suspicion in an active and practical form — an inquisitorial visit to his squalid lodgings, the Sanctuary — and the end of Larry the Bat!

If, as he had thought only a few hours before, he was through forever with his dual life, that would not have mattered, the underworld would have been welcome to make what it chose of it — but now the preservation of the character of Larry the Bat was more vital and necessary to him than it had ever been before. It was a means of defense and offense against these men who lurked now outside his doors. It was the sole means now of communication with her; for, warned both by Jason's words, and what must be an obvious fact to her, that their plans had miscarried, that it was dangerous to communicate with him as Jimmie Dale, she would expect him, count on him to make that move. There would be no longer either reason or attempt on her part to maintain the mystery with which she had heretofore surrounded herself, the crisis had come, she would be watching, waiting, hoping, seeking for him more anxiously and with far more at stake than he had ever sought for her — until now!

He got up impulsively from his chair, and, in the blackness, began to pace the room. The next move was clear, pitifully clear; it had been clear from the first, it had been clear even in that ride in the car — it was so clear that it seemed veritably to mock him as he prodded his brains for some means of putting it into execution. He must get to the Sanctuary, become Larry the Bat — but how? *How!* The question seemed at last to become resonant, to ring through the room with the weight of doom upon it.

Schemes, plans, ideas came, bringing a momentary uplift — only to be discarded the next instant with a sort of bitter, desperate regret. These men were not men of mere ordinary intelligence; their cleverness, their power, the amazing scope of their organisation, all bore grim witness to the fact that they would be blinded not at all by any paltry ruse.

He could walk out of the house in the morning as Jimmie Dale without apparent hindrance — that was obvious enough. And so long as he pursued the usual avocations of Jimmie Dale, he would not be interfered with — only *watched*. It was useless to consider that plan for a moment. It would not help him to reach the Sanctuary — without leading them there behind him! True, there was always the chance that he might shake them off his trail, but he could hardly hope to accomplish anything like that without their knowing that it was done *deliberately* — and that he dared not risk. The strongest weapon in his hands now was his secret knowledge that he was being watched.

That telephone there, for instance, that most curiously kept on insisting in his mind that it, and it alone was the way out, was the last thing he could place in jeopardy. Besides, there was another reason why such a plan would not do; for, granting even that he succeeded in eluding them on the way, and managed to reach the Sanctuary, his freedom of action would be so restricted and limited as to be practically worthless—he would have to return to his home here again within a reasonable time as Jimmie Dale, within a few hours at most—or again they would be in possession of the fact that he had discovered their surveillance.

That, it was true, had been his original plan when he had entered the house half an hour previously, but it was an entirely different matter now. Then, he had counted on *getting away* without their knowing it, before they, as he had fondly thought, would have had a chance to establish their espionage, and when they would have had no reason to suspect, for a time at least, that he was not still within the house, when they would have been watching, as it were, an empty cage.

He stopped in his walk, and, after a moment, dropped down into the lounging chair again. That was it, of course. An empty cage! If he could escape from the house! Not so much without their seeing him; that was more or less a mechanical detail. But escape—and leave them in possession of a sort of guarantee or assurance that he was still there! That would give him the freedom of action that he must have. He smiled with bitter irony. That solved the problem! That was all there was to it—just that! It was very simple, exceedingly simple; it was only —impossible!

The smile left his lips, and once more his hands, clenched fiercely. No; it was not impossible! It *must* be done—if he was to win through, if he was even to save himself! It must be done—or *fail* her! It *could* be done; there was a way—if he could only see it!

CHAPTER VII

THE "HOUR"

(Saturday 10/16/1915)

As the minutes passed, many of them, Jimmie Dale sat there motionless, staring before him at the desk that was faintly outlined in the unlighted room. Then somewhere in the house a clock struck the hour. Five o'clock! He raised his head. *Yes!* It could be done! There was a way! He had the germ of it now. And now the plan began to grow, to take form and shape in his mind, to dovetail, to knit the integral parts into a comprehensive whole. There was a way — but he must have assistance. Jason — yes, assuredly. Benson, his chauffeur — yes, equally as trustworthy as Jason. Benson was devoted to him; and moreover Benson was young, alert, daring, cool. He had had more than one occasion to test Benson's resourcefulness and nerve!

Jimmie Dale rose abruptly, went to the rear window, and, parting the curtains cautiously, stood peering down into the courtyard. Yes, it was feasible; even a little more than feasible. The garage fronted the driveway, of course, to give free entrance and egress to the cars, but where the wall of the garage and the rear wall of the house overlapped, as it were, the space between them was not much more than ten yards; and here the shadows of the two walls, mingling, lay like a black, impenetrable pathway — not like that other shadow he had seen moving at the side of the garage, and that, if not for the moment discernible, was none the less surely still lurking there!

Satisfied, Jimmie Dale swung briskly from the window, and, going now to his bedroom across the hall, undressed and went to bed — but not to sleep. There would be time enough to sleep, all day, if he wished; now, there were still the little details to be thought out that, more than anything else, could make or wreck his plans. A point overdone, the faintest suggestion of a false note where men of the calibre of those against whom he was now fighting for his life were concerned, would not only make his scheme abortive, but would place him utterly at their mercy.

It was nine o'clock when he rang for Jason.

"Jason," he said abruptly, as the other entered, "I want you to telephone for Doctor Merlin."

"The doctor, sir!" exclaimed the old man anxiously. "You're — you're not ill, Master Jim, sir?"

"Do I look ill, Jason?" inquired Jimmie Dale gravely.

"Well, sir," admitted Jason, in concern; "a bit done up, sir, perhaps. A little pale, sir; though I'm sure — "

"I'm glad to hear it," said Jimmie Dale, sitting up in bed. "The worse I look, the better!"

"I — I beg pardon, sir?" stammered Jason.

"Jason," said Jimmie Dale, gravely again, "you have had reason to know that on several occasions my life has been threatened. It is threatened now. You know from last night that this house is now watched. You may, or you may not have surmised — that our telephone wires have been tapped."

"Tapped, sir!" — Jason's face had gone a little gray.

"Yes; a party line, so to speak," said Jimmie Dale grimly. "Do you understand? You must be careful to say no more, no less than exactly what I tell you to say. Now go and telephone! Ask the doctor to come over and see me this morning. Simply say that I am not feeling well; but that, apart from being apparently in a very nervous condition, you do not know what is the matter."

"Yes, sir — good Lord, sir!" gasped Jason — and left the room to carry out his orders.

An hour later, Doctor Merlin had been and gone — and had left two prescriptions; one written, the other verbal. With the written one, Benson, in his chauffeur's livery, was dispatched to the drug store; the verbal one was precisely what Jimmie Dale had expected from the fussy old family physician: "Two or three days of quiet in the house, James; and if you need me again, let me know."

"Now, Jason," said Jimmie Dale, when the old man had returned from ushering Doctor Merlin from the house, "our friends out there will be anxious to learn the verdict. I was to dine with the Ross-Hendersons [59] to-morrow night, was I not?"

"Yes, sir; I think so, sir."

"Make sure!" said Jimmie Dale. "Look in my engagement book there on the table."

Jason looked.

"Yes, sir, that's right," he announced.

---

[59] Possibly they are related to the Ross-Logan family mentioned in Chapter Ten, Part One of this novel.

"Very good," said Jimmie Dale softly. "Now go and telephone again, Jason. Present my regrets and excuses to the Ross-Hendersons, and say that under the doctor's orders I am confined to the house for the next few days—and, Jason!"

"Yes, sir?"

"When Benson returns with the medicine let him bring it here himself—and I shall want you as well."

Jimmie Dale propped himself up a little wearily on the pillows, as Jason went out of the room. After all, his condition was not entirely feigned. He was, as a matter of fact, pretty well played out, both mentally and physically. Certainly, that he should require a doctor and be confined to the house could not arouse suspicion even in the minds of those alert, aristocratic thugs of the Crime Club, prone as they would be to suspect anything—a man who had been knocked unconscious in an automobile smash the night before, had been in a fight, had been subjected to a terrific mental shock, to say nothing of the infernal drug that had been administered to him, might well be expected to be indisposed the next morning, and for several mornings following that! It might, indeed, even cause them to relax their vigilance for the time being—though he dared build nothing on that. Well, he had only to coach Benson and Jason in the parts they were to play, and the balance of the morning and all the afternoon was his in which to rest.

He reached over to the table, picked up a pencil and paper, and began to jot down memoranda. He had just tossed the pencil back on the table as the two men entered.

Jason, at a sign, closed the door quietly.

Jimmie Dale looked at Benson half musingly, half whimsically, for a moment before he spoke.

"Benson," he said, "the back seat of the large touring car is hinged and lifts up, once the cushion is removed, doesn't it?"

"Yes, sir," Benson answered promptly.

"And there's space enough for, say, a man inside, isn't there?"

"Why, yes, sir; I suppose so—at a squeeze"—Benson stared blankly.

"Quite so!" said Jimmie Dale calmly. "Now, another matter, Benson: I believe some chauffeurs have a habit, when occasion lends itself, of taking, shall we say, their 'best girl' out riding in their masters' machines?"

"*Some* might," Benson replied, a little stiffly. "I hope you don't think, sir, that—"

"One moment, Benson. The point is, it's done—quite generally?"

"Yes, sir."

"And you have a 'best girl,' or at least could find one for such a purpose, if you were so inclined?"

"Yes, sir," said Benson; "but—"

"Very good!" Jimmie Dale interrupted. "Then to-night, Benson, taking advantage of my illness, and to-morrow night, and the nights after that until further notice, you will acquire and put into practice that reprehensible habit."

"I—I don't understand, Mr. Dale."

"No; I dare say not," said Jimmie Dale—and then the whimsicality dropped from him. "Benson," he said slowly, "do you remember a night, nearly four years ago, the first night you ever saw me? You had, indiscreetly, I think, displayed more money than was wise in that East Side neighbourhood."

"I remember," said Benson, with a sudden start; then simply: "I wouldn't be here now, sir, if it hadn't been for you."

"Well," said Jimmie Dale quietly, "the tables are turned to-day, Benson. As Jason already knows, this house is watched. For reasons that I cannot explain, I am in great danger. Bluntly, I am putting my life in your hands—and Jason's."

Benson looked for an instant from Jimmie Dale to Jason, caught the strained, troubled expression on the old man's face, then back again at Jimmie Dale.

"D'ye mean that, sir!" he cried. "Then you can count on me, Mr. Dale, to the last ditch!"

"I know that, Benson," Jimmie Dale said softly. "And now, both of you, listen! It is imperative that I should get away from the house; and equally imperative that those watching should believe that I am still here. Not even the servants are to be permitted a suspicion that I am not here in my bed, ill. That, Jason, is your task. You will allow no one to wait on me but yourself; you will bring the meal trays up regularly—and eat the food yourself. You will answer all inquiries, telephone and otherwise, in person—I am not seeing any one. You understand perfectly, Jason?"

"I understand, Master Jim. You need have no fear, sir, on that score."

"Now, you, Benson," Jimmie Dale went on. "A few minutes ago I sent you out in your chauffeur's togs with that prescription. You were undoubtedly observed. I wanted you to be. It was quite necessary that they should know and be able to recognise you again—to disabuse their minds later on of the possibility that I might be masquerading in your clothes; and also, of course, that they should know who you were, and what your position was in the household. Very well! To-night, at eight o'clock exactly, you are to go out from the back door of the house to the

306

garage. On the way out – it will be quite dark then – I want you to drop something, say, a bunch of keys that you had been jingling in your hand. You are to experience some difficulty in finding it again, move about a little to force any one that may be lurking by the garage to retreat around the corner. Grumble a bit and make a little noise; but you are not to overdo it – a couple of minutes at the outside is enough, by that time I shall be under the car seat. You will then run the machine out to the street and stop at the curb, jump out, and, as though you had forgotten something, hurry back to the garage. You must not be away long – enough only to permit, say, a passer-by to glance into the car and satisfy himself that it is empty. You understand, of course, Benson, that the hood must be down – no closed car to invite even the suggestion of concealment – that would be a fatal blunder. Drive then to the young lady's home by as direct a route as you can – give no appearance of being aware that you are followed, as you will be, and much less the appearance of attempting to elude pursuit. Act naturally. Between here and your destination I will manage readily enough to leave the car. You will then take the young lady for her drive – that is what they will be interested in – your motive for going out to-night. And, as I said, take her driving again on each succeeding night – establish the *habit* to their satisfaction."

Jimmie Dale paused, glanced at the paper which he still held in his hand, then handed it to Benson.

"Just one thing more, Benson," he said: "Listed on that paper you will find a different rendezvous for each night for the next five nights, excluding to-night, which, after you have returned the young lady to her home, you are to pass by on your way back here. See that your drive is always over in time for you to pass each night's rendezvous at half past eleven sharp. Don't stop unless I signal you. If I am not there, go right on home, and be at the next place on the following night. I am fairly well satisfied they will not bother about you after to-night, or to-morrow night at the most; but, for all that, you must take no chances, so, except in the route you take in going to the young lady's, always avoid covering the same ground twice, which might give the appearance of having some ulterior purpose in view – even in your drives, vary your runs. Is this clear, Benson?"

"Yes, sir," said Benson earnestly.

"Very well, then," said Jimmie Dale. "Eight o'clock to the dot, Benson – compare your time with Jason's. And now, Jason, see that I get a chance to sleep until dinner time to-night."

The hours that followed were hours of sound and much-needed sleep for Jimmie Dale, and from which he awoke only on Jason's entrance that evening with the dinner tray.

"I've slept like a log, Jason!" he cried briskly, as he leaped out of bed. "Anything new – anything happened?"

"No, sir; not a thing," Jason answered. "Only, Master Jim, sir" – the old man twisted his hands nervously – "I – you'll excuse my saying so, sir – I do hope you'll be careful to-night, sir. I can't help being afraid that something'll happen to you, Master Jim."

"Nonsense, Jason!" Jimmie Dale laughed cheerfully. "There's nothing going to happen – to me! You go ahead now and stay with the servants, and get them out of the road at the proper time."

He bathed, dressed, ate his dinner, and was slipping cartridges into the magazine of his automatic when, within a minute or two of eight o'clock, Jason's whisper came from the doorway.

"It's all clear now, Master Jim, sir."

"Right!" Jimmie Dale responded – and followed Jason down the stairway, and to the head of the cellar stairs.

Here Jason halted.

"God keep you, Master Jim!" said the old man huskily.

"Good-night, Jason," Jimmie Dale answered softly; and, with a reassuring squeeze on the other's arm, went on down to the cellar.

Here he moved quickly, noiselessly across to the window – not the window of the night before, but another of the same description, almost directly beneath the one in his den above, that faced the garage and lay in the line of that black shadow path between the two buildings. Deftly, cautiously without sound, a half inch, an inch at a time he opened it. He stood listening, then. A minute passed. Then he heard Benson open and shut the back door; then Benson in the yard; and then Benson's voice in a muttered and irritable growl, talking to himself, as he stamped around on the ground.

With a lithe, agile movement, Jimmie Dale pulled himself up and through the window – and began to creep rapidly on hands and knees toward the garage. It was dark, intensely dark. He could barely distinguish Benson's form, though, as he passed the other, the slight sounds he made drowned out by the chauffeur's angry mumblings, he could have reached out and touched Benson easily.

He gained the interior of the garage, and, as Benson, came on again, stepped lightly into the car, lifted the seat, and wriggled his way inside.

It was close, stuffy, abominably cramped, but Jimmie Dale was smiling grimly now. Thanks to Benson, there wasn't a possibility that he had been seen. He both felt and heard Benson start the car. Then the car moved forward, ran the length of the driveway, bumped slightly as it made the street – and stopped. He heard Benson jump out and run back – and then he listened intently, and the grim smile flickered on his lips again. Came the sound of a footstep on the sidewalk close beside the car—then silence—the car shook a little as though some one's weight was on the step—then the footsteps receded—Benson returned on the run—and the car started forward once more.

Perhaps ten minutes passed. Three times the car had swerved sharply, making a corner turn. Then Jimmie Dale pushed up the seat, and, protected from observation from behind by the back of the car itself, crawled out and crouched down on the floor of the tonneau.

"Don't look around, Benson," he said calmly. "Are we followed?"

"Yes, sir." Benson answered. "At least, there's always been a car behind us, though not the same one. They're pretty clever. There must be three or four, each following the other. Every time I turn a corner it's a different car that turns it behind me."

"How far behind?" Jimmie Dale asked.

"Half a block."

"Slow down a little," instructed Jimmie Dale; "and don't turn another corner until they've had a chance to accommodate themselves to your new speed. You are going too fast for me to jump, and I don't want them to notice any change in speed, except what is made in plain sight. Yes; that's better. Where are we, Benson?"

"That's Amsterdam Avenue ahead," replied Benson.

"All right," said Jimmie Dale quietly. "Turn into it. The more people the better. Tell me just as you are about to turn."

"Yes, sir," said Benson; then, almost on the instant, "All ready, sir!"

Jimmie Dale's hand reached out for the door catch, edged the door ajar, the car swerved, took the corner—and Jimmie Dale stepped out on the running board, hung there negligently for a moment as though chatting with Benson, and then with an airy "good-night" dropped nonchalantly to the ground, and the next instant had mingled with the throng of pedestrians on the sidewalk.

A half minute later, a large gray automobile turned the corner and followed Benson—and Jimmie Dale, stepping out into the street again, swung on a downtown car. The road to the Sanctuary was open!

In his impatience, now, the street car seemed to drag along every foot of the way; but a glance at his watch, as he finally reached the Bowery, and, walking then, rapidly approached the cross street a few steps ahead that led to the Sanctuary, told him that it was still but a quarter to nine. But even at that he quickened his steps a little. He was free now! There was a sort of savage, elemental uplift upon him. He was free! He could strike now in his own defense—and hers! In a few moments he would be at the Sanctuary; in a few more he would be Larry the Bat, and by to-morrow at the latest he would see — The Tocsin. After all, that "hour" was not to be taken from him! It was not, perhaps, the hour that she had meant it should be, thought and prayed, perhaps, that it might be! It was not the hour of victory. But it was the hour that meant to him the realisation of the years of longing, the hour when he should see her, see her for the first time face to face, when there should be no more barriers between them, when —

"Fer Gawd's sake, mister, buy a pencil!"

A hand was plucking at his sleeve, the thin voice was whining in his ear. He halted mechanically. A woman, old, bedraggled, ragged, was thrusting a bunch of cheap pencils imploringly toward him — and then, with a stifled cry, Jimmie Dale leaned forward. The eyes that lifted to his for an instant were bright and clear with the vigor of youth, great eyes of brown they were, and trouble, hope, fear, wistfulness, ay, and a glorious shyness were in their depths. And then the voice he knew so well, the Tocsin's was whispering hurriedly:

"I will be waiting here, Jimmie — for Larry the Bat."

CHAPTER VIII

THE TOCSIN

(Saturday 10/16/1915)

It was only a little way back along the street from the Sanctuary to the corner on the Bowery where as Jimmie Dale he had left her, where as Larry the Bat now he was going to meet her again; it would take only a moment or so, even at Larry the Bat's habitual, characteristic, slouching, gait — but it seemed that was all too slow, that he must throw discretion to the winds and run the distance. His blood was tingling; there was elation upon him, coupled with an almost childlike dread that she might be gone.

"The Tocsin! The Tocsin!" he kept saying to himself.

Yes; she was still there, still whiningly imploring those who passed to buy her miserable pencils — and then, with a quick-flung whisper to him to follow as he slouched up close to her, she had started slowly down the street.

"The Tocsin! The Tocsin! The Tocsin!" — his brain seemed to be ringing with the words, ringing with them in a note clear as a silver bell. The Tocsin — at last! The woman who so strangely, so wonderfully, so mysteriously had entered into his life, and possessed it, and filled it with a love and yearning that had come to mold and sway and actuate his very existence — the woman for whom he had fought; for whom he had risked, and gladly risked, his wealth, his name, his honour — everything; the woman for whose sake he, the Gray Seal, was sought and hounded as the most notorious criminal of the age; she whose cleverness, whose resourcefulness, whose amazing intimacy with the hidden things of the underworld had seemed, indeed, to border on the supernatural; she, the Tocsin — the woman whose face he had never seen before! The woman whose face he had never seen before — and who now was that wretched hag that hobbled along the street before him, begging, whining, and importuning the passers-by to purchase of her pitiful wares!

He laughed a little — buoyantly. He had never pictured a first meeting such as this! A hag? Yes! And one as disreputable in appearance as he himself, as Larry the Bat, was disreputable! But he had seen her eyes! Inimitable as was her disguise, she could not hide her eyes, or hide the pledge they held of the beauty of form and feature beneath the tattered rags and the touch of a master in the make-up that brought haggard want and age into the face — and dimly he began to divine the source, the means by which she had acquired the information that for years had enabled her to plan their coups, that had enabled him to execute them under the guise of crime, that for years had seemed beyond all human reach.

Where was she going? Where was she taking him? But what did it matter! The years of waiting were at an end – the years of mystery in a few moments now would be mystery no more!

Ah! She had turned from the Bowery, and was heading east. He shuffled on after her, guardedly, a half block behind. It was well that Jimmie Dale had disappeared, that he was Larry the Bat again – the neighbourhood was growing more and more one that Jimmie Dale could not long linger in without attracting attention; while, on the other hand, it was the natural environment of such as Larry the Bat and such as she, who was leading him now to the supreme moment of his life. Yes, it was that – the fulfillment of the years! The thought of it alone filled his mind, his soul; it brushed aside, it blotted out for the time being the danger, the peril, the deadly menace that hung over them both. It was only that she, the Tocsin, was here – only that at last they would be together.

On she went, traversing street after street, the direction always trending toward the river – until finally she halted before what appeared to be, as nearly as he could make out in the almost total darkness of the ill-lighted street, a small and tumble-down, self-contained dwelling that bordered on what seemed to be an unfenced store yard of some description. He drew his breath in sharply. She had halted – waiting for him to come up with her. She was waiting for him – *waiting* for him! It seemed as though he drank of some strange, exhilarating elixir – he reached her side eagerly – and then – and then – her hand had caught his, and she was leading him into the house, into a black passage where he could see nothing, into a room equally black over whose threshold he stumbled, and her voice in a low, conscious way, with a little tremour, a half sob in it that thrilled him with its promise, was in his ears:

"We are safe here, Jimmie, for a little while – but, oh, Jimmie, what have I done! What have I done to bring you into this – only – only – I was so sure, so sure, Jimmie, that there was nothing more to fear!"

The blood was beating in hammer blows at his temples. It seemed all unreal, untrue that this moment could be his, that it was not a dream – a dream which was presently to be snatched from him in a bitter awakening. And then he laughed out wildly, passionately. No – it was true, it was real! Her breath was on his cheek, it was a living, pulsing hand that was still in his – and then soul and mind and body seemed engulfed and lost in a mad ecstasy – and she was in his arms, crushed to him, and he was raining kisses upon her face.

"I love you! I love you!" he was crying hoarsely; and over and over again: "I love you! I love you!"

She did not struggle. The warm, rich lips were yielding to his; he could feel the throb, the life in the young, lithe form against his own. She was his—his! The years, the past, all were swept away—and she was his at last—his for always. And there came a mighty sense of kingship upon him, as though all the world were at his feet, and virility, and a great, glad strength above all other men's, and a song was in his soul, a song triumphant—for she was his!

"You!" he cried out—and strained her to him. "You!" he cried again—and kissed her lips and her eyelids and her lips again.

And then her head was buried on his shoulder, and she was crying softly; but after a moment she raised her hands and laid them upon his face, and held them there, and because it was dark, dared to raise her head as well, and her eyes to look into his.

Then for a long time they stood there so, and for a long time neither spoke—and then with a little startled, broken cry, as though the peril and the menace hanging over them, forgotten for the moment, were thrust like a knife stab suddenly upon her, she drew herself away, and ran from him, and went and got a lamp, and lighted it, and set it upon the table.

And Jimmie Dale, still standing there, watched her. How gloriously her eyes shone, dimmed and misty with the tears that filled them though they were! And there was nothing incongruous in the rags that clothed her, in the squalour and poverty of the bare room, in the white furrows that the tears had plowed through the grime and make-up on her cheeks.

"You wonderful, wonderful woman!" Jimmie Dale whispered.

She shook her head as though almost in self-reproach.

"I am not wonderful, Jimmie," she said, in a low voice. "I"—and then she caught his arm, and her voice broke a little—"I've brought you into this—probably to your death. Jimmie, tell me what happened last night, and since then. I—I've thought at times to-day I should go mad. Oh, Jimmie, there is so much to say to-night, so much to do if—if we are ever to be together for—for always. Last night, Jimmie—the telephone—I knew there was danger—that all had gone wrong—what was it?"

His arms were around her shoulders, drawing her close to him again.

"I found the wires tapped," he said slowly.

"Yes, and—and the man you met—the chauffeur?"

"He is dead," Jimmie Dale answered gently.

He felt her hand close with a quick, spasmodic clutch upon his arm; her face grew white—and for a moment she turned away her head.

"And—and the package?" she asked presently.

313

"I do not know," replied Jimmie Dale. "He did not have it with him; he—"

"Wait!" she interrupted quickly. "We are only wasting time like this! Tell me everything, everything just as it happened, everything from the moment you received my letter."

And, holding her there in his arms, softening as best he could the more brutal details, he told her. And, at the end, for a little while she was silent; then in a strained, impulsive way she asked again:

"The chauffeur—you are sure—you are positive that he is dead?"

"Yes," said Jimmie Dale grimly; "I am sure." And then the pent-up flood of questions burst from his lips. Who was the chauffeur? The package, the box numbered 428, and John Johansson? And the Crime Club? And the issue at stake? The danger, the peril that surrounded her? And she—above all—more than anything else—about herself—her strange life, its mystery?

She checked him with a strangely wistful touch of her finger upon his lips, with a queer, pathetic shake of her head.

"No, Jimmie; not that way. You would never understand. I cannot-"

"But I am to know—now! Surely I am to know *now!*" he cried, a sudden sense of dismay upon him. Three years! Three years—and always the "next" time! "I must know now, if I am to help you!"

She smiled a little wanly at him, as she drew herself away, and, dropping into a chair, placed her elbows on the rickety table, cupping her chin in her hands.

"Yes; you are to know now," she said, almost as though she were talking to herself; then, with a swift intake of her breath, impulsively: "Jimmie! Jimmie! I had thought that it would be all so different when—when you came. That—that I would have nothing to fear—for you—for me—because—it would be all over. And now you are here, Jimmie—and, oh, thank God for you!—but I feel to-night almost—almost as though it were hopeless, that—that we were beaten."

"Beaten!" He stepped quickly to the table, and sat down, and took one of her hands away from her face to hold it in both his own. "Beaten!" he laughed out defiantly; then, playfully, soothingly, to reassure her: "Jimmie Dale and Larry the Bat and the Gray Seal and the Tocsin—*beaten!* And after we have just scored the last trick!"

"But we do not hold many trumps, Jimmie," [60] she answered gravely. "You have seen something of this Crime Club's power, its methods, its merciless, cruel, inhuman cunning, and you, perhaps, think that you understand—but you have not begun to grasp the extent of either that power or cunning. This horrible organisation has been in existence for many years. I do not know how many. I only know that the men of whom it is composed are not ordinary criminals, that they do not work in the ordinary way—to-day, they set the machinery of fraud, deception, robbery, and murder in motion that ten years from now, and, perhaps, only then, will culminate in the final success of their schemes—and they play only for enormous stakes. But"—her lips grew set—"you will see for yourself. I must not talk any longer than is necessary; we must not take too much time. You count on three days before they begin to suspect that all is not right with Jimmie Dale—I know them better than you, and I give you two days, forty-eight hours at the outside, and possibly far less. Jimmie"—abruptly—"did you ever hear of Peter LaSalle?"

"The capitalist? Yes!" said Jimmie Dale. "He died a few years ago. I know his brother Henry well—at the club, and all that."

"Do you!" she said evenly. "Well, the man you know is not Peter LaSalle's brother; he is an impostor—and one of the Crime Club."

"Not—Peter LaSalle's brother!"—Jimmie Dale repeated the words mechanically. And suddenly his brain was whirling. Vaguely, dimly, in little memory snatches, events, not pertinent then, vitally significant now, came crowding upon him. Peter LaSalle had come from somewhere in the West to live in New York; and very shortly afterward had died. The estate had been worth something over eleven millions. [61] And there had been— he leaned quickly, tensely forward over the table, staring at her. "My God!" he whispered hoarsely. "You are not, you cannot be—the—the daughter—Peter LaSalle's daughter, who disappeared strangely!"

"Yes," she said quietly. "I am Marie LaSalle."

---

[60] There are multiple references in the series to Dale playing bridge and the Tocsin is clearly familiar with the game too. Packard was a regular player.

[61] $269 million in 2018 dollars.

CHAPTER IX

THE TOCSIN'S STORY

(Saturday 10/16/1915)

LASALLE! The old French name! That old French inscription on the ring: *"Sonnez le Tocsin!"* Yes; he began to understand now. She was Marie LaSalle! He began to remember more clearly.

Marie LaSalle! They had said she was one of the most beautiful girls who had ever made her entree into New York society. But he had never met her—as Marie LaSalle; never met her—until now, as the Tocsin, in this bare, destitute, squalid hovel, here at bay, both of them, for their lives.

He had been away when she had come with her father to New York; and on his return there had only been the father's brother in the father's place—and she was gone. He remembered the furor her disappearance had caused; the enormous rewards her uncle had offered in an effort to trace her; the thousand and one speculations as to what had become of her; and that then, gradually, as even the most startling and mystifying of events and happenings always do, the affair had dropped into oblivion and had been forgotten by the public at least. He began to count back. Yes, it must have been nearly five years ago; [62] two years before she, as the Tocsin, and he, as the Gray Seal, had formed their amazing and singular partnership, that—he started suddenly, as she spoke.

"I want to tell you in as few words as I can," she said abruptly, breaking the silence. "Listen, then, Jimmie. My mother died ten years ago. I was little more than a child then. Shortly after her death, father made a business trip to New York, and, on the advice of some supposed friends, he had a new will drawn up by a lawyer whom they recommended, and to whom they introduced him. I do not know who those men were. The lawyer's name was Travers, Hilton Travers." She glanced curiously at Jimmie Dale, and added quickly: "He was the chauffeur—the man who was killed last night."

---

[62] Marie LaSalle wouldn't have been the only significant disappearance in the final months of 1910. In December of that year Dorothy Arnold also vanished mysteriously in New York City. Like Marie she was a wealthy young heiress but her disappearance was never solved.

"You mean," Jimmie Dale burst out, "you mean that he was – but, first, the will! What was in the will?"

"It was a very simple will," she answered. "And from the nature of it, it was not at all strange that my father should have been willing to have had it drawn by a comparative stranger, if that is what you are thinking. Summarised in a few words, the will left everything to me, and appointed my Uncle Henry as my guardian and the sole executor of the estate until I should have reached my twenty-fifth birthday. [63] It provided for a certain sum each year to be paid to my uncle for his services as executor; and at the expiration of the trust period – that is, when I was twenty-five – bequeathed to him the sum of one hundred thousand dollars."

Jimmie Dale nodded. "Go on!" he prompted.

"It is hard to tell it in logical sequence," she said, hesitating a moment. "So many things seem to overlap each other. You must understand a little more about Hilton Travers. During the five years following the signing of the will father came frequently to New York, and became, not only intimate with Travers, but so much impressed with the other's cleverness and ability that he kept putting more and more of his business into Travers' hands. At the end of that five years, we moved to New York, and father, who was then quite an old man, retired from all active business, and turned over a great many of his personal affairs to Travers to look after for him, giving Travers power of attorney in a number of instances. So much for Travers. Now about my uncle. He was my father's only brother; in fact, they were the only surviving members of their family, apart from very distant connections in France, from where, generations back, the family originally came." Her hand touched Jimmie Dale's for an instant. "That ring, Jimmie, with its crest and inscription, is the old family coat of arms."

"Yes," he said briefly; "I surmised as much."

"Strange as it may seem, in view of the fact that they had not seen each other for twenty years," she went on hurriedly "my father and my uncle were more than ordinarily attached to each other. Letters passed regularly

---

[63] In Packard's radio adaptation of the Gray Seal's premiere he says there is a five-year age difference between Jimmie and Marie. But if she is twenty-one here then she would have only been around sixteen at the time of her disappearance. Which means that it was about age eighteen that she first blackmailed the Gray Seal into doing her bidding. That same radio script notes that Herman Carruthers is five years older than Dale when the first chapter of this novel clearly indicates they are the same age. Having Marie be just two or three years younger than Dale is more plausible but that's still just a supposition.

between them, and there was constant talk of one paying the other a visit—but the visit never materialised. My uncle was somewhere in Australia, my father was here, and consequently I never saw my uncle. He was quite a different type of man from father—more restless, less settled, more rough and ready, preferring the outdoor life of the Australian bush to the restrictions of any so-called civilisation, I imagine. Financially, I do not think he ever succeeded very well, for twice, in one way or another, he lost every sheep on his ranch and father set him up again; and I do not think he could ever have had much of a ranch, for I remember once, in one of the letters he wrote, that he said he had not seen a white man in weeks, so he must have lived a very lonely life. Indeed, at about the time father drew the new will, my uncle wrote, saying that he had decided to give up sheep running on his own account as it did not pay, and to accept a very favourable offer that had been made to him to manage a ranch in New Zealand; and his next letter was from the latter country, stating that he had carried out his intentions, and was well satisfied with the change he had made. The long-proposed visit still continued to occupy my father's thoughts, and on his retirement from business he definitely made up his mind to go out to New Zealand, taking me with him. In fact, the plans were all arranged, my uncle expressed unbounded delight in his letters, and we were practically on the eve of sailing, when a cable came from my uncle, telling us to postpone the visit for a few months, as he was obliged to make a buying trip for his new employer that would keep him away that length of time—and then"—her fingers, that had been abstractedly picking out the lines formed by the grain of the wood in the table top, closed suddenly into tight-clenched fists—"and then—my father died."

Jimmie Dale turned away his head. There were tears in her eyes. The old sense of unreality was strong upon him again. He was listening to the Tocsin's story. It was strange that he should be doing that—that it could be really so! It seemed as though magically he had been transported out of the world where for years past he had lived with danger lurking at every turn, where men set watch about his house to trap him, where the denizens of the underworld yowled like starving beasts to sink their fangs in him, where the police were ceaselessly upon his trail to wreak an insensate vengeance upon him; it seemed as though he had been transported away from all that to something that he had dreamed might, perhaps, sometime happen, that he had hoped might happen, that he had longed for always, but now that it was his, that it also was full of the sense of the unreal. And yet as his mind followed the thread of her story, and leaped ahead and vaguely glimpsed what was to come, he was conscious in a sort of premonitory way of a vaster peril than any he had ever known, as though forces, for the moment masked, were arrayed against him whose strength and whose malignity were beyond human parallel. In what a strange, almost incoherent way his brain was working! He roused himself a little and looked around him – and, with a shock, the starkness of the room, the abject, pitiful air of destitution brought home to him with terrific, startling force the significance of the scene in which he was playing a part. His face set suddenly in hard lines. That she should have been brought to assume such a life as this – forced out of her environment of wealth and refinement, forced in her purity to rub shoulders with the vile, the dissolute, forced to exist as such a creature amid the crime and vice, the wretched horror of the underworld that swirled around her! There was anger now upon him, burning, hot – a merciless craving that was a savage, hungry lust for vengeance.

And then she was speaking again:

"Father's death occurred very shortly after my uncle's message advising us to postpone our trip was received. On his death, Travers, very naturally, as father's lawyer, cabled my uncle to come to New York at once; and my uncle replied, saying that he was coming by the first steamer."

She paused again – but only for an instant, as though to frame her thoughts in words.

"I have told you that I had never seen my uncle, that even my father had not seen him for twenty years; and I have told you that the man you know as Henry LaSalle is an impostor – I am using the word 'uncle' now when I refer to him simply to avoid confusion. You are, perhaps, expecting me to say that I took a distinctive dislike to him from the moment he arrived? On the contrary, I had every reason to be predisposed toward him; and, indeed, was rather agreeably surprised than otherwise – he was not nearly so uncouth and unpolished as, somehow, I had pictured his life would have made him. Do you understand, Jimmie? He was kind, sympathetic; and, in an apathetic way, I liked him. I say 'apathetic' because I think that best describes my own attitude toward every one and everything following father's death until – *that night.*"

She rose abruptly from her chair, as though a passive position of any kind had suddenly become intolerable.

"Why tell you what my father and I were to each other!" she cried out in a low, passionate voice. "It seemed as though everything that meant anything had gone out of my life. I became worn out, nervous; and though the days were bad enough, the nights were a source of dread. I began to suffer from insomnia – I could not sleep. This was even before my supposed uncle came. I used to read for hours and hours in my room after I had gone to bed. But" – she flung out her hand with an impatient gesture – "there is no need to dwell on that. One night, about a week after that man had arrived, and a little over a month after father had died, I was in my room and had finished a book I was reading. I remember that it was well after midnight. I had not the slightest inclination to sleep. I picked up another book—and after that another. There were plenty in my room; but, irrationally, of course, none pleased me. I decided to go down to the library—not that I think I really expected to find anything that I actually wanted, but more because it was an impulse, and furnished me for the moment with some definite objective, something to do. I got up, slipped on a dressing gown, and went downstairs. The lights were all out. I was just on the point of switching on those in the reception hall, when suddenly it seemed as though I had not strength to lift my hand, and I remember that for an instant I grew terribly cold with dread and fear. From the room on my right a voice had reached me. The door was closed, but the voice was raised in an outburst of profanity. I—I could hear every word.

"'If she's out of the way, there's no come-back,' the voice snarled. 'I won't listen to anything else! Do you hear! Why, you fool, what are you trying to do—hand me one! Turn everything into cash, and divvy, and beat it—eh? And I'm the goat, and I get caught and get twenty years for stealing trust funds—and the rest of you get the coin!' He swore terribly again. 'Who's taken the risk in this for the last five years! There'll be no smart Aleck lawyer tricks—there'll be no halfway measures! And who are you to dictate! She goes out—that's safe—I inherit as next of kin, with no one to dispute it, and that's all there is to it!'

"I stood there and could not move. It was the voice of the man I knew as my uncle! My heart seemed to have stopped beating. I tried to tell myself that I was dreaming, that it was too horrible, too incredible to be real; that they could not really mean to—to *murder* me. And then I recognised Hilton Travers' voice.

"'I am not dictating, and you are not serious, of course,' he said, with what seemed an uneasy laugh. 'I am only warning you that you are forgetting to take the real Henry LaSalle into account. He is bound to hear of this eventually, and then—'

"Another voice broke in—one I did not recognise.

"'You're talking too loud, both of you! Travers doesn't understand, but he's to be wised up to-night, according to orders, and—'

"The voice became inaudible, muffled—I could not hear any more. I suppose I remained there another three or four minutes, too stunned to know what to do; and then I ran softly along the hall to the library door. The library, you understand, was at the rear of the room they were in, and the two rooms were really one; that is, there was only an archway between them. I cannot tell you what my emotions were—I do not know. I only know that I kept repeating to myself, 'they are going to kill me, they are going to kill me!' and that it seemed I must try and find out everything, everything I could."

She turned away from the table, and began to pace nervously up and down the miserable room.

Jimmie Dale rose impulsively from his chair – but she waved him back again.

"No; wait!" she said. "Let me finish. I crept into the library. It took me a long time, because I had to be so careful not to make the slightest noise. I suppose it was fully six or seven minutes from the time I had first heard my supposed uncle's voice until I had crept far enough forward to be able to see into the room beyond. There were three men there. The man I knew as my uncle was sitting at one end of the table; another had his back toward me; and Travers was facing in my direction – and I think I never saw so ghastly a face as was Hilton Travers' then. He was standing up, sort of swaying, as he leaned with both hands on the table.

"'Now then, Travers,' the man whose back was turned to me was saying threateningly, 'you've got the story now – sign those papers!'

"It seemed as though Travers could not speak for a moment. He kept looking wildly from one to the other. He was white to the lips.

"'You've let me in for – *this!*' he said hoarsely, at last, 'You devils – you devils – you devils! You've let me in for – murder! Both of them! Both Peter and his brother – *murdered!*'"

She stopped abruptly before Jimmie Dale, and clutched his arm tightly.

"Jimmie, I don't know why I did not scream out. Everything went black for a moment before my eyes. It was the first suspicion I had had that my father had met with foul play, and I –"

But now Jimmie Dale swayed up from his chair.

"Murdered!" he exclaimed tensely. "Your father! But – but I remember perfectly, there was no hint of any such thing at the time, and never has been since. He died from quite natural causes."

She looked at him strangely.

"He died from – inoculation," she said. "Did – did you not see something of that laboratory in the Crime Club yourself the night before last – enough to understand?"

"Good God!" muttered Jimmie Dale, in a startled way then: "Go on! Go on! What happened then?"

She passed her hand a little wearily across her eyes – and sank down into her chair again.

"Travers," she continued, picking up the thread of her story, "had raised his voice, and the third man at the table leaned suddenly, aggressively toward him.

"'Hold your tongue!' he growled furiously. 'All you're asked to do is sign the papers—not talk!'

"Travers shook his head.

"'I won't!' he cried out. 'I won't have any hand in another murder—in hers! My God, I won't—I won't, I tell you! It's horrible!'

"'Look here, you fool!' the man who was posing as my uncle broke in then. 'You're in this too deep to get out now. If you know what's good for you, you'll do as you're told!'

"Jimmie, I shall never forget Travers' face. It seemed to have changed from white to gray, and there was horror in his eyes: and then he seemed to lose all control of himself, shaking his fists in their faces, cursing them in utter abandon.

"'I'm bad!' he cried. 'I've gone everything, everything but the limit—everything but murder. I stop there! I'll have no more to do with this. I'm through! You—you pulled me into this, and—and I didn't know!'

"'Well, you know now!' the third man sneered. 'What are you going to do about it?'

"'I'm going to see that no harm comes to Marie LaSalle,' Travers answered in a dull way.

"The other man now was on his feet—and, I do not know quite how to express it, Jimmie, he seemed ominously quiet in both his voice and his movements.

"'You'd better think that over again, Travers!' he said. 'Do you mean it?'

"'I mean it,' Travers said. 'I mean it—God help me!'

"'You may well add that!' returned the other, with an ugly laugh. He reached out his hand toward the telephone on the table. 'Do you know what will happen to you if I telephone a certain number and say that you have turned—traitor?'

"'I'll have to take my chances,' Travers replied doggedly. 'I'm through!'

"'Take them, then!' flung out the other. 'You'll have little time given you to do us any harm!'

"Travers did not answer. I think he almost expected an attack upon him then from the two men. He hesitated a moment, then backed slowly toward the door. What happened in the next few moments in that room, I do not know. I stole out of the library. I was obsessed with the thought that I must see Travers, see him at all costs, before he got away from the house. I reached the end of the hall as the room door opened, and he came out. It was dark, as I said, and I could not see distinctly, but I could make out his form. He closed the door behind him — and then I called his name in a whisper. He took a quick step toward me, then turned and hurried toward the front door, and I thought he was going away — but the next instant I understood his ruse. He opened the front door, shut it again quite loudly, and crept back to me.

"'Take me somewhere where we will be safe — quick!' he whispered.

"There was only one place where I was sure we would be safe. I led him to the rear of the house and up the servants' stairs, and to my boudoir."

She broke off abruptly, and once more rose from her chair, and once more began to pace the room. Back in his chair, Jimmie Dale, tense and motionless now, watched her without a word.

"It would take too long to tell you all that passed between us," she went on hurriedly. "The man was frankly a criminal — but not to the extent of murder. And in that respect, at least, he was honest with himself. Almost the first words he said to me were: 'Miss LaSalle, I am as good as a dead man if I am caught by the devils behind those two men downstairs.' And then he began to plead with me to make my own escape. He did not know who the man was that was posing as my uncle, had never seen him before until he presented himself as Henry LaSalle; the other man he knew as Clarke, but knew also that 'Clarke' was merely an assumed name. He had fallen in with Clarke almost from the time that he had begun to practise his profession, and at Clarke's instigation had gone from one crooked deal to another, and had made a great deal of money. He knew that behind Clarke was a powerful, daring, and unscrupulous band of criminals, organised on a gigantic scale, of which he himself was, in a sense — a probationary sense, as he put it — a member; but he had never come into direct contact with them — he had received all his orders and instructions through Clarke. He had been told by Clarke that he was to cultivate father following the introduction, to win father's confidence, to get as many of father's affairs into his hands as possible, to reach the position, in fact, of becoming father's recognised attorney — and all this with the object, as he supposed of embezzling from father on a large scale. Then father died, and Travers was instructed to cable my uncle. He knew that the man who answered that summons was an impostor; but he did not know, until they had admitted it to him that night, that both my father and my uncle had been murdered, and that I, too, was to be made away with."

She looked at Jimmie Dale, and suddenly laughed out bitterly.

"No; you don't understand, even yet, the patient, ingenious deviltry of those fiends. It was they, at the time the new will was drawn, who offered to buy out my real uncle's sheep ranch in that lonely, unsettled district in Australia, and offered him that new position in New Zealand. My uncle never reached New Zealand. He was murdered on his way there. And in his place, assuming his name, appeared the man who has been posing as my uncle ever since. Do you begin to see! For five years they were patiently working out their plans, for five years before my father's death that man lived and became known and accepted, and *established* himself as Henry LaSalle. Do you see now why he cabled us to postpone our visit? He ran very little risk. The chances were one in a thousand that any of his few acquaintances in Australia would ever run across him in New Zealand; and besides, he was chosen because it seems there was a slight resemblance between him and the real Henry LaSalle — enough, with his changed mode of living and more elaborate and pretentious surroundings, to have enabled him to carry through a bluff had it become necessary. He had all of my uncle's papers; and the Crime Club furnished him with every detail of our lives here. I forgot to say, too, that from the moment my uncle was supposed to have reached New Zealand all his letters were typewritten — an evidence in father's eyes that his brother had secured a position of some importance; as, indeed, from apparently unprejudiced sources, they took pains to assure father was a fact. This left them with only my uncle's signature to forge to the letters — not a difficult matter for them!

"Believing that they had Travers so deeply implicated that he could do nothing, even if he had the inclination, which they had not for a moment imagined, and arrogant in the belief in their own power to put him out of the way in any case if he proved refractory, they admitted all this to him that night when he brought up the issue of the real Henry LaSalle putting in an appearance sooner or later, and when they wanted him to smooth their path by releasing all documents where his power of attorney was involved. Do you see now the part they gave Travers to play? It was to put the stamp of genuineness upon the false Henry LaSalle. Not but that they were prepared with what would appear to be overwhelmingly convincing evidence to prove it if it were necessary; but if the man were accepted by the estate's lawyer there was little chance of any one else questioning his identity."

She halted again by the table — and forced a smile, as her eyes met Jimmie Dale's.

"I am almost through, Jimmie. That night was a terrible one for both of us. Travers' life was not worth a moment's purchase once they found him — and mine was only under reprieve until sufficient time to obviate suspicion should have elapsed after father's death. We had no proof that would stand in any court — even if we should have been given the chance to adopt that course. And without absolute, irrefutable proof, it was all so cleverly woven, stretched over so many years, that our charge must have been held to be too visionary and fantastic to have any basis in fact.

"All Travers would have been able to advance was the statement that the supposed Henry LaSalle had admitted being an impostor and a murderer to him! Who would believe it! On the face of it, it appeared to be an absurdity. And even granted that we were given an opportunity to bring the charge, they would be able to prove by a hundred influential and well-known men in New Zealand that the impostor was really Henry LaSalle; and were we able to find any of my uncle's old acquaintances in Australia, it would be necessary to get them here – and not one of them would have reached America alive.

"But there was not a chance, not a chance, Jimmie, of doing that – they would have killed Travers the moment he showed himself in the open. The only thing we could do that night was to try and save our own lives; the only thing we could look forward to was acquiring in some way, unknown to them, the proof, fully established, with which we could crush them in a single stroke, and before they would have time to strike back.

"The vital thing was proof of my uncle's death. That, if it could be obtained at all, could only be obtained in Australia. Travers was obliged to go somewhere, to disappear from that moment if he wanted to save his life, and he volunteered to go out there. He left the house that night by the back entrance in an old servant's suit, which I found for him – and I never heard from him again until a month ago in the 'personal' column of the *Morning News-Argus,* through which we had agreed to communicate.

"As for myself, I left the house the next morning, telling my pseudo uncle that I was going to spend a few days with a friend. And this I actually did; but in those few days I managed to turn all my own securities, that had been left me by my mother and which amounted to a considerable sum, into cash. And then, Jimmie, I came to – this, I have lived like this and in different disguises, as a settlement worker, [64] as a widow of means in a fashionable uptown apartment, but mostly as you see me now – for five years. [65] For five years I have watched my supposed

---

[64] A likely location for Marie to be a settlement worker (i. e. a social worker) would have been the Henry Street Settlement on the Lower East Side of Manhattan. We know from later books in this series that she has some familiarity with nursing so perhaps she learned it there.

[65] Considering the number of times Marie has come up so close to Dale that she could speak to him or slip an envelope into his hand or clothing, there were probably more than just these three

uncle, hoping, praying that through him I could get to know the others associated with him; hoping, praying that Travers would succeed; hoping, praying that we would get them all—and watching day after day, and year after year the 'personal' column of the paper, until at last I began to be afraid that it was all useless. And there was nothing, Jimmie, nothing anywhere, and I had no success" — her voice choked a little.

"Nothing! Even Clarke never went again to the house. You can understand now how I came to know the strange things that I wrote to the Gray Seal, how the life that I have led, how this life here in the underworld, how the constant search for some clew on my own account brought them to my knowledge; and you can understand now, too, why I never dared to let you meet me, for I knew well enough that, while I worked to undermine my father's and my uncle's murderers, they were moving heaven and earth to find me.

"That is all, Jimmie. The day before yesterday, a month after Travers' first message to let me know that he was coming, [66] there was another 'personal' giving me an hour and a telephone number. He was back! He had everything—everything! We dared not meet; he was afraid, suspicious that they had got track of him again. You know the rest. That package contained the proof that, with Travers' death, can probably never be obtained again. Do you understand why *they* want it—why it is life and death to me? Do you understand why my supposed uncle offered huge rewards for me, why secretly every resource of that hideous organisation has been employed to find me—that it is only by my *death* the estate can pass into their hands, and now—"

She flung out her hands suddenly toward Jimmie Dale. "Oh, Jimmie, Jimmie, I've—I've fought so long alone! Jimmie, what are we to do?"

He came slowly to his feet. She had fought so long—alone. But now—now it was his turn to fight—for her. But how? She had not told him all—surely she had not told him all, for everything depended upon that

---

identities for her. And the disguises she used had to allow her to blend into settings as diverse as a Broadway theater and a Badlands dance hall.

[66] Was it that communication from Travers on September 14th, with its promise of a possible end to her life in the shadows, that three days later caused a distracted Marie to leave her ring behind for Jimmie to find ("The Thief" Chapter Seven, Part One)? And the reason why she later chose to visit him in person at his home when a phone call would have worked as well ("The Stool-Pigeon" Chapter Eleven, Part One)?

package. There had been so much to tell that she had not thought of all, and she had not told him the details about that.

"That box—No. 428!" he cried quickly. "What is that? What does it mean?"

She shook her head.

"I do not know," she answered.

"Then who is this John Johansson?"

"I do not know," she said again.

"Nor where the Crime Club is?"

"No"—dully.

He stared at her for a moment in a dazed way.

"My God!" Jimmie Dale murmured.

And then she turned away her head.

"It's—it's pretty bad, isn't it, Jimmie? I—I told you that we did not hold many trumps."

CHAPTER X

SILVER MAG

(Saturday 10/16/1915)

THERE was silence between them. Minute after minute passed. Neither spoke.

Jimmie Dale dropped back into his chair again, and stared abstractedly before him. "We do not hold many trumps, Jimmie — we do not hold many trumps" — her words were repeating themselves over and over in his mind. They seemed to challenge him mockingly to deny what was so obviously a fact, and because he could not deny it to taunt and jeer at him — to jeer at him, when all that was held at stake hung literally upon his next move!

He looked up mechanically as the Tocsin walked to a broken mirror at the rear of the miserable room; nodded mechanically in approval as she began deftly to retouch the make-up on her face where the tears had left their traces — and resumed his abstracted gaze before him.

Box number four-two-eight — John Johansson — the Crime Club — the identity of the man who was posing as Henry LaSalle! If only he could hit upon a clew to the solution of a single one of those things, or a single phase of one of them — if only he could glimpse a ray of light that would at least prompt action, when every moment of inaction was multiplying the odds against them!

There were the men who were watching his house at that moment on Riverside Drive — he, as Larry the Bat, might in turn keep watch on them. He had though of that. In time, perhaps, he might, by so doing, discover the whereabouts of the Crime Club. In time! It was just that — he had no time! Forty-eight hours, the Tocsin insisted, was all the time that he could count upon before they would become suspicious of Jimmie Dale's "illness," before they would discover that they were watching an empty house!

He might — though this was even more hazardous — make an attempt to trace the wires that tapped those of his telephone through the basement window that gave on the garage driveway. And what then? True, they could not lead very far away; but, even if successful, what then? They would not lead him to the Crime Club, but simply to some confederate, to some man or woman playing the part of a servant, perhaps, in the house next door, who, in turn, would have to be shadowed and watched.

Jimmie Dale shook his head. Better, of the two, to start in at once and shadow those who were shadowing his house. But that was not the way! He knew that intuitively. He hated to eliminate it from consideration, for he had no other move to take its place—but such a move was almost suicide in itself. Time, and time alone, was the vital factor. They, the Tocsin and he, must act quickly—and *strike* that night if they were to win. His fingers, the grimy fingers, dirty-nailed, of Larry the Bat, that none now would recognise as the slim tapering, wonderfully sensitive fingers of Jimmie Dale, the fingers that had made the name of the Gray Seal famous, whose tips mocked at bars and safes and locks, and seemed to embody in themselves all the human senses, tightened spasmodically on the edge of the table. Time! Time! Time! It seemed to din in his ears. And while he sat there powerless, impotent, the Crime Club was moving heaven and earth to find what *he* must find—that package—if he was to save this woman here, the woman whom he loved, she who had been forced, through the machinations of these hell fiends, to adopt the life of a wretched hag, to exist among the dregs of the underworld, whose squalour and vice and wantonness none knew better than he!

Jimmie Dale's face set grimly. Somewhere—somewhere in the past five years of this life of hers in which she had been fighting the Crime Club, pitting that clever brain of hers against it, *must* lie a clew. She had told him her story only in baldest outline, with scarcely a reference to her own personal acts, with barely a single detail. There must be something, something that perhaps she had overlooked, something, just the merest hint of something that would supply a starting point, give him a glimmer of light.

She came back from across the room, and sank down in her chair again. She did not speak—the question, that meant life and death to them both, was in her eyes.

Jimmie answered the mute interrogation tersely.

"Not yet!" he said. Then, almost curtly, in a quick, incisive way, as the keen, alert brain began to delve and probe: "You say this man Clarke never returned to the house after that night?"

She nodded her head quietly.

"You are sure of that?" he insisted.

"Yes," she said. "I am sure."

"And you say that all these years you have kept a watch on the man who is posing as your uncle, and that he never went anywhere, or associated with any one, that would afford you a clew to this Crime Club?"

"Yes," she said again.

It was a moment before Jimmie Dale spoke.

"It's very strange!" he said musingly, at last. "So strange, in fact, that it's impossible. He must have communicated with the others, and communicated with them often. The game they were playing was too big, too full of details, to admit of any other possibility. And the telephone as an explanation isn't good enough."

"And yet," she said earnestly, "possible or impossible, it is nevertheless true. That he might have succeeded in eluding me on occasions was perhaps to be expected; but that in all those years I should not catch him once in what, if you are correct, must have been many and repeated conferences with the same men is too improbable to be thought of seriously."

Jimmie Dale shook his head again.

"If you had been able to watch him night and day, that might be so," he said crisply. "But, at best, you could only watch him a very small portion of the time."

She smiled at him a little wanly.

"Do you think, Jimmie, from what you, as the Gray Seal, know of me, that I would have watched in any haphazard way like that?"

He glanced at her with a sudden start.

"What do you mean?" he asked quickly.

"Look at me!" she said quietly. "Have you ever seen me before? I mean as I am now."

"No," he answered, after an instant. "Not that I know of."

"And yet" – she smiled wanly again – "you have not lived, or made the place you hold in the underworld, without having heard of Silver Mag."

"You!" exclaimed Jimmie Dale. "You – Silver Mag!" He stared at her wonderingly, as, crouch-shouldered now, the hair, gray-threaded, straggling out from under the hood of a faded, dark-blue, seam-worn cloak, she sat before him, a typical creature of the underworld, her role an art in its conception, perfect in its execution. Silver Mag! Yes, he had heard of Silver Mag – as every one in the Bad Lands had heard of her. Silver Mag and her pocketful of coin! Always a pocketful of silver, so they said, that was dispensed prodigally to the wives and children temporarily deprived of support by husbands and fathers unfortunate enough in their clashes with the law to be doing "spaces" up the river – and therefore the underworld swore by Silver Mag. Always silver, never a bill; Silver Mag had never been seen with a banknote – that was her eccentricity. Much or little, she gave or paid out of her pocketful of jangling silver. She was credited with being a sworn enemy of the police, and—yes, he remembered, too—with having done "time" herself. "I don't quite understand," he said, in a puzzled way. "I haven't run across you personally because you probably took care to see that I shouldn't; but— it's no secret—every one says you've served a jail sentence yourself."

"That is simply enough explained," she answered gravely. "The story is of my own making. When I decided to adopt this life, both for my own safety and as the best means of keeping a watch on that man, I knew that I must win the confidence of the underworld, that I must have help, and that in order to obtain that help I must have some excuse for my enmity against the man known as Henry LaSalle. To be widely known in the underworld was of inestimable value—nothing, I knew, could accomplish that as quickly as eccentricity. You see now how and why I became known as Silver Mag. I gained the confidence of every crook in New York through their wives and children. I told them the story of my jail sentence—while I swore vengeance on Henry LaSalle. I told them that he had had me arrested for something I never stole while I was working for him as a charwoman, and that he had had me railroaded to jail. There wasn't one but gave me credit for the theft, perhaps; but equally, there wasn't one but understood, and my eccentricity helped this out, my wanting to 'get' Henry LaSalle. Well—do you see now, Jimmie? I had money, I had the confidence of the underworld, I had an excuse for my hatred of Henry LaSalle, and so I had all the help I wanted. Day and night that man has been watched. He receives no visitors—what social life he has is, as you know, at the club. There is not a house that he has ever entered that, sooner or later, I have not entered after him in the hope of finding the headquarters of the clique. Even the men and women, as far as human possibility could accomplish it, that he has talked to on the streets have been shadowed, and their identity satisfactorily established—and the net result has been failure; utter, absolute, complete failure!"

Jimmie Dale's eyes, that had held steadily on her face, shifted, troubled and perplexed, to the table top.

"You are wonderful!" he said, under his breath. "Wonderful! And— and that makes it all the more amazing, all the more incomprehensible. It is still impossible that he has not been in close and constant touch with his accomplices. He *must* have been! We would be blind fools to argue against it! It could not, on the face of it, have been otherwise!"

"Then how, when, where has he done it?" she asked wearily.

"God knows!" he said bitterly. "And if they have been clever enough to escape you all these years, I'm almost inclined to say what you said a little while ago—that we're beaten."

She watched him miserably, as he pushed back his chair impulsively and, standing up, stared down at her.

"We're against it — *hard!*" he said, with a mirthless laugh. Then, his lips tightening: "But we'll try another tack — the chauffeur — Travers. Though even here the Crime Club has a day's start of us, even if last night they knew no more about the whereabouts of that package than we know now. I'm afraid of it! The chances are more than even that they've already got it. If they were able to catch Travers as the chauffeur, they would have had something tangible to work back from" — Jimmie Dale was talking more to himself than to the Tocsin now, as though he were muttering his thoughts aloud. "How did they get track of him? When? Where? What has it led to? And what in Heaven's name," he burst out suddenly, "is this box number four-two-eight!"

"A safety-deposit vault, perhaps, that he has taken somewhere," she hazarded.

Jimmie Dale laughed mirthlessly again.

"That is the one definite thing I do know — that it isn't!" he said positively. "It is nothing of that kind. It was half-past ten o'clock at night when I met him, and he said that he had intended going back for the package if it had been safe to do so. Deposit vaults are not open at that hour. The package is, or was, if they have not already got it, readily accessible — and at any hour. Now go over everything again, every detail that passed between you and Travers. He let you know that he was back in New York by means of a 'personal,' you said. What else was in that 'personal' besides the telephone number and the hour you were to call him? Anything?"

"Nothing that will help us any," she replied colourlessly. "There were simply the words 'northeast corner of Sixth Avenue and Waverly Place,' and the signature that we had agreed upon, the two first and two last letters of the alphabet transposed — BAZY."

"I see," said Jimmie Dale quickly. "And over the 'phone he completed his message. Clever enough!"

"Yes," she said. "In that way, if any one were listening, or overhead the plan, there could be little harm come of it, for the essential feature of all, the place of rendezvous, was not mentioned. It has not been Travers' fault that this happened — and in spite of every precaution it has cost him his life. He wanted nothing to give them a clew to my whereabouts; he was trying to guard against the slightest evidence that would associate us one with the other. He even warned me over the 'phone not to tell him how, where, or the mode of life I was living. And naturally, he dared give me no particulars about himself. I was simply to select a third party whom

I could trust, and to follow out his instructions, which were those that I sent to you in my letter."

Jimmie Dale began to pace nervously up and down the room.

"Nothing else?" he queried, a little blankly.

"Nothing else," she said monotonously.

"But since last night, since you knew that things had gone wrong," he persisted, "surely you traced that telephone number — the one you called up?"

"Yes," she said, and shrugged her shoulders in a tired way. "Naturally I did that — but, like everything else, it amounted to nothing. He telephoned from Makoff's pawnshop on that alley off Thompson Street, and — "

"*Where!*" Jimmie Dale, suddenly stock-still, almost shouted the word. "He telephoned from — where! Say that again!"

She looked at him in amazement, half rising from her chair.

"Jimmie, what is it?" she cried. "You don't mean that — "

He was beside her now, his hands pressed upon her shoulders, his face flushed.

"Box number four-two-eight!" He laughed out hysterically in his excitement. "John Johansson — box number four-two-eight! And like a fool I never thought of it! Don't you see? Don't you know now yourself? *The underground post office!*"

She stood up, clinging to him; a wild relief, that was based on her confidence in him, in her eyes and face, even while she shook her head.

"No," she said frantically. "No — I do not know. Tell me, Jimmie! Tell me quickly! You mean at Makoff's?"

"No! Not Makoff's — at Spider Jack's, on Thompson Street!" — he was clipping off his words, still holding her tightly by the shoulders, still staring into her eyes. "You know Spider Jack! Jack's little novelty store! Ah, you have not learned all of the underworld yet! Spider Jack is the craftiest 'fence' in the Bad Lands — and Makoff is his partner. Spider buys the crooks' stuff, and Makoff disposes of it through the pawnshop — it's only a step through the connecting back yard from one to the other, and — "

"Yes — but," she interrupted feverishly, "the package — you said — "

"Wait!" Jimmie Dale cried. "I'm coming to that! If Travers stood in with Makoff, he stood in with Spider Jack. For years Spider has been a sort of clearing house for the underworld — for years he has conducted, and profitably, too, his underground post office. Crooks from all over the country, let alone those in New York, communicate with each other through Spider Jack. These, for a fee, are registered at Spider's, and given a number – a box number he calls it, though, of course, there are no actual boxes. Letters come by mail addressed to him – the sealed envelope within containing the actually intended recipient's name. These Spider either forwards, or delivers in person when they are called for. Dozens of crooks, too, unwilling, perhaps, to dispose of small ill-gotten articles at ruinous 'fence' prices, and finding it unhealthy for the moment to keep them in their possession, use this means of depositing them temporarily for safe-keeping. You see now, don't you? It's certain that's where Travers left the package. He used the name of John Johansson, not to hoodwink Spider Jack, I should say, but as an added safeguard against the Crime Club. Travers must have known both Makoff and Spider Jack in the old days, and probably had reason, and good reason, to trust them both – possibly, a crook then himself, as he confessed, he may have acted in a legal capacity for them in their frequent tangles with the police."

"Then," she said – and there was a glad, new note in her voice, "then, Jimmie – Jimmie, we are safe! You can get it, Jimmie! It is only a little thing for the Gray Seal to do – to get it now that we know where it is."

"Yes," he said tersely. "Yes – if it is still there."

"Still there!" – she repeated the words quickly, nervously. "Still there! What do you mean?"

"I mean if they, too, have not discovered that he was at Makoff's – if they have not got there first!" he said grimly. "There seems to be no limit to their cleverness, or their power. They penetrated his disguise as a chauffeur, and who knows what more they have learned since last night? We are fighting them in the dark, and – *what's that!*" he whispered tensely, suddenly – and leaning forward like a flash, as he whipped his automatic from his pocket, he blew out the lamp.

The room was in darkness. They stood there rigid, silent, listening. Her hand found and caught his arm.

And then it came again – a low sound, the sound of a stealthy footstep just outside the window that faced on the storage yard.

CHAPTER XI

THE MAGPIE

(Saturday 10/16/1915)

A MINUTE passed — another. The automatic at Jimmie Dale's hip, the muzzle just peeping over the table top, held a steady bead on the window. Came the footstep again — and then suddenly, a series of low, quick tappings upon the windowpane. The Tocsin's hand slipped away from his arm. Jimmie Dale's set face relaxed as he read the underground Morse, and he replaced his revolver slowly in his pocket.

"The Magpie!" said Jimmie Dale, in an undertone. "What's he want?"

"I don't know," she answered, in a whisper. "He never came here before. There's a back way out, Jimmie, if you —"

"No," he said quickly. "We've enemies enough, without making one of the Magpie. He knows some one is here with you — our shadows were on the blind. Don't queer yourself. Let him in. I'll light the lamp."

He struck a match, as she ran from the room, and, lifting the hot lamp chimney with the edge of his ragged coat, lighted the lamp. He turned the wick down a little, shading and dimming the room — and then, as he flirted a bead of moisture from his forehead, whimsically stretched out his hand to watch it in the lamplight.

"That's bad, Jimmie," he muttered gravely to himself, as he noted an almost imperceptible tremour. "Got a start, didn't you! Under a bit of a strain, eh? Well" — grimly — "never mind! It looks as though the luck had turned Makoff and Spider Jack!"

His hand reached up to his hat, jerked the brim at a rakish angle over his eyes — and he sprawled himself out on a chair. He heard the Tocsin's voice at the front door, and a man's voice, low and guarded, answer her. Then the door closed, and their steps approached the room. It was rather curious, that — a visit from the Magpie! What could the Magpie want? What could there be in common between the Magpie and Silver Mag? The Magpie, alias Slimmy Joe, was counted the cleverest safe worker in the United States, barring only and always one — a smile flickered across the lips of Larry the Bat — one whose pre-eminence the Magpie, much to his own chagrin, admitted himself — the Gray Seal!

He looked up, twisting the stub of a cigarette between his grimy fingers and fumbling for a match, as the Tocsin and, behind her, the Magpie, short, slim, and wiry, shrewd-faced, with sharp, quick-glancing little black eyes, entered the room.

"'Ello, Larry!" grinned the Magpie. "Got yer breath back yet? I felt it through de windowpane when youse let go at de lamp!"

"'Ello, Slimmy!" returned Jimmie Dale ungraciously, speaking through the corner of his mouth. "Ferget it!"

"Sure!" said the Magpie unconcernedly. He stared about him, and finally, drawing a chair up to the table, sat down, motioned the Tocsin to do the same, and leaned forward amiably. "I didn't mean to throw no scare into youse," he said, in a conciliating tone. "But I had a little business wid Mag, an' I was kind of interested in whether she was entertainin' company or not—see? I didn't know youse an' Mag was workin' together."

"Mabbe," observed Jimmie Dale, as ungraciously as before, "mabbe dere's some more t'ings youse don't know!"

"Aw, cough up de grouch!" advised the Magpie, with a hint of impatience creeping into his voice. "Youse don't need to be sore all night! I told youse I wasn't tryin' to hand youse one, didn't I?"

"Never mind Larry, Slimmy," put in the Tocsin petulantly. "He's down on his luck, dat's all. He ain't had de price of a pinch of coke fer two days."

"Oho!" exclaimed the Magpie, grinning again. "So dat's wot's givin' youse de pip, eh, Larry? Well, den, say, youse can take it from me dat mabbe youse'll be glad I blew around. I was lookin' fer a guy about yer size fer a little job to-night, an' I was t'inkin' of lettin' Young Dutchy in on it, but seem' youse are here an' in wid Mag, an' dat I got to get Mag in, too, youse are on if youse say de word."

"Wot's de lay?" inquired Larry the Bat, unbending a little.

The Magpie cocked his eye, and stuck his tongue in his cheek.

"*Good*-night!" he said tersely. "Nothin' like dat! Are youse on, or ain't youse?"

"Well, den, wot's in it fer me?" persisted Larry the Bat.

"More'n de price of a coke sneeze!" returned the Magpie pertinently. "Dere's a century note fer youse, an' mabbe two or t'ree of dem fer Mag."

Larry the Bat's eyes gleamed avariciously.

"Aw, quit yer kiddin'!" he said gruffly. "A century note—fer me!"

"Dat's wot I said! Youse heard me!" rejoined the Magpie shortly. "Only if it listens good to youse now, I don't want no squealin' after the divvy. I'm takin' de chances, youse has de soft end of it. One century note fer youse—an' de rest is none of yer business! Dat's puttin' it straight, ain't it?

Well, wot do youse say, an' say it quick — 'cause if youse ain't comin' in, youse can beat it out of here so's I can talk to Mag."

"Dere ain't nothin' I wouldn't take a chance on fer a hundred plunks!" declared Larry the Bat, with sudden fervency — and stared, anxiously expectant, at the Magpie. "Sure, I'm on Slimmy! Sure, I am! Cut it loose! Spill de story!"

"Well, den," said the Magpie, "I wants — "

"Youse ain't through yet!" interrupted the Tocsin tartly. "I ain't heard youse askin' me nothin'! I ain't on me uppers like Larry, an' mabbe de price don't cut so much ice — see?"

"Aw," said the Magpie, with a smirk, "I don't have to ask youse on dis lay. Dis is where youse'd come in on it fer marbles. Say, dis is where we gets de hook into a guy by de name of Henry LaSalle! Get me?"

Henry LaSalle! Under the table, Jimmie Dale's hand clenched suddenly; but not a muscle of his face moved, save, as with the tip of his tongue, he shifted the butt of the cigarette that was hanging royally from his lower lip to the other corner of his mouth.

"Sure! She's 'got' youse, Slimmy!" he flung out, with a grin, as the Tocsin wrinkled up her face menacingly and began to mumble to herself. "He's de guy dat handed her one when she was young, an' she's been layin' fer him ever since! Sure! I know! Ain't I worked him fer her till I wears me shoes out tryin' to get somet'ing on him! Sure, she's in on it! Go on, Slimmy, wot's de lay? Wot do I do fer dat century?"

The Magpie hitched his chair closer to the table and, as his sharp, little, ferret eyes glanced around the room, motioned the two to bring their heads nearer.

"One of me influential broker friends down on Wall Street put me wise," he said, with a wink. "Dat's good enough fer youse two, as far as dat goes. But take it from me, I got it dead straight." He lowered his voice "Say, he's one of de richest mugs in New York, ain't he? Well, he's been sellin' stocks an' bonds all day, t'ousands an' t'ousands of dollars' worth — fer cash."

"All dem t'ings is always sold fer cash," remarked Larry the Bat fatuously.

"Aw, forget it!" said the Magpie earnestly. "Fer *cash,* I said — de coin, de long green — understand? He wasn't shovin' no checks fer what he sold into de bank except to get dem cashed. Dat's wot he's been doin' all day — gettin' de checks cashed, an' gettin' de money in big bills — see! I know of one bunch of eighty t'ousand — an' dat's only one!"

"Wot fer?" inquired Larry the Bat. It was the question that was pounding at his brain, as he stared innocently at the Magpie. What did it mean? Why was Henry LaSalle turning, and, if the Magpie was right, feverishly turning every security he could lay his hands on into cash? And then, in a flash, the answer came. *They had not found the package!* Equally to them, as to the Tocsin, sitting there before him, it meant life and death. If the package were found by the Tocsin instead of themselves, the game was up! They were preparing for eventualities. If they were forced to run at a moment's notice, they at least were not going to run empty-handed! Far from empty-handed, it seemed! It would not be difficult for the estate's executor to realise a vast sum in short order on instantly marketable, gilt-edged securities — say, half a million dollars. Not very bulky, either — in large bills! Five thousand hundred-dollar bills would make half a million. It was astonishing how small a hand bag, say, might hold a fortune! "Wot fer, Slimmy?" he inquired again, wiggling his cigarette butt on his tongue tip. "Wot'd he do dat fer?"

"How de hell do youse suppose I knows!" demanded the Magpie, politely scornful. "Dat's his business — dat ain't wot's worryin' me!"

"No — sure, it ain't!" admitted Larry the Bat ingratiatingly. "But go on, keep movin', Slimmy! Wot's he done wid de stuff?"

"Done wid it!" echoed the Magpie, with a short laugh. "Wot do youse t'ink! He's been luggin' it home to his swell joint up dere on de avenoo, an' crammin' his safe full of it."

Larry the Bat sucked in his breath.

"Gee, dat's soft!" he murmured, and then suddenly, as though with painful inspiration: "Say, Slimmy — say, are youse sure youse ain't been handed a steer?"

The Magpie grinned wickedly.

"I ain't fallin' fer steers!" he said shortly. "Dis is on de level."

Jimmie Dale lurched up from his chair, and, leaning over the lamp chimney, drew wheezily on his cigarette to get a light. His eyes sought the Tocsin's face. To all intents and purposes she was entirely absorbed in the Magpie. He sat down again to gape, with well-stimulated, doglike admiration, at Slimmy Joe. *Was this, too, a plant?* Why had the Magpie come to *them* with this story of Henry LaSalle? And then, the next instant, as the Magpie spoke, his suspicions were allayed.

"Let's get down to cases!" the Magpie invited crisply. "I didn't blow in here just by luck. Dis Henry LaSalle is de guy youse worked fer once, ain't he, Mag? Dat's de spiel, ain't it? — he sent youse up fer pinchin' de tacks out of his carpets!"

"I never pinched nothin'!" snarled Silver Mag truculently. "He's a dirty liar! I never did!"

"Cut it out! Cut it out! Can dat!" complained the Magpie patiently. "De point is, youse worked in his house, didn't youse?"

"Sure I did!" snapped the Tocsin, sullenly aggressive; "but – "

"Well, den, dat's wot I want, dat's wot I come fer, Mag – a plan of de house. See?"

Jimmie Dale could feel the Tocsin's eyes upon him, questioning, searching, seeking a cue. A plan of the house – yes or no? And a decision on the instant!

"Sure!" said Larry the Bat brightly. "Dat's wot I was t'inkin' youse were after all de time. Say, youse are all right, Slimmy! Youse are de kind to work wid! Go on, Mag, draw de dope fer Slimmy. Dat's better dan tryin' to put one over on de swell guy. Dis'll make him squeal fer fair!"

The Magpie produced a pencil and a piece of paper from his pocket, and laid them on the table in front of the Tocsin.

"Dere youse are," he announced. "Help yerself, an' go to it, Mag!"

The Tocsin, evidently not quite certain of her part, wet the pencil doubtfully on the end of her tongue.

"I ain't never drawed plans," she said anxiously. "Mabbe" – she glanced at Jimmie Dale – "mabbe I dunno how to do it *right*."

"Aw, go ahead!" nodded Larry the Bat. "Youse can do it right, Mag. Youse don't have to make no oil paintin'! All de Magpie wants is de doors an' windows, eh, Slimmy?"

"Sure," agreed the Magpie encouragingly. "Dat's all, Mag. Just mark de rooms out on de first floor, an' de basement. Youse can explain wot youse 're doin' as youse goes along. I'll get youse."

The Tocsin cackled maliciously in assent; and then, while the Magpie got up from his chair and stood peering over her shoulder, she began to draw labouriously, her brows knitted, the pencil hooked awkwardly between cramped-up forefinger and thumb.

Larry the Bat, slouched forward over the table, his chin in his hands, appeared to watch the proceedings with mild interest – but his eyes, like a hawk's, were following every line on the paper, transferring them to his brain, photographing every detail of the plan in his mind. And as he watched, there seemed something that was near to the acme of all that was ironical in the Magpie standing there, his sharp, little, black eyes drinking in greedily the Tocsin's work, in the Tocsin herself aiding and abetting in the projected theft – *of her own money!* How far would he let the Magpie go? He did not know. Perhaps – who could tell! – all the way. Between now and then there lay that package! If it were at Makoff's, at Spider Jack's, if he could find it, get it – the Magpie as a temporary custodian of the estate's money would at least preclude its loss by flight if the Crime Club took alarm too quickly. Larry the Bat's eyes, under half-closed lids, rested musingly on the Magpie's face. The Magpie would not get very far away with it! On the other hand, if he failed at Spider Jack's, if, after all, he was wrong, and the package had never been there, or if they had forestalled him, turned the trick upon him, already secured it, then — Larry the Bat's lips, working on his cigarette, formed in a twisted smile — then, well then, that was quite another matter! Perhaps he and the Magpie might not agree so far! A half million dollars was perhaps not much out of eleven millions, but it was a salvage not to be despised! Why did he say half a million! Well, why not? If the Magpie knew of a single transaction of eighty thousand, and there had been many transactions during the day, a half million was little likely to prove an exaggeration — and the less likely in view of the fact that, if those in the Crime Club were preparing for an emergency, they would not stint themselves in the disposal of securities.

The Magpie was keeping up a running fire of questions, as the Tocsin toiled on with her pencil. Where did the hall lead to? How many windows in the library? Did she remember the kind of fastenings? Did the servants sleep in the basement, or above? And finally, twice over, as she finished the clumsy drawing and pushed it toward him, he demanded minute details of the position of the safe.

"Aw, dat's all right, Slimmy!" Larry the Bat cut in airily. "If youse ferget anyt'ing when youse get in dere, youse can ask me. I got it cinched!"

The Magpie folded the paper and stowed it carefully away in his pocket.

"Ask youse, eh!" he grunted sarcastically. "An' where do youse t'ink youse'll be about dat time?"

"In dere wid youse, of course," replied Larry the Bat promptly. "Dat's wot youse said."

"Yes, youse will — *not!*" announced the Magpie, with cold finality. "Do youse t'ink I want to queer myself! A hot one youse'd be on an inside job! Youse'll be *outside,* wid yer peepers skinned for de bulls — youse an' Mag here, too. See! Get dat straight. While I'm on de job youse two plays de game. Now youse listen to me, both of youse. Don't start nothin' unless youse has to. If it's a cinch I got to make a get-away, youse two start a drunk fight. Get me? Youse know de lay. T'row de talk loud — an' I'll fade. Dat's all! We'll crack de crib early — it'll be quiet enough up dere by one o'clock."

One o'clock! Larry the Bat shook his head. What time was it now? It was about nine when he had first met the Tocsin, then the Sanctuary, then the long walk as he had followed her — say a quarter of ten for that. And he had certainly been here with her not less than an hour and a half. It must be after eleven, then. One o'clock! And before that must come

Makoff and Spider Jack! The night that half an hour ago had seemed so sterile, was crowding a program of events upon him now – too fast!

"Nothin' doin'!" he said thoughtfully. "Youse are in wrong dere, Slimmy. One o'clock don't go! Say, take it from me, I've watched dat guy too many nights fer Mag. 'Tain't often he leaves de club before one o'clock – an' he ain't never in bed before two."

"All right," agreed the Magpie, after a moment's reflection. "Youse ought to know. Make it three o'clock." He pulled a cigar from his pocket, lighted it, and, leaning back in his chair, stuck his feet up on the table. "If youse don't mind, Mag, I'll stick around a while," he decided calmly. "Mabbe de less I'm seen to-night de better – an' I guess dere won't be nobody lookin' fer me here."

Larry the Bat coughed suddenly, and rose up a little heavily from his chair. He had not counted on that! If the Magpie was settling down for a prolonged stay, it devolved upon him, Jimmie Dale, to get away, and at once – and without exciting the Magpie's suspicions. He coughed again, looked nervously from the Tocsin to the Magpie – stammered – swallowed hard – and coughed once more.

"Well, wot's bitin' youse?" inquired the Magpie ironically.

"Nothin'," said Larry the Bat – and hesitated. "Nothin', only –" He hesitated again; and then, the words in a rush:

"Say, Slimmy, couldn't youse come across wid a piece of dat century now?"

"Wot fer?" demanded the Magpie, a little aggressively.

Larry the Bat cleared his throat with a desperate effort.

"Youse knows," he admitted sheepishly. "Just gimme de price of one, Slimmy – just one."

"Coke!" exploded the Magpie. "An' get soaked to de eyes – not by a damn sight!"

"No! Honest to Gawd, no, Slimmy – just one!" pleaded Larry the Bat.

"Nix!" said the Magpie shortly.

Larry the Bat thrust out a hand before the Magpie's eyes that shook tremulously.

"I got to have it!" he declared, with sudden fierceness. "I *got* to – see! Look at me! I ain't goin' to be no good to-night if I don't. I tell youse, I got to! I ain't goin' to t'row youse down, Slimmy – honest, I ain't! Just one – an' it'll set me up. If I don't get none I'll be on de rocks before mornin'! Dat's straight, Slimmy – ask Mag, she knows."

"Aw, let him go get it!" broke in the Tocsin wearily. "Dat's de best t'ing youse can do, Slimmy – dey're all alike when dey gets in his class."

"Youse cocaine sniffers gives me de pip!" snorted the Magpie, in disgust. He dug down into his pocket, produced a bill, and flung it across the table to Larry the Bat. "Well, dere youse are; but youse can take it from me, Larry, dat if youse gets whiffed" – he swore threateningly – "I'll crack every bone in yer face! Get me?"

"Slimmy," said Larry the Bat fervently, grabbing at the bill with a hungry hand, "youse can count on me. I'll be up dere on de job before youse are. Three o'clock, eh? Well, so long, Slimmy" – he slouched eagerly to the door. "So long, Mag" – he paused on the threshold for a single, quick-flung, significant glance. "See youse on de avenoo, Mag – I'll be up dere before youse are. So long!"

"Oh, so long!" said the Tocsin contemptuously.

And, an instant later, Jimmie Dale closed the outer door behind him.

CHAPTER XII

JOHN JOHANSSON — FOUR-TWO-EIGHT

(Saturday 10/16/1915 to Sunday 10/17/1915)

N EARLY midnight already! It was even later than he had thought. Larry the Bat pressed his face against a shop's windowpane on the Bowery for a glance at a clock that had caught his eye on the wall within. Nearly midnight!

He slouched on again hurriedly, still debating in his mind, as he had been debating it all the way from the Tocsin's, the question of returning again to the Sanctuary. So far, the way both to Spider Jack's and the Sanctuary had been in the same direction — but the Sanctuary was on the next street.

Jimmie Dale reached the corner — and hesitated. It was strange how strong was the intuition upon him to-night that bade him go on and make all speed to Spider Jack's — while equally strong was the cold, stubborn logic that bade him go first to the Sanctuary. There were things that he needed there that would probably be absolutely essential to him before the night was out, things without which he might be so badly handicapped as to invite failure from the start; and yet — it was already midnight!

Ostensibly both Makoff and Spider Jack closed their places at eleven. But that might mean anything — depending upon their own respective inclinations, or on what of their own peculiar brand of deviltry might be afoot. If they were still about, still in evidence, he was still too early, midnight though it was; though, on the other hand, if the coast was clear, he could ill afford to lose a moment of the time between now and the hour that the Magpie had planned for the robbery of Henry LaSalle, for it would not be an easy matter, even once inside Spider Jack's, to find that package — since it was Spider's open boast that things committed to his care were where the police, or any one else, might as well whistle and suck their thumbs as try to find them!

And then, with sudden decision, taking his hesitation, as it were, by the throat, Jimmie Dale hurried on again — to the Sanctuary. At most, it could delay him but another fifteen minutes, and by half-past twelve, or a quarter to one at the latest, he would be at Spider Jack's.

Disdaining the secrecy of the side door on the alley, for who had a better right or was better known there than Larry the Bat, a tenant of years, he entered the tenement by the front door, scuffled up the stairs to the first landing, and let himself into his disreputable room. He locked the door behind him, lighted the choked and wheezy gas jet, in a single, sharp-flung glance assured himself that the blinds were tightly shut, and, kneeling in the far corner, threw back the oilcloth and lifted up the loose section of the flooring beneath. He reached inside, fumbling under the neatly folded clothes of Jimmie Dale, and in a moment laid his leather girdle with its kit of burglar's tools on the floor beside him; and beside that again an electric flashlight, a black silk mask, and – what he had never expected to use again when, early the night before, he had, as he had believed, put it away forever – the thin, metal insignia case of the Gray Seal. Another moment, and, with the flooring replaced, the oilcloth rolled back into position, he had stripped off his coat and was pulling his spotted, greasy shirt off over his head; then, stooping quickly, he picked up the girdle, put it on, put on his shirt again over it, put on his coat, put the metal case, the flashlight, and the mask in his pockets – and once more the Sanctuary was in darkness.

It was perhaps fifteen minutes later that Jimmie Dale turned into the upper section of Thompson Street. Here he slowed his pace, that had been almost a run since he had left the Sanctuary, and began to shuffle leisurely along; for the street, that a few hours before would have been choked with its pushcarts and venders, its half naked children playing where they could find room in the gutters, its sidewalks thronged with shawled women and picturesquely dressed, earringed, dark-visaged men, a scene, as it were, transported from some foreign land, was still far from deserted; the quiet, if quiet it could be called, was but comparative, there were many yet about, and he had no desire to attract attention by any evidence of undue haste. And, besides, Spider Jack's was just ahead, making the corner of the alleyway a few hundred feet farther on, and he had very good reasons for desiring to approach Spider's little novelty store at a pace that would afford him every opportunity for observation.

On he shuffled along the street, until, reaching Spider Jack's, a little two-storied, tumble-down brick structure, a muttered exclamation of satisfaction escaped him. The shop was closed and dark; and, though Spider Jack lived above the store, there were no lights even in the upper windows. Spider Jack presumably was either out, or in bed! So far, then, he could have asked for nothing more.

Jimmie Dale edged in close to the building as he slouched by, so close that his hat brim seemed to touch the windowpane. It was possible that from a room at the rear of the store there might be a light with a telltale ray perhaps filtering through, say, a door crack. But there was nothing – only blackness within.

He paused at the corner of the building by the alleyway. Down here, adjoining the high board fence of Spider Jack's back yard, Makoff made pretense at pawnbrokering in a small and dingy wooden building, that was little more pretentious than a shed – and in Makoff's place, so far as he could see, there was no light, either.

Jimmie Dale's fingers were industriously rolling a cigarette, as, under the brim of his slouch hat, his eyes were noting every detail around him. A yard in against the wall of Spider Jack's, the wall cutting off the rays of the street lamp at a sharp angle, it was shadowy and black – and beyond that, farther in, the alleyway was like a pit. It would take less, far less, than the fraction of a second to gain that yard, but some one was approaching behind him, and a little group of people loitered, with annoying persistency, directly across the way on the other side of the street. Jimmie Dale stuck the cigarette between his lips, fumbled in his pockets, and finally produced a box of matches. The group opposite was moving on now; the footsteps he had heard behind him, those of a man, drew nearer, the man passed by – and the box of matches in Jimmie Dale's hand dropped to the ground. He reached to pick them up, and in his stooping posture, without seeming to turn his head, flung a quick glance behind him up the street. No one, for that fraction of a second that he needed, was near enough to see – and in that fraction of a second Jimmie Dale disappeared.

A dozen yards down the lane, he sprang for the top of the high fence, gripped it, and, lithe and active as a cat, swung himself up and over, and dropped noiselessly to the ground on the other side. Here he stood motionless for a moment, close against the fence, to get his bearings. The rear of Spider Jack's building loomed up before him – the back windows as unlighted as those in front. Luck so far, at least, was with him! He turned and looked about him, and, his eyes growing accustomed to the darkness, he could just make out Makoff's place, bordering the end of the yard – nor, from this new vantage point, could he discover, any more than before, a single sign of life about the pawnbroker's establishment.

Jimmie Dale stole forward across the yard, mounted the three steps of the low stoop at Spider Jack's back door, and tried the door cautiously. It was locked. From his pocket came the small steel instrument that had stood Larry the Bat in good stead a hundred times before in similar circumstances. He inserted it in the keyhole, worked deftly with it for an instant – and tried the door again. It was still locked. And then Jimmie Dale smiled almost apologetically. Spider Jack did not use ordinary locks on his back door!

The discountenanced instrument went back into his pocket, and now Jimmie Dale's hand slipped inside his shirt, and from one of the little, upright pockets of the leather belt, and from still another, and from after that a third, came the vicious little blued-steel tools. The sensitive fingers travelled slowly up and down the side of the door – and then he was at work in earnest. A minute passed – another – there was a dull, low, grating sound, a snick as of metal yielding suddenly – and Jimmie Dale was coolly stowing away his tools again inside his shirt.

He pushed the door open an inch, listened, then swung it wide, stepped inside, and closed it behind him. A round, white beam of light flashed in a quick circle – and went out. It was a sort of storeroom, innocent enough and orderly enough in appearance, bare-floored, with boxes and packing cases piled neatly against the walls. In one corner a staircase led to the story above – and from above, quite audibly now, he caught the sound of snoring. Spider Jack was in bed, then!

Directly facing him was the open door of another room, and Jimmie Dale, moving softly forward, entered it. He had never been in Spider Jack's before, and his first concern was to form an intimate acquaintanceship with his surroundings. Again the flashlight circled, and again went out.

"No windows!" muttered Jimmie Dale under his breath. "Nothing very fancy about the architecture! Three rooms in a row! Store in front of this room through that door of course. Wonder if the door's locked, though it's a foregone conclusion the package wouldn't be in there."

Not a sound, his tread silent, he crossed to the closed door that he had noticed. It was unlocked, and he opened it tentatively a little way. A faint glow of light diffused itself through the opening. Jimmie Dale nodded his head and closed the door again. The street lamp, shining through the shop windows, accounted for the light.

And now the flashlight played with steady inquisitiveness about him. The room in which he stood seemed to combine a sort of office, with a lounging room, in which Spider Jack, no doubt, entertained his particular cronies. There was table in the centre, cards still upon it, chairs about it. Against the wall farthest away from the shop stood a huge, old-fashioned cabinet; and a little farther along, anglewise, partitioning off the corner, as it were, hung, for some purpose or other, a cretonne curtain. Also, against the wall next to the lane, bringing a commiserating smile to Jimmie Dale's lips as his eyes fell upon it, was a clumsy, lumbering, antique safe.

Jimmie Dale's eyes returned to the curtain. What was it doing there? What was it for? Instinctively he stepped over to examine it. A single glance, however, as he lifted it aside, sufficed. It was nothing but a make-shift clothes closet. He turned from it, switched off the flashlight, and stood staring meditatively into the darkness. In a strange house, with the knowledge to begin with that what he sought was carefully hidden, it was no sinecure to find that package. He had never for a moment imagined that it would be. But of one thing, however, there was no uncertainty in his mind—he would get the package!—by search if possible, by other means if search failed. It was now close to one o'clock. If by two o'clock his efforts had been fruitless, Spider Jack would hand over the package—at the revolver point! It was quite simple! Meanwhile—Jimmie Dale shrugged his shoulders, and, going over to the safe, knelt down in front of it—meanwhile, as well begin here as anywhere else.

The trained fingers closed on the handle—and on the instant, as though in startled amazement, shifted to the dial. They came back to the handle—a wrench—then a low, amused chuckle—and the door swung open. The great, unwieldy thing was only a monumental bluff! It not only had not been locked, but it *could not* be locked—the mechanism was out of order, the bolts could not be moved by so much as a hair's breadth!

Still chuckling, Jimmie Dale shot the flashlight's ray into the interior of the safe—and the chuckle died on his lips, and into his face came a look of strained bewilderment. Inside, everything was in chaos, books, papers, a miscellany of articles, as though they had first been ruthlessly pulled out on the floor, then gathered up in an armful and crammed back inside again. For an instant he did not move, and then a queer, hard, mirthless smile drew down the corners of his mouth. With a sort of bitter, expectant nod of his head, he turned the light upon the door of the safe. Yes, there were the scratches that the tools had left; and, as though in sardonic jest, the holes, where the steel bit had bored, were plugged with putty and rubbed over with some black substance that was still wet and came off, smearing his finger, as he touched it. It could not have been done long ago, then! How long? A half hour—an hour? Not more than that!

Mechanically he closed the door of the safe, rose to his feet and, almost heedless of noise now, the flashlight ray dancing before him, he jumped across to the old-fashioned cabinet and pulled the door open. Here, as within the safe, all inside, plain evidence of thorough, if hasty, search, was scattered and tossed about in hopeless confusion.

He shut the cabinet door; the flashlight went out; and he stood like a man stunned, the sense of some abysmal disaster upon him. He was too late! The game was up! If it had ever been here, the package was gone now—*gone!* The Crime Club had been here before him!

"The game was up! The game was up!"—his mind seemed to keep on repeating that. The Crime Club had beaten him by an hour, at most, and had been here, and had searched. It was strange, though, that they should have been at such curious pains to cover their tracks by leaving the room in order, by such paltry efforts to make the safe appear untouched when the first glance that was at all critical would disclose immediately what had been done! Why should they need to cover their tracks at all; or, if it was necessary, why, above all, in such a pitifully inadequate way! His mind barked back to the same ghastly refrain—"the game was up!"

No! Not yet! There was still a chance! There was still Spider Jack! Suppose, in spite of their search, they had failed to find the package! Jimmie Dale's lips set in a thin line, as he started abruptly toward the door. There was still that chance, and one thing was grimly certain—Spider Jack would, at least, show him where the package *had been!*

And then, halfway to the door, he halted suddenly, and stood still—listening. An electric bell was ringing loudly, imperiously, somewhere upstairs. Followed almost immediately the sound of some one, Spider Jack presumably, moving hurriedly about overhead; and then, a moment later, steps coming down the staircase in the adjoining room.

Jimmie Dale drew back, flattening himself against the wall. Spider Jack entered the room, stumbled across it, in the darkness, fumbled for the door that led into his little shop, opened it, passed through, fumbled around in there again, for matches evidently, then lighted a gas jet in the store, and, going to the street door, opened it.

Jimmie Dale had edged along the wall a little to a position where he had an unobstructed view through the open doorway connecting the shop and the room in which he stood. Spider Jack, in trousers and shirt, hastily donned, no doubt, as he had got out of bed, was standing in the street doorway, and beyond him loomed the forms of several men. Spider Jack stepped aside to allow his visitors to enter—and suddenly, a cry barely suppressed upon his lips, Jimmie Dale involuntarily strained forward. Three men had entered, but his eyes were fixed, fascinated, upon only one—the first of the three. Was it an hallucination? Was he mad—dreaming? It was Hilton Travers, *the chauffeur*—the man whom he could have sworn he had last seen dead, lashed in that chair, in that ghastly death chamber of the Crime Club!

"Rather rough on you, Spider, to pull you out of bed at this hour," the chauffeur was saying apologetically.

"Oh, that's all right, seein' it's you, Travers," Spider Jack answered, gruffly amiable. "Only I was kind of lookin' for you last night."

"I know," the chauffeur replied; "but I couldn't connect with my friends here. Shake hands with them, Spider—Bob Marvin—Harry Stead."

"Glad to know you, gents," said Spider Jack, with a handgrip apiece.

The chauffeur lowered his voice a little.

"I suppose we're alone here, eh, Spider? Yes? Well, then, you know what I've come for—that package—Marvin and Stead, here, are the ones that are in on it with me. Get it for me, will you, Spider?"

"Sure—Mr. Johansson!" Spider grinned. "Sure! Come on into the back room and make yourselves comfortable. I'll be mabbe five minutes, or so."

Jimmie Dale's brain was whirling. What did it mean? He could not seem to understand. His mind seemed to refuse its functions. Travers, the chauffeur—*alive!* He drew in his breath sharply. That curtain in the corner! He must see this out now! They were coming! Quick, noiseless, he stole along the side of the wall, reached the corner, and slipped in behind the curtain, as Spider Jack, striking a match, entered the room.

Spider Jack lighted the gas, and, as the others followed behind him, waved them toward the chairs around the table.

"I'll just ask you gents not to leave the room," he said meaningly, over his shoulder, as he stepped toward the rear door. "It's kind of a fad of mine to keep some things even from my wife!"

"All right, Spider—I understand," the chauffeur returned readily.

Jimmie Dale's knife cut a tiny slit in the cretonne on a level with his eyes. The three men had seated themselves at the table, and appeared to be listening intently. Spider Jack's footsteps echoed back as he crossed the rear room, sounded dull and muffled descending the stoop outside, and died away.

"I told you it wasn't in the house!" the man who had been introduced as Stead laughed shortly. "We wasted the hour we had here."

The third man spoke crisply, incisively, to the chauffeur.

"Turn down that gas jet a little! You've got across with it so far—but you can't stand a searchlight, Clarke!"

And at the words, in a flash, the meaning of it, all of it, to the last detail that was spelling death, ruin, and disaster for her, the Tocsin, for himself as well, burst upon Jimmie Dale. That *voice!* He would have known it, recognised it, among a thousand—it was the masked man of the night before, the leader, the head of the Crime Club! And it was not Travers there at all! He remembered now, too well, that second room they had showed him in the Crime Club—its multitude of disguises, though in this case they had the dead man's clothes ready to their hands—the leader's boast that impersonation was but child's play to them! And now he understood why they had covered up the traces of their search in only so curiously inadequate a manner. They had failed to find the package, and, as a last resort, had adopted the ruse of impersonating Hilton Travers, the chauffeur, which made it necessary that when they called Spider Jack from his bed, as they had just done, that Spider Jack, at a *casual* glance, should notice nothing amiss—but it would be no more than a casual glance, for, who should know better than they, he would not have to go for the package to any place that they had disturbed! And he, Jimmie Dale, could only stand here and watch them, helpless, powerless to move! Three of them! A step out into the room was to invite certain death. It would not matter, his death – if he could gain anything for her, for the Tocsin, by it. But what could he gain – by dying? He clenched his hands until the nails bit into the flesh.

Spider Jack re-entered the room, carrying what looked like a large, bulky, manila envelope, heavily sealed, in his hand. He tossed it on the table.

"There you are, Travers!" he said.

"I wonder," suggested the leader pleasantly, "if, now that we're here, Travers, your friend would mind letting us have this room for a few minutes to ourselves to clean up the business?"

"Sure!" agreed Spider Jack cordially. "You're welcome to it! I'll wait out here in the store until you say the word."

He went out, closing the door after him. The leader picked up the package.

"We'll take no chances with this," he said grimly. "It's been too close a call. After we've had a look at it, we'll put it out of harm's way on the spot, here, while we've got it – before we leave!"

He ripped the package open, and disclosed perhaps a dozen official-looking documents, besides a miscellaneous number of others. He took up the first of the papers, glanced through it hurriedly, then tossed it to the pseudo chauffeur.

"Tear it up, and tear it up – *small!*" he ordered tersely. The next, after examining it as he had the first, he tossed to the other man. "Go ahead!" – curtly. "Work fast! From the looks of these, Travers had us cold! There's proof enough here of LaSalle's murder to send us all to the chair!"

He went on glancing through the documents; and then suddenly, joining the others in their work, began to rip and tear at the papers himself.

A sort of cold horror had settled upon Jimmie Dale, and his forehead was clammy wet. The inhuman irony of it! That he should stand there and watch, impotent to prevent it, the destruction of what he would have given his life to secure! [67] And then slowly, a grim, hard, merciless smile

---

[67] A wonderful reminder here that while Dale is an accomplished hero, he is still very human. Why doesn't he confront the trio and save those all-important documents? Yes, he is outnumbered but even so he's armed and would have had the advantage of surprise. It's because the horrific experiences he had as a recent prisoner of the Crime Club have temporarily sapped his nerve more than he consciously realizes.

came to his lips. He had recognised the leader's voice—now he would recognise the leader's *face*. At least, that was left to him—perhaps the master trump of all. It would not be very hard to find the Crime Club now—with that man to lead the way!

The scraps of paper, tiny shreds, mounted into a heap on the table—and with the last of the contents of the package destroyed, the leader stood up.

"Put these pieces in your pockets; we don't want to leave them here," he directed quietly. "And then let's get out."

In scarcely a moment, the last scrap of paper had vanished. The three men walked to the door, passed through it, and joined Spider Jack in the store—and Jimmie Dale, slipping out from behind the curtain, gained the door of the rear room, crept through it, reached the stoop, and then, darting like the wind across the yard, was over the fence in a second, and in another was out of the alleyway and on the street.

He was in time—in plenty of time. They had just left Spider Jack's, and were, perhaps, fifty yards or so ahead of him. He slouched on behind them—the cold, grim smile on his lips once more. It was the Crime Club now, that hell's cradle where their devil's schemes were hatched, that was the one thing left to him; they would lead him to that, and then—and then it would be his turn to *strike!*

They turned the first corner. And suddenly, as the racing engine of an automobile caught his ear, he broke into a run, and dashed around the corner after them—in time to see them jump into a car, and the car speed off along the street! He halted, as though he were suddenly dazed—started involuntarily to run forward again—stopped with a hollow laugh at the futility of it—and stood still and motionless on the sidewalk.

And then he swayed a little, and his face grew gray. Failure, defeat, ruin—in that moment he knew them all to their bitterest dregs. How could he go to her! How could he face her, and tell her that they were beaten, that the last hope was gone, that he had failed!

"God!" he cried aloud, and clenched his hands.

Then deep in his consciousness a thought stirred, and he swept a shaking hand across his eyes. Why had it come again, that thought! Did it mean that *he* must play—the last card! There was a way—there had always been a way. The way the Crime Club took—*murder*. It was their own weapon! If the man who posed as Henry LaSalle were killed! If that man—were killed!

"The Magpie was to be there at three!" he muttered—and started mechanically back along the street.

CHAPTER XIII

THE ONLY WAY

(Sunday 10/17/1915)

IT was a horrible thing—and it grew upon him. In a blind, mechanical way, his brain receptive to nothing else, Jimmie Dale walked on along the street. To kill a man! Death he had faced himself a hundred times, witnessed it a hundred times in its most violent forms, had seen murder done before his eyes, had been in straits where, to save his own life, it had seemed the one last desperate chance—and yet his hands were still clean! [68] To kill a man in fair fight, in struggle, when the blood was hot, was terrible enough, a possibility that was always before him, the one thing from which he shrank, the one thing that, as the Gray Seal, he had always feared; but to kill a man deliberately, to creep upon his victim with hideous, cold-blooded premeditation—he shivered a little, and his hand shook as he drew it nervously across his eyes.

But there was no other way! Again and again, insidiously grappling with his revulsion, with the horror that the impulse to murder inspired, came that other thought—there was no other way. If the man who posed as Henry LaSalle were *dead!* If he were dead! If he were dead! See, now, what would happen if that man were dead! How clear his brain was on that point! The whole plot would tumble like a house of cards about the heads of the Crime Club. The courts would require an auditing of the estate by a trustee of the courts' own appointing, who would continue to administer it until the Tocsin's twenty-fifth birthday, or until there was tangible evidence of her death—but the Tocsin, automatically with her pseudo uncle's death, could publicly appear again. Her death could no longer benefit the Crime Club, since it, the Crime Club, with the supposed uncle dead, could not profit through the false Henry LaSalle inheriting as next of kin! It was the weak link, the vulnerable point in the stupendous scheme of murder and crime with which these hell fiends had played for and won, so far, the stake of eleven millions. Not that they had overlooked

---

68 Was Jimmie Dale's strong aversion to killing a factor in Doc Savage's similar code of conduct nearly twenty years later? The Gray Seal first appeared in the Street & Smith magazine *People's Ideal Fiction Magazine* and Doc was also a Street & Smith character.

or been blind to this, they were too clever, too cunning for that — it was only that they had planned to accomplish the Tocsin's death, as they had her father's and uncle's, and *establish* the false Henry LaSalle in undisputed possession and ownership of the estate — and had failed in that — up to the present. But the material results remained the same, so long as the Tocsin, to save her life, was forced to remain in hiding, so long as proof that would convict the Crime Club was not forthcoming — *so long as that man lived!*

Time passed to which Jimmie Dale was oblivious. At times he walked slowly, scarcely moving; at times his pace was a nervous, hurried stride, that was almost a run. And as he was oblivious to time, so was he oblivious to his surroundings, to the direction which he took. At times his forehead was damp with moisture that was not there from physical exertion; at times his face, deathly white, was full as of the vision of some shuddering, abhorrent sight; at times his lips were thinned into a straight line, and there was a glitter in the dark eyes that was not good to see, while his hands at his sides clenched until the skin, tight over the knuckles, was an ivory white. To kill a man!

What other way was there? The proof that it had taken Hilton Travers years to obtain, the proof on which the Tocsin's life depended, was destroyed utterly, irreparably. It could never be duplicated — Hilton Travers was dead — *murdered.* Murder! That thought again! It was their own weapon! Murder! Would one kill a venomous reptile in whose fangs was death? What right had this man to life, whose life was forfeit even under the law — for murder? Was she to drag on an intolerable existence among the dregs and the scum of the underworld, she, in her refinement and her purity, to exist among the vile and dissolute, in daily, hourly peril of her life, because the weapons that these inhuman vultures had used to rob her, to destroy those she loved, to make of her life a hideous, joyless thing, should not be used against them?

But to kill a man! To steal upon a man with cold intent in the blackness of the night — and take his life! To be a murderer! To know the horror of blood forever upon one's hands, to rise, cold-sweated, in the night, fearful of the very shadows around one, to live with every detail of that fearsome act sweeping like some dread spectre at unexpected moments upon the consciousness! He put up his hands before his face, as though to blot out the thought from him. Mind and soul recoiled before it — to kill a man!

He walked on and on, until at last, conscious of a sense of fatigue, he stopped. He must have come a long way, been walking a long time. Where was he? He looked about him for a moment in a dazed way — and suddenly, with a low cry, shrank back. As though he had been drawn to it by some ghastly magnet, he found himself standing in front of the LaSalle mansion, on Fifth Avenue. No, no; it was not for that he had come—to kill a man! It was only—only to get that money. Yes—he remembered now—that money from the safe, before the Magpie got it. The Magpie was to be there at three o'clock—and the Tocsin was to be there, too. The Tocsin! That package! He had failed! It had been her one hope, and—and it was gone. What could he say to her? How could he tell her the miserable truth? But—but he had not come there in the dead of night to kill a man, these other things were what had—

"Jimmie!" It was a quick-breathed whisper. A hand was on his arm.

He turned, startled. It was the Tocsin—Silver Mag.

"Jimmie!" in alarm. "Why are you standing here like this? You may be *seen!*"

Seen! Suppose he *were* seen? He shuddered a little.

"Yes; that's so!" he said hoarsely. He glanced numbly up and down the wide, deserted, but well-lighted, avenue. It was no place, that most aristocratic section of the city, for such as Silver Mag and Larry the Bat to be seen at that hour of night, or, rather, morning. And if anything *happened* inside that house! "I—I didn't think of that," he said mechanically.

"Come across the street—under the stoop of that house there." She had his arm, and was half dragging him as she spoke, the alarm in her voice intensified. And then, a moment later, safe from observation: "Jimmie, Jimmie, what is the matter? What has happened? What makes you act so strangely?"

"Nothing," he said. "I—"

"*Tell* me!" she insisted wildly.

And then, with a violent effort, Jimmie Dale forced his mind back to the immediate present. He was only inspiring her with terror—and there was the Magpie—and that money in the safe!

"Where is the Magpie?" he asked, with quick apprehension. "Am I late? Is he in there already?"

"No," she said. "He hasn't come yet."

"What time is it?" he demanded anxiously.

"About half-past two," she replied. "But, Jimmie—"

"Wait!" he broke in. "Where is he now? You were both together! And you were both to be here at three. What are you doing here alone at half-past two?"

A strange little exclamation, one almost of dismay, it seemed, escaped her.

"The Magpie left my place an hour ago—to get his kit, I think. And I came here at once because that was what you and I understood I was to do, wasn't it? Jimmie, you frighten me! You are not yourself. Don't you remember the last words you said, as you nodded to me behind the Magpie's back – that you would be here *before* us? There was no mistaking your meaning – if I could get away from him, I was to come here and meet you."

Jimmie Dale passed his hand nervously across his eyes. Of course, he remembered now! What a frightful turmoil his brain had been in!

"Yes; of course!" He tried to speak nonchalantly. "I had forgotten for the moment."

She caught his arm in a quick, tight hold, shaking him in a terrified way.

"*You* – forget a thing like that! Jimmie – something terrible has happened. Can't you see that I am nearly mad with anxiety! What is it? What is it? That package, Jimmie – is it the package?"

He did not answer. What could he say? It meant life, hope, joy, everything that the world held for her – and it was gone.

"Yes – it *is* the package!" she whispered frantically. "Quick, Jimmie! Tell me! It – it was not there? You – you could not find it?"

"It was there," he said, as though the words were literally forced from him.

"Then? Then – *what*, Jimmie?" The clutch on his arm was like a vise.

"They got it," he said. It was like a death sentence that he pronounced. "It is destroyed."

She did not speak or move – save that her hands, as though nerveless and without strength, fell away from his arms, and dropped to her sides. It was dark there under the stoop, though not so dark but that he could see her face. It was gray – gray as death. And there was misery and fear and a pitiful helplessness in it – and then she swayed a little, and he caught her in his arms.

"Gone!" she murmured in a dead, colourless way – and suddenly laughed out sharply, hysterically.

"Don't! For God's sake, don't do that!" he pleaded wildly.

She looked at him then for a moment in strange quiet – and lifted her hand and stroked his face in a numbed way.

"It – it would have been better, Jimmie, wouldn't it," she said in the same monotonous voice, "it would have been better if – if I had never found out anything, and they – they had done the same to me that they did to – to father."

"Marie! Marie!" It was the first time he had ever spoken her name, and it was on his lips now in an agony of tenderness and appeal. "Don't! You mustn't speak like that!"

"I'm tired," she said. "I – I can't fight any more."

She did not cry. She lay there in his arms quite still – like a weary child.

The minutes passed. When Jimmie Dale spoke again it was irrelevantly – and his face was very white:

"Marie, describe the upper floor of that house over there for me."

She roused herself with a start.

"The upper floor?" she repeated slowly. "Why – why do you ask that?"

"Have *you* forgotten in turn?" he said, with a steady smile. "That money in the safe – it's yours – we can at least save that out of the wreck. You only drew the basement plan and the first floor for the Magpie – the more I know about the house the better, of course, in case anything goes wrong. Now, see, try and be brave – and tell me quickly, for I must get through before the Magpie comes, and I have barely half an hour."

"No, Jimmie – no!" She slipped out of his arms. "Let it alone! I am afraid. Something – I – I have a feeling that something will happen."

"It is the only way." He said it involuntarily, more to himself than to her.

"Jimmie, let it alone!" she said again.

"No," he said. "I am going – so tell me quickly. Every minute that we wait is one that counts against us."

She hesitated an instant – and then, speaking rapidly, made a verbal sketch of the upper portion of the house for him.

"It's a very large house, isn't it?" he commented innocently – to pave the way for the question, above all others, that he had to ask. "Which is your uncle's, I mean that man's room?"

"The first on the right, at the head of the landing," she answered. "Only, Jimmie, don't – don't go!"

He drew her close to him again.

"Now, listen," he said quietly. "When the Magpie comes and finds I am not here, lead him to think that the money he gave me was too much for me; that I am probably in some den, doped with drug – and hold him as long as you can on the pretext that there is always the possibility I may, after all, show up before he goes in there. You understand? And now about yourself – you must do exactly as I say. On no account allow yourself to be seen by *any one* except the Magpie. I would tell you to go now, only, unless it is vitally necessary, we cannot afford to arouse the Magpie's suspicions – he'd have every crook in the underworld snarling at our heels. But you are not to wait, even for him, if you detect the slightest disturbance in that house before he comes. And, equally, after he has gone in, whether I have come out or not, at the first indication of anything unusual you are to get away at once. You understand — Marie?"

"Yes," she said. "But — but, Jimmie, you — "

"Just one thing more." He smiled at her reassuringly. "Did the Magpie say anything about how he intended to get in?"

"Yes — by the side away from the corner of the street," she said tremulously. "You see, there's quite a space between the house and the one next door; and, besides, the house next door is closed up, there's nobody there, the family has gone away for the summer. The library window there is low enough to reach from the ground."

For a moment longer he held her close to him, as though he could not let her go — then bent and kissed her passionately. And in that moment all the emotions he had known as he had walked blindly from Spider Jack's that night surged again upon him; and that voice was whispering, whispering, whispering: "It is the only way — it is the only way."

And then, not daring to trust his voice, he released her suddenly, and stepped back out from under the stoop — and the next instant he was across the deserted avenue. Another, and he had slipped through the iron gates that opened on the street driveway — and in yet another he was crouched close up against the front door of the LaSalle mansion.

It was a large house, a very large house, one of the few that, even amid the wealth and luxury of that quarter, boasted its own grounds, and those so restricted as scarcely to deserve the name; but it was set far enough back from the street to escape the radius of the street lamps, and so guarantee in its shadows security from observation. It was not the Magpie's way, the front door — the obvious to the Magpie and his ilk was a thing always to be shunned. Jimmie Dale's lips were set in a grim smile, as his fingers worked with lightning speed, now taking this instrument and now that from the leather pockets in the girdle beneath his shirt — the penitentiaries were full of Magpies who shunned the obvious!

Very slowly, very cautiously the door opened. He listened breathlessly, tensely. The door closed again — behind him. He was inside now. Stillness! Blackness! Not a sound! A minute went by — another. And then, as he stood there, strained, listening, the silence itself began, it seemed, to palpitate, and pound, pound, pound, and be full of strange noises. It was a horrible thing — to kill a man!

CHAPTER XIV

OUT OF THE DARKNESS

(Sunday 10/17/1915)

A MOMENT later, Jimmie Dale stepped forward through the vestibule. He was quite calm now; a sort of cold, merciless precision in every movement succeeding the riot of turbulent emotions that had possessed him as he had entered the house.

The half hour, the maximum length of time before the Magpie would appear, as he had estimated it when out there under the stoop with the Tocsin, had dwindled now to perhaps twenty minutes, twenty-five at the outside. Twenty-five minutes! Twenty-five minutes was so little that for an instant the temptation was strong upon him to sacrifice, rather than any of those precious minutes, the Magpie instead! And then in the darkness, as he stole noiselessly across the hall, he shook his head. It would be a cowardly, brutal thing to do. What chance would a man with a record like the Magpie's stand if caught there? How easy it would be to shift the murder of the supposed Henry LaSalle to the Magpie's shoulders! Jimmie Dale's lips closed firmly. Self-preservation was, perhaps, the first law, but he would save the Magpie if he could—the Magpie should have his chance! The man might be a criminal, might deserve punishment at the hands of the law, his liberty might be a menace to the community—but he was not a murderer, his life forfeit for a crime he had never committed!

If he, Jimmie Dale, could only in some way have arranged with the Tocsin out there to keep the Magpie away altogether! But it could not be done without arousing the Magpie's suspicions; and, as a corollary to that, afterward, with the subsequent events, would come—the deluge! The law of the underworld was clear, concise, and admitting of no appeal on that point; to double cross a pal meant, sooner or later, a knife thrust, a blackjack, or—But what difference did it make what form the execution of the sentence took? And, since, then, that was out of the question, since he could not keep the Magpie away without practically risking his own life, the Magpie at least must have his chance.

Jimmie Dale was at the library door now, that, according to the plan the Tocsin had drawn for the Magpie, and as he remembered her description when she had told him her story earlier in the evening, was just at the foot of the staircase. How dark it was! Though the stairs could be only a few feet away, he could not see them. And how intense the silence was again! Here, where he stood, the slightest stir from above must have reached him – but there was not a sound.

His hand felt out for the doorknob, found it, turned it, and pushed the door open. He stepped inside the room and closed the door behind him. The safe, according to the Tocsin's plan again, was in that sort of alcove at the lower end of the library. Jimmie Dale's flashlight played inquisitively about the room. There was the window, the only one in the room, the window through which the Magpie proposed to enter; there was the archway of the alcove, with its – no, there were no longer any portières; and there was the safe, he could see it quite plainly from where he stood at the upper end of the room.

The flashlight went out for the space of perhaps thirty seconds – thirty seconds of absolute silence, absolute stillness – then the round, white ray of the light again, but glistening now on the nickel knobs and dial of the safe – and Jimmie Dale was on his knees before it.

A low, scarcely breathed exclamation, that seemed to mingle anxiety and hesitation, escaped him. He, who knew the make of every safe in the country, knew this one for its true worth. Twenty-five minutes! Could he open it in that time, let alone with any time to spare! It was not like the one in Spider Jack's; it was the kind that the Magpie, however clever he might be in his own way, would be forced to negotiate with "soup," and, with the attendant noise, double his chance of discovery and capture – and the responsibility for what might have happened *upstairs!* No; the Magpie must have his chance! And, besides, the money in the safe apart, why should not he, Jimmie Dale, have his own chance, as well? All this would help. The motive – robbery; the perpetrator, there was grim mockery on his lips now as the light went out and the sensitive fingers closed on the knob of the dial, the perpetrator – the Gray Seal. It would afford excellent food for the violent editorial diatribes under which the police again would writhe in frenzy!

Stillness again! Silence! Only a low, tense breathing; only, so faint that it could not be heard a foot away, a curious scratching, as from time to time the supersensitive fingers fell away from the dial to rub upon the carpet – to increase even their sensitiveness by setting the nerves to throbbing through the skin surface at the tips. And then Jimmie Dale's head, ear pressed close against the safe to catch the tumbler's fall, was lifted – and the flashlight played again on the dial.

"Twenty-eight and a quarter – left."

How fast the time went – and how slowly! Still the black shape crouched there in the darkness against the safe. At times, in strange, ghostly flashes, the nickel dial with the ray upon it seemed to leap out and glisten through the surrounding blackness; at times, the quick intake of breath, as from great exertion; at times, faint, musical little clicks, as, after abortive effort, the dial whirled, preparatory to a fresh attempt. And then, at last – a gasp of relief:

"Ah!"

Came the sound, barely audible, as of steel sliding in well-oiled grooves, the muffled thud of metal meeting metal as the bolts shot back – and the heavy door swung outward.

Jimmie Dale stretched his cramped limbs, and wiped the moisture from his face – then set to work again upon the inner door. This was an easier matter – far easier. Five minutes, perhaps a little more, went by – and then the inner door was open, and the flashlight's ray was flooding the interior of the safe.

A queer little sound, half of astonishment, half of disappointment, issued from Jimmie Dale's lips. There was money here, a great deal of money, undoubtedly, but there was no such sum as he had, somehow, fantastically imagined from the Magpie's evidently overcoloured story that there would be; there was money, ten packages of banknotes neatly piled in the bottom compartment – but there was no half million of dollars! He picked up one of the packages hurriedly – and drew in his breath. After all, there was a great deal – the notes were of hundred-dollar denomination, and on the bottom were two one-thousand-dollar bills! Calculated roughly, if each of the other nine packages contained a like amount, the total must exceed a hundred thousand.

And now Jimmie Dale began to work with feverish haste. From the leather girdle inside his shirt came the thin metal insignia case – and a gray seal was stuck firmly on the dial knob of the safe. This done, he tucked away the packages of banknotes, some into his pockets and some inside his shirt; and then quickly ransacked the interior of the safe, flauntingly spilling the contents of drawers and pigeonholes out upon the floor.

He stood up, and, leaving the safe door wide open, walked back across the room to the window, unfastened the catch, and opened the window an inch or two. The way was open now for the Magpie! The Magpie would have no need to make any noise in forcing an entrance; he would be able to see almost at a glance that he had been forestalled – by the Gray Seal; and that, as far as he was concerned, the game was up. The Magpie had his chance! If the Magpie did not take the hint and make his escape as noiselessly as he had entered – it was his own fault! He, Jimmie Dale, had given the Magpie his chance.

Jimmie Dale turned from the window, and made his way out of the library to the foot of the stairs, leaving the library door open behind him. How long had he been? Was it more or less than the twenty-five minutes?

He did not know—only, as yet, the Magpie had not come, and now perhaps it did not make so much difference.

Where was he going now? His foot was on the first stair—and suddenly he drew it back, the cold sweat bursting out on his forehead. Where was he going now? *"The first room on the right at the head of the landing."* From his inner consciousness, as it were, the answer, in all the bald, naked horror that it implied, flashed upon him. The first room on the right—*that* man's room! God, how the darkness and the stillness began to palpitate again, and suddenly seem to shriek out at him over and over the one single, ghastly word—*murder!*

It had been with him, that thought, all the time he had been working at the safe; but it had been there then only subconsciously, like some heavy, nameless dread, subjugated for the moment by the work he had had to do which had demanded the centred attention of every faculty he possessed. But now the moment had come when there was only *that* before him, only that, nothing else—only that, the man upstairs in the first room to the right of the landing!

Why did he hesitate? Why did he stand there while the priceless moments before daylight came were passing? The man was a murderer, a blotch on society, and, his life already forfeited, he was living now only because the law had not found him out—the man was a criminal, bloodstained—and his life, because he had taken her father's life and had tried to take the Tocsin's own life, stood between her and every hope of happiness, robbing her even literally, in a material sense, of everything that the world could hold for her! Why did he hesitate? It was that man's life—or hers! It was the only way!

He put his foot upon the bottom step again—paused still another instant—and then began stealthily to mount the stairs. The darkness! There had never been, it seemed, such darkness before! The stillness—he had never known silence so heavy, so full of strange, premonitory pulsings; a silence that seemed so incongruously full of clamouring whispers in his ears! It must be those imagined whispers that were affecting his nerve—for now, as he gained the landing and slipped his automatic from his pocket, his hand was shaking with a queer twitching motion.

For an instant, fighting for his self-composure, he stood striving to locate his surroundings through the darkness. The staircase was a circular one, making the landing nearly at the front of the house, and rearward from this, the Tocsin had said, a hallway ran down the centre, with rooms on either side. The first room to the right, therefore, should be just at his hand. He reached out, feeling cautiously—there was nothing. He edged to the right—still nothing; edged a little farther, a sense of bewilderment growing upon him, and finally his fingers touched the wall. It was very strange! The hallway must be much wider than he had understood it to be from what she had said!

He moved along now straight ahead of him, his hand on the wall, feeling for the door – and with every step his bewilderment increased. Surely there must be some mistake – perhaps he had misunderstood! He had come fully twice the distance that one would expect – and yet there was no door. Ah, what was that? His fingers closed on soft, heavy velvet hangings. These could hardly be in front of a door, and yet – what else could it be? He drew the hangings warily apart, and felt behind them. It was a window; but it was shuttered in some way evidently, for he could not see out.

Jimmie Dale stood motionless there for fully a minute. It seemed absurd, preposterous, the conviction that was being forced home upon him – that there were no rooms on the right-hand side of the corridor at all! But that was not like the Tocsin, accurate always in the most minute details. The room must be still farther along. He was tempted to use his flashlight – but that, as long as he could feel his way, was an unnecessary risk. A flashlight upstairs, where a sleeping-room door might be ajar, or even wide open, where some one wakeful, *that* man himself, perhaps, might see it, was quite another matter than a flashlight in the closed and deserted library below!

He went on once more, still guiding himself by a light finger touch upon the wall, passed another portière similar to the first, and, after that, another – and finally stopped by bringing up abruptly against the end wall of the house. It was certainly very strange! There *were* no rooms on the right-hand side of the corridor. And here, hanging across the end wall, was another of those ubiquitous velvet portières. He parted it, and, a little to his surprise, found a window that was not shuttered, but that, instead, was heavily barred by an ornamental grille work. He could see out, however, and found that he was looking directly out from the rear of the house. A lamp from the side street threw what was undoubtedly the garage into shadowy outline, and he made out below him a short stretch of yard between the garage and the house. He remembered that now – she had described all that to the Magpie. There was no driveway between the front and the rear. The house being on the corner, the entrance to the garage was directly from the side street. Yes, she had described all that exactly as it was, but – he dropped the portière and faced around, carrying his hand in a nonplused way to his eyes – but here, upstairs, within the house, it was not as she had said it was at all! What did it mean? She could not have blundered so egregiously as that, unless – he caught his breath suddenly – unless she had done so intentionally! Was that it? Had she surmised, formed a suspicion of what was in his mind, of what he meant to do – and taken this means of defeating it? If so – well, it was too late for that now! There was one way – only one way! Whatever the cost, whatever it might mean for him – there was only one way out for her.

His flashlight was in his hand now, and the round, white ray shot down the corridor – seemed suddenly to falter unsteadily – swept in through an open door that was almost beside him – and then, as though a nerveless hand held it, the ray dropped and played shakily on the toe of his boot before it went out.

A stifled cry rose to his lips. Something cold, like a hand of ice, seemed to clutch at his heart. Those portières, the wide, richly carpeted corridor! It was the corridor of the night before! That room at his side was the room where he had seen Hilton Travers, the chauffeur, dead, lashed in a chair! He felt the sweat beads burst out anew upon his forehead.

It was the Crime Club!

CHAPTER XV

RETRIBUTION

(Sunday 10/17/1915)

HIS brain seemed to whirl, staggered as by some gigantic, ghastly mockery. The Crime Club! *Here!* He had thought to creep upon that man — and he had run blindly into the very heart and centre of these hell fiends' nest!

Silently he stood there, holding his breath as he listened now, motionless as a statue, forcing his mind to *think.* He remembered that last night his impression of the place had been that it was more like some great private mansion than anything else. Well, he had been right, it seemed! He could have laughed aloud — sardonically, hysterically. It was not so strange now that there were no rooms on the right-hand side of the corridor! And what could have suited their purpose better, what, by its very location, its unimpeachable character, could be a more ideal lair for them than this house! And how grimly simple it was now, the explanation! In the five years that the false Henry LaSalle had been in possession, they had cunningly remodelled the upper floor — that was all! It was quite clear now why the man never entertained — why he had never been caught or found or known to be in communication with his fellow conspirators! It was no longer curious that one might watch the door of the house for months at a stretch and go unrewarded for one's pains, as the Tocsin had done, when access to the house by those who frequented it was so easy through the garage on the side street — and from the garage, if their work there was in keeping with their clever contrivances within the house, by an underground connection into, say, the cellar or basement!

Again Jimmie Dale checked that nervous, unnatural inclination to laugh aloud. Was there anything, any single incident, any single detail of all that had transpired, that was not explained, borne out, as it could be explained and borne out in no other way save that the Crime Club should be no other than this very house itself? It was the exposition of that favourite theory of his — it was so obvious that therein lay its security. He had mocked at the Magpie not many moments before on that score — and now it was the beam in his own eye! It was so obvious now, so glaringly obvious, that the Crime Club could have been nowhere else; so obvious, with every word of the Tocsin's story pointing it out like a signpost — and he had not seen it!

364

And then suddenly every muscle grew strained and rigid. *Was there some one in the corridor?* Was it some one moving — or was it only fancy? He listened — while he strained his eyes through the darkness. There was no sound; only that abnormal, heavy silence that — yes, he remembered that, too, now — that had clung about him last night like a pall. He could see nothing, hear nothing — but intuitively, bringing a cold dismay, the greater because it was something unknown, intangible, he *felt* as though eyes were upon him, that even in the darkness he was being watched!

And as he stood there, then, slowly there crept upon Jimmie Dale the sense of peril and disaster. It was not intuition now — it was certainty. He was trapped! It was the part of a fool to imagine that with their devil's cunning, their cleverness, their ingenuity, he, or any one else, could enter that house unknown to its occupants! Had he made electric contact when he had opened the front door, and rung a signal here, perhaps, upstairs — had he set some system of alarm at work when he had touched that window? What did it matter — the details that had heralded his entrance? He was certain now that his presence in the house was known. Only, why had they left him so long without attack? He shook his head with a quick, impatient movement. That, too, was obvious! He was under observation. Who was he? Why had he come? Was he simply a paltry safe-tapper — or was he one whom they had a real need to fear? And then, too, there might well be another reason. It was far from likely, in fact unreasonable, to imagine that all the men he had seen here the night before were in the house now. Not many of them, if any, would *live* here, for *constant,* daily coming and going, even through the garage, could not escape notice; and, of the servants, probably a lesser breed of criminal, some of them, at least, no doubt, were engaged at that moment in watching his own house on Riverside Drive! There was even the possibility that the man posing as Henry LaSalle was, for the time being, here alone.

He shook his head again. He could hardly hope for that — he had no right to hope for anything more now than a struggle, with an inevitably fatal ending to himself, but one in which at least he could sell his life as dearly as possible, one in which, perhaps, he might pay the Tocsin's score with the man he had come to find! If he could do that — well, after all, the price was not too great!

There were no tremours of the muscles now. It was Jimmie Dale, the Gray Seal, every faculty alert, tense, keyed up to its highest efficiency; the brain cool, keen, and active — fighting for his life. The front door through which he had entered was an impossibility; but there was the window in the library that he had opened — if they would let him get that far! That was as good a chance as any. If he made an effort to find, say, a way to the flat above and chanced some means of escape there, it would in no wise obviate an attack upon him, and he would only be under the added disadvantage of unfamiliar surroundings.

Feeling out with his left hand, his automatic thrown a little forward in his right, he began to retrace his way along the blank wall of the corridor, pausing between each step to listen, moving silently, his tread on the heavy carpet as noiseless as though it were some shadow creeping there.

Stillness—utter, absolute! Always that stillness. Always that sense of danger around him—the tense, bated expectancy of momentary attack—a revolver flash through the darkness—a sudden rush upon him. But still there was nothing—only the darkness, only the silence.

He gained the head of the stairs and began to descend—and now the strain began to tell upon his nerves again. Again he was possessed of the mad impulse to cry out, to do anything that would force the issue, that would end the horrible, unbearable suspense. Why did that revolver shot not come? Why had they not yet rushed upon him? Why were they playing with him as a cat with a mouse? Or was it all wild, fanciful imagination? *No!* What was that again! He could have sworn this time that he had heard a sound, but he could neither define its character, nor locate the direction from which it had come.

He was at the foot of the stairs now; and, guiding himself by the wall, moving now barely an inch at a time, he reached the library door that he had left open, and stole in over the threshold. Halfway down the room and diagonally across from where he stood was the window. In a moment now he could gain that, but they would never let him go so easily—and so it must come now, in that next moment, their attack! Where were they? Where were they now? The table—he must remember not to bump into the table! A pause between each step, he was crossing the room. He was halfway to the window. Had it been all fancy, was he to—And then Jimmie Dale stood motionless. *Some one had closed the library door softly!*

Stillness again! A sort of deadly calm upon him, Jimmie Dale felt out behind his back for the big library table that he had been circuiting—if the window were wide open it might be done, but to jump for it and stand silhouetted there during the pause necessary to fling the window up was little less than suicidal. He edged back noiselessly until his fingers touched the table; then, lowering himself to his knees, he backed in underneath it, and lay flat upon the floor. It was not much protection, but it had one advantage: if they switched on the lights it would show an *empty* room for the first instant, and that instant meant—the first shot!

Where were they now? By the library door? How many of them were there? Well, it was their move! Two could play at cat and mouse until—until *daylight!* That wasn't very far off, now, and when that came he might still have the first shot, but after that—he turned his head quickly toward the window. There was a faint scratching noise as of finger nails gripping the sill; then the window, very slowly, almost silently, was pushed steadily upward, and a dark form loomed up outside; and then, crawling through, a man dropped, as though his feet were padded like a cat's on the floor inside the room. The Magpie!

A flashlight's ray shot out—and, with a twisted smile propped now on his left elbow to give free play to his revolver arm, Jimmie Dale followed the white spot eagerly with his eyes. But it did not circle around; instead, the light was turned almost instantly toward the lower end of the room—and, a second later, was holding steadily on the open door of the safe, and the litter of papers on the floor.

Came a savage growl of amazed fury from the Magpie: then his step down the room; and, as he reached the safe, a torrent of unbridled blasphemy—and then, in a sort of staggered gasp, as he leaned suddenly forward examining the knob of the dial:

"The Gray Seal!"

A moment the Magpie stood there; and then, cursing again in abandon, turned, and started back for the window, his flashlight dancing before him—and stopped, a snarl of fury on his lips. The flashlight was playing full on Jimmie Dale under the table!

"Larry the Bat! The Gray Seal! By God!" choked the Magpie. "You—you—" The Magpie's flashlight, as he shifted it from his right hand to his left and wrenched out his revolver, had fallen upon two men crouched close against the wall by the library door—and he screamed out in an access of fury. "De double cross! A plant! De bulls! You damned snitch, Larry!" screamed out the Magpie—and fired.

The bullet tore into the carpet beside Jimmie Dale. Came answering shots from the men by the door; and then the Magpie, emptying his automatic at the two men as he ran, the flame tongues cutting vicious lanes of fire through the darkness, dashed for the window. There was a cry, the crash of a heavy body pitching to the floor—and the Magpie had flung himself out through the window, and in the momentary ensuing silence within the room came the sound of his footsteps running on the gravel below.

There was a low moan, the movement as of some one staggering and lurching around—and then the lights went on. But for an instant Jimmie Dale did not move. He was staring at the form of a man still and motionless on the floor in front of him—the man who had posed as Henry LaSalle. Dead! The man was dead! His mind ran riot for a moment. Where were the others—were there only these two? Only these two in the house! Only these two—and one was dead! And then Jimmie Dale was on his feet. One was dead—but there was still the other, the man who was reeling there, back turned to him, by the electric-light switch. But even as Jimmie

Dale sprang forward, this second man, clawing at the wall for support, slipped to his knees and fell upon the carpet.

Jimmie Dale reached him, snatched the revolver from his hand, and bent over him. It was the man whose name he did not know, but whose face he had reason enough to know too well – it was the leader of the Crime Club.

The man, though evidently badly wounded, smiled defiantly in spite of his pain.

"So you're the Gray Seal!" he flung out contemptuously. "A clever enough safe-cracker – but only a lowbrow, like the rest of them. Another illusion dispelled! Well, you've got the money – better run, hadn't you?"

Jimmie Dale made no answer. Satisfied that the man was too badly hurt to move, he went and bent over the silent form in the centre of the room. A moment's examination was enough. "Henry LaSalle" was dead.

He stood there looking down at the man. It was what he had come for – though it was the Magpie, not himself, who had accomplished it! The man was dead! The words began to run through his mind in a queer reiteration. The man was dead – the man was dead! He checked himself sharply. He must think now – think fast, and think *right*.

The Magpie knew that Larry the Bat was the Gray Seal – and as fast as the Magpie could get there, the news would spread like wildfire through the underworld. "Death to the Gray Seal! Death to the Gray Seal!" He could hear that slogan ringing again in his ears, but as he had never heard it before – with a snarl of triumph now as of wolves who at last had pulled their quarry down. He had not a second to spare – and yet – that man wounded there on the floor! What of him – guilty of murder, the brains of this inhuman, monstrous organisation, the one to whom, more even than to that dead man, the Tocsin owed the horror and the misery and the grief and despair that had come into her life! What of him? What of the Crime Club here? What of this nest of vipers? Were they to escape? Were they to –

With a sudden, low exclamation, Jimmie Dale jumped for the table, and, snatching up the telephone, rattled the hook violently.

"Give me" – his voice came in well-simulated gasps, each like a man fighting for every word – "give me – police – headquarters! Quick! *Quick!* I've – been – shot!"

The wounded man on the floor raised himself on his elbow.

"What are you doing?" he demanded in a startled way. "Are you mad! Thank your stars you were lucky enough to get out of this alive – and get out now, while you have the chance!"

Jimmie Dale pressed his hand firmly over the mouthpiece of the telephone.

"I'll go," he said, with a cold smile, "when I've settled with you – for the murder of Henry LaSalle."

"That man!" ejaculated the man scornfully, pointing to the form on the floor. "So that's your game! Going to try and cover your tracks! Why, you fool, I *live* here! Do you think the police would imagine for an instant that I killed him?"

"I said – *Henry LaSalle,*" said Jimmie Dale evenly.

The man came farther up on his elbow, a sudden look of fear in his face.

"What – what do you mean?" he cried hoarsely.

But Jimmie Dale was talking again into the telephone – gasping, choking out his words as before:

"Police headquarters? I'm Henry LaSalle. Fifth Avenue. I – I've been shot. Take down this statement. I'll – I'll be dead before you get here – I'm not the real Henry LaSalle at all. We murdered Henry LaSalle – in Australia, and murdered Peter LaSalle here. We – we tried to kill the daughter, but she ran away. This house has been our headquarters for the last five years. The man who shot me to-night is the leader of the gang. We quarrelled over the division of a haul. He's here on the floor now, wounded. Get them all, get them all, damn them! – do you hear? – get them all! They're out of the house now, but lay a trap for them. They always come in through the garage on the side street. Oh, God, I'm done for! Break down the west walls of the rooms upstairs – if – you – want proof of what – the gang's been doing. Hurry! Hurry! I'm – I'm – done for – I – "

Jimmie Dale permitted the telephone to drop with a clash from his hand to the table.

The face of the man on the floor was livid.

"Who are you? In God's name, who are you?" he cried out wildly.

"Does it matter?" inquired Jimmie Dale grimly. "Your game is up. You'll go to the chair for the murder of 'Henry LaSalle' – if it is by proxy! Those rooms upstairs alone are enough to damn you, to prove every word of that dying 'confession' – but to-morrow, added to it, will come the story of Marie LaSalle herself."

For a moment the man hung there swaying on his elbow, his face working in ghastly fashion – and then suddenly, with a strange laugh, he carried one hand swiftly to his mouth – and laughed again – and before Jimmie Dale could reach him was lifeless on the floor.

A tiny vial rolled away upon the carpet. Jimmie Dale picked it up. A drop or two of liquid still remained in it – colourless, clear, like that liquid this same man had dropped into the rabbit's mouth the night before, like the liquid in the glasses they had carried into that third room, like the liquid that his man had said was from a formula of their own, that was instantaneous in its action, that defied detection by autopsy!

The set, stern features of Jimmie Dale relaxed. It was justice – but it was also death. In a surge of emotion, the events of scarcely more than twenty-four hours, began to crowd upon him – and then, ominously dominant, above all else, that slogan of the underworld, "Death to the Gray Seal!" came ringing once more in his ears. It brought him, with a startled movement of his hand across his eyes, to a realisation of his own desperate position. Yes, yes, he must go! The way was clear now for the Tocsin – clear now for her!

He dropped the vial into his pocket, and, running to the safe, quickly scraped the gray seal from the dial's knob; then he drew the packages of money from his shirt and pockets and tossed them on the floor among the litter of papers already there – she would get it back again when it had served its purpose, it would be self-evident that it was the proceeds of that day's sale of the estate's securities over which the "quarrel" had occurred!

And now the window! He ran to it, closed it, and *locked* it; then, laying the revolver he had taken from the leader down beside the man, he stepped across the room again and drew the body of "Henry LaSalle" closer to the table – as though the man had fallen there when the telephone had dropped from his hand.

It was done now! On the floor beside him lay each man's weapon – and both of the revolvers had been discharged several times. Jimmie Dale paused on the library threshold for a final survey of the room. It was done! The way was clear – for her. And now if he could only save himself! There was no chance for Larry the Bat! Could he save – *Jimmie Dale!*

He crossed the hall, a queer, half-grim, half-wistful smile on his lips, unlocked the front door, stepped out, locked it behind him – and in another moment, doubling around the corner, was running along like a hare along the side street.

CHAPTER XVI

"DEATH TO THE GRAY SEAL!"

(Sunday 10/17/1915)

O<small>N</small> Jimmie Dale ran. Across on Fourth Avenue he swung on a car that took him to Astor Place. Then striking east once more, making a detour to avoid the Bowery, he ran on at top speed again. To reach the Sanctuary, not before the Magpie should have spread the alarm, that was impossible, but to reach it before the underworld should have had time to recover its breath, as it were, before the underworld should have had time to act — that was his only chance! The Magpie had, at the outside, a start of fifteen minutes; but he, Jimmie Dale, had probably retrieved five minutes of that in the time he had made in getting downtown. That left the Magpie ten to the good. How long would it take the Magpie to bring the underworld swarming like hornets around the Sanctuary?

On Larry the Bat ran. At the Sanctuary were the clothes, the belongings of Jimmie Dale. Could he save Jimmie Dale! If he could get there, change, and get out again, the way was clear for him — as clear as for the Tocsin now. In a few hours the police would have every member of the Crime Club in the trap; there would be no watch any more around his house on Riverside Drive; and he would be free to return there and resume his normal life as Jimmie Dale again if he could make the Sanctuary in time! But let the Magpie get there first, let the underworld tear the place to pieces in its fury as it would do, let them discover that hiding place under the flooring, for instance, and the Gray Seal would not be merely Larry the Bat, but Jimmie Dale as well, and — a cry escaped him even as he ran — it meant ruin, the disgrace of an honoured name, death, crimes without number at his door. Crimes! The Gray Seal had never committed a crime! [69] But the crimes attributed to the Gray Seal he could not disprove, not one of them! He had meant them to appear as crimes — and he had succeeded so well that the Gray Seal's name, execrated, was a synonym for the most callous, dangerous, and unscrupulous criminal of the age!

He was gasping for breath as finally, making for the side door, he darted into the alleyway that flanked the Sanctuary. What story would the

---

[69] Even if it could somehow be proved in court that Dale's many, many illegal activities were actually altruistic acts, an argument could still be made that the Gray Seal's widely-publicized exploits would have increased sales profits for safe manufacturers like Jimmie's father.

Magpie tell? Not the truth, of course – that would let the Magpie in for what had happened that night, for the Magpie must be well aware that he had shot at least one of the two men in that room. But the truth wasn't necessary; it was foreign, and had no bearing on the one outstanding fact – the Gray Seal was Larry the Bat. At the present moment the Magpie had a double incentive for "getting" the Gray Seal – the Gray Seal was the only one who could prove murder against him that night in the LaSalle mansion. And afterwards, when the police version of the affair was made public, the Magpie, to save himself, would be careful enough to do or say nothing to contradict "Henry LaSalle's" confession!

Larry the Bat slipped in through the door, halted there, listened; and then began to mount the rickety stairs, with his silent tread. At the top he paused again. Nothing – no sound! They were not here yet – so far he was in time! He stepped to the Sanctuary door, unlocked it, passed into the squalid, miserable room that had harboured him for so long as Larry the Bat, locked the door behind him, crossed quickly to the window to make sure that the shutters were closed – and then, for the first time, as the gray light streaked in through the interstices, he was conscious that it was already dawn. So much the more need for haste then!

He whipped out his revolver and laid it at his hand on the dilapidated table; then the flooring in the corner was up in an instant, and he began to strip off the rags of Larry the Bat. Boots, mismated socks, the torn, patched trousers, the greasy flannel shirt, the threadbare coat, the nondescript slouch hat were thrown in a pile on the floor; and with them, from their hiding-place, the grease paints and heterogeneous collection of make-up accessories. This done, he began to slip on the clothes of Jimmie Dale; and, when half dressed, turned to the table again to remove the characteristic grime, stain, and paint of Larry the Bat from face, hands, wrists, throat, and neck. This was a longer, more arduous task. He reached for the cracked pitcher to pour more water into the basin – and, snatching up his revolver instead, whirled to face the door.

Some one was outside! He had caught the creak of a footstep upon the stairs. In a flash he was across the room and crouched by the door. Yes, the step was nearer now – at the head of the stairs – on the landing. His revolver lifted, holding a steady bead on the door panel. And then there came a low voice:

"Jimmie! Jimmie! Are you there? Quick, Jimmie! Are you there?"

The Tocsin! What was she doing here! Why had he not warned her up there on the avenue, fool that he was, that of all places she was to keep away from here!

She slipped into the room as he unlocked the door.

"They're coming, Jimmie!" she panted breathlessly. "There's not an instant to lose! Listen! When the Magpie ran from the house, I ran with him — but it" — she tried to smile — "it wasn't to obey you, to run away — I had made up my mind I wouldn't do that — it was to find out from him what had happened. He told me you were the Gray Seal. He did not suspect me. He thinks you were no more than just Larry the Bat to me, as you were to everybody else. He went straight to Chicago Ike's gambling rooms and found the Skeeter's gang there — you know them, Red Mose, the Midget, Harve Thoms, and the Skeeter — you remember your fight with them over old Luddy's diamonds! Well, they have not forgotten, either! They are on their way here, now! The news that you are the Gray Seal is travelling like lightning all through the underworld — there will be a mob here on the Skeeter's heels. So, Jimmie — quick! Run!"

Run! Half Larry the Bat, half Jimmie Dale — and run! In another five minutes, perhaps — yes. But there probably would not be five minutes — and she — if she were found here!

"Yes," he said quietly. "I'll get away in a moment. You go at once. I'll" — he was smiling at her reassuringly — "I'll meet you at — "

She looked at him then for an instant — interrupting him quickly, as she shook her head.

"I didn't notice, Jimmie. You cannot go like that — can you? It would be even worse than being caught as Larry the Bat. Hurry then — I am not going without you."

"No!" he said. "Go now! Go at once, Marie — while you can. You have risked your life as it is to come here and tell me this. For God's sake, go now!"

The great, brown eyes were smiling bravely through a sudden mist. She shook her head again.

"Not without you, Jimmie."

It brought a fierce, wild throb of joy upon him — and then a cold, sickening fear.

"Listen!" he cried out desperately. "You must go now! You cannot take any chances now, Marie. Everything is right for you. That man who posed as your uncle is dead — the leader of the Crime Club is dead. Don't you understand what that means! You have only to be Marie LaSalle again and claim your own. I cannot tell you all now — there's no time. That house was the Crime Club itself. The police will get them all. Don't you see! Don't you see! Everything is clear for you now — and now go! Go — you must go!"

She was staring at him, a strange wonder in her face.

"Clear! All clear — for me! I — I can go back to — to my own life again!"

It was as though she were whispering some amazing thing of unbelievable joy to herself.

"*Yes!*" he cried out again. "Yes! But go – go, Marie!"

But now, for answer, suddenly she reached out and took the key from the door and put it in the pocket of her dress.

"We will go together, Jimmie – or not at all," she said simply. "We are wasting precious moments. Hurry and dress!"

He hesitated miserably. What could he do – if she *would* not go! And it was true – the moments were flying. Better, rather than futile argument, to use them as she said. There was still a chance! Why not! Five minutes! He could do better than that! He *must* do better than that!

Without a word, he ran back across the room. In frantic haste, from face, hands, wrists, and neck came the stain. There was still time. She was standing there by the door, listening. She, the Tocsin, she whom he loved, she who, all through the years that had gone, had been so strangely elusive and yet so intimately a part of his life, *she* was standing there now, here with him – in peril with every second that passed!

He had only to slip on his coat and vest now – and make a bundle of Larry the Bat's things on the floor, so that he could carry them away to destroy them. He stooped to gather up the clothes – and straightened suddenly – and jumped toward the door again.

"They are coming, Jimmie!" she called, in a low voice. But he had already heard them – the stairs were creaking loudly under the tread of many feet. He pushed the Tocsin hurriedly back against the wall at the side of the door.

"Stand there!" he said, under his breath. "Out of the line of fire! Don't move!"

There was a rush against the door – and then a voice growled:

"Aw, cut dat out! Wot do youse want to do – scare him away by bustin' it! Pick de lock, an' we'll lay for him inside till he shows up."

It was the Skeeter's voice. The Skeeter and his gang – the worst apaches in the city of New York! Professional assassins, death contractors, he had called them – and the lowest bidders! A man's life any time for twenty-five dollars! No, they were not likely to forget the affair of the pushcart man, to forget old Luddy and his diamonds, to forget – the Gray Seal! And they were only the vanguard of what was to come!

Some one was working at the lock now. There was one way to stop that. It would not take them long to find out that he *was* there once the door was opened! Better know it with the door *shut!* Jimmie Dale lifted his revolver coolly and fired through the panel.

A burst of yells answered the shot; and among them, high above the others, the Magpie's scream:

"We got him! We got him! He's dere now!"

And then it seemed that pandemonium broke loose—there was a volley of shots, the bullets splintering through the door panels as from a machine gun, so fast they came—and then another rush against the door.

Flat on the floor, but well back and to one side, Jimmie Dale fired steadily—again and again.

Came screams of pain, yells, and oaths—and they fell back from the door.

And now from above, from overhead, came tumult—windows thrown up, the stamp of feet, cries of fright. And from the street, a low, sullen roar. The underworld was gathering fast!

Once more the rush upon the door—and Jimmie Dale, a grim, twisted smile upon his lips, emptied his revolver into the panels. Once more they fell back—and then there came the Skeeter's voice, snarling like an infuriated beast:

"He'll get de lot of us like dis! Cut it out! Besides, we'll have de bulls down here in a minute—an' he's *our* meat, not theirs. Dey'd be too damned soft wid him—dey'd only send him to de chair. Youse chase upstairs, Mose, an' pass de word to beat it—an' beat it quick. We'll *burn* de skunk out—dat's wot. An' de bulls can stand alongside an' watch, if dey likes—but he's our meat."

Jimmie Dale did not dare to look at the Tocsin's face. Mechanically he refilled the magazine of his automatic—and lay there, waiting. The roar from the street grew louder. They seemed to be fighting out there, as though an inadequate number of police were trying to disperse a mob—and not succeeding! Pretty soon, with the riot call in, there would probably be a battle—for the Gray Seal! Sublime irony! It was death at the hands of either one!

Children whimpered on the stairs outside, men swore, women cried, feet shuffled hurriedly by as the tenement emptied. Occasionally, a pertinent invitation to him to remain where he was, there was a vicious rip through the panel, and the drumming whir of a bullet flying through the room. And then a curious, ominous crackling sound—and then the smell of smoke.

Jimmie Dale stood up, his face drawn and haggard. The tenement would go like matchwood, burn like a bonfire, with any kind of a start—and there was no doubt about the start! The Skeeter, the Magpie, and the rest would have seen that it had headway enough to serve their purpose before either firemen or police could thwart them. He, Jimmie Dale, could take his choice: walk out into a bullet, or stay there and – he smiled miserably as his eyes fell upon the pile of Larry the Bat's clothing on the floor. There was no longer need to worry about *its* destruction – the fire would take care of that only too well! And then a low, bitter cry came to his lips, and he clenched his hands. If it were only himself – only himself! He crossed to the Tocsin and caught her in his arms.

"Oh, my God – Marie!" he faltered.

The cape and hood had fallen from her, and with the hood had fallen the gray-streaked hair of Silver Mag – and now as she smiled at him it was from a face that was very beautiful and very brave and very full of tenderness.

And he held her there – and neither spoke.

It seeped in under the threshold of the door, it came from everywhere, filling the room – the black, strangling smoke. Outside in the hall all was silence now – save for that crackle of flame that grew in volume, that came now in quick, sharp reports, like revolver shots. From out in the street swelled a cry: "Death to the Gray Seal!" Then the clang of bells, the roar and rattle of fire apparatus, strident voices bellowing orders, and the crowd again, blood hungry: "Death to the Gray Seal!"

There was a chance, just one – if the fire had no headway along the upper end of the landing – and if they had not thought to set a watch for him *above!* They – the Magpie, the Skeeter, and his gang – must have been driven even out of the house now by the smoke and flame.

"Give me the key, I am going to open the door, Marie," he said quietly. "Cover your face with a handkerchief, anything, and run to the *left* to the next flight of stairs. There are two flats above this – we'll make the roof if we can. Now – are you ready?"

It was an instant before she answered, an instant in which she lifted her face to his, and held his face between her two hands – and then:

"I am ready, Jimmie."

He flung open the door, his arm around her to help her forward – and instinctively, with a cry, fell back for a moment. With the inrush of the draft poured the smoke, and through it, lurid, yellow, showed the flames leaping from the stair well.

And then all was blind madness. Together they ran. At the foot of the stairs she fell, recovered herself, staggered up another – and fell again. He caught her up in his arms and, staggering now as she had staggered, went on. His lungs seemed to be bursting. His limbs grew weak and trembled under him. He could not see or breathe. The nauseating fumes suffocated him, bringing an intolerable agony. He gained the first landing above. There was one more – one more! If he could only rest here for a moment!

Yes, that was it—rest. It wasn't so bad here now. She stirred in his arms, struggled to her feet—and he was helping her on again, and up the next flight of stairs.

And suddenly he found himself laughing in hysteria—for they were climbing a half stair, half ladderway at the end of the upper landing, and the open skylight was above them, and they were drinking in the pure, fresh air—and now they were out upon the roof, and the roar from the street was in their ears, like the roar of great waters from some canyon far below. Jimmie Dale tried to speak, and found his lips were cracked and dry. He wet them with his tongue.

"Don't stand up—we'd be seen—*crawl*," he mumbled hoarsely.

It took a long time—over one roof, and then another, and yet another—and then through the skylight of a tenement whose occupants were either craning from the front windows, or were on the street below. It was, perhaps, half an hour—and then they, too, were standing in the street, and all about them the crowd was shouting in wild excitement.

Up the block, inside the fire lines, the Sanctuary was blazing furiously—and now suddenly the wall seemed to bulge outward. It brought a yell from the crowd:

"Death to the Gray Seal!"

She pulled at his arm.

"Let us get away! Let us get away, Jimmie!" she whispered frantically.

A strange smile was on Jimmie Dale's lips.

"We're safe now—for always," he whispered back. "Look!"

The Sanctuary wall bulged farther outward, seemed to hang an instant hesitant in mid-air—and fell with a mighty crash.

The Gray Seal was dead!

THE END

Volume Two of the Complete Adventures of Jimmie Dale will include *The Further Adventures of Jimmie Dale* and *Jimmie Dale and the Phantom Clue*, the final two battles of the Gray Seal and the Tocsin against the agents of the Crime Club.

AVAILABLE NOW

THE FIRST NEW GRAY SEAL NOVEL IN
MORE THAN EIGHTY YEARS!

JIMMIE DALE, ALIAS THE GRAY SEAL

By Michael Howard

In the summer of 1912 New York City was being terrorized by a bizarre organization of metal-clawed criminals who ascend stone walls as easily as others climb stairs. Dubbed the Spider Gang by the press, they roamed over every part of Manhattan from neighborhoods of squalid tenements to the most luxurious mansions of the rich. It wasn't wealth that they sought however, instead it was the City's most beautiful women who were being carried off for some sinister purpose.

IN BOTH ELECTRONIC AND PRINT
EDITIONS

For further information about the Gray Seal check out his very own page on Facebook:

https://www.facebook.com/JimmieDaleGraySeal/

Made in United States
Orlando, FL
28 January 2022

14161153R00209